House de Gracie

By

DENNIS MAULSBY

THE HOUSE DE GRACIE

For more information: www.neoleafpress.com

First Edition: March 2020

ISBN: 978-1-945663-27-7

Acknowledgments:

Grateful acknowledgment is made to the publishers of books, periodicals, and anthologies in which these extracts or earlier versions of them have appeared.

- The World War II episode has been published as a stand-alone short story in the 2014 Anthology of the Military Writers Society of America's *All Gave Some* under the title "The Graceful Raven."
- An extract entitled "Amtrak Dream" (flash fiction 500 words) received an honorable mention in the 2015 Soul-Making Keats Literary Competition – the annual community arts outreach program of the National Federation of American Pen Women.
- The first chapter under the title "The Dive Bar" has been published as a standalone short story in Main Street Rag's 2017 fall anthology *Of Burgers & Barrooms*.
- A short story extract entitled "Near Ypres" has been published by the Military Writers Society of America as part of their 2018 anthology.
- The short story extract "Monkey See, Monkey Go" received a recognition award from Ageless Authors in 2019.

Other Books by Dennis Maulsby

Poetry
Near Death/Near Life

Short Stories
Free Fire Zone Winterset

Author's note:

My gratitude to the book's French language editor, Marilyn Baszczynski.

DEDICATION

My thanks and gratitude to Robin Sprafka and Rick Hildreth whose insight and humor were the gifts that made this book easier to write.

1

AS THE TAXI SWAYED, Major Hugh de Gracie closed his good eye and drifted off into a resurrected memory of his first tour in 2010 and the patrol with his driver Sergeant Murphy. The pair drove a Humvee then, the fifth and last vehicle of the group taking supplies to an outlying Afghan patrol base. They passed the time telling each other riddles. Known as Riddler, Murphy could spew forth an inexhaustible supply, especially dirty ones.

*

"What's a mixed feeling?" the three-striper asked. Hugh's answer, "Seeing your mother-in-law backing off a cliff in your new car."

Hugh's comeback was, "What is the definition of *macho?*" Murphy's answer, "Jogging home after a vasectomy.

"What is the difference between 'oooooh' and 'aaaaah'?" the

1

sergeant then inquired.

After a respectable silence, Hugh said, "I give up."

"About three inches," came the laughing response.

An IED exploded on the lonely stretch of road, flipping the lead vehicle onto the roadside. Its fuel tank ignited with a whoosh and a bang.

Hugh bailed out of their tail-end Humvee, Beretta in hand. A 7.62 mm round from a Dragunov sniper rifle hit him smack in the middle of his chest. The impact slammed him onto the hood of the Humvee. He dropped to his knees. The pistol fell from a palsied hand onto the red-brown earth of the roadbed.

Murphy ran over, grabbed his wrists, and started dragging him to cover. A second round caught the sergeant in the unprotected area below the armpit. The slug tumbled through both her lungs, exiting on the other side.

Face in the gravel and dirt, Hugh heard the bass chug-chug-chug of the Ma Deuce fifties and the tenor chatter of the M-240's mounted on the remaining vehicles establish fire superiority. Three minutes later, the action ended. A woof of wind blew over and around the vehicles, sucking up fine particles of dust to mix with black ash and the odors of burnt pork and cordite.

The ceramic plate in Hugh's armored vest had saved his life. Other than temporarily knocking the wits out of him, and a saucer-sized bruise, there was no damage. He rode back to base holding Murphy, keeping pressure on the bandages over the holes where bloody foam bubbled out of his chest. They failed to find the killers.

◈

Hugh woke and stared out the cab window, the deep-tearing vacuum of her loss in his heart. The fender-dinged, yellow taxi pulled to the curb. Salt-streaked tires slopped icy mush up over the curb. Spring had come late this year. The day's earlier snow and sleet marking the end of a rough winter passage.

The cabby turned his head. "This is the place, Major. They stay open till 4 a.m., then it's just a short walk up 8th Avenue to the 31st Street entrance to Penn Station."

Hugh leaned forward and read the meter. His hand reached into an internal jacket pocket, paper rustled, and bills passed to the front seat.

The Crown Vic cab pulled away, leaving the tall, green-uniformed soldier standing on the sidewalk holding an old-fashioned double-handled black leather briefcase. Across the street stood the Conlaoch Tavern, a New York City dive bar, recommended by the Sikh cabby while imitating an Irish accent: *"A fine public house, it is, run fer the last twenty years by a native of the old sod. A good, safe place, fer sure, ta pass the time till yer train. And they do not water the liquor."*

The lines had produced a little trickle of humor, the sight of a bearded, turbaned man tonguing the brogue. Hugh hoped the tavern name wasn't a bad omen: Con meant chief and laoch warrior in Gaelic. The two words in combination referred to a legendary Irish hero accidentally killed by his own father. Toward the end of the next twenty hours Hugh would be back in his father's house, a house he'd been glad to leave over ten years ago.

The Major stared at the lighted sign running the fifty-foot length of the two-story building. The first-floor façade was done in Anglo-Irish pub style with plastered panels framed in dark beams and matching leaded glass windows. Despite the winter dirt and grit coating the structure, it was the bright spot in the block.

Overflowing dumpsters peeked out of the mouths of alleys. The adjacent buildings were dark, making it hard to tell if they were abandoned, or if the owners just didn't believe in security lights. He raised his left hand, exposing a stainless-steel Rolex Submariner – its illuminated dial displayed 12:15.

He would kill four hours here, and then walk up to Penn station to await his 8:00 a.m. departure on Amtrak's Adirondack train. Now, he needed a drink. The fever was starting to take him. Hugh needed to take his pills. He needed to recover from the ten-hour flight from Germany in a ready for retirement, rattletrap C-130 that had left him weak and shaky.

The tar-thick, bitter Air Force coffee and the white bread baloney sandwiches rationed out by the plane's crew chief had barely sustained him. The loadmaster had noticed his fidgeting in the ass-biting canvas-bottomed seats, and let him stretch out on a bed made from quilted cargo wraps and a military-issue wool blanket, all smelling of diesel and lube oil. The vibration of the turbo-prop engines, transmitted through the aluminum and titanium metal of the plane, became muted as it passed through the heavy quilts and made his muscles relax. He slept.

The army medics hadn't wanted to release him this soon, but his disability discharge had come through. After ten years of service, the military couldn't use what was left of him. In the old days, they would have said he had been invalid-ed out.

A city trash truck dashed by, raising a spindrift of muddy haze that chilled his hands and cheeks. Moisture collected into drops and rolled off the high gloss toes of his oxford low quarter shoes.

The fever generated by his illness took him and made the world seem surreal. In the dim light, the street's icy paving stones looked like worn molars taken from the jawbones of mammoths. The city's warm breath fogged up out of iron gratings set in the street and sidewalks. The vapor flashed gold then white, in time to the wink of beer signs in the pub's windows. Hugh shivered. The spray of Taliban shrapnel in his legs and thighs began to burn in the chilled wind.

He adjusted the switchblade knife, now closed to half its five-inch length, resting in the hollow of his back. Hugh's old drill sergeant mentor had insisted, never go without a weapon.

Opening the bar door, he was immediately immersed in the warm beefy rasp of male chatter, their voices a blend of rumor and gossip.

Hands waved, fingers flexed and pointed, their seated bodies black paper cutouts backlighted by a Miller Lite clock, Budweiser Clydesdale revolving lamps, and Guinness stained glass. Logos on beer taps advertised Murphy's, O'Hara's, Harp, and Smithwick's.

The Major waited for his eyes to adjust to the dark wood interior. On his way to the bar, he memorized the location of the back exit, the toilets, the clusters of patrons, and any blind spots. Most of the good places where he could get his back to a wall taken, he took a stool center right at the bar. Hugh placed his briefcase between his legs.

An occasional glance in the full-length mirror mounted along the back wall allowed him to observe his rear, establishing a defensive perimeter. Removing his beret exposed half-inch long black hair that blended into shorter hair on the sides and back. He combed both hands through the prickly fuzz, massaging scalp and neck muscles drawn tight enough to generate a headache.

The men's room door opened, letting loose a wink of brighter light. Seconds later, the whiff of urine came, smelling hot against the cool blasé odors of beer and tobacco. Movement in his peripheral vision announced the arrival of the bartender.

A mature female voice produced the obligatory, "What's your pleasure, soldier?"

He turned his head.

Her eyebrows lifted in response to the black patch secured over his right eye and the scars that radiated out over the eyebrow and cheek.

"I need a pilsner or pale ale in a bottle, your recommendation, and a shot of rye."

Her eyebrows returned to their normal position. "You look like a Wild Turkey guy to me."

"That will be just fine. I'll need something to eat. Is there a menu?"

"Take your choice." She pulled a handful of dog-eared pasteboards from underneath the counter and fanned them like playing cards. "Pizza, hoagies, hamburgers, Chinese, Thai... I call in your order, and they deliver right to your stool."

Hugh ordered pizza, remembering the Big Apples' denizens' method of eating the famed best pizza in the world. You munched on a folded slice held in one hand, leaving the other free to punctuate your conversation. He rubbed his chin. A female in close proximity made him self- conscious about his day-old bristle.

The bartender returned from the telephone with a long-necked bottle of City Island pale ale, placed a napkin and a tall thin-walled Weizen glass on the bar. She read from the ale's label, "A handcrafted amber, a classic American-style ale with a citrus-y finish." She noticed his hands shake as he reached for the bottle. "Want me to pour? You're building a boiler maker, right? By the way, I'm Gabby, short for Gabriella, but also because I can talk the talk."

He extended his arm across the bar and clasped her fingers, keeping her hand palm-down — half handshake, and half hand-kiss — and found her bones and muscles firm, the skin cool and wet from the bottle's condensation. "I am Hugh, Hugh de Gracie."

She smiled, showing teeth white but with irregular spacing – no braces during her childhood. He marked clear skin with a tiny mole or two.

Light brown hair, probably her birth color, done up in a Swedish braid, complemented the oval of her face. She dressed simply in dark Irish green slacks, a long-sleeved French-cuffed white shirt, and a matching green scarf knotted around her neck. The overall impression: Gabby was an approachable person, living comfortably outside of most women's irrational quest for the perfection of bone, flesh, and mind papered to their egos by corporate marketing.

She nodded and turned to the tiered shelves of liquor bottles. Her hips swayed in the millennia-old way women's curves react when conscious of a man's attention. She returned with a shot glass of amber-dark brown rye, caught up his glass, and transferred the hundred-proof liquor.

Hugh grasped Gabby's wrist and pulled the liter-sized glass to his nose, the remembered whiskey scent sharp and bracing. His brain separated out the elements – honey with mint, sour apple, sandalwood, menthol, and sun-dried oak. She raised the bottle of pale ale, tilted his glass to a sixty-degree angle, and used a gentle pour to keep the two liquids from mixing.

Resting on the bar, the glass showed the mixing colors of the mysterious dark brown nestled in the small diameter bottom of the Weizen, and the light translucent ale rested on top. A just-right two inches of foam crowned the top. Hugh raised it in both hands. Lips and nose savored the bubbles, then hit the liquid ale under the foam. The twin stimuli of scent and taste caused a rush of pleasure. He sat the glass down and rubbed his upper lip. On a scale of one to ten, one being scratching an annoying itch and ten being sex, the moment was an eight.

Gabby's years of bartending had made her an excellent observer, able to wring details out of patrons' body posture, dress, and voice. She had an interesting enigma before her. The soldier's shirt and jacket fit loosely. He must have recently lost weight. Over his left pocket rested three rows of military ribbons, which must mean a lot of past action. The shoulder patches were also indecipherable, except the one on the right. It carried crossed red bayonets on a blue shield with two curved ribbons above, one reading "Ranger," the other "Mountain." She had seen one like it as a child when she had gotten into her grandfather's old military locker.

This patch indicated Hugh had seen combat with the Tenth Mountain Division based out of Fort Drum, New York, trained for arctic and high altitude fighting. She knew from her grandfather's war stories that he had served with that unit in the Italian mountain campaigns of World War II. In recent years, the two had followed his old division's operations in Desert Storm, Haiti, Bosnia, and Kosovo. More recently, grandfather had mentioned the Tenth's deployments to Iraq and Afghanistan.

She also recognized the winged badge centered over the other ribbons announcing his qualification as a paratrooper. Gabby's eyebrows lifted as she noticed the blue and white ribbon with a red stripe in the middle. Grandfather also had one, the silver star, an award only given for gallantry in combat.

Noticing her stare, Hugh spoke up, "Don't get taken with all the fruit salad. The longer you're in the service, the more weight they make you carry." He pointed to a bottom ribbon, one with a broad middle red stripe and smaller alternating red and white stripes on the edges. "I got this one for painting the rocks circling the Headquarters' flagpole."

Hugh watched the corners of Gabby's lips rise. "I've got a wall in my apartment that needs painting. Perhaps, you could help."

Hugh noticed movement in the mirror. The pizza boy had arrived with his food.

Gabby left to fill orders from the servers.

The sausage, onion, and mushroom with extra cheese went down quickly, interspersed with sips of ale. For dessert, he drank the last swallow of the ale then the rye. The tart, astringent tang of the ale, made the whiskey taste as sweet as liquid sugar. He pulled up the briefcase, released the latch, opened its clamshell-hinged mouth, and extracted three orange plastic pill bottles.

Gabby returned from the stock room.

Hugh motioned towards the containers. "Could I have a water please?"

She used the mix gun to fill a glass and slid it over with raised eyebrows.

"Not to worry, it's not contagious. Just something I picked up in

Afghanistan. This medicine controls it."

He remembered a nightmare from his second tour. The days he spent as a Taliban prisoner in the cave, to the point even the soft flutter of bat wings overhead – more active at dusk and dawn – had begun to haunt him. The doctors in Germany, an expert with exotic diseases, diagnosed a new trans-species virus, probably infecting him through inhaling the aerosol of bat urine, or entering his system through untreated wounds. It was an old story – viruses originating in other mammals mutating and jumping into humans. No current antiviral medicines could touch this stuff. They finally hit upon a cocktail of three drugs that repressed the virus and strengthened his resistance. The docs had been clear that treatment was only delaying the inevitable. The one-of-a-kind disease would soon kill him.

"So, are you headed home?" Gabby asked.

"Going north on the Adirondack almost to Canada, Hugh replied. "The family manse is up in the mountains near Port Henry." Hugh felt eyes on the back of his neck, glanced in the bar mirror, and noticed a thin man alone at a two-chair table, a hoodie keeping his face in shadow.

"I've always wanted to take a trip up that way." Gabby's fingers stroked the wooden bar rail lightly, the nature of her motion suggestively erotic. "See all the old Victorian mansions along the Hudson Valley and water ski on Lake Champlain."

A bit of sweat glistened on Hug's upper lip, sexual fantasies formed in his mind. The conversation continued, nuggets of personal anecdotes and emotion surfacing.

Gabby moved down the bar from time to time to fill orders, but it was a slow night.

She explained that Tuesdays after midnight was typically dead, especially if there was no event scheduled up the street at Madison Square Garden. She lived in the apartment over the bar and offered to let him rest upstairs until his train was due.

9

In spite of the signals she was sending, Hugh had to refuse. At the end of the story, they would both be disappointed and embarrassed, given his weakness. He was in no shape to satisfy a woman.

At ten minutes to four, he and the hoodie-man found themselves the only remaining customers. Hugh pulled out his stash of bills and peeled off two twenties.

Gabby ran hot water in the stainless-steel bar sinks to soap and rinse glasses and pitchers.

He reached across to hold Gabby's wet hand one last time. Her goodbye smile made him second-guess whether he should have accepted her offer.

On his way out, he noticed the hoodie-man had already left. The tavern door slipped out of his fingers, closing with a click of its lock. The cold pushed its way through the wool fabric of his uniform, insulation value negated by the sweaty humidity absorbed in the bar's interior. Hugh moved better than when he had arrived, his body generating energy from pizza, ale, and whiskey calories. Shadow and light alternated as he moved in and out of the amber circles cast by streetlights. The tap of his jump boots sent out sonar sounds to echo back from the brick and stone of the surrounding buildings.

Looking ahead, he paused when he spotted hoodie-man standing, one hand in his garment's front pouch, under the streetlight at the corner of Eighth Avenue and Thirty-First Street. Hugh retrieved the knife from the hollow of his back and slipped it up his right sleeve.

Entering the cone of light, his fever made him feel distant in time, as though the two of them were meeting in the blood and sand of an arena, crowds waiting hushed just outside the glare to bet and exult. Hugh walked from the perimeter to the center. He faced the man and waited.

The hoodie-man moved, breaking the dream. He drew a Colt Cobra snub-nosed .38 revolver, took a step closer, and motioned a give me gesture with an open left hand.

A police siren wailed two blocks away.

The hoodie-man looked.

Hugh didn't. The switchblade dropped out into his fingers. The blade snapped open. Light reflecting off the tip of the four-inch blade marked a silver arc to the handle of the pistol. The cutting edge slashed up along the snub-nose's grip.

A fan of sparks flew.

The pistol fell, clinking on the sidewalk. Fingers sliced from the thief's gripping hand left a swirl-pattern of twitching pink caterpillars on the concrete. Stuck in the trigger guard, three knuckles of the index finger spasmed, a three-inch-long dying worm too weak to depress the trigger. The hoodie-man looked down at the gun, held up his hand, sobbed, and ran loose-legged into the dark, shaking blood from an appendage now possessing only a thumb.

The rumble-sway of the train, the rhythm of iron wheels clipping welds between rails, the sun's early spring heat, all combined to make his head nod, and his eyes flutter. Hugh felt somewhat better, having stripped to the waist for a wash and a shave in the Penn Station men's room. Now, at least, his body odor wouldn't offend fellow passengers. Although, someone setting close would still detect the faint petroleum smell absorbed by his uniform during the C-130 flight. Perhaps it would pass for some new ultra-masculine deodorant. Anticipating long lines in the train's Amcafe food service car, he had stocked his briefcase with two plastic-wrapped sandwiches and a variety of candy bars.

Hugh had forgotten how frequently the Adirondack stopped. The first leg was from Penn Station to Yonkers, only fourteen miles — hardly enough to get up to full speed before slowing to pick up passengers. Then eighteen slow clacky-clack miles unrolled to Croton-on-Hudson; afterward the third leg lengthened to forty miles between there and Poughkeepsie. After that, came ten more stops and one hundred eighty-six miles to Port Henry where, if he was lucky, his father would have received his last letter and would find him at the circa 1888 slate-roofed station.

The gray granite building was classified as Romanesque revival architecture, but to Hugh's eyes, it resembled an old hay barn except for the conical-roofed round tower built into a trackside corner of the structure. According to the Amtrak route guide in his lap, it now had no ticket office, no restrooms, no payphone, no Wi-Fi, and no ATM. The only facility it retained from its active railroad days was a restored waiting room. The Moriah County Senior Citizens Center used the remainder of the building. The Center caretaker opened and closed the room as needed for train passengers. In a flash of fantasy, Hugh imagined departed old folks' souls waiting patiently at the station for a heaven-bound train.

The scenery hadn't amounted to much yet, mostly the industrial backside of several centuries of decaying American capitalism. He let the scenery wash through his mind without thought until they hit West Point with its gray stone battlements. The army officers' school was still surrounded by 16,000 acres of forested land. He thought he caught sight of a figure high up on the crenelated walls of the school's Fort Putnam, probably the ghost of its first Colonial commander, Benedict Arnold. He had known a large number of Ring Knockers, some good, and some bad. Being a mustang and coming up from the ranks, he could not readily identify with their credo.

He remembered the old army proverb about the types of officers. There were smart, dumb, aggressive, and lazy officers. The combination was crucial. The worst were dumb and aggressive, dropping their ill-led units into untenable, killing situations. Next came dumb and lazy. Their units rarely prepared and usually got their dicks stuck in a meat grinder on their first battlefield. Smart and aggressive was somewhat better. The troops well prepared but thrust into the forefront of the battle resulting in a high rate of casualties.

The best was smart and lazy. These officers figured out ways to accomplish missions with a minimum expenditure of men and equipment. Most of the Pointers he had rubbed shoulders with fit into one of the two aggressive categories.

The train car jiggled on its suspension as it ran over a curved section of track. Hugh opened his eyes and watched the Hudson River drift by through the window. He wished for more foot room. The train was composed of cylindrical-roofed cars, the coaches having more than thirty double pairs of forward-facing seats separated by an aisle down the middle. Their blue, fabric-covered seats were now slick with the wear of many backsides. An overlay of cheap flowery perfume tried to hide the commercial-grade cleanser the clean-up crews used. From the looks of the dirt ingrained in the crack between floor and wall, there must not be much time during the turnaround for attention to detail.

Hugh took a last look around, leaned back, and drifted off into fever-induced sleep. He woke with the train taking on passengers at the Albany station.

A pair of older women, one with a man-short hairstyle, had taken seats across the aisle.

"You just get back from overseas?" the end one asked as she took in his uniform. Ethel and I are glad you returned in one pi–" She bit off the last word as Hugh turned his head and exposed the eye patch and scars. "Damn, I fucked up, sorry."

"I appreciate the sentiment. You've not given offense."

"It's still bad luck on me. This is a special day. We're traveling to Canada to be married. They allow same-sex marriage, and better yet, the state of New York recognizes its legality." Ethel looked past her partner and gave him a shy smile.

She waved a bridal bouquet.

Hugh responded. "Congratulations, and I hope you have many happy years together."

"The name's Jean Wicowski. I'm a doctor, and Ethel's my operating room nurse. We office in Manhattan. I'm a board-certified surgeon specializing in aesthetic plastic surgery."

Hugh raised his eyebrows, looked confused. "I don't follow."

"Well, to put it in the vernacular, we do everything from tummy tucks and eyelid surgery to boob jobs and butt implants with a little rhinoplasty thrown in." She focused on his scars. "I could probably do something about those." Jean stepped into the aisle. "May I?"

Without waiting for a reply, she cupped his chin in her fingers and raised his head, her other hand lifted the patch. "Humm, someone did a crude job of removing the eye – not a bullet or shrapnel, but purpose work with a knife. The scars can be removed, and the eyelid reconstructed. You feel a little feverish."

She looked at the ribbons on his chest, touched the Combat Infantry Badge with its flintlock rifle resting on a blue panel backed by a wreath then resumed her seat.

Hugh felt a great wave of sadness.

Jean seemed to share the feeling. She fumbled in her purse, found a business card, and handed it over. "Call me in a month for an appointment. I'll do you much better than the VA – no charge. I have many friends in the service. You folks keep us safe. It's a debt beyond our ability to repay."

Hugh nodded his head. "Thank you."

He leaned back in his seat, trying to relax; mind and muscles tense from confronting his injury, something he had been avoiding. Closing his eye, he started the relaxing methods his father had taught him. Starting with breathing, Hugh filled his lungs with long slow breaths then reduced their duration. Mentally, he started with his scalp, making it relax, then to other muscles progressing down his body from head to toes. His exit medical examination in Germany came back to him.

"Son, I'm Doctor Jeskie. I head up this mess they call a military hospital. Normally, being a colonel — don't get up — I rarely have the pleasure of working with patients: only reams of paper, forms, books of regulations, nonsense letters from Congressmen, and the like."

Hugh felt a developing admiration for the colonel: a short, thin man with a shock of one hundred percent white hair outfitted in the traditional white coat, neck-hung stethoscope, and medical files under one arm. Like many military medical personnel, their concern for patients had priority over army regulations and procedures. He had heard the nurses referring to their leader with respect as "The Great White Father."

"It appears we have a personal connection. I knew your father and served with him in a MASH unit in Korea during that, uh, police action. An excellent chest-cutter and a good friend."

Emboldened Hugh asked, "Was it anything like the TV series?"

The Colonel chuckled. "Worse, if my memory serves me. Your dad and I covered a lot of ground and a lot of women in the peninsula and in Japan. He and I had a few narrow escapes in the war's ice and fire – and in the back alleys of Tokyo. I visited your home in New York several times after we rotated back, but it has been a decade since our last contact. Can you courier a personal communication to him?"

"Yes, sir. I can take a message with me if you wish."

"Good, I anticipated that. Here's a letter for your father." The doctor handed Hugh an envelope. "Now, about your situation. The flesh wounds you will survive. You can live with the shrapnel in your legs and thighs. The only problem is if some of it starts to migrate. I've already talked with the folks at the Albany VA Hospital. Your post-army treatment will be directed out of there, although their satellite facility at Saranec Lake will handle your primary care. You'll need periodic x-rays. The skin around the eye will need

15

reconstruction. Your father can find someone for that. I don't expect the VA has anyone with the credentials.

"The very bad news: the zoonotic virus you contracted is strange beyond anything we've ever seen. It is not contagious, except through the exchange of blood. Your broken nose, eye damage, even the shrapnel penetrations could have provided the entry for virus-laden bat urine. The drugs will temporarily keep it at bay and extend your life, but soon the disease will have its way."

"Will you be telling my father?"

"No. Doctor-patient confidentiality prohibits that. You need to decide how much to tell him, but I don't think you will fool him for long. You will hand-carry your personnel and medical records. If you wish, you can let him see those before you turn them in at Albany. I've listed my email and snail-mail address and cell phone number in my letter. I can tell him the details with your permission."

The Colonel reached into his pocket, "Oh, one last thing, the lonely fairy godmother that resides in the basement of the Pentagon has touched you with her wand." He opened his hand to display a pair of gold oak leaves. "These were mine, and I am glad to pass them on to a deserving soldier. Your promotion to major just came through, so your disability pension will be figured on a higher pay scale."

❧

Hugh's body felt the train slowing, little jerks and skids as the brakes were applied. Waking to an increase in his fever, he pulled a bottle of water from the briefcase, took his medication, and polished off a sandwich. The faces in the seat across the aisle had changed again, the closest one now containing a very young black soldier. Hugh noticed his uniform mostly blank of any ribbons and patches. A newbie, he thought, probably near the beginning of his service. The shoulders of his greens sported a shiny new gold stripe with a single rocker underneath, a private first class, and pinned over this left pocket was an expert rifleman badge.

Sweat popped out on the PFC's forehead, and his muscles grew stiff. He tried to come to attention in his seat as he noticed Hugh's inspection. A major wasn't as close to God as a general, but infinitely closer than the boy's third from the bottom rank, especially one with a chest full of medals and combat scars.

Hugh caught his eyes and smiled, "Relax trooper, this is not a formal occasion. What's your TIS?"

"Close to ten months, sir. Just returning home on leave."

The young'un must be aggressive and good, Hugh thought. It usually took a year or better to make PFC. A flash of brass on his lapels showed crossed rifles. "You took your basic and advanced training at Fort Benning?"

"Yes, sir, and I hope to return there next year for jump training."

Hugh rubbed his chin and looked at the soldier's nametag, "Thinking of making the army your life choice, Private First-Class Jefferson?"

"Yes, sir, I'm taking all the course work I can. Aim to get my college degree over time."

"I'm also a graduate of Benning's school for boys and girls."

"I know, sir."

Getting tired of all the *yes sirs*, Hugh extended his hand across the aisle. "Well, it's a pleasure to meet a fellow lifer. Hugh de Gracie is the name. And, how do you know I was at Benning?"

Emboldened by the informality, Jefferson replied, "Sergeant Major Jonsey has told us stories about Coup de Grace, sir."

"Aha, you're serving with my old unit the Tenth Mountain Division, and you've been exposed to that rascal son-of-a-bitch Jonsey, also known as my best friend. Whatever he's been telling you is probably a mess of lies and make-believe.'

"He told us of how you trained and served together. And, how his association with you made you — in his words, sir — 'the fine man you became.' "

Hugh made a sham choking noise and frowned. "Well, this is your lucky day, Jefferson, since I will now tell you the true story of how we started, instead of the bullshit you have probably heard." Clearing his throat, Hugh began the tale.

"We hated each other the very first time our eyes met. We fought and schemed against each other every day and hour of our Basic Combat Training and Advanced Individual Training. That bastard Jonsey scuffed my spit shined shoes just before inspection, and I loosened the blanket on his bed so the Drill Instructor's quarter didn't bounce. He put a frog under my sheets, stroking its belly to put it in a trance that lasted long enough for me to get in bed before it started kicking. Scared the shit out of me. The next night, his arm hanging out of the bed, I placed his hand in a helmet full of warm water. He pissed his pants and soaked the sheets."

Jefferson's eyes widened at this.

"The tit-for-tat went on for some time. He pushed me into quicksand during our escape and evasion training, and I messed up his rope at the repelling tower causing him to fall the last ten feet. The DI noticed the escalating disruption. It was affecting the entire unit. People were taking sides.

"The cadre started an unofficial contest. We were pitted against each other, the first time in pugil training. Jonsey pinned my first lunge under his right arm and pivoted his stick to catch me on the head with the simulated butt, making my vision star. I started our second go with a feigned kick to the asshole's groin. His reaction opened him up to a bayonet thrust to the sternum."

Again, Jefferson looked shocked.

"When he complained about the move being unfair, the DI responded, 'There is nothing fair in combat!' We went for two out of three. I blocked his short-thrust opening, moved in close, stepped on his toe pinning him, reversed, and brought the long end of the pugil up between his legs. He dropped his stick and got me in a chokehold. I gave him a fist in a kidney, hip threw him, and started punching. It took four guys to get us apart.

"The DI yelled, 'You don't have to give him the coup de grace.' The phrase, meaning deathblow in French, stuck and ever since then, in military circles I have been known as Coup, instead of Hugh.

"The DI spent some time with us laying down the law. If our conflict continued one of us would be set back and have to go through training all over again. He'd give us one more chance. He made us battle buddies. As you are aware, this meshed our lives. We were expected to assist each other both in and out of combat. We pushed it, of course, in hand-to-hand we tried for real damage. After one session, he had an eye swelled shut, and I had cracked ribs. We competed at the rifle range and tied at expert."

Jefferson smiled at this.

"Our fellow trainees finally had had enough," Hugh went on. "They woke us one midnight, placed sheathed M-9 bayonets in our hands, and told us to go at it. If this didn't settle our dispute, they would beat us both black and blue as many times as it took to keep us cooperative. I remember Jonsey's smile as he hefted his weapon. He'd had lots of knife experience growing up in Bed-Stuy. What he didn't know was the immersion in blade training I'd had since I was seven years old. We cut and poked at each other, not making much progress, until Jonsey tore off the sheath, exposing the naked seven-inch blade.

"He feinted right and thrust left. Taking a short step back to move out of his lunge, I let the knife-tip make only a tiny prick of pain on my stomach skin. I hooked the guard of my bayonet, fingers and all, around his guard. When he pulled back the hilt jerked out of his hand, and the bayonet fell to the floor. The look of surprise on his face was well worth the sprung knuckle I received during the unorthodox maneuver."

19

Jefferson let out a chuckle as he nodded.

"After that, we entered a period of uneasy peace, not fighting, but not cooperating. To everyone else it was a great relief. The real bond between us became established after graduation in a back alley across the river from Benning in Columbus.

"I'd fallen in with bad company in a seedy bar just outside the city limits. A gang of six dragged me through the back door. I broke a civilian wrist, a few fingers, and a nose among my attackers before they pinned me. Just as I was about to be beaten silly, I felt their hands being ripped off me. Jonsey pulled me up. 'Coup, if anyone is going to kill you, it's going to be me.'

"Back to back, we cleaned out the alley, leaving crumpled bodies scattered among the trashcans. Just warmed up, we went inside and punched out the remaining four customers and the bartender. Jonsey served up victory drinks from behind the bar, occasionally tapping the supine bartender with a bung starter to keep him quiet. We had a long talk and decided since there was much to be admired about each other after all, that we should be blood brothers — we certainly had enough of each other's blood smeared on us."

The train pulled into a station. The PFC started to rise; this was his stop. Seeing the gravity in Hugh's distant stare, he sat back.

Hugh blinked then looked Jefferson in the eye. "That was the beginning. We served together for the next five years, took Ranger and jump training together, faced enemies in combat, and saved each other's asses many times. We parted when I left for OCS, but we buddied up and fought together again later. However, that's another story. Is that version close to what he tells?"

"Pretty close, sir," Jefferson pulled his camouflage-pattern backpack from the overhead rack, "but he claims you two finished off about twice the number of gang members and that he put down two opponents for every one you did."

Hugh laughed and clapped his hands. "Of course, of course."

Jefferson straightened to attention and drew his flattened right hand up to his eyebrow.

Hugh returned the salute.

The PFC spun and rushed for the exit as the train began to grind forward.

Hugh's stomach rumbled. Penn Station's cellophane-wrapped ham salad on white was struggling through his digestive system. He flushed. Soon a chill would follow. The Army-prescribed medication had lost its punch. The alternating hot and cold sessions must mean the virus was gaining control. He looked to the left. A scholarly couple had taken the seats vacated by the soldier. The man's dark hair scalloped back from his forehead, signaling male pattern baldness. His sharp nose, thin cheeks, and blue eyes shielded by wire-rimmed bifocals placed him in middle age.

His female companion possessed a pug nose pressed between plump cheeks. Breasts and rump strained against her clothes. Either recent weight gain or lack of funds had kept her attire from keeping up with a changing body. Hugh caught a flash of a wedding ring as the woman waved her hands, sprinkling complaints in Canadian French.

The seatback in front of him bumped against his knees. A female squirmed, hands over her head. She pulled her tresses back with one hand, while the other secured a twisted rubber band around a gathered knot of hair to create a ponytail.

Hugh's eyebrows went up. "Nora." he hissed. The shade of those deep burgundy tresses, whether natural or dyed, brought back a strong memory-picture of his former tutor.

He sniffed the air. The woman's aroma came from some standard commercial perfume. A common floral-rose scent — probably the ever-popular Burberry Body or some copy — not Nora's dry, aromatic scent, reminiscent of quality aged whiskey given off by her

Clinique. He hadn't been exposed to the fragrance since he left home — a bouquet that challenged men to move closer and breathe deep.

A high school girl's pixie face appeared over the seat top, "Sorry, didn't mean to bump you." She flashed teeth in their perfection that spoke of wealthy parents.

With this advance, Hugh concluded the seat bumping and hair alteration had been part of an elementary scheme to open a flirtation. A flutter or two of eyelashes thickened with mascara, and the opening moves would be complete. Wait for it, he thought, here it comes.

Her lashes flickered.

His smile confined to his mind, he nodded, remained silent, and turned his head to look out the window, cutting off any continuation of the girl's opening gambit.

She was too young and predictable. Hugh liked women whose experience in the stumble-tumble of adult business and romance allowed them a realistic worldview. Free-thinkers able to live up to their own expectations, not those of others. Age rarely a factor, his mind paraded the images of past enchanting women ranging from twenty to sixty; the first of which, and the best in many ways, had entered his life ten years ago. The train rumbled on. On the river's surface, thousands of concave pockets formed by the action of wind and current reflected sunlight to form diamond-points of brilliance. Their hypnotic flashes took him back.

*

When he was four, the loneliness began with his Mother's death in a woman versus taxi smashup while on a New York City shopping trip. At eighteen, he had felt way overdue to leave the family's isolated mountain estate and enter the world.

Margaret, the gaunt mouse-haired daughter of the stable master, became a full-time nanny and nurse. Recently widowed, his Margy was available to fill the vacuum of the lost mother, and he filled her loss of husband and childlessness. Father refused to let him attend public or even private school. His only child should not face the world unprepared and unprotected.

She was the constant in a world where tutors came and went in an annual stream as he grew and passed the annual tests required by the state for the homeschooled. Consistent with his father's admiration of the ancient Spartans, he was turned over to the men at age seven. Margy was pushed into the background, retreating to the kitchen. Hugh had never forgiven his father for the forced separation, another reason he departed for the military upon reaching legal age.

Nora O'Connell arrived his last year, a full-bodied woman with master's degrees in history and philosophy. She soon established a standard in his mind by which he measured all subsequent encounters with females. Her dresses, knee-length or below, were not provocative, but the athletic body beneath moved in delightful ways, whether cultivated or natural unknown. Hugh became intensely enamored with the deep red of her hair, the sprays of freckles on cheeks and arms, and the play of muscles as she walked or gestured. Her athleticism no sham, she worked out with him in the gym, dojo, and fencing salon. She taught him new gymnastic tricks, matched him move for move in martial arts, and consistently beat him with the foil, but just as consistently lost to him in saber duels.

When he was alone at night, her avatar dominated his fantasies during frequent autoerotic moments. Yet what came to intrigue him most was the animated intellectual behind the outward beauty, especially in their final month together.

Hugh's last assignment in philosophy had also been a revelation and a test. Nora handed him a few photocopied pages. "I want you to read and give me your opinion on Arthur Schopenhauer's treatise On Women. Your account will be presented verbally without notes. I have selected a copy in the original German, which your language instructor assures me you can read adequately."

A week later, sunlight streaming in through skylights to reflect off a Revere silver coffee pot and translucent Ming china cups, the pair settled at a table in the library where she took Hugh's oral report.

"I start by saying Schopenhauer writes in the manner of his time, the turn of the nineteenth century. The propositions and conclusions he drew are backed only by what he feels are reasoned observations, not by the statistical analysis that would be required today.

"Overall, the philosopher posits that women are by nature best suited to be subordinate to men. This, he claims, is quickly seen as when a woman reaches a state of complete independence, she immediately attaches herself to some man. In his words: 'If she is young, it will be a lover, if she is old, a priest.'"

Nora looked up at him. "Has he no admiration for women then?" Nora questioned.

"A misogynist he may very well be," Hugh responded. "However in the introduction of his treatise, he quotes Victor Joseph Etienne de Jouy: Without women, the beginning of our life would be helpless, the middle, devoid of pleasure, and the end, of consolation. He also suggests women need to be consulted in difficult times. According to him, women are more perceptive of the present than men, and their more sober judgment can bring men back to '…the right standpoint, so as to recover the near and simple view.'"

"So, women have a place in a culture's political life?"

"Not on an independent basis. Schopenhauer points to historical examples of women gaining political power, which resulted in disasters, such as the fall of Sparta and the French revolution. This ignores, of course, all the failures of states and empires caused by men."

"So, what is the purpose of women in the philosopher's world?"

"This was the most interesting part. He refers to nature, having evolved women's abilities, personalities, and bodies into focusing on the survival of the species, everything else becoming secondary. He says: 'Nature has equipped women, as she does all her creatures, with the weapons and implements requisite for the safeguarding of her existence, and for just as long as necessary for her to have them.' This was a wow moment for me. Schopenhauer seems to have anticipated Darwin."

"An excellent observation. Whatever you think about his conclusions," Nora said, "the man had a massive influence as a precursor to evolution theory and modern psychology. So, let's hear how Schopenhauer's writing affected your personal beliefs about the role of the genders."

Hugh nodded. "He seems very prejudiced and quaint to me. The early loss of his father, the dislike of his mother, and his rejection by desirable women must have shaped him and his writings. He seems to have missed the experience of unconditional passion and love, a familiarity I wish to have someday. As to gender roles, I am sure our brains and bodies are wired differently, but how much is the question. I believe women and men can do equally well in politics, science, and the arts. There are many modern examples. I would hate a world with only male or only female philosophies dominant."

Nora looked at him closely and, in a smooth story teller's voice, replied, "There is an old tale. Long, long ago, before recorded history began, men and women were one creature. The male and female characteristics combined in complete harmony, their lives peaceful and fulfilled. The gods observing from their heaven became jealous, and with lightning bolts split the creatures into man and woman. Ever since that day, remembering the harmony, we instinctively seek to rejoin."

Hugh remained quiet, trying to imagine such a being. He felt her warm hand grasp his.

"This concludes your baptism in philosophy. You have now added Schopenhauer to your earlier immersions in Descartes, Voltaire, Kant, Hegel, Russell, Thoreau, Marx, and Sartre. We will mark the accomplishment. This is Friday evening. Instead of training on Saturday and Sunday as usual, I have convinced your father and Uncle Frank to give you a weekend off."

Hugh detected a new sway to her hips as she exited, leaving the familiar trail of beguiling perfume. Taking a sip of coffee, he grimaced and almost spit it out. It had sat untouched until it grew cold.

🍃

He surfaced for a moment in the contemporary world of Amtrak and pulled tissues from his briefcase to wipe the fever-sweat from his forehead and cheeks. Shivering, a chill spell began. He pulled his jacket lapels closer and retreated back into memory.

🍃

Hugh lay in his bed with a wool blanket pulled snugly up to his armpits. The last cool temperatures of spring seeped through the curved walls in his third-story tower room, the cold resisted only by ash-covered embers in the corner ceramic fireplace and the kerosene lamp on the bed table. A copy of the third book of Ovid's *Ars Amatoria — The Art of Love*, in the original Latin — propped on his chest.

The two-thousand-year-old poetic sex-manual had survived fire, plague, and government censorship to continue to offer men and women proven ways of seduction and romantic intrigue. Publius Ovidius Naso was one of the first to move man-woman relationships away from force and possession to concepts of mutual fulfillment. Hugh read aloud. "'Odi concubitus, qui non utrumque resolvunt' I abhor intercourse which does not relieve both." He hoped he would live long enough to shed his virginity and thoroughly explore the author's suggestions and advice about sex.

A tap on the door brought him fully awake. It creaked open and Nora entered, dressed in a puff-sleeved peasant blouse. An ankle-length pleated skirt swirled around her hips and bare feet as she crossed the room. A chevron-patterned shawl around her shoulders had allowed her to navigate the unheated stairs without producing a full crop of goosebumps.

Starting to rise, Hugh remembered he slept naked, and only changed position to rest propped on one arm, the other pulling his blanket tight. The book slid off to flop on the floor.

Nora retrieved the text and read its title. "A good book to prepare for tonight," she said as the shawl slipped from her shoulders.

The irises of Hugh's eyes widened. Her face warmed in the glow of the lamp. Moving to the side of the bed, she tugged on a pink ribbon, releasing the bow holding the blouse and exposing the curve of breasts. The blouse came up and over her head – she posed for him arms held high like a ballerina, this most beautiful and erotic position of women that lifted the breasts and pulled in the stomach. Hugh shivered. His body began to react. The teacher's arms came down, releasing the blouse to join the shawl. Her hands moved to unbutton the skirt.

"Books prepare you, but experience makes you an expert," Nora said in a husky voice. The skirt dropped. She placed one bare knee on the bed. Hugh sensed his teeth were clenched and tried to relax them. His head only two feet from her charms, his eyes followed the peach fuzz on her lower belly down into mysterious pelvic hair. Nora was a natural redhead. Hugh expanded his gaze to drink in her breasts and the curve of her hips.

She let him look a few seconds more. With a slight tightening occurred in the corners of her lips, his teacher pulled up the blanket and slipped in beside him. Holding his head in her hands, she leaned forward to kiss his eyelids, whispering, "Ovid also said, 'If you want to be loved, be loveable.'"

*

Sitting in the rocking, vibrating train, Hugh reflected on all she had taught him. His first big surprise being how much of a sex organ human skin was, and the corollary: any place there were nerves, arousal could be augmented or achieved. Over the next month, they made love many times and, in many places. When the weather finally warmed enough, they joined bodies in grassy protected places on the mansion grounds or in the house lap pool.

He discovered the value of lips, tongue, and teeth. As a history teacher and gymnast, she took him to ecstatic highs achieved through bodily positions described in ancient books, some techniques even incorporating aspects of meditation, yoga, and mindfulness. One thing she never did was fake an orgasm. Unable to bring those to her at first, she worked Hugh with gentle patience, building his self-esteem as a lover and his desire to please, until he could release the music from her again and again.

The only puzzle in retrospect was why no one said or did anything, as little as they hid their relationship from father, uncle, and others. The answer, of course, Hugh mused, they knew and approved. In fact, to this day, he remained unsure whether she had been hired to provide him with that final polish. Given the dreadfully ignorant sexual performance of other men his age, it had been a gift beyond compare.

Nora had stayed until the day he left. He stood at the door facing her, a small green duffle bag at his feet. With one last embrace, she recited a verse from an old poem:

> *Kiss me, and say good-bye;*
> *Good-bye, there is no word to say but this,*
> *Nor any lips left for my lips to kiss,*
> *Nor any tears to shed, when these tears dry;*
> *Kiss me, and say good-bye.*

As the train rocked, Hugh's head slumped. His temperature kicked up a notch and he lapsed into a deep, fever-induced dream. Mind swimming, he faced off against his Uncle Frank in a strange dojo, the atmosphere hot and humid, the cotton fabric of his white judogi sweat-stuck to his back and sides. The two bowed and advanced. Hugh felt the elasticity of the wooden floor give against his bare feet. Medium height and stocky, looking like he was mostly chest and arms, Uncle Frank grasped fistfuls of the cloth covering Hugh's chest and left elbow.

He reciprocated.

They danced back and forth, each feeling for a split-second imbalance or weakness on their opponent's part. Hugh could see his uncle's prizefighter nose, broken many times, and the sweat-curled black chest hair exposed in the neck 'V' of his jacket. The familiar smell of the garlic and wine that flavored his food spiced his breath and body odor.

"Recite the rules!" Uncle Frank shouted in his ear.

Hugh couldn't remember them. He looked for the sign, the place where the *dōjō kun* — the rules of the house — were posted. Attention distracted, his opponent stepped in and used an *O-goshi* hip throw to smack him to the floor. He gasped.

Uncle pinned him and repeated, "Recite the rules!" Using his advantageous position, Uncle Frank slid his body to a right angle and placed an arm around the back of Hugh's neck. Hands came together, fingers locked, positioning his right bicep across Hugh's throat. Tightening, the *shime-waza* chokehold immediately began shutting off his air. Then the arms relaxed.

He could breathe, and "Recite the rules!" came again. Over a pinning shoulder, Hugh focused on the sign. The usual rules of the House de Gracie dojo were: Show courtesy, respect, and honesty towards others/Develop confidence through knowledge, honesty, and strength/Never use violence for personal gain/Seek perfection of character. The lettering on this sign was different, strange, yet familiar.

The lettering on this sign was different, strange, yet familiar. Muscles squeezed. His air cut off, Hugh slapped his Uncle's back with one hand in surrender. He took a breath and read off the first rule: *La pluy nous a buez et lavez*, translated as "Rain has drained and washed us." A flex of bicep encouraged him to speak the second line: *Et le soleil dessechiez et noircis*, "And the sun has dried and blackened us." The third line: *Pies, corbeaulx nous ont les yeux cavez*, "Magpies and crows have pecked out our eyes." Hugh silently read the fourth line, *Et arrachié la barbe etles sources*, "And torn off our beards and eyebrows."

He recognized the lines as coming from the five-hundred-year-old poem *Ballad of the Hanged* by François Villon. Hugh realized this was a dream. The vision of the dojo, Uncle, and the rules was trying to tell him something. He felt stupid, couldn't fathom it. In a normal voice, he said *"C'est des conneries!"* then shouted the same in English: "This is bullshit!"

Muscles tightened, air shutoff, he struggled and jerked at his Uncle's hair and judogi. His sight necked down to a pinpoint. Lungs sent last panic messages to his brain. Legs and arms lost direction and quivered. The point of light grew closer. He rushed upwards as though erupting from a dark well.

Someone shook his left arm, "Sir, *Monsieur*, wake up." Only his weakness kept his reflexive open palm jab from reaching the man's jaw. The man ignored the defensive move.

"You're burning up. Here, drink." The balding Canadian from across the aisle removed the cap and passed him a plastic water bottle.

Hugh took the container with both shaking hands and drank great gulps, excess water dribbling down the corners of his mouth to wet his shirt and tie. His mind returned to the reality of the Amtrak train.

"C'est un rêve très remarquable. We couldn't help hearing your dream-talk, most of it in a French that hasn't been spoken for centuries. I am Louis, *professeur de langues anciennes* with the University of Montreal."

His wife giggled and spoke from her window seat, *"Mais tres moderne — le mots grossiers à la fin."*

Hugh blushed. Evidently, Louis, his wife, and everyone else within range of his command voice had heard his recitation of the dream rules and the swearing at the end. He had picked up this French from his Uncle Frank, which usually left native French speakers puzzled and goggle-eyed after a few minutes of conversation. Up to this point, he had thought it some bastard dialect with its frequent straight-from-the-Latin borrowings and archaic words. His mind presented another bit of old French for his defense. *Hony soyt qe mal y pense.* Shame be to him who thinks evil of it.

The train began to slow. Over the car's speakers, the conductor announced Port Henry the next station stop. He reached for his briefcase and beret. The professor looked disappointed, but Hugh was relieved there would be no further exploration of his *langue ancienne.* The railcar ceased moving with a jerk, not as smooth a stop as most.

Hugh rose and fell back into his seat. He tried again, pulling himself upright with arms somewhat stronger than his rubbery legs. He buttoned his jacket to meet military specifications before leaving the car and entering the public eye. It was a conditioned reflex, past inspections by numerous keen-eyed drill sergeants surfacing in his subconscious mind. But his wrinkled pants, scuffed boots, and cheek bristles wouldn't pass their scrutiny. The lack of a shower and clean clothes left him surrounded by a body odor fug of nasty proportions. The door opened. He experienced a head-spin of vertigo. The descent down the stairs to the platform seemed yards distant. Taking the first step as a leap of faith, Hugh felt a wave of darkness lap over him. His foot twisted, and he crumpled forward.

His body smacked into something solid, yet fluid. He heard a grunt. Arms encircled his chest and held him upright. With the help of this support, he pulled his feet together and managed a shaky stance. Someone grabbed his chin and moved his face from side-to-side. Gentle fingers ran over his scars and eye patch.

"*La Vierge Marie, Joseph, et Jésus, quel fils de salope* did this to you?"

Hugh felt great relief. The distinctive bastard French-English chatter was his Uncle Frank's. Among friends at last, strong arms pulled him into a hug.

"*Tu me rends heureux.* I am happy again to have you back. You shake. What is the matter, boy?"

The familiarity resurrected a little boy's personality. "*Malade*, I am sick, *mon oncle*."

"*Allon nous-en*, let us get you to your father, *tout de suite*." Frank took the briefcase in one hand and Hugh's arm in the other.

With his uncle supporting him, the pair eked out a slow progression across the platform to the rear of the station. Waiting there stood two matched roan horses harnessed to the de Gracie House's tan and black brougham, its box-shaped body enclosed by two doors with side windows and glazed front and back windscreens.

The carriage could seat two on the cushioned bench seat, and two more could be squeezed in on an extra pair of foldaway seats in the front corners. The squared-off cab rested on a wood and iron frame that morphed upward into a triangular beak that could swivel on its attachment to the front wheels. Unlike a more traditional coach, this design feature and the lack of fenders allowed the rig to turn sharply. A desired characteristic, given the acute angles of the mountain switchbacks they would traverse to reach the family home.

He noticed the de Gracie family crest on the door panel was freshly painted. It consisted of a shield with a multi-branched tree of life placed on an azure field. The tree's leaves were tiny *Fleur de Lys*, given the fact they were downplayed probably referred to some ancient back-bedroom connection with European royalty. A banner across the bottom displayed the family motto: *Nous servons, que nous soyons servis*. He whispered the meaning, "We serve, that we may be served."

Hugh heard a whine and a deep-throated half-bark. A pair of tails thumped the sidewalk. He recognized two of the estate's Irish Wolfhounds. Both sat, dog-rumps quivering, eager to be released from the "stay" command they had been given. The female held the reins to the horses in her mouth.

He knew them, both companions of his youth, the male named *Loup-garou* and the female *Alys*. The dogs were a product of the House's breeding program that went back hundreds of years. Noted for their loyalty, trainability, and intelligence, the puppies fetched premium prices. The one-hundred-and-fifty-pound male displayed such cleverness and understanding of humans that many of the household thought him a man changed into a wolf, hence his French name, meaning werewolf. Even in his fever-induced weakness, Hugh felt uneasy; something was wrong about the dogs. Loup and his mate would be in their twenties, entirely too old for a breed that averaged an eight-year lifespan.

Cold early-spring air insinuated itself through his sweat-dampened clothes. Hugh started to shake so badly he lost control of his legs and arms. His companion opened the carriage door.

Hugh tried to pull himself up and failed.

Uncle turned, lifted him in his arms, and placed him on the bench seat. "*Mon Dieu, mon petit coq*, you have lost a lot of weight. You feel as light as a dust bunny."

He placed Hugh's feet on a metal box fastened to the floor – the container for hot bricks heated feet and cab. He felt like a little boy again as uncle tucked a wool blanket around his hips and legs.

With one whistle the big gray-black wolfhounds leapt into the cab.

Taking positions one on each side of Hugh, they pushed against his body, propping him upright and sharing their body heat. The warmth was so welcome Hugh didn't mind their carnivore breath. He put a hand on each head, jaws big enough to cut through his thigh in one bite opened in toothy smiles.

The brougham rocked as uncle climbed into the driver's seat. With a jerk, the horses pulled the ancient carriage into the town's nightly five-minute traffic jam consisting of homeward bound folks, whose lack of curiosity indicated they had seen this sight many times before.

The rhythmic sound of the horses' hoofs and the sway of the vehicle put him to sleep. He roused whenever the vehicle broke rhythm to reverse direction at the bends of the mountain switchbacks.

The dogs' excitement brought him fully awake as they neared the gate in the estate's outer wall. The setting sun, though blocked by the west side of the mountain, still cast bright indirect light, making the long shadows of the wall and the chateau within creep across road and fields. Skeletal and leafless in its winter gray and black, the outer barrier's sinister mass appeared more threatening than usual. An intertwined curtain of thirty-foot tall blackthorn tree — their needle-studded trunks and branches crisscrossed — was so thick and grown together that only something the size of a squirrel could crawl through.

The coach entered a set of masonry-pillared double gates that pierced the twenty-foot thick interlocked growth.

Gravel crunched under the iron-rimmed wheels as the carriage moved up a drive that bisected an open area the size of three football fields fronting the manse. The horses raised their heads and picked up speed, anticipating their stables.

Uncle cursed and pulled back on the reins.

The mansion's great door stood open, its dark mouth framed by striated tan-and-cinnamon colored walls. The ivy vines that stretched up to the third story and curled around the protruding three towers had just begun to leaf again.

This scene brought a frisson of foreboding. Hugh remembered times in his room or traveling the many stairways when he did not feel completely alone. Always he felt the sensation of an omnipresent directionless presence watching and analyzing – the sensation scary sometimes, on other occasions reassuring. As the carriage drew closer, Hugh could see a dozen figures, men and women recognizable from their dress, waiting at the bottom of the steps.

The brougham skittered to a halt. Individual pieces of gravel popped from under its iron-rimmed tires to rattle against the coach's underbody. The right-side door opened and the dogs bounded out.

Hugh centered mentally and drew on the last of his energy reserves. Abandoning the briefcase, he slid out of the carriage. Knees buckled and he fell forward into the arms of the man he hadn't seen for ten years.

"Father, father…"

2

A time to be born, and a time to die; a time to
plant, and a time to pluck up that which is planted;
Ecclesiastes: 3:2

HUGH THOUGHT HE DREAMED. He felt no sense of passing time as his mind flooded with memories – vivid, erotic, and serene, of the last twenty-eight years. Episodes played themselves out, intervals between them skipped past at blurry velocity. It was as though someone, some entity, watched a film of his life, stopping at the most entertaining spots and fast-forwarding past the mundane.

The decade of his youthful Spartan schooling flashed by. The years of learning to live with and function in spite of pain and hardship, hunger, thirst, cold, and lack of sleep. Father and Uncle awarded punishments for failing to struggle to the utmost.

His time in the military rolled by, the training, some as dangerous as combat. The long periods of boredom, the loneliness – all punctuated by the controlled panic of battle. The culmination came with an exhaustive, full-color, detailed replay of his capture and mutilation in Afghanistan.

In this dream, wind-boosted dust flicked against eyes and filled the nostrils of the travelers. The powdered soil contained traces, accumulated over thousands of years, of all those that had come to this land to die. The desiccated chalky bones and corroded war wreckage of Macedonians, Arabs, Persians, Mongols, British, Soviets, and more recently NATO forces littered the country's mountains, deserts, and fertile valleys. Eyes teared, noses ran, and mouths spit to clear the metallic-tasting paste formed as the air-borne grit mixed with human secretions.

The land they passed through had been deforested, the trees turned into lumber and shipped to Pakistan, leaving the unshaded, uprooted soil to erode and powder. Hugh de Gracie nuzzled into the mane hair of the donkey he straddled, hoping it would serve as a filter.

He and the dun-gray jack had become friends. Wounds acquired in the ambush prevented his walking any distance, so he rode tied to the strongest of his captors' pack animals, feet roped under its belly, and hands tied together around its neck. Riding bareback created agony. Between the flat donkey back keeping his legs spread out, and the grinding shrapnel lodged in his calves, thighs, and buttocks, no relief could be realized. Another layer of anguish had been added after his previous escape attempt.

The first night they had hunkered down in an orchard whose figs, apricots, peaches, and plums would be ripe in another month. The Taliban fighters made a primitive camp and unpacked simple journey food of dates, smoked mutton strips, and cheese curds. A kettle of cracked wheat steamed over a guarded fire of dry animal dung. Before they staked out his feet and hands for the night, he slopped part of the contents of his half-cooked bowl of gruel over the fuzzy local-made rope tying his hands.

Back on the donkey at the break of day, he held the bindings up to the animal's white muzzle. He heard a sniff and a tongue licked the rope. From his previous tour of being embedded with Afghan government forces, he knew donkeys didn't require much graze. They only needed to consume less than two percent of their mass daily, but they took six hours or better, depending on the quality of the forage, to eat enough. This Taliban party was moving too fast to allow that. Hugh felt the jack's teeth start to chew on the ropes. He worked his feet, trying to stretch the bonds on his ankles.

Thirty minutes later, hands and feet free, he spun off his mount and rolled down the mountainside, rock outcroppings biting his hips and shoulders as he spun. He came to a sudden racking stop against a cluster of white poplar stumps, knocking the breath out of him. Shouts came from back on the trail. Pebbles and fist-sized rocks rattled down as his pursuers scrabbled after him. Hugh rose on all fours, groaned, and staggered upright. Limping around the tree stubs, he tried sliding his feet through the loose rocks and gravel bending his body and knees as though he was back home doing stem-christies on the ski slopes surrounding Lake Placid. The tactic failed.

The hillmen, active in these mountains since birth, ran him down. Back on the trail, they removed his boots and socks then whipped the bottoms of his feet with canes. Father's Spartan training from his seventh to eighteenth year had taught him ways to ignore or deal with physical hurt. Hugh used every trick he knew to dim a burning agony so intense unbidden tears trickled out of the corners of his eyes.

Convinced their captive would not be walking for a few weeks, they tied him back on the donkey. He pushed the throbbing hurt down to a dull background ache and went back to observing the men, filing away their features and personality quirks. Hugh paid special attention to their voices, memorizing their lift, fall, and peculiarities. In his previous tour, he had picked up quite a bit of Pushto and was able to follow many of the conversations without his captors being aware.

The five Taliban fighters, led by their commander Fahad, were all related. Hugh recognized their use of specific Pushto words for kin, and always they used the familiar forms of address not used in conversation with the unrelated or even with friends. It made sense. Blood relatives could be trusted the most. The oldest, Uncle Maahir, a man of no-nonsense personality, possessed a reputation as an experienced fighter with the scars to prove it. Next came the leader's younger brother, a slender youth whose joy in life was reciting poetry, both classical and verses of his own creation. They called him Nazim, but Hugh couldn't tell if that was his birth name or a nickname, since Nazim translated as poet.

Squat cousin Abdul normally stayed on his farm and tended crops and animals, coming on raids and resupply treks only when they needed his donkeys. The fifth member of the party was a foreign fighter, an arrogant Saudi named Aziz, who seemed even more out of place among the group than Hugh. Related only by marriage, he was a younger brother to Fahad's fourth wife. The leader gained power in the traditional tribal way by multiple marriages into powerful and rich clans.

Fahad, whose name translated as lynx, the only one who spoke English, did so proficiently. His command of the language combined with light skin and green eyes made it possible for him to pass for a European. Walking alongside Hugh's donkey, he bragged in perfect Midwestern American about his time living in the United States on a student visa. He had received his BA and law degree from the University of Iowa. His years there had not made him a fan of American culture and politics, much the opposite. The government was much too secular, the women shamefully unrestrained, and the people fat and corrupt.

"Unbelievers will never defeat us. Your fort was correctly located to shut off our movement of supplies and fighters, but poorly built.

Before you arrived, with only a few men, we kept your infidel soldiers afraid and shivering in their holes."

It was true. The high command had sent Hugh to Combat Outpost Barracuda to get the failing platoon to accomplish its mission of interdicting a major Taliban supply route. He arrived to find the sandbagged and bunkered outpost completely open to plunging fire from the surrounding pine and poplar-covered mountains. Even the latrines were exposed and couldn't be used until nightfall. Men huddled shoulder-to-shoulder in shelters with overhead cover during the daylight hours – the whole affair more like a submarine than a ground base. Low morale resulted in the defenders renaming the base "The Alamo" and starting a pool to guess the date when the Taliban would overrun them.

Hugh, accompanied by two handpicked NCO's, reorganized and refortified the base, zeroed their 81mm mortars on probable sniper locations and led four-man teams on night patrols. Using advanced night vision devices, they set up successful ambushes and shut down the trails leading into the valley. Some patrols moved into hiding positions and waited until daylight allowed them to call fire down on the snipers. The mortars' airbursts threw shrapnel in a fifty-meter cone on enemy positions, chopping them to pieces or driving them out of cover to be killed or captured. Within a month, enemy activity virtually ceased.

The Taliban commander's countermove had been well-conceived and executed. He offered himself as bait, allowing false information on his whereabouts to be delivered to the local Afghan police, who passed it on to the Americans. Hugh led a six-man night patrol intending to capture Fahad. His position behind the point man on the narrow trail put him in the blast circle of an IED that filled his legs and buttocks with shrapnel and set off the L-shaped enemy ambush.

Knocked unconscious, he awoke tied to the donkey. The remnants of the Taliban force scurried away, cursing the incoming artillery that had prevented them from finishing off the American squad. However, they had achieved their primary objective with his capture.

Just before nightfall the second day, the party halted. The men combat alert, each one faced a different direction, Kalashnikovs ready, while the leader scouted ahead. Hugh's animal stiffened and let out an ee haw, ee haw, quickly answered by another donkey further up. The men laughed and relaxed. The leader returned, indicating their base and its caretaker remained secure.

Based on the duration of the trip and the steady upward climb, Hugh knew they must be well into the no-mans-land between the border of Kunar province and the Pakistani tribal lands.

Near a cave mouth, the Taliban fighters unloaded the donkeys while two grabbed Hugh under the arms and dragged him underground. The skin on his trailing bare toes became scratched and bloody scraping the uneven rock floor as they moved past defensive firing positions and storage alcoves cut into the interior stone. They continued around two right-angle turns, through a thick ironbound wooden door, and into a natural cavern. Stripped naked and tossed on a mound of smelly pudding-soft material, his ropes were exchanged for padlocked wrist gauntlets welded to chains attached to iron wedges hammered into cracks in the rock.

The door slammed, bolts shot home leaving him in complete blackness and silence.

Hugh worked on reducing pain and controlling his breathing. The noise of his gasping and heart-pounding interfered with the senses needed to understand the new surroundings. After minutes of calming meditation, he mentally checked what sensory input remained. The air, cool on his skin and in his lungs, indicated a temperature of around fifty-five degrees – he was below the frost line where the thermometer remained stable regardless of the outside weather. He wouldn't freeze. Breathing very slowly, he listened, detecting a delicate fluttering noise higher up in the cave. The noise came again in separate fragments from most of the compass points.

Bats, he concluded. If so, the night flyers must have a route out of the cave. Hugh's fingers dug in the squashy gunk surrounding him and raised a sample to his nose – fecal matter.

Damn! He rested on bat shit. Shit that must have built up to a considerable depth over the centuries. In some places in this country, the natives mined the guano for crop fertilizer, a valuable commodity. Perhaps he should feel wealthy. Something with multiple legs ran up his thigh. He slapped it. Running his fingertips over the stunned creature helped him form a picture in his mind. He detected multiple legs and a hard-shelled body. Beetles and other insects must be working the dung. Well, at least he wouldn't starve, his early family training had included sampling a full menu of insects – a good source of protein.

Hugh shook his chains and listened for the echo. It was a big cave. Using fingernails to test the padlocks and chains, he felt crusted rust scales on the surface of the native-forged iron. However, sound metal underneath retained its strength — no hope of breaking it without tools. Following the shackles down to the floor, he rubbed his fingertips over the metal stakes and the chains' connecting links. Might be some hope there. Former prisoners had rubbed the inside of the links back and forth against the hole in the piton, thinning their diameter. Jerking and pulling on the fetters one at a time produced no movement: the metal wedges adhered to the rock as strongly as Arthur's sword in the anvil. Hugh began scraping the bottom link of the right wrist chain against its connecting stake. He had all the time in the world.

After what seemed like a long time, bolts slammed back, and the door opened letting Fahad and Aziz enter. "Hold up the light, Brother," the leader commanded. "Let us see how the kafir is doing."

Hugh sat up and covered eyes, not used to the brightness of the lantern.

Aziz, his face etched into a permanent scowl, fingered the hilt of the jambiya dagger stuck under his two-inch-wide leather belt. The double-edged steel blade was forged with an exaggerated upward curve ending in a sharp point, resembling a very large filleting knife.

Given its age and decoration, Hugh guessed this one had the traditional rhinoceros horn handle. Silver filigree work covered the cedar wood sheath, which was also inset with pearls and small rubies, all in all, a piece of work-worn by a very high-status individual.

Fahad noticed his interest. "My brother-in-law's knife has passed to him through his father from his grandfather. He is Hashimite, and can trace his bloodline directly to the family of the prophet Muhammad, peace be upon his name. It is his pride and joy, for as you have probably noticed he has few other positive characteristics."

Hugh waited in silence – his eyes now adjusted to the light level. "Were you satisfied with your four-legged transport on the trip here?"

"If it was good enough for Jesus, it was good enough for me."

Fahad tried another tack: "You don't seem concerned about your lack of clothing."

"I am as the one God we both worship made us – in his image. Why should I be embarrassed?"

Not happy that attempts to humiliate the prisoner had little effect, he swung a wooden-stocked AK-47. The steel butt plate smashed across the bridge of Hugh's nose, breaking the cartilage. "Smart-ass answers I can get from any dirt-ragged hairy *imam*, I don't need them from you." He gave an order to Aziz in Arabic and took the lantern from him.

The brother-in-law unsheathed his dagger, stepped forward, and grabbed a handful of Hugh's hair, pulling him forward and face up. The jambiya slashed downward, opening a furrow across Hugh's forehead into the right eyebrow then dropping to nick the eyelid before continuing to cut into his cheek. The return backhand cut a groove riding the cheekbone, the upward curve of the blade tip pierced the eye before cutting the socket flesh above it to the bone.

Hugh's scream contained equal parts of anger and pain.

"I will be gone for the next three days into Pakistan. Think about your loss. Your value to me is small now that we have removed you from your soldiers. If you are not completely cooperative upon my return… Well, you have other pairs of things that can be reduced to singles." Fahad tossed the prisoner a palm-sized pasteboard box.

The two turned and exited, leaving a shaking Hugh bleeding in the blackness. The box contained a compressed Russian gauze bandage dating back to their failed occupation, which he unfolded and pressed over his wound. The cotton pad staunched the blood flow. The adrenaline reaction and the collective pain, now from many sources, made Hugh's body shudder. Turning his head, he threw up.

Struggling to keep from going into shock, he rested for twenty minutes before tying the bandage's tails around his head.

He must bear the pain. Using thumbs and index fingers, he pushed his nose back into position and then returned to rasping the right-hand chain's last link against its piton. There was no question now. He must escape before Fahad returned. All he had to do was break the chain on each of his arms, learn to walk again, get through a bolted door, and bare-ass naked kill four Afghan guerillas — while struggling with impaired depth perception.

Alone in the dark, the whisper of bat wings overhead, Hugh took inventory. He stretched – no bones were broken. Wiggling fingers first, he then manipulated his wrists, elbows, shoulders, hips, knees, and ankles – all worked unimpeded. No crucial internal organs had been injured. Outside of the pain coming from numerous locations, he retained a workable body – minus an eye.

Standing, a spasm of agony rushed up to his brain from injured feet. One foot took a forward step, the other followed. He shuffled forward and back the two paces the chain allowed and then sat abruptly.

His checklist complete, Hugh concluded that his body would do mostly what he commanded. At an Army field hospital, the triage system would have marked him last for treatment. Dealing with the throbbing agony in feet, nose, and eye while trying to function both mentally and physically became his primary problem. His early Spartan upbringing and Army training had conditioned him to withstand hurt. From the age of seven, he had been forced to compete with full-grown men. Running, wrestling, punching, and kicking against his larger opponents had accelerated his ability to take punishment and his fighting capabilities. These came at the cost of bruises, contusions, sprains, and broken bones.

His relatives and military instructors told him warriors expected pain to accompany combat. Pain that couldn't be ignored could be diminished through the meditative techniques taught him by his father and uncle. And he possessed one asset his captors didn't – desperation. Full of fear and anger, Hugh was only one adrenaline rush away from becoming a berserker.

Human nature gave him an escape chance the afternoon of the next day. Aziz couldn't leave him alone. Rejected from the company of his fellows due to a combination of obnoxious behavior and the Afghan's deep-grained distrust of outsiders, he turned to Hugh to provide a diversion. Holding a lantern in one hand, he wielded one of the canes they had used on his feet, lashing forearms and shoulders.

Hugh scuttled back, forcing his tormentor to step into the range of his chained arms. He grabbed the cane, jerked the little man forward, and used a right foot hooked around his ankles to trip him. The dropped lantern made a soft angled landing in the bat guano. Its canted light cast struggling shadows against the cave wall.

Hugh howled and shouted, "Don't beat me, don't beat me!" to cover the noise of the struggle from the guard on the other side of the door. Pulling Aziz close, he rolled on top, pinning his lighter adversary on his back, neutralizing the Kalashnikov slung over the

Saudi's shoulder.

Aziz opened his mouth to yell.

Hugh used his only weapon. He jammed a handful of bat shit into the man's open jaws, then another handful, and a third. Mouth and throat stuffed full, the Saudi's face turned blue, his feet kicked. Fingernails tore at Hugh's neck. Arab muscles twitched and relaxed, arms fell askew.

He held the body down for a five-minute count to be sure. Hugh searched the man's clothes for the padlock keys. No luck. He set the kerosene lamp upright, burning a finger on the hot reflector shade. A flicker of motion caught his eye. He thought Aziz had moved. Panicky, his hands squeezed the Saudi's throat. Looking closer, a centipede finished twisting its way out of the dirt in the Saudi's overstuffed mouth and scurried away.

Full of adrenaline, he pulled the AK-47 from under Aziz and slammed its steel butt plate against the pitons, while yelling as though still being beaten. Hammered back and forth, the rocks released their grip on the stakes. A quick plan formed, he couldn't use the assault rifle on the door guard, the firing would alert the others, and he would remain trapped in the back portion of the cave. Hugh used some of the bat guano to blacken his face and neck.

Relieving Aziz of his *jambiya* dagger he shut off the lantern. Pulses of pain clawed up Hugh's legs as he raised the Saudi's dead body, a flash of dizziness came and passed. Straining to hold the body upright next to the door, he pounded on the wood with one fist and imitated the Saudi's voice, demanding it open.

Nazim, the poet, pushed the door wide. A body smacked against him. Instinctively he reached out and grasped the dead weight, reeling backwards. The deadweight pinning him, the boy's mind had still not grasped the situation when a razor-sharp blade cut his throat.

Hugh retrieved the keys and the chains came off.

As Hugh crept up the tunnel, he smelled cooking. Someone

prepared *kofta challow*, a lamb, onion, garlic, and rice dish. The scent made him salivate. Blood rushed from his head to his stomach. Feeling faint, he leaned against the cool rock wall to steady himself before resuming a quiet limp through the upper passageway, pausing to examine each alcove. Near the cave entrance, he found farmer Abdul bent over a cooking pot.

Uncle Maahir must be out on sentry duty.

Hugh stepped behind the cook and butt-stroked the back of his head with the AK-47, producing a satisfying crunch. Remembering the words of his Uncle Frank, never leave a live enemy behind your back, he knelt and used the knife.

Unable to resist tasting a mouthful of stew, he swallowed without chewing. It was too hot and burned all the way down. He grabbed a water jug and drank a cupful, used more to wash his face, arms, and hands. Squeezing into Abdul's too small shirt and coat, he filled a bowl with the lamb-rice mixture and waved it out the entrance showing only an extended arm mimicking Abdul's voice, shouting in Pushto, "Food, food." When Uncle Maahir's silhouette showed in the cave entrance, Hugh put two bullets center mass in compliance with army training, and one final round in the forehead, obeying his boyhood lessons. Leaving the body to bleed out, he finished the kofta challow.

Lining up the corpses, he selected clothing. Nazim's salwar pants had the right waist and length, Uncle Maahir's larger chest made his kameez long shirt and shearling vest fit. Aziz's belt and knife completed the costume. Hugh had trouble with Abdul's *pakul* cap until he remembered the bag-like hat's sides needed to be rolled up to form a thick band that rested on the head like a beret. No footwear fit his swollen feet, so they remained bare.

A quick tour outside located a camouflaged wooden gate between two boulders, which opened into the donkey corral. The jack recognized him. Separating from the others, it pranced up on its straight-sided petite hoofs and showed brown-stained ivory teeth in a grotesque smile.

Hugh rubbed its head. He decided to name him *Koshan*, which meant hard-working in Pushto.

He stopped many times to rest while preparing his get-away. After satisfying the donkeys' immediate needs with grain and water, he assembled packs of food, drink, and ammunition. Animal feed, hand grenades, and an extra Kalashnikov were added, making up two sixty-pound burdens. Crawling when his feet needed relief, Hugh placed explosives found in the storage alcoves in key places, connected them with a central fuse.

Koshan and two loaded pack donkeys waited outside the cave while Hugh lit what he hoped was a fifteen-minute fuse. Limping up to the jack, he made a clumsy belly-first mount. The animals trotted off, needing no urging and no guidance. The intelligent beasts knew the way they had traveled many times. Despite their fast exit, the little party of man and donkeys felt the shake of the blast and were enveloped in a wing-edge of the windborne dust cloud from the exploded cave.

Two days passed. Hugh watched as the startled sentries at Combat Outpost Barracuda saw and heard what appeared to be a tall Afghan man, bandage over one eye, riding a donkey and singing *The Hallelujah Chorus* from Handel's *Messiah* at the top of his lungs.

Weeks later, in Germany, Hugh received a packet containing an extract from an official report from his friend Lieutenant Reynolds. He and Bobby had gone through Officers' Candidate School together and then transferred to Military Intelligence. They had both received orders for Afghanistan at the same time. A handwritten note accompanied the envelope.

Coup,
Hope you are doing well. Gloria and my daughters are already planning a feast of your favorite foods for the next time we are all

together.

    *I am directing Specialist Cararia, who is transferring to your
location, to hand deliver this interrogation transcript outside official
channels, otherwise you may go unwarned.*

    *You evidentially stirred up quite a hornet's nest with your escape.
Whether you deserve it or not, you have acquired an implacable enemy.
Remember what Winston Churchill said in his memoirs:*

    *"The Pathan tribes are always engaged in private or public war.
Every man is a warrior, politician, and a theologian. Every house is a
real feudal fortress... Every family cultivates its vendetta; every clan,
its feud... Nothing is ever forgotten and very few debts are left
unpaid."*

    *The family and I will never forgive you, you slippery bastard, if you
let this Afghani son of a bitch get the better of you. Let me know if
there is some further way I can help.*
Best of luck to you,
Bobby

Hugh set down the note and began to read a smudged extract of a
prisoner interrogation translated into English. He noted the
transcriber had added explanatory notes in parenthesizes where
needed.

INTERROGATOR: You were with Taliban Commander Fahad during
   his return from the Pakistan tribal areas?

PRISONER: Yes, a party of twenty men, eight donkeys, and
   two dogs over the mountains with supplies.

INTERROGATOR: What were your plans?

PRISONER: Commander Fahad planned on resting for a day at
   the cave base, questioning an infidel Captain, and then
   hitting the American fort with the fish name-the thin
   one with the sharp teeth. A good name.
   (PRISONER SMILES)
   Fahad said we would pull those teeth.

INTERROGATOR: The attack didn't happen. What disrupted the
   plan?

PRISONER: We found the cave blocked with fallen rubble.
   (PRISONER FROWNS)

It took three days to dig it out. Most of the stores and equipment were destroyed. The cool of the mountain preserved the bodies. They didn't smell much.

INTERROGATOR: What was Fahad's reaction?

PRISONER: I was sad to see it.
(PRISONER'S FACE EXPRESSES A VARIETY OF EMOTIONS)
Fahad was beyond rage. His relatives were dead. His cousin, the Saudi jihadi, had been choked with filth and the crawling things of the deep earth.
(PRISONER SHUDDERS)
May Allah preserve him, a bad way to go. His heavenly virgins will reject him. The killer is a demon.
(PRISONER PAUSES THEN CONTINUES)
All of us heard Fahad curse himself for keeping the infidel officer alive. He raised the shiny metal tags he had taken from the prisoner listing the man's name, special number, and religion. Squeezing them in a raised fist, he vowed to God that a blood feud would exist between him and the American, ending only when the man and his family were exterminated from the earth or until the end of time.

INTERROGATOR: What happened next?

PRISONER: The men refused to be led by the Commander. He had allowed a single, crippled, one-eyed man to kill his relatives and defeat his plans.
(PRISONER SHOWS DISTASTE)
His nang (PASHTUN CONCEPT OF PERSONAL HONOR) was stained.

INTERROGATOR: What will Fahad do now?

PRISONER: What can he do? Fahad must restore nang (HONOR) through badal (PASHTUN CONCEPT OF REVENGE). He must do this by shedding the blood of the American and his family, at least in equal measure to what the commander has lost. Failure to restore honor is beghairat (PASHTUN CONCEPT OF SHAME, DISHONOR). He and his family will never be accepted again until that is accomplished.

INTERROGATOR: Is there anything short of bloodletting that can balance the scales?

PRISONER: The American and his family have no standing in our land. The normal ways, a Jirga (GROUP OF ELDERS) ruling, Nanawatay (AN ACT OF HUMILIATION AND REQUEST FOR

ASYLUM OR MERCY BY THE AMERICAN TO FAHAD'S FAMILY),
payment of blood money, are not available for the killer.

INTERROGATOR: Where is Fahad now?

PRISONER: I know not. It is said that he went to beg help
from his Saudi relatives.

INTERROGATOR: Who are these Saudis?

PRISONER: Fahad never told us. They are rumored to possess
great wealth and know the ways of the infidel world.

Hugh dropped the papers on the bedsheets. He wondered, what
the hell had he gotten himself into?

The recollections continued. Drawn out of him by some alien
force, the memories came back. The hospital in Germany, his plane-
train trip home, and the confrontation with the hoodie-man flickered
past in noir-movie black and white. Someone patted forehead and
cheeks with a cool damp cloth. His nose fed him the familiar musty
book scent of his old tower room mixed with a blended woman and
dog smell arousing him from deep slumber to that in-between place
of comfortable rest and the growing desire to wake.

Hugh felt a strong yearning to stretch muscles – arms, back, and
legs motionless too long. Flexing fingers, he raised a forearm,
something cord-like impeded the action. Trying to pull away, hands
pinned his arm and chest. He panicked, kicked, and bucked.

"Alys, fetch the Father, Loup, help me hold him."

A heavy weight fell across his legs; pushing against it, he tried to
free his right arm from under the blanket.

"Hugh, stay quiet," came a matronly command. "You will pull out
your intravenous needle. You are home, remember, you are home."
The voice, the voice so familiar – Margy, his Margy.

Relaxing, his eye opened to a dark room, bars of light across the
floor led back to curtained cross-shaped slit windows.

Margy, his former nanny, knelt beside the bed, she reached up and tousled his hair, and smiled. Her curls were whiter than he remembered, but her skin still looked smooth with only laugh-wrinkles at the corners of her eyes. A burst of sniffing attracted his attention. Loup pushed his soccer ball-sized head forward and laid it on his stomach. Hugh managed to finally extract his right arm and scratched behind an ear as big as his hand. Muzzle lifted, mouth opened, and a tongue licked the blanket.

"Okay, monster. You've had your fun, off me now."

Turning to his surrogate mother, "May I sit up?" Hugh asked.

Alys trotted in, her claw tips tapping on the floor. "*Pas encore, mon fils*, not just yet," came a voice from the doorway. His father, Aubert Renée Phillipe de Gracie, stepped in and made a circuit of the room, opening curtains. "Watch your eye, it will be bright."

Hugh could only see the shadowy silhouette of a man as it approached the threesome at the bed, the extra light reflected off a white medical smock.

Margy and dogs retreated, the woman bent to pick up a fallen lap blanket and resumed her seat in a mission-style oak rocker.

Loup and Alys flopped at her side. Their bodies made bass drum thumps on the bare wood floor. Heads up, they followed the proceedings.

In his role as doctor, Aubert ran through the bedside ritual of checking pulse, lungs, and temperature. After taking a pulse and sticking an overly cold stethoscope on his chest, he ran a digital thermometer across Hugh's forehead and nodded.

Clicking on a small penlight, he checked Hugh's single iris and pupil and then ran a hand under Hugh's neck and down to the small of his back between body and bed. Hugh's skin started to tickle and itch.

"Pulse is normal, lung sounds normal and your fever is gone… temperature normal. Eyes… eye is clear. Let me remove the intravenous needle. You needed extra fluids to resist dehydration.

And, now, we will allow you to sit up, *doucement*, gently."

Margy pulled extra pillows out of an armoire.

The two lifted Hugh, propping him up against the headboard. Adjusted to the increased light, his father's appearance became clear. His hair, more salt and pepper than ten years ago as it should be, but other features, those mirroring his son's, remained unchanged. The high-unlined forehead, slim black eyebrows, dark brown eyes, and level teeth, they shared. The differences between them came from Hugh's mother's genetic contribution – fuller lips, higher cheekbones, and different-shaped ears. He smiled, noticing the noses, originally different, but now battered by events to look the same. Both broken several times — Father's a true prizefighter's memorial — received during his early fascination with boxing and Hugh's in military training accidents, bar fights, and lately with the help of his captors. Aubert showed little sign of age, moving with the muscular poise of a much younger man.

In his mind, Hugh ran over the numbers. As a surgeon, Father had served in a MASH unit during the Korean War. In the ordinary course of events, his Bachelor's Degree would have taken four years, medical school another four years, one year for an internship, and six or so years for a residency added up to twelve years – he would have gone to the war aged thirty-something. The misnamed police action ended in 1953, some sixty years ago. No, this couldn't be a man in his nineties. Another thought struck. Hugh would have been conceived when Father was in his sixties.

Interrupting the thought thread, his father handed him a glass of orange liquid and said, "*Ça va*? Take a nip and tell me how you feel?"

Hugh's hands shook as he sipped, the slightly acidic beverage reactivated his taste buds, and he drank more. The beverage was *citron, une spécialité de la maison de Gracie*, a citrus tasting drink high in vitamin C and electrolytes. Hugh had not found it anywhere else during his travels. His stomach growling as it received the liquid, he realized that he was ravenous.

"I feel…" He almost upended the glass. "I feel very weak, but clear-headed and free of pain. But my neck and back itch."

"Must be from lying in one position for so long. You have slept for three days. In addition, you are forty pounds under your normal fighting weight of one hundred eighty-five. Do not worry, we will feed you, exercise you, and whip you back into shape. In the meantime, Margy will apply some salve to ameliorate your itch."

Hugh leaned forward. Margy peeled back his bed shirt. Lips tightened as she rubbed ointment on tiny penetrations, each with their dot of congealed blood, which covered every inch of his skin from neck to buttocks.

"What about the virus?" Hugh asked. "The medication was failing."

Aubert held up a finger-length wood-grained ampoule sealed on the ends with a waxy substance. He stood and walked to the stand-alone ceramic fireplace nestled in an inside corner of the room. Unlatching the door, he used a poker to stir the embers on the grate, causing them to blaze up. He added three more sticks of wood. The flames grew and crackled as they engulfed the added fuel. He dropped the capsule in the center of the fire.

"*Il n'y a plus de souci.* It is not a concern any longer."

3

A time to kill, and a time to heal, a time to break down, and a time to build up.

Ecclesiastics: 3:3

HUGH LEAPT BACKWARDS. It wasn't enough. His opponent's blade flicked across the back of his hand, leaving a dripping red slash. Switching the dagger from right to left grip, he assumed a balanced stance, grateful for the early training that allowed him to be ambidextrous with weapons. Only six weeks since his return to the family home, he had not fully recovered his strength and agility. Endurance was also questionable. Only seven minutes into the fight and his feet and hands had begun to shake. Initially, he held the dagger point straight out, the blade locked into his grip, arm and knife forming a spear that could slide between ribs or deeply penetrate human soft tissue. Any substantial strike would have ended the dance of death immediately.

His antagonist, smart and experienced, false-signaled him into too long an extension, parried his move, and inflicted a cut. The easy way no longer an option, the fight would revert to a series of cuts and slashes. Whoever received the most would weaken from blood loss and shock to eventually fall victim to the other.

An attack came. Hugh parried, reversed the handle. Blade now down in a stabbing position, he dropped to one knee and cut forward and back on his rival's upper thigh. A crooked leg smacked against Hugh's head spinning him face down. A shin pinned his body flat. His opponent's knife blade half-slashed, half-stabbed across his spine where it joined his neck. He felt liquid trickle down his shoulder. Properly executed, the cut, if shallow, would leave him a paraplegic, if deeper a quick death. He had lost.

A curt laugh and Uncle Frank grabbed his hand and pulled. "How are your feet?"

"A little tingling in the toes, but good. I'm surprised, though. The Army docs thought there would be permanent nerve damage from the caning."

Uncle handed him back the double-weighted, blunt practice dagger. The dull wooden blades had felt strips glued along the edges. Soaked in red dye, they left incontestable marks.

"The first three minutes, good, very good. Remember, focus only on knife and you ignore natural weapons, such as feet, head, knees, fist... With only one eye, you must also move to keep opponent from striking on the blindside. Your endurance not back yet. I tell the kitchen to increase your protein. Also, more distance running."

Hugh groaned, but there was little in Uncle's prescription to which he could legitimately object. With a show of surface bravery, he said, "You want to go another round?"

"*Non, mon petit coq*, we meet with your father. Clean up, change clothes, join us in the library."

While Hugh was glad to feel more normal, sources of irritation had emerged. *Mon petit coq*, for example, my little rooster, his uncle's pet name for him as a child. Margy fussed over him as though he hadn't yet graduated into long pants. The cooks, maids, stable master, gardeners, armorer — all members of the de Gracie family — referred to him as Master Hugh or the young master, outdated terms rarely used in most of the world. In this isolated bubble, it meant a male child under eighteen, or tagged him as the heir designate, probably both in their minds.

He was an adult, damn it, in age and by accomplishment. They didn't know his successes in the last ten years. A Master's Degree in History through the Army Bootstrap Program, his rise through the ranks from private to field grade officer, the responsibility for millions of dollars of equipment, and leading troops through life and death situations in Bosnia, Kuwait, Iraq, and Afghanistan. Thinking of it philosophically, he reckoned this must be the natural way of things – family and friends' strongest memories always behind the curve. When they looked at him, what did they see? For a horrified moment, he wondered if they pictured him as a drooling toddler wandering the halls in droopy diapers. No, please, *le bon Dieu*.

Approaching the library for the first time in ten years, Hugh tapped his memory of the room, one of his favorites. Dark oak bookshelves ran from floor to ceiling equipped with the traditional sliding ladders allowing access to the twenty-foot high tops. Above that, a surrounding balcony with more books reached by a wrought iron spiral staircase. Light streamed in from translucent panels set in the ceiling and through French doors set in the inside wall, which opened up into inner grounds.

He remembered happy times in that central garden, especially after hard winters.

Protected from the winds and warmed in close association with interior loggias that ran around three sides, the trees and plants flowered and leafed two or three weeks in advance of their wild cousins outside on the mountain. There was a high-walled English hedge maze with core mother-tree grown fountain, dwarf crab apple trees with white, purple, and pink flowered branches all out of the same trunks. Vines with twisted together wrist-thick stocks grew up the columns of the peristyle, or covered porch, that circled the garden. Wisteria, clematis, honeysuckle, and trumpet creepers drew hummingbirds and butterflies. The estate's hives were moved inside from their cold weather storage areas allowing the bees to get an early start. Perennial flowerbeds would feature multi-colored violets, red trillium, colt lilies, hepatica, iris, and blue cohosh.

Hugh recalled that at this time of year, the library's atmosphere would smell like a blend of tobacco, book glue, and wisps of May's blended perfume from the adjacent plantings and blossom-covered trees. He entered. Tables of various sizes sat on hand-woven braided wool rugs. Ladder-back chairs, some with arms and cushions, provided seating. Extra chairs hung from rungs set into cream-colored walls decorated with stylized fern wreath stencils.

A soft command to shut the door came from his right. Uncle Frank and Father sat, comfortably slouched, wearing jeans and long-sleeved shirts unbuttoned at the neck, drinking from mugs.

"Would you partake of a beverage with us?" Father asked.

Hugh raised a wooden pitcher and looked inside, the amber color and spicy rich scent identified it as his uncle's small beer. Early in the day for modern folks to imbibe alcoholic beverages, the drink dated from centuries ago, prior to the invention of treated water or pasteurized milk.

Consumed at breakfast and lunch, germ-free small beer with its alcohol content of one and a half to two percent didn't interfere with the work of the day.

Mistaking his hesitation for reluctance, his uncle spoke, "I brewed it, from a recipe I... our family received in 1757 from *Le Générale* George Washington himself. Of course, he was not a general then, that honor or one should say that testing came later. The brew consists of boiled barley hops, molasses, and the finest Belgian yeast."

Father frowned at Frank's slip of the tongue, motioning for his son to take a seat.

Hugh picked up a mug, surprised by its three-quarter pound weight. Taking a second look, he found solid sterling silver, its outside cool and beaded with condensation. The older menfolk waited while he poured and took a sip – very pleasant, with a sweet brown sugar aftertaste.

"My son, it is time to tell you the family secret, or secrets, if you wish. I do not know a good way to relate our story in a manner immediately believable, so I will proceed in the same fashion as my father told me. I have asked your Uncle Frank to join us for two reasons: first, he will support my tale, so you will not conclude that I am completely insane, and secondly, he will fill in anything I miss. He has been in on past generation father-son conversations many times."

Hugh sat up straight in his chair and pulled his feet together. The breeze off the courtyard ruffled the hairs on his arms, generating a few goosebumps. Instinct told him something strange was forthcoming. Pushing the stein away, he rested his forearms on the table.

"You are familiar with the symbol of our house, a great leafed tree. We call it the *Arbre-mère*, or Mother-tree. Such trees have been known for all the thousands of years humans have been extant under one name or another, mostly as The Tree of Life. The motif and the legends appear again and again in religion, art, and mythology."

From a side table, Aubert picked up the family bible, opened to a bookmarked passage and read,

"The Lord God made trees grow up from the ground, every kind of tree, pleasing to the eye and good for food; and in the middle of the garden (Eden) he set the tree of life, and the tree of the knowledge of good and evil."

Aubert glanced over the book. "You know, of course, what

happened next. God created Adam and Eve and forbade them to eat from the last two trees. However, it happened. They disobeyed and ate from the tree of knowledge. In violation of His command, God assigned punishment, but the reason He drove them from the garden was not entirely due to this violation."

Hugh nodded though he wondered what his uncle was trying to say.

Aubert ran his finger down the page, again reading aloud, "But God said, 'The man has become like one of us, knowing good and evil; what if he now reaches out and takes fruit from the tree of life also, and eats it and lives forever?'"

Finally, Aubert shut the book and set it beside him. "God could not trust man any longer, out of the Garden Adam and Eve went, a cherubim and a fiery sword left to guard the remaining tree. Predating the Bible, references to the Tree of Life and its gifts of immortality and healing are found in most world cultures, even those as geographically separated as Native Americans and Sumerians, and as far back as humankind's earliest preserved writing, Gilgamesh. In some instances, gods and leaders spring from trees as did the Egyptian Isis and Osirus, the Iranian myth of Mashy and Mashyane, and the origin of the Turkic people from a man found in a pod hanging from The Tree."

Hugh broke in on his father's explanation, "Immortality and health, I can see why it would be desirable to be close to such a creation, but where is our connection? It must be something serious to be part of our family crest."

"This will be thirsty work. Frank, can you procure more beverage?"

"*Sûrement*, we have a superfluity of the beer." He grasped the pitcher and hustled out the door.

Father and son let loose suppressed laughter. "Superfluity?" Hugh sputtered, "What's going on?"

"Your Uncle recently decided to increase the depth and breadth of his English vocabulary. Be prepared for assaults of multisyllabic words sprinkled within his normal conversation."

"How long has this been going on?"

"Long enough to drive most of the house half crazy. Be warned."

"So, our family crest features a Tree of Life…" Hugh raised his eyebrows and held his hands palms up.

The residual smile left his father's face. "Son, we are people of The Tree. There was a reason why a botanist was always among your tutors during your schooling. For thousands of years, perhaps hundreds of thousands or more your ancestors have lived in harmony with Trees of Life."

The lingering tickle of humor in Hugh's mind vanished, replaced with a sliver of fear that caused him to bend forward, legs pulled back, and forearms extended on the table, ready to react physically, the fight or flight response fluttering in the back of his brain.

His father went on, "You know the definition of symbiosis, two organisms dependent upon each other, in mutually beneficial ways. The relationships include associations where one partner lives on the other or inside the other. For example, we humans have harmless bacteria that live inside us, assisting in our digestion, and protecting us from their evil relatives. There are many other examples: mistletoe and trees, clownfish and anemones, and some fungi and plants. The example that fits us best is the relationship some ants have with varieties of acacia and cecropia plants. The trees provide shelter inside themselves. In exchange, the ants attack any animal attempting to eat the trees. They also trim back competing vegetation around the plants. As an additional bonding mechanism, the trees provide food for the ants."

Hugh sat stunned, not liking where this conversation was going — too surreal — the tenets of his ordered world started to tumble. His jaw dropped. He stared at his father.

Uncle Frank reappeared, noted his paling face, topped off his stein, and motioned him to drink. "You should close your mouth, such a perfect *gobemouche*, flies will find a home."

Hugh drank deep and replaced the mug on the table. The continuing breeze from the courtyard began evaporating the wetness under his arms. His nostrils flared as they reacted to the peppery adrenaline smell of his sweat.

"As for us, we have a much more complicated relationship, evolved over what may be hundreds of thousands of years, almost infinitely intricate."

"Who is the 'us'?"

"The *Arbre-mére*, all of your ancestors historically, and currently everyone living here, including your Uncle Frank, you, and I."

"We have a symbiotic relationship with a tree?" Hugh mentally ran through his recollection of the trees in the chateau grounds, coming up blank. He sat up straight, instinctively raised his arms into a defensive position, and looked at Uncle Frank, who cocked his head, raised his shoulders, and nodded yes. "What tree?" He gasped, half knowing the answer, feeling like an idiot.

"This one." Aubert raised both arms, waved them like wings in quarter-circles, encompassing the floor, walls, and ceiling. "We live inside this one."

Hugh lay in bed, unable to sleep, mind restless with new knowledge, trying to fit it into the recollections of his early years. He remembered times when clues about the true nature of House de Gracie had been apparent but ignored. Baby and toddler days focused on people: mother, father, Uncle Frank, Margy, and the others, not so much on surroundings. By the time he reached the exploring age of young males, the house and its features seemed familiar and natural, not requiring questioning or analysis. Yet there were signs, such as the time he had discovered the way into the many tunnels and caverns underneath the chateau. A kerosene lamp carried from his room illuminated rough-cut stone burrows and the ramps and crude stairs connecting them.

Somewhere water rushed down raceways creating a droning noise and sending vibrations up through the rock floor into the soles of his feet. He was deep into the mountain.

Covering much of the surface area of walls and floors, knotty hose-like tubes of varying thicknesses ran, branched, and split, their organic round shapes reminding him of plant roots. He brought the light close to one half-round, half-flattened roll and placed a palm on its surface. It felt solid, substantial, and large enough around to hold his entire body in its interior. Hugh pressed a temple and ear against a knobby projection. A mild hum vibrated through his skin and skull, relaxing him. His skin tingled where it rubbed against the bulge. He felt himself drift into a pleasant reverie. Light grew, pictures formed.

Women moved heads and hands, accenting conversations. Their red, blue, and ivory blouses or bodices puff-sleeved and beribboned featured gowns drawn tight at the waist with angle-length skirts fluffed out by multiple petticoats. One of them moved among eight seated guests refilling cups, offering a china teapot with a jade-green painted dragon curled around its barrel.

In voices muted and unintelligible to Hugh's ears, the women engaged in lively conversation. They knitted, sewed, or tatted, fingers moving faster or slower in time with the speed of the banter, stopping entirely for moments of laughter. The clothes, as well as the furniture and decorations, were old fashioned to his eyes. A mahogany empire sofa dominated the room. Its side tables held oil lamps with milk-white glass shades decorated with hand-painted flowers and vines. Walnut armchairs, several wooden folding chairs with seats of floral-patterned carpet, and a rocker with cutout scrollwork forming the arms had been arranged in sewing circle fashion.

Heavy velvet drapes hung on each side of the windows, a mother-in-law's tongue plant in a brass container sat on a cast iron half-table complementing a three-foot-tall potted Norfolk pine across the room. An upright piano decorated with arabesque carvings leaned against one wall, sheet music propped in its holder. A Boston fern atop one corner spread its fronds to soften the piano's sharp angles.

Heads turned towards twin double-hung windows as horses and men in blue uniforms flashed by outside. A team of four pulling a caisson with an attached twelve-pounder bronze Napoleon cannon brought up the rear. A rolling rattle of iron-rimmed wheels on cobblestones vibrated the window glass. Two women threw open the door without knocking and rushed in from the outside, hands held feather and lace decorated hats on their heads. Four-foot diameter layered hoop skirts flared out behind, exposing shoes and ankles.

Flush-cheeked and panting, they waved a folded newspaper. One opened the paper and began to read aloud. Hugh could make out the name on the masthead: *The Daily National Republican*, dated July 3, 1863. He squinted in an attempt to make out the subtitles. In inch-high type the word EXTRA was readily legible, underneath that heading in a smaller font: TWELVE O'CLOCK, THE SITUATION, lower down another title: THE REBEL INVASION, Battle of Gettysburg. He strained to read the normal-sized print and failed. Sweaty-palmed female hands flipped the newspaper to expose a bottom column entitled Casualties in the Army.

The woman in the rocker groaned and bent over as a name was read, two others rushed to her side. Arranged in sausage-shaped curls, the grieving woman's gold-blonde hair bounced and shook in time to sobs and fists pounding her knees. A boy and a girl appeared, rushed to her side, their facial features seeming familiar to Hugh, even in the contortions of grief. The heat from his lantern started burning his fingers, his head jerked, and the pseudo-dream faded out. The young Hugh sat the lamp down, blinked, and rubbed his temple. The skin itched where it had touched the root. His hand came away with a drop of blood.

There was no reason for him to daydream of a time and place of which he had no knowledge or apparent connection. The experience spooked him. In the following years, he continued to explore the above ground space of the mansion, including three secret passageways, but he never returned to the underground maze. However, the memory of his subterranean wandering supported his father's revelation, where there were roots there must be a plant. The massive roots he had seen would support a giant plant.

After lunch the day of the library disclosure, Father had taken Hugh on a tour of the grounds, letting him see with new eyes. The chateau's curious facade included two small towers flanking a larger central tower. The connecting sidewalls folded back into right angles at the ends of the shorter towers and ran back until they blended into the bare rock of the mountain peak. Facing the front door, the dogs Loup and Alys flanking them, Father had Hugh examined the buff-brown striated walls, their surfaces broken only by the squared-off columns of the three towers and arched mullioned windows set in symmetrical patterns delineating each of the three stories.

"As you can see, the faux-stone bark has long raised irregular strips angling downward, the channels between catch rainwater, guide it to the ground, and eventually to the roots. Under this surface layer, we find a thick protective cork, then the *phloem*, and the *xylem*. As you remember, the xylem are long tubes that transport water and minerals throughout the organism. The phloem, in a similar fashion, sends organic nutrients, particularly sucrose — products of photosynthesis — all over the tree."

Hugh looked up at the tower tops, "Quite a way to raise water."

"A three-hundred-foot-tall redwood can raise five hundred gallons of nutrient-suffused water each day. Capillary action, evaporation through the leaves' *stomata*, and the cohesion of water molecules all have been presented as explanations."

Humans and dogs left the porch and followed the flagstone path circling the chateau's foundations, the flat limestone surfaces still wet from last night's rain with greening Irish moss pushing up between the cracks. Up against the walls grew a multicolored three-foot thick hedge of rose bushes. Flowers in shades of white, yellow, and red attracted multitudes of bees and other pollinating insects. The murmur of their work combined with the perfume relaxed the men. As they strolled, Aubert pointed out hidden characteristics, beginning with the ivy looking leaves now covering the outside walls.

"The three-lobed leaves, which in shape resemble the fleur de lis, are not ivy. They are the Mother-tree's."

The pseudo-vines, not fully leafed yet, crawled up the walls in long rows looking like green-haired Rastafarian dreadlocks.

"These leaves and those on the twenty-foot thick thornwall that surrounds the chateau grounds provide an immense surface area for photosynthesis. Notice the thick leaf cover on the outer-barrier tops. What appears to be individual grown-together trees are propagative, budded from the Mother-tree's roots. In a smaller tree, they would be called suckers."

Father and son rounded an end tower, entered a sunlit terra cotta tiled patio, and took seats at a cast iron table decorated with curly leafed vines.

Wearing a plain ivory-colored apron tied over a flowered housedress, Margy came out a side door carrying a tray that contained a pitcher of The House citron and a plate of orange-frosted scones. She joined the men.

Father poured for all three.

Hugh sipped and noticed off-white low-to-the-ground forms moving towards them. Something taller and dun-gray lifted its head and sampled the breeze. It froze for a moment and then broke into a jerky gallop followed by the other shapes.

An *ee haw*, *ee haw*, broke the conversation. The group on the patio was assaulted by a flock of small-sized sheep led by a donkey. Hugh leaped up to embrace the grinning jack. "Koshan, good man, how did you get here?" His nose prickled with the familiar musky tart-apple smell of the equine's skin. Missing was the odor of infected places where the saddle pad had been misplaced or slipped, allowing the wooden pack frame to rub sores on the animal's hide.

"Well, it took a considerable amount of bribe money over the last month and a half," Father injected. "A present for you and a reward for a faithful animal. We will match him up with a jenny soon."

After rubbing Koshan's ears and feeding him a scone, Hugh looked around, "Sheep. We keep sheep?"

Margy rubbed a finger alongside a largish nose before speaking. "Between the chateau and the outer thornwall there is a grassy area in excess of three football fields. These miniature Shetland sheep keep the grass short." She wagged a finger at one of the diminutive wooly ones, "Be wary of the ram — for all his small size, he can give you quite a butt with those curly horns."

"We try to be as self-sufficient and self-reliant as possible," Father added. "We walk softly on the earth, hence sheep rather than exhaust spewing mowers." He continued the thought. "The *Arbre-mère*, with a little help, can provide anything any plant can offer and more. For example, the citron we are enjoying is one of the fluids the mother-tree produces."

Hugh nodded. "Yes, this discussion brings to mind some burning questions. Why am I in such good health, when the experts and modern treatment couldn't cure me?"

"There is truth in the myths about the trees of life offering healing and longevity. Remember your itching backside upon your first awakening. The Mother-tree filtered the virus out of your blood using fine root hairs inserted through the pores of your skin, collecting the virus in a wooden tube of its making. The one I tossed in the fire. It has also used growth hormones to help your body repair the scars circling your right eye, which now can hardly be seen, unless you blush or are angry."

"Can it regrow my eye?"

Aubert's lips pressed together then opened. "No. At this time, the *Arbre-mère* cannot create complex organs. In the last fifteen years, I have become educated in genetics and have recently immersed myself in stem cell research. Someday perhaps I can show it the way."

Hugh frowned. "Why wasn't I told of all this during my childhood?"

"Your rebellious streak. Not everyone born here stays. You were determined to leave. We do not tell our secrets to those who might disclose them to outsiders. I had to be sure. General knowledge of our relationship would surely result in us becoming specimens for study. Or, being overwhelmed by people, governments, or corporations demanding the secrets of long-life and medical cures. They would let nothing stand in their way. The Mother-tree, your family, all would be destroyed."

"And you are sure of me now?"

Aubert opened his hands. "Your return is a good omen. The timing is right. But more about that later."

Margy pulled a small bottle out of the pocket of her smock, shook it, making a metallic rattle, and handed it to Hugh. "It took longer, but the Mother-tree has similarly removed the last of the shrapnel from your flesh."

He stared at the clear glass bottle, big and round as a tennis ball, half its volume glittered with bits of gray-black metal pieces, some tiny as a grain of sand, the biggest the diameter of a dime. Hugh shook the bottle, the noise mimicking maracas, a mystified smile on his face. "Bodies it can heal, but what about minds?" The memories, the horrors. He thought of the violent loss of friends, exploded blood and flesh, his torture, and the killings.

"Your dreams have been peaceful since your return. We have

made it so. Adequate sleep, exercise, and a balanced diet we can accomplish, blanking your memories we would not do. The sum of your experiences is what you are. Change that, and you have someone incomplete who is apt to repeat disastrous errors once learned to avoid."

"How do you know about my dreams?"

"We dream to communicate with the Mother-tree. Our word for it is *rêvè-souche*. Through the centuries, it is how we learned to serve and how she learned to serve. The entirety of our lives and all of your ancestors are recorded in her. We can play them back."

"The first few days of my return I dreamt a detailed account of the ten years I was away."

"Those events are part of her now."

A flare of anger made Hugh's brows come together, his fists clench, and heartbeat increase. "What right did you have to pry out the intimate details of my entire adult life?"

The dogs raised their heads at the voice tone. Koshan nuzzled his shoulder.

"*Mon fils*," Aubert leaned forward and placed his hands over Hugh's, "you were dying, we had to know the background. In addition, you are de Gracie and bound to the tree-human partnership mind and body. You judge the intrusion by the standards of the outside world. It is not a question of a violation of ethics or privacy. The Tree of Life possesses no double nature, no good, and evil, no light and dark, no duality. It only offers a oneness."

Hugh saw a strange scene in his mind, as though viewing a movie.

The mountain was tree and brush-covered, although here and there varicolored rock faces poked through where they had been pushed up by ancient tectonic forces or exposed through erosion. From the looks of the mature foliage and the patches of blackberry brambles, it was late summer. Old growth sugar maple, American beech, and bigtooth aspen struggled against each other for the sun. A number of bark-less weathered blowdowns provided cover and concealment for skunks, rabbits, and possums, but their entwined bleached-gray limbs and roots blocked straight-line travel, requiring many detours.

A lone white man stopped and listened. Long strings of tat-tat-tats to his right announced the presence of a black-backed woodpecker. Earlier in the day, he had flushed a covey of spruce grouse. Fortunately for them, he needed the quantity of meat a deer would provide. He would waste no energy for a few pounds of bird flesh.

Pleased with his new garments, presents from his recent Mohawk bride, Ahladita, he adjusted the belt around his buckskin jacket. The loincloth and leggings were comfortable, allowed a full range of movement, and protected his skin from thorns and ticks – in this wild country much superior in design and material to European wool and linen. The moccasins allowed feet to feel the terrain better and were quieter when moving through the brush-choked mountainside. The woodpecker's rattle stopped, a gray jay hunkered in an alert position on the upper limb of a white pine, staring west. The collective little noises of the forest ceased. The hunter put arrow to bowstring, adjusted the wheellock pistol in his belt, and moved in the direction indicated by the bird, placing each foot to make the least noise. He pushed down a leafy tree branch, caught the coppery scent of fresh blood, and looked out over a young meadow of grass, low shrubs, and foot-high saplings, its acre-sized open area created last year by a lightning started fire.

His back to the observer, a native crouched out in the low grass, bent over a deer carcass, right elbow moving in a pattern suggesting a skinning knife in his hand. The man's head was bald except for a thick close-cropped rectangular patch of hair on the back crown. The short mane lengthened as it approached the neck where it split into three braids. Hairstyle and the tattoos visible on shoulders and cheeks identified the hunter as a Mohawk. The man in the tree line recognized Ojas, one of the young bucks of his wife's tribe. Easing the arrow off his bowstring, he opened his mouth to shout a greeting.

A flicker of motion flashed across his vision. Ojas jerked and screamed, the fletched part of an arrow jutted from the Indian's upper back. A trio of Algonquians, enemies of the man's tribe, charged across the clearing whooping and waving weapons. Ojas stood, turned, and raised a yard-long wooden war club with a blunt stone attached to its end. The enemy arrow had entered his upper back muscles, pierced the scapula, and continued through thick fan-shaped chest muscles. Eight inches of shaft and arrowhead protruded from his front, impeding the use of his left arm.

The white man fired his ready arrow at the rearmost attacker, missing the body but impaling a knee. The warrior fell. Dropping the bow, he pulled his pistol, slapped the hammer forward, aimed, and snapped the trigger. The powder in the pan flashed but the main charge failed to ignite. A misfire. Throwing the pistol aside, he drew a bone-handled long-knife and leaped forward.

Ojas swung his club underhanded, coming up under the first enemy's spear. The polished granite stone connected, stopped the man in full stride, shattering his Adam's apple, jaw, and the roof of his mouth. The falling body curled around the weapon, pulling it from the Mohawk's grip. Knife lost somewhere around the deer, Ojas faced the second warrior unarmed.

Grabbing the wrist of the enemy's knife hand, the Mohawk began a shuffling, grunting, twisting dance with his Algonquian opponent. The man was shorter, but Ojas' leverage advantage was erased by the arrow still jutting from his breast. Where was the third enemy? The Mohawk's body began to weaken, struggle to the end he must, but the deathmatch would end soon. The short man slipped and the tip of the imbedded arrow sliced across his chest leaving a six-inch-long scratch. Ojas realized that he was not without a weapon. He pulled back his left leg feinting a stumble. The Algonquian leaned in anticipating a kill. Ojas' right arm stretched out his opponent's knife hand. Left hand slipped behind the man's head pulling it down and forward. In one jerking move, the Mohawk drove the arrow protruding from his chest through the eye socket of his enemy into the brain.

The connected pair fell forward. Ojas, face contorted with pain, looked up seeking the third Algonquian. He spotted the man he knew as Frank, drawing a knife across the throat of the last enemy.

Letting the dead body flop forward, Frank grinned, saluted with his bloody knife, and shouted, "*Shay-cone*, brother-in-law. Rest. I'll patch you up shortly."

✏

Hugh blinked as the *rêve* ended. He waited until the prickling sensation slowed, indicating the fine root hairs had withdrawn from his body, then stretched and groaned as muscles complained of inactivity. During the last week, he had learned that all the beds and couches in the chateau contained ganglions of Mother-tree nerves, allowing it to connect and communicate with anyone at rest. The bathroom sinks, toilets, and shower/tubs were also specially grown artifacts, the tree providing water and recycling the effluent. To reduce the possibility of fire in an all-wooden structure, hot water came from integrated solar-heated rooftop tanks. A recent innovation he wished had been available when he was growing up. The memory of all those cold showers made his whole-body shudder. All other furniture and furnishings had either been handmade on the estate or imported from outside contractors and not grown by the Mother-tree.

On a couch near him, a grinning Uncle Frank knocked out situps. "Come on, *pauvre naze*, pushups," he commanded.

Groaning, Hugh turned over and began a quick twenty, letting his Uncle's insult, which translated as "useless and probably stupid," roll off his ego. In the Army, he'd been worked over by experts, whose insults weren't buffered by family love.

"What did you learn from this… this training film?"

For the third time in a week, Uncle Frank was drawing on the Mother-tree's recorded memories for quasi-classroom training. The pair *rêvèrent* or dreamed together with the tree.

"I learned you can't count on technology — the pistol misfired."

Hugh stopped at the top of a pushup and continued. "That you shouldn't be hunting alone in disputed territory, a second person could have stood watch."

Another extension and stop. "You are never without weapons. Even those of your enemies can be used."

His arms lowered then lifted his body. "Intelligence is better than strength. It was interesting seeing the scene played out from both the European hunter and Native American perspectives."

"The Mother-tree has the recorded memories of both men. What you saw was a composite," Uncle replied.

A final pushup, elbows locked. "And, you sure are a dead-ringer for your ancestor. A wheellock pistol marks that action as Sixteenth Century."

Frank's eyebrows went up, his lips pressed together. He started to respond, then shook his head. "*Maintenant*, showers and *le déjeuner*, then the library for more instruction from The Father."

❦

The rain splatted and snare-drummed against the hallway skylights, formed rivulets, and hissed its way down the grooves in the outside walls, walls that Hugh now knew to be the striated bark of the Mother-tree. The water soaked into the ground or filled the ponds of the inner courtyard. Overflow joined other rivulets to gush down rocky, mountain draws. Liquid fingers rushed together to fill the creeks and streambeds. The combined thousands of gallons raced down to lose themselves in the great mass of Lake Champlain. The storm's lightning and falling water had cleared the air. Hugh's nostrils tingled with ozone residue as he took deep exhilarating breaths of storm-cleansed air.

Tucked along the joint between library walls and ceiling, translucent globes glowed, providing full spectrum light, mimicking the sun with all its useful wavelengths for plants and animals. Uncle Frank and Hugh entered through the garden's French doors to find Father bent over a round table.

A silver tray containing a carafe of water stood at one side, its accompanying glasses spread out on the table surface pinning open maps with curled edges.

The three men examined them in silence. All described or plotted the family freehold in different ways. A U.S. Government geodesic map detailed the elevations and steepness of the mountain with thin lines that traced its curves and twists. The lines closed together where it became steepest and spread apart to distinguish gentler slopes. A second map consisted of a large aerial photo blowup, taken on an early morning so shadows helped delineate walls and upright features.

The third — the most interesting — yellowed with age, had been hand drawn with pen and ink on what must be vellum. Elevation and distance markings accompanied a detailed sketch of the mansion and the surrounding thornwall, showing cross-shaped firing slits where now existed standard windows. In the map's corner, Hugh noted the date 1763, a compass rose, and a legal description. A signature inscribed in lacy calligraphy swooped across the bottom: a fancy looped first name initial 'G', then a last name beginning with a scrolled 'W', later an 'f' where there should be an 's' and fancy loops on an 'h' and a 't'. It took him a moment to decipher the name G. Washington.

Catching his revelation, the Father said, "It is George Washington's all right. Most people don't realize he did survey work when he wasn't fighting, politicking, or working his plantation."

Hugh rubbed his fingers over the signature.

"Careful, son, our skin oil can damage it."

"Don't tell me one of our ancestors hired a young Washington to map our holdings?"

"Yes, this piece is from our family collection, most of which is located in a humidity-controlled vault in a New York City bank. I will take you there someday. It is stuffed with marvelous things: correspondence and papers from all the presidents, many famous inventors, religious leaders, and notable military people. The entire collection was valued last year at over fifty million dollars."

Hugh felt like someone had just smacked him between the eyes with a two by four. He would need to find out more about the family's finances.

Pulling a two-lobed leather pouch and an old-fashioned white clay pipe from his jacket pocket, a bored Uncle Frank announced, "Well, while you two engage in egregious conversation, I smoke on the porch."

Hugh dropped into a cushioned chair and watched his uncle slip out through the French doors and disappear. *"Mon Dieu –* egregious, where is he getting these words? And, what is he doing still smoking?"

"I caught him opening the library's unabridged Oxford dictionary to random pages last week. His smoking habit dates back many decades. But do not worry, the Mother-tree cleans his lungs periodically. Now, while you still see things through fresh eyes and before we give you any more details on the nature of our symbiosis, I desire your opinion as a military man. From what you have observed and learned in the two months you have been back, how would you plan an attack on our little fortress?"

Hugh's military-trained mind had already worked over that question. He picked up the aerial photo, and said, "We are located at the peak of a three-thousand-foot mountain, the only way up being a cross-country jaunt through intertwined old growth trees and brush that haven't been cut back for centuries. An attacker might advance up our series of very sharp-angled switchbacks, which any modern vehicle can barely navigate. However, they would be strung out and subject to ambush. Any force reaching the top must then breach a twenty-foot thick wall of interlocked dagger-sprouted trees. The amount of C-4 or comparable explosive to blow through would be immense, although the Air Force has blockbusters that could do it. However, a narrow breach would channelize your breakthrough, so one inside man with a rapid-fire weapon could eliminate any rush of troops."

"So, you think it would be impossible?"

"No, a suitably trained ground force, like my Tenth Mountain Division, backed by a preplanned artillery barrage, airstrikes, and helicopter assault over the thornwall, would level the chateau and be camped on its ruins in four hours. Unless there are other defenses you haven't told me about."

"Your assessment is correct, but in that instance, I hope they would ask us to surrender before attacking. We would give up. However, there are some additional hidden factors. Do you remember what kind of minerals form the Adirondacks?"

"These are young, pushed up mountains made of very old rock. If I remember correctly my old textbook said from these kinds of basement rock you could extract iron ore, quartz, garnets, zircons, and titanium oxides."

His father nodded. "The Mother-tree's roots have been mining the mountain for almost five hundred years. Among other things, it has incorporated a great deal of titanium mesh into its wooden flesh. In its unalloyed form, the metal is stronger than most steels and forty-five percent lighter. The thornwall and the walls of the chateau itself will stop or absorb the projectiles of most handguns and rifles. Ten years ago, we re-glazed the windows replacing the glass, which the

Mother-tree cannot grow, with laminated sheets of Lexan, a bullet-resistant plastic."

"Anything more?" Hugh asked.

"A couple of items. First, the grassy area inside the thornwall is laced with pitfalls and traps, which can be activated in an emergency. They consist of two basic types. One is a twelve-foot deep human-diameter pit with crumbly sides that will collapse smothering their catch. Another consists of a checkerboard network of stingers, something one of our marine biologist ancestors coaxed the mother-tree to grow based on the stinging nematocyst capsules of jellyfish. Treading on a surface trigger launches an eight-foot-long wooden penetrator-rod into the air. Finally, any force coming through the outer wall will face a spirited resistance by the de Gracie family, all of whom are well trained in weapons use and hand-to-hand combat."

"What about fire, the Mother-tree is still wood after all. Can we be burnt out?"

"Yes, but there are defenses. Remember the tree is pumping water constantly. Penetrate its tubes and water will spray out. The designs on all the inner walls, such as the wreaths on these library walls, are not wallpaper. They are very thin membranes, which burn out quickly, releasing water from the Mother-tree's organic piping."

"So, short of a modern army's combined arms attack, this would be a tough nut to crack."

"It is improbable we would face such a major peril. However, we must not forget. You made a powerful enemy in Afghanistan who has the financial backing and leadership skills to come after us. Fahad is also used to fighting in the mountains and he has already had eight months to prepare.

"Realistically, his response would include assassination teams or a commando raid in force. Hugh, I want you and your uncle to consider every possibility of such attempts and determine a defense. In your final report, include a list of any additional equipment and protective modifications needed, along with estimated costs."

4

A time to weep, and a time to laugh;
a time for mourning, and a time for dancing;
Ecclesiastes 3:4

AUBERT RENEÈ PHILLIPE DE GRACIE — The Father, as he was called by his clan — stood in the lowest level of the tree-mined underground caverns. A long line of crystal-paneled eggshell-like covered pedestals stretched out before him, in part resembling the catacombs of the Old World. Instead of enclosing dusty bones, remnants of mummified skin, and rotting shrouds, these capsules contained the living "sleeping beauties" of de Gracie house. Aubert wondered if, as there was in most of the old stories, a grain of truth in that fairytale. Someone in the past, he mused, must have acquired knowledge of a European *Arbre-mere*'s ability to keep its symbiotes in perfect suspension for centuries at a time, and worked it into a peasant tale. The fact that the Sleeping Beauty story also described the enchanted maiden as resting in a castle surrounded by thorny vines added credibility to his thinking.

He held up a battery-powered LED lantern, much brighter than the kerosene lamps they had replaced five years ago. An additional benefit of the upgrade was that they presented no chance of an accidental fire, reducing the primary domestic threat to the Mother-tree.

Beside him, Margy shivered and clasped her arms across her chest, the reaction due both to the chill of the vault and her fear of this dark place of entombed, suspended humanity.

Over one arm, she held a long, Turkish bathrobe embroidered with the blue and green family crest, while pushing a lightweight wheelchair with an ergonomic S-shaped seat.

They walked down the line, the muted echo of their footsteps and the wheels' click-spin merged to produce a shuffling bat wing noise. Remarkably dry for this deep in the rock, the air bathed them in a cool, antiseptic scent. They stopped at the twelfth pedestal – its glassine panels peppered on the inside with tiny drops of condensate. The lantern light produced a distorted view of the supine human shape inside.

"I believe this is the one." Aubert looked at the inscription on a brass plate. "Yes, *c'est elle.*" he read, "Catherine Désirée de Gracie, born 1843, resting since 1865. Margy, help me."

The pair unsnapped the metal fastenings and raised the hinged upper case. Aubert took in a fast breath, he heard Margy gasp, reacting to her first time at a resurrection.

Before them lay a five-foot-four-inch naked female body looking like the marble-carved goddess of a Renaissance sculptor, even down to a whiteness that mimicked the purest marble of the period.

There was a more mundane explanation. Aubert knew the accumulation of dead skin cells caused the bleached flour look. The body was in a kind of stasis, all functions slowed by the tree, with heart rate and blood pressure hardly measurable. Yet, the person lived and the production of skin cells, the growth of finger and toenails, hair, and other such things continued, albeit at a dramatically slower pace. This de Gracie woman had been suspended near one hundred and fifty years, her hair now flowed around her shoulders and crept down to her calves in tangled frizzed-together gold locks.

Margy made a mental list. *First, those horrid nails must be clipped – the fingernails and toenails have grown straight out for three inches and then curled into spirals. Baths and oils for the skin, and the hair, oh, the hair — never combed — draping over her shoulders in two thick matted and snarled cables. I wonder if the hair detangle products used on the carriage horse's tails will help, and we will need thinning shears for the mats and impossible tangles. I will save as much as I can.*

Fifteen years ago, Aubert had completed the DNA sequencing necessary to confirm she possessed the recessive genes needed to endow future children with the ability to *rêver* or dream with the tree. The gene allowing closeness to the Mother-tree must come from both parents. In Désirée's case, the test was hardly needed since her offspring clearly possessed the talent, six generations of breeding by her children proved its truth. The House de Gracie used linebreeding, bringing in fresh genetic stock from outside the family for three generations and then using selective inbreeding to preserve the characteristics needed to continue the strong bond between tree and human. The interim out-breeding and the distance between related parents prevented negative genetic anomalies.

Aubert, like his predecessors, had observed the benefits of long-term care by the Mother-tree. Chickenpox marks, acne scars, and other imperfections would be healed. Once the dead skin was scrubbed off, the woman's complexion would be classical peaches and cream, although it would be tender and sun-sensitive for the first month. He looked down. This one had delivered two children in her early life, but the stretch marks had been eradicated. He wondered if the hymen had been regrown – hopefully not, since they would be presenting her as a widow.

The woman's toes bent. Elongated nails clicked against the faux-stone slab. Muscles on her calves twitched under the ash-pale skin, the involuntary muscle reaction flowed in a wave up her thighs, buttocks, and back ceasing at the scalp. The tree kept the muscles from atrophy and prevented bedsores with pulses of electric stimulation. The exercise, done at regular intervals twenty-four hours a day, produced superb muscle tone and flexibility, in many cases generating a potential for athletic ability not enjoyed in the subject's previous life.

Aubert knew that physically, Désirée would be perfect for her coming role. Her belly flat, breasts taut, hips slim, and her muscles toned into a sinuosity that would massively blow the fuses of every male libido within sight.

The big worry was the woman's state of mind. Awakening one hundred fifty years in the future was shock enough, but — despite her perfectly healthy body — Catherine Désirée de Gracie carried nasty psychological baggage. He had sampled her recorded dreams. Those and others of her day told the story. After losing her husband at the Battle of Gettysburg, she fell deeper into an addiction shared by many women of the Victorian period. A common treatment to relieve painful menstruation — labeled then as "female problems" — was a tincture of opium and alcohol known as "laudanum." From his medical student days, Aubert knew it as one of the few effective painkillers of the time, which could be purchased in unrestricted amounts from local pharmacists.

Even before the loss of her husband, monthly use of the liquor put Désirée well on her way to joining the 200,000 opiate addicts of her era, three-quarters of whom were women. After his death, she collapsed into profound craving, neglecting her children and her family duties.

Scandalously, two short, but affectionless love affairs marked her mourning period, each with men of lesser quality who took advantage of her vulnerable condition. This stopped abruptly when her father shot one of the miscreants in a duel. Aubert had visited his great-great-great- great grandfather's memory of the duel several times to admire the calm emotional state as he put a fifty-eight-caliber lead ball into his opponent's forehead.

Well aware of her problem by this time, the family narrowly prevented a suicide attempt and she was placed in the Mother-tree's care until a cure might be available. Cleansed of her addiction, sustained, and preserved by the tree, the root cause of depression and loss remained to be treated. Over the last decade and a half through mutual dreaming, Aubert had used modern psychology to ease much of her illness. He also allowed her access to dream-records of her children and their descendants to help deter her sense of loss and guilt when she would awake, still alive many years after their demise. Through these, she had also gained some perception of the modern world.

Even so, he thought, to dream it is one thing, to be immersed in it another. Given his familiarity with her emotional problems, he guessed the odds were only fifty-fifty that she would adapt to this new world and fulfill her purpose. A movement of her chest caught his eye. The tree had started the awakening. Aubert brushed the powdery dead cells off her sternum and used a stethoscope to listen to the gradual increase in heart rate. With his hand on her forehead, he felt her temperature, now rising from its century and a half harmony with the forty-five degrees of the ambient air and the surrounding rock. In another fifty-five minutes, Désirée would be in her room. Six to eight hours later, she might be alert enough to converse.

*

Margy held Désirée's forehead while she threw up in a kidney-shaped stainless-steel pan, the third time in the last two hours. It was typical of the awakened, their stomachs and digestive systems struggling to reactivate after many years of little use. Aubert had also warned that there would be a period of diarrhea before body systems came into harmony. In doctor mode, he prescribed liquids with dissolved salt and sugar to maintain hydration. He would allow regular food in a few hours. Désirée would take her first solid breakfast in one hundred and forty-eight years.

Margy assisted her patient to lay back, thinking she would need a second bath and a massage before the meal. An application of Mother-tree derived skin conditioner with fatty acid oils, vitamins, proteins, and antioxidants would be doubly beneficial at this stage of recovery, since much of what is applied to the skin is absorbed directly into the bloodstream.

Uncle Frank appeared carrying a battery-powered combination television and DVD player with a fancy rabbit-eared antenna and a Port Henry Dollar Store shopping bag. He raised his eyebrows.

Margy pointed to a table at the foot of the bed.

"*Je suis naze*, I have been running up and down this grand *téton* of a mountain buying this and fetching that," he complained. "Such expeditious shopping has worn me out."

"Were you able to get all the DVDs on Aubert's list?"

"*Nom d'un chen,* woman," he waved several rolled-up pages, "only a fistful could be found in our small town. I have ordered the rest from Amazon and Netflix. What does Aubert wish to do, blow her mind?" He read from the list, "History Channel and Public Television documentaries, fashion shows, and classic movies heavy on romance. The women in them, oh the women: Mae West, Jean Harlow, Grace Kelly, Elizabeth Taylor, Katherine Hepburn, and Vivien Leigh – the combination of glamour and intellect beyond compare. He sets our resurrected one examples *très difficile* to match."

"I believe he knows her potential better than you, grandfather. You were suspended in the Mother-tree during her time. Now, move along, *Allez faire vos corvées*."

Aubert knocked – time for his daily visit. Thirty days into her recovery now, Désirée had adapted well enough to discuss her mission.

Margy opened the door. On the television screen, in the background, a reporter ducked and interrupted his spiel as an explosion down the street behind him threw up dust and fragments. Young Middle Eastern men with AK-47s fired streams of tracers into a building.

A few abandoned crumbs of scrambled eggs on the plate in front of her, Désirée sat at a card table staring out a sun-flecked window. She had retreated once again into a dissociative state, a neutral and thoughtless condition. These short protective retreats, designed by nature to numb the mind, allowed humans to blank the internal distress felt when the nervous system became overwhelmed with stimulation. It was a natural defensive mechanism, which acted as a buffer between her adapting Nineteenth-Century personality and modern times.

A good sign – they had become less frequent over the last couple of weeks. However, Aubert needed to remember this de Gracie came from an era where females of her class were sheltered from direct experience of baser happenings. In this world of daily exposure to much that was nasty and brutal, she would be vulnerable until she grew some emotional calluses.

Margy handed him a mug of coffee, used the remote to shut off the TV, and left the room.

Aubert pulled up a chair, put his hand on Désirée's, and waited.

Her fingers twitched. Head turned. "Tell me, how does it work? The television."

He smiled. "While I have a general knowledge of the theory, I would be hard pressed to explain it, especially since the technical words do not exist in your vocabulary. Just let me assure you it is not magic, modern industry manufactures them, just as factories in your time made complicated mechanisms, such as telegraphs, steam engines, and revolvers."

Désirée pointed to a stack of DVDs. "I am amazed to see many of the books I have read now done up into this age's movies. The Shakespeare plays, Dickens' novels, Shelly's *Frankenstein*, and Melville's *Moby Dick* for a few. I never liked his novel in print, I like it better in moving pictures."

"*Alors, en vérité*, the critics of your time received it not well at all. What were your favorite writings back in the 1860s?"

"Hugo's *Les Misérables*, of course, and poetry by Whitman and a new one named Dickinson." Her face and voice grew more animated as she recited, "Inebriate of air am I, And debauchee of dew, Reeling, thro' endless summer days, From inns of molten blue." Désirée's tone calmed as she completed her recitation. "Also, quite thrilling, Jules Verne's *Voyage au Centre de la Terre* and *De la Terre à la Lune*."

Aubert nodded. "Only ten of Dickinson's poems were published during her lifetime, and now we have hundreds. One of my favorites seems to fit our family, 'Because I could not stop for death, He kindly stopped for me, The Carriage held but just Ourselves, And Immortality.' I'll have a book of her complete poems brought up to you."

"Please make it soon."

"Now to business. I am sure you have wondered why you have been awakened at this time. You know from the dreaming, of the lives of your children and their modern descendants."

She pulled an embroidered handkerchief from a pocket, pressed it against her eyes.

Firming her lips, she asked, "Yes, I am what – your great-great-great grandmother?"

"Add another great and you are correct."

In her mind still twenty-two, Désirée stared at the eighty-seven-year-old multi-great grandson before her, who looked to be in his fifties. Her eyes unfocused as she slipped into another dissociative state. Hands folded in her lap, the thought of it all overwhelming.

Aubert sipped lukewarm coffee and waited.

One of the chateau's cats, an orange and black calico, pushed the door open and paused, one paw lifted as she noticed Aubert. Catching the bacon smell of breakfast, the young kit, tail up, made a quick dance across the polished wood floor ending in a leap into Désirée's lap. The impact, as light as it was, brought the woman back into the current reality. Her hand moved to stroke the furry head and back.

"*Chatte d'Espagne*, back again?"

The cat poked its head up, ears aloft, and stared into her breakfast plate. A bit of laughter came with a bit of bacon presented. The cat pawed the offering and then nibbled it with dainty teeth.

"Normally, we do not feed the animals at the table."

"Oh, but his one is so thin, and is so companionable. I need a little someone to practice my affections on."

"I cannot refuse," he hesitated and rubbed his chin, "to pamper you." Aubert almost called her *grand-mère*, even though it was important for her to think of herself as a young 21st Century woman. Wishing to keep the conversation light, he asked, "Do you have a favorite among the DVDs?"

"They are all entertaining and interesting, especially the man-woman relationships. The women display a freedom of voice and body that, to me, is both alarming and enviable. Must I become like them?"

Aubert smiled and hunched his shoulders. "As much as you dare."

"Well, my favorite is *Gone With the Wind*, although the man's ears seem a little large for my taste. It attempts to recreate my time, of course, although the dresses are somewhat exaggerated."

"And Scarlett?"

"She is very much like we de Gracie women, dedicated to the preservation of her house above all. I think we would be friends. Although, I have not loved as she did."

From examining her life-dreams in the tree's records, Aubert knew that Désirée, a product of her time, had not been sexually awakened. American Victorian women of her class had very little knowledge of sex and reproduction going into marriage. Their female relatives, embarrassed about the subject and ignorant themselves, offered little help during this major adjustment. Aubert was dismayed to discover that, for the most part, men felt sex with their wives a duty to be done quickly and without foreplay. They sought satisfaction with frequent trips to brothels and bawdy houses. Civil War Washington, DC during Désirée's time possessed over four hundred and fifty such domiciles with another seventy-five in nearby Alexandria.

Contrary to Aubert's training, most of those in the male-dominated medical profession of the era thought sex a necessary evil and did not even believe females could have orgasms. Non-aroused wives found intercourse painful and distasteful. Dealing with the resulting neglect, depression, and sometimes hysteria, women sought out so-called doctors to be relieved by manipulation. Aubert remembered a copy of a handbill displayed in his medical school museum in which one popular practitioner, advertised home visits offering gentle massage: "For all DISEASE OF the MID-QUARTERS, From NECK to KNEE."

Aubert mentally added a visit to a female sex therapist to the list of things Désirée needed. He would be sending her to New York City for a month of shopping, dance lessons, charm school, and entertainment. The absence would also keep Hugh from meeting her until she was prepared and committed.

Intertwining his fingers to keep them from displaying his nervousness, Aubert broached the real reason for her resurrection. "From your identification with Scarlett O'Hara, I am glad to see you still feel the de Gracie obligation to serve. Now, do you have any idea why we have brought you back at this time?"

"I believe so," Désirée speculated. "During the last part of my long sleep, I sensed a small but growing excitement in the Mother-tree. As happens every century and a half, she will produce a seed that must be carried away to a distant fertile and secret location by an expedition from this house."

Aubert smiled at her deft perception. "We project eighteen to twenty years yet before it happens, but we must prepare now. Children must be conceived to replace those that will leave. The new colony will need two to three new fertile couples along with a few old hands."

"So, I am brought here to be the broodmare again. You try to remind me of my duty." Désirée groaned. "I did not enjoy either the making or birthing of my children. My time of the month produces horribly painful cramps, bloating, and crazy thoughts. You would make me go through that again?"

"These are different times. The tree synthesizes hormones…"

Désirée's face wrinkled in confusion.

Aubert rephrased, "Ah… medications that either completely prevent your monthly trial or moderate it. None of the currently active de Gracie women are experiencing a period, not for years. The pain of childbirth can also be greatly eased."

"Why me? Why not your *arriére-arriére-arriére-grand-tante* Mathilde, as I remember she could crank out babies with great regularity?"

"Mathilde might have been a better choice, but she did not survive the birth of her ninth child. Unlike her, you possess a second chance. My advice. Shuck off your old-world husk — your mistakes, while fresh in your mind, are impossibly distant. They cannot hurt you, unless you repeat them."

"I do not know. It is so confusing… and frightening. In my mind, the old-world blends with the new, which one is real?"

He took her small hand in his. "There will be time to try things out, to test yourself, and to find balance. Preparations are complete. I am sending you to New York City for immersion into today's culture. Margy, whom you know, and Ojas, one of our people you have yet to meet, will accompany you. They know the outside well. Margy lived far from our little enclave for many years before returning. Ojas, during his past periods of awakening, worked as one of the Mohawk ironworkers that built almost all of New York's skyscrapers and bridges. Recently, he served as head of security at one of the Native American casinos. Margy will show you the wonders of the Big Apple while Ojas protects you from the dangers."

Désirée wiggled her shoulders. "Do I have a choice?"

Her many times removed offspring nodded. "Indeed, you do. Here are your options as I see them. Take your place among us and serve, return to suspended rest to be awakened at a future date, or cut all ties with us, and find your own way in these modern times."

Aubert could see the fire kindle within her, chin up, brow wrinkled, and lips thinned. He grinned internally – she was a de Gracie woman after all. Those normally hidden flames, a familiar characteristic, had bred true in her female offspring. He felt more hopeful.

Her shoulders settled. Her head lifted. "I will think about those options. Perhaps, I will create possibilities of my own. In the meantime, I want one of those money things. I want…" She switched to the Canadian French words from the TV. "*Je veux une carte de paiement.*"

"A charge card?" Aubert sighed. There were too many bankcard ads on the major networks. "*Mais certainement, cœur de ma famille.*"

"Make it American Express, no limit," Désirée said, with a grin of her own.

◆

Hugh was once again immersed in a memory of an ancestor.

Captain Alain Michel de Gracie's bunker shook as another shell exploded nearby. He sat on the creaky wreck of an old folding chair with his feet propped on the splintered remains of an ammunition box, the combination of which kept him above the mud, water, and sewage of the bunker floor. No one else had this much luxury – rank has its privileges, he thought with sarcasm, surveying the torn and mud-splattered ruin of his uniform.

The April weather had consisted of rain and more rain, filling the shell holes between the Allied and German lines, until they became ponds and lakes. The artillery of both sides roiled and churned the water and dirt of these Belgian fields into an almost impassable morass. Runoff raised the water level in the trenches making resupply difficult and skyrocketing cases of trench foot from feet too long immersed. Soldiers' excrement, washed out of latrines, joined the mix to make the smell almost unbearable.

Just when it seemed the shelling was letting up, a wracking explosion assaulted his ears, shook the bunker, and collapsed the chair, dropping him into the muck. Adding a final insult, it shotgunned wet pellets of sand and dirt over the interior of the shelter, spotting and stinging his face.

A hand clamped on his shoulder and helped pull him to his feet. "That was a good close one."

While the darkness in the bunker kept him from seeing the facial expression on his helper, he detected an attempt to hide humor in the voice. Watching an officer take a pratfall in shitty mud was an enlisted man's dream, even one as close to him as Ojas.

"What has it been, three hours of bombardment, so far?"

He heard a grunt of agreement. The two had enlisted together in 1914, running off from the family mansion in a patriotic fever to join the Canadian Army, given that the United States had not yet entered the war. Following the English tradition, each officer was allowed a batman, a combination bodyguard, valet, and runner, so they had been allowed to serve together.

Eighteen months of combat and they were still a partnership, although patriotism had long since been replaced with anger and frustration. The failings of the high command in the trench battles around Ypres had transformed their attitudes. With no innovative tactics, the generals and marshals' brains stuck in the Napoleonic Era, a horrific *danse macabre* had developed, affecting both sides.

Following earth-shattering barrages of thousands of artillery shells, chorus lines of Allied soldiers would advance through the no-man's land between the trenches to be met with pre-registered fire from enemy machine guns and cannon. Even when penetrations occurred, the lack of reliable communications kept victories from being reinforced in time to smash through second and third lines of resistance. German attacks experienced the same dismemberment and annihilation, both sides capable of defensive fires that created thousands of casualties. One battle of attack and counterattack concluded last week had racked up over forty thousand losses equally divided between the two warring parties.

Alain could see no end of it. Even desperate attempts to use new technology failed to have a lasting impact on the great amoeba of death that stretched from the Channel to the Swiss border. The Germans, with an extensive chemical industry, had recently added chlorine poison gas to the mix of weapons. Breathing the gas created hydrochloric acid in the lungs, destroyed delicate tissue, and caused asphyxiation. Initial counter-tactics involved Allied soldiers being issued thick gauze bandages soaked in urine to be tied around the nostrils and mouth, the urea, and water content chemically neutralizing the gas.

"Barrage over, time to take a look," Ojas announced.

Alain shouted at the first sergeant, "Roust them out. Attack coming."

He splashed out of the bunker and leaped up on the trench's firing platform. "Oh God, here it comes." Released from canisters all along the German first-line trench, thin earth-hugging clouds of yellow-green gas crept across the shell holes and shredded vegetation of no man's land. Dropping useless binoculars, he shouted, "Gas! Gas!"

All along the line, men paused, removed their short-brimmed helmets, and tied gauze pads over mouths and noses. Ojas handed him one. Alain's brow wrinkled. The liquid smelled suspiciously fresh. He looked at his companion, who grinned and winked.

The Germans, using real gasmasks, would be advancing behind the cloud, using it for cover. He counted in his head the seconds they would need to come within range. Machine guns opened fire at his order, blindly spraying bullets at five hundred rounds per minute knee-high across the battlefield. Their lead ribbons interlocked at the edges of their traverse. A minute later, he ordered rifle fire into the cloud as it luffed over the parapet and dropped to fill the low places in his company's portion of the trench. A whiff of chlorine slipped around his mask, the gas's distinctive odor, an odd combination of pepper and pineapple.

His eyes began to sting. Germans had included tear gas among the chlorine to attack unprotected eyes. Alain heard some scuffles further down in the trench, signaling possible panic among some of his Canadians.

In as calm a voice as he could generate, "Sergeants, attend to your men. Keep them firing."

Pulling out his .455 Webley revolver, he discontinued the countdown with a shout, "Watch yourselves, they'll be here anytime now."

Upon the heels of that remark, gray-clad soldiers began to fall into the trench. A heavy body carried Alain to the dugout bottom, pinning him in the liquid mud. He punched his pistol barrel into the enemy's kidney and fired three times. Two others, wearing German coalscuttle helmets loped out of the chlorine fog, their gasmasks making them look like nightmare wolves.

Still immobilized by the first dead man, he raised the pistol only to have it slapped out of his hand by a German wielding a short-handled shovel like an axe. The man slipped. Alain ripped off the enemy soldier's mask. Stripped of his protection from the gas, the soldier panicked and ran off, replaced by three others with bayoneted rifles.

Alain imagined the long steel blades stabbing into muscle and bone. He made one last effort to buck the dead body off. The nearest soldier paused, squinted, and started his thrust. Out of the miasma came a spinning propeller. It stopped abruptly. A tomahawk-like hatchet materialized, embedded in his attacker's neck just below the chin. The man fell back in a nerveless slump, blocking the companions behind him.

A terrible, eardrum-shattering Mohawk screech blew down the trench, paralyzing the Germans. The angel of death swept out of the green fog, a razor-sharp bayonet in each hand striking and slashing. The closest two enemy storm troopers went down in sprays of blood, coughing and groaning in the knee-high pools of swirling gas. Shirtless and helmetless, with gleaming eyes, spiral tribal tattoos exposed, Ojas chased the remaining Germans into the vapor. Alain could hear the thump of falling bodies and Teutonic screams and curses as the warrior progressed down the trench. He wiggled out from under the corpse, jerked the tomahawk from the dead man partially submerged in the trench bottom's muddy brown soup, and followed.

❦

Body oiled with sweat, Hugh woke from the war experience of his great, great grandfather into which the *Arbre-mère* had inserted him. Rubbing his empty eye socket, he thought how strange it was to have binocular vision again in these dreams. The glowing hands of his Rolex showed three a.m. A better timing for the vision would have been six o'clock, his normal rising time. Too many years in the army — imaginary bugles blew in his mind at that time each day — a bad conditioned reflex to have for a civilian. But the Mother-tree was trying to tell him something important.

The gas, it had to be the poison gas. The Mother-tree and, for that matter, all of them were vulnerable to chemical attack. He'd discuss it with father in a few hours. Much too excited to sleep, he turned on the battery-powered lamp attached to the bed's headboard and pulled a copy of *Masnavi I Ma'navi* from the side table, a translation of the seven-hundred-year-old book of Sufi-mysteries written by Jalaluddin Rumi. His recent experience confirmed dialogue with the Mother-tree improved with an understanding of meditation and the mystic practices of such religious sects as Quakers, Zen Buddhists, Kabbalists, and Sufis. Had the *Arbre-mères* of previous times influenced such movements? After all, the Buddha had reached his goal of enlightenment after meditating for forty days under the bodhi tree of his childhood. Was it a Mother-tree? The thought being unprovable, he opened the book and lost himself in its poetry-structured stories and parables.

Hugh stood in the depths of the shadow-darkened underground passageway, waiting for his father and uncle. Remnants of a rushed shower collected on the ends of his still wet combed- back hair dripped to his neck and slipped down underneath his T-shirt. The cold runnels made his muscles quiver and twitch. Recollections of his scary childhood experiences in these depths magnified the reaction. He needed a haircut. Used to short army-burrs, longer locks became a nuisance when exercising or working. In addition, there was always the warrior's fear of an enemy grabbing a fistful in a close-quarter fight.

He wondered what surprises his father and uncle would spring on him now. Much appeared to have been hidden from him. The old resentment, started in his teens, resurfaced. His face twisted into a grimace. Despite the miraculous healing he had undergone, perhaps thinking he could just reassimilate into his family had been a mistake.

Earlier in the day, Hugh had jogged and wind-sprinted around the circular path paralleling the thornwall. The wolfhounds, Loup and Alys, flanked him. The trio completed four laps before exiting out the front gate. They ran down the mountain, taking a side path leading to the outside livestock barns and secluded meadows. The day had started well. He was putting on muscle mass, his recovery almost complete.

Everyone worked every job on the de Gracie holdings. Today he took his turn milking one of the family's small Brown Swiss cows, developed in their country of origin for mountain living and cold climates. Bred down in size over the centuries, the miniature animals, forty to forty-two inches high at the hip, took less food than the full-sized variety. The six cows gave one to one and a half gallons of butterfat rich liquid each per milking, plenty enough for drinking, cooking, and making butter and cheese for the dozen active de Gracie's.

At first, he thought he'd lost his touch, the nervous cow stomped her hoof and refused to produce.

With a laugh, Jeannine, *une cousine au deuxième ou au troisième degré*, the daughter of Old Alphonse the caretaker of the armory, provided Hugh with a dollop of skin softener. Seems *la vache* Isabella didn't like the rough calluses on his finger pads.

Sitting on the low stool, hands maintaining the proper rhythm, and head pressed against the warm-ribbed skin, he fell into a care-easing meditation. Sensed through ear and cheek contact, the gurgle of the cow's multiple stomachs, the swish of tail, and beat of heart produced a pleasurable rhythm.

Jeannine emptied a bucket of milk into the top kettle of a hand-cranked separator, then stopped to tie up raven-black hair. She watched through glazed over green eyes as Hugh's arm and back muscles rippled. Attracted to his large chested, slim-hipped body and man-of-the-world personality, she had hoped for an intimate rendezvous in the soft hay of the barn. Normally, the Mother-tree's active humans could hook-up as they desired, either in long-term partnerships or temporary connections for the joy and stress-relieving aspects of sex.

However, Jeannine and all the other de Gracie women had been warned that Hugh was untouchable. Any attempt on their part to initiate any *petit divertissement* would be punished. The family leaders wanted him undistracted and in a high state of need when he met Désirée. Jeannine sighed and bent to work the crank on the old cast-iron machine. After a few seconds, skim milk flowed from one nozzle and cream from a second.

After the milking, Hugh mucked out the stalls. Even that brought back satisfying feelings, the pitchfork a familiar tool to the muscle-memory of arms and hands. His nose picked up the tang of digested hay and grass-rich must, not unpleasant to those raised with it. The straw and manure mixture were dumped in piles and mixed with other vegetation to ferment and decay into compost that would be carted up to the entry points of the Mother-tree's roots. In a concentric circle paralleling the path inside the thornwall were evenly spaced boxy granite-looking benches.

Removing the tops allowed material to be dropped down into the root region, where it would be taken up and recycled. Father and Uncle Frank had explained all this as they continued to replace his youthful ignorance of the Mother-tree. Someday his dead husk would take that path to follow those of his ancestors in returning his water and minerals back to the mother that had provided them.

Two sets of echoing footsteps brought him out of his recollection of earlier hours and back into the caverns. Raising the lantern brought out more detail on the locked iron-faced door to his front. A mystery room, he had never been into the space behind.

His uncle's voice came from behind him. "*Alors, mon petit coq*, finished doing some useful work today? That will not let you out of the session I have planned for this afternoon. Quarterstaffs, perhaps, or close-in knife work. What do you think?" Uncle Frank paused, held up his lantern to allow Hugh's father to key the door.

It opened out into the passageway, exposing heavy well-oiled hinges.

The men bent over to enter the five-foot-tall opening. Uncle Frank closed and latched it from the inside. They hung the lanterns on hooks hammered into the rock of the low ceiling. Light played on shelves lining the walls of the ten-by-ten room, a cabinet-high table taking up the middle space. Father pulled out a drawer, removed a cream-colored wool blanket, and shook it out over the tabletop.

"Today we make you aware of the de Gracie family finances. Soon you will have full authorization and access to all our assets, which take many forms. As you might expect, our five hundred years of existence has allowed us to take advantage of historical periods of growth, originally in the purchase and resale of real estate, and later with investments in commodities and equities. The beginning investment capital came from this mountain and the *Arbre-mère's* interaction with it."

Father made a circuit of the room, selecting bags and boxes from the shelves.

An arm around Hugh's shoulders, Uncle Frank whispered in his ear, "There is no worry. We possess *gros*, *énorme*, and sybaritic riches."

Hugh blinked. Sybaritic? *Uncle has made it to the 'S' section of the dictionary*, he thought.

Bags and boxes deposited on the table, father opened the neck of one five-pound sack displaying a black powder. "We talked before about the Mother-tree's ability to mine elements out of the mountain in the normal course of her root growth. This is pure titanium. It has become valuable in the production of airplanes and aerospace devices. The price has risen from fifteen dollars a pound in 2003 to fifty dollars per pound today and it continues to go up. We have over five hundred years of slow accretion stored up, something close to a billion dollars."

He opened another bag, "The income from titanium has recently become useful, but the most valuable asset, especially in the family's early days, was this." He grasped Hugh's hands and poured a teaspoon of fine granulated metal into his palms.

Its weight and the light reflecting from the material gave him a clue. "Why, it's gold."

"The Mother-tree collects it in such quantities as to be an embarrassment. A small amount is stored here, larger sums in New York and Swiss banks, and more in registered gold depositories around the world. Historically, our needs have been small and not much of the accumulation has been spent. The value has increased 650% in the last decade."

Hugh stared at the golden sand. It felt like six plus ounces, which at today's value meant he held seven to eight thousand dollars' worth of the metal.

Uncle Frank spoke, "In the past, the gold funded purchases of property, most of which has been sold at large profits over the decades to simplify our record-keeping and the demand of maintenance. We still own a good chunk of land about Port Henry, a high-rise apartment building in New York City, and recreational properties in Florida, California, Canada, and Monaco, near the French Riviera. Our land in Cuba was nationalized by the Castro government in 1959."

Hugh interrupted with a rush, "I thought New York has a law that all gold and silver are property of the state."

"Quite correct," his father replied, "but due to some generous gifts to early state legislators, we were grandfathered in. Our income from cash flow and sale of assets is held in both domestic and foreign banks, much of it liquid, the rest in T-bills, stock, and commodity portfolios under the care of professional management."

"Doesn't all this affluence bring us to the attention of various government agencies and private individuals?"

"Most of our wealth is held within various straw companies, the trail to which we make more intricate each year. Tracing it all back to us would be impossible for most and unlikely for those with more capability. Plus, we pay our fair share of taxes, which keeps the IRS at bay."

Uncle Frank held open the neck of the gold sack and motioned Hugh to replace the sample in his hands. "Show him the bodacious stones in the boxes, Aubert."

"The Adirondacks are also known for precious jewels." Aubert shook his head at Frank but smiled and said, "They are bodacious indeed."

The tops of boxes removed, small piles of various-sized uncut garnets and zircons in shades of vermilion and greenish-blue spilled out on the wool blanket. "These stones accompany gold recovery. Most are not gemstone quality, but sometimes we get a few or they combine in a configuration to attract the interest of mineral collectors."

"*Mon petit-fils*, show him the good ones," Frank urged. "I am excited to see them myself."

Father paused and opened some larger boxes, exposing faceted multi-caret gems. "These are Herkimer diamonds, quartz crystals formed in cavities of our mountain over many ages. Single specimens have eighteen facets, sixteen sides, and two terminations and may be clear, smoky, or colored with rare impurities."

Hugh's fingers touched and prodded the cache. They varied in length from a few tenths of an inch to over eight inches. Many were as transparent as diamonds, but others were colored by contaminates. He raised one to his eye. It seemed to have a liquid center. A bubble moved as he turned it.

"That one, called an *enhydros*, is very valuable with its inner liquid capsule – very rare," Aubert said saw what Hugh held. "And this one," he added, lifting two three-inch crystals grown together in a Siamese twin configuration, "they call a soul mate."

"And what is all this — the diamonds, minerals, land, artifacts — worth?"

His father's face grew serious. The tenor of his voice dropped as he spoke. "All that, and more that you will learn about later, comes to many billions of dollars. If Forbes magazine knew about us, we would rank in the top ten of the wealthiest enterprises in the world. You must promise not to tell anyone about us. Outside knowledge of the family's wealth and the Mother-tree's capabilities would result in our destruction."

Uncle Frank consulted his watch, a gift from Hugh – a Rolex matching the one he wore.

He placed one hand on Hugh's shoulder. "Time, my friends, for me to beat the spurs off this splendiferous Chanticleer. More information the boy can get by studying the family financial portfolio."

5

*A time to scatter stones, and a time to gather them;
a time to embrace, and a time to abstain from
embracing;*

Ecclesiastes: 3:5

"WHEN ARE YOU GOING TO TELL HIM EVERYTHING?"

Aubert took a deep breath, and looked down at the path. He remained silent, contemplated Frank's question, and listened to the crunch of pea gravel under their feet and the early morning birdcalls. He recognized the song of a wood thrush, quickly overlaid by the chittering of gray squirrels in the thornwall.

"Most of the facts about the Mother-tree and our relationship with it comes to Hugh as real eye-openers. In effect, the disclosures assault him in a series of *force majeures* – shocking revelations that force him to go back and reinterpret his memories of this place and its people. I am afraid pushing him too fast will, at the least, keep him confused when we need him the most, or at worst, push him into a neurotic state requiring professional treatment. He is the one who has the knowledge, training, and command experience to lead us against the threat posed by Fahad."

"Do we have any indication of when the terrorist will make a stab at us?"

"There is little information – the detail in Hugh's dreams of his captivity is not enough. We know of the Taliban commander's determination, and his marriage connection to Saudi oil money, but not the name of the family. In the past, our isolation has been our greatest protection. We have never developed the outside contacts or infrastructure to chase down what will be highly secret preparations. We are limited to a defensive strategy – not the best option."

The two men approached and worked their way through cropping miniature sheep, keeping a wary eye on the ram. Recently sheared, the ram and his ewes looked strangely thin and naked. Koshan, long velvet donkey ears flicked forward, clopped alongside the humans long enough to receive an apple and sugar cubes.

Aubert said, "There have been signs. Three days ago, a buzzing single-engine airplane spiraled overhead for over thirty minutes. I suspect aerial reconnaissance. The manager of our motel in Port Henry reports pairs of young men going bird watching in the adjacent mountains, their cameras equipped with impressive long-range lenses. I believe we have been staked out. Fahad will not try anything until his reconnaissance is complete."

"Do you wish me to disabuse the scouts of their mission?"

"No, let them think they have the element of surprise. Besides, their photos will reveal nothing serious about our defenses and the true nature of the Mother-tree."

"Well, at least Hugh is ready in body – everything rebuilt after his illness. His strength and agility are superb. He will soon be leading me *par le bout du nez* in the dojo. Have you heard how our Désirée is progressing?"

"The reports I am receiving by satellite phone indicate she has thrown herself into the free-wheeling culture of the Big Apple. I have faith that in the end she will accept her mission to bond with Hugh and to keep him with us. However, the situation is still worrisome."

☙

The first night of *The New Impressionists*, a showing of nine major New York artists, was invitation-only. Male and female heads turned as a woman led her entourage of two past security guards at the art gallery door. A red and blue flowered blouse and spruce green military-style jacket, complete with epaulets and brass buttons, complemented the invitee's designer jeans.

Laser measurement must have been required to fit the jeans to her body. Feet sheathed in black stiletto-heeled boots carried her forward to view the first canvas. Her blonde-gold hair pulled back and tied, formed an Angelina Jolie ponytail, whose end brushed the small of her back. She tilted her head to one side, allowing the long tresses to swirl.

The gallery owner, thin and in his late thirties, brushed past her two companions. "*Madame Terrenèe*," he took her hand in the French manner and bowed over it, "*Je m'appelle* Harold Moore. *Bienvenue à ma boutique.*"

"Please call me Catherine, Mr. Moore. You speak French?"

"Only a few words memorized in anticipation of your arrival. Are you having a good time in our city?"

"Oh, yes. Last night we attended a showing of *Les Misérables*. I had read the book, of course, but it was many years ago."

"Ha, yes, another revival of Les Miz. I don't think it will ever go away."

"Did you know, Mr. Moore, that it was the most celebrated novel of the Civil War?"

"No, do tell."

"There was a popular joke about it. A Southern Belle went into a bookstore in Atlanta, wagged her bustle, and asked for a copy of that fashionable book about General Lee's faintin' miserable soldiers."

The art dealer responded with polite laughter.

The lady's muscular companion moved into their space cutting off further conversation and hand-fondling. Ojas' gray Ralph Lauren suit and open-necked black silk shirt stood in contrast to the tattoos on his cheeks and hands. The shaved head with the wedge of hair and braids in the back appeared to disconcert the owner.

Harold bowed to leave, then turned. "The letter from your bankers has established your credit." He waved toward the paintings. "Please let me know if there is anything you like."

Désirée's other attendant, Margy, dressed in a version of the little black dress, stood inconspicuous in a corner testing the quality of the gallery's champagne. Her frown marked it as only a modest vintage and she returned the still half-filled glass to a passing waiter. Chaperon duties were a mixed blessing for the former nanny. It was a joy for her to see Catherine Désirée Terrenèe, renamed for her new femme fatale role as a distant de Gracie cousin, experience the delights of the modern world. The entire de Gracie family knew her origin, but Hugh would not make the connection, the made-up last name meant, "born from the earth," a clue describing her awakening.

After a week of shyness and hesitation, the girl — her companions finding it hard to think of her as *La Grand-mère* — had thrown herself into shucking off her stodgy Victorian ways. The makeup consultant had been both astonished and disappointed – astonished at her customer's excellent complexion and disappointed that it would require few purchases of cosmetics. She would receive few commissions for this day's work. Shaping of the eyebrows, mascara, blush, lip-gloss, and lessons in their application was all that was necessary.

Margy secured a supply of Clinique Aromatics Elixir perfume, Hugh's first lover's favorite scent. In a subtle manner, it should draw his attention to Désirée.

The hairdressers provided shampoo and conditioners, and suggested hairstyles suitable for Désirée's hip-length gold hair. All this had been fun, but the tour of fashion houses, while it had not impressed poor bored Ojas, had almost driven the two women into a bacchanalian frenzy. The wardrobe they would be taking back became quite extensive, some of which utilized techniques and fabrics only accessible by innovative technology such as lasers and 3D printers.

Margy and Ojas had set up a daily schedule of exercise and martial arts training for their charge. The payoff came early. Désirée had been attacked by three men while jogging in the cloudy gray twilight of Central Park, not far from the de Gracie fifty-fourth floor penthouse. Ojas tackled the first two muggers, breaking a knee on the first one and an arm on the other. He found the last man on his knees crying, Désirée twisting his wrist with a one-handed disarm. He pulled the creature into the bushes. Using a handful of hair, he twisted the man's head to one side, and listened to the crack as the knife-edge of his hand broke the man's jaw at the hinge.

Her horseback riding, tennis, swimming, fencing, and time at the shooting range went without incident. She was quite good at these, having had an indulging Nineteenth-Century father, who allowed her some tomboy moments normally denied to Victorian women. Fine-tuning was required for her to ride, straddling a horse instead of using a sidesaddle. An active woman during her era, she also possessed skill at lawn tennis, canoeing, ice-skating, archery, and dancing. In addition, she played a mean game of croquet, which had been introduced into America in 1860. In the evenings, Désirée feasted on plays and musicals seeing *Annie,* two versions of Les Miz, *Richard III, The Glass Menagerie, Forever Tango,* and many others. In between, the trio took trips to the ballet, the Philharmonic, and the museums.

Her visits to the sex therapist required the greatest adjustment. In addition to office visits twice a week, she completed assigned homework in the form of explicit DVDs and books, most of which caused considerable blushing and raised eyebrows. At week three, she began to ask Margy questions.

"Before you were married, did you know about sex?"

"Yes, my mother and aunts explained the basics to me some years before I met my husband." Margy chuckled, "They had a book we read together, but nothing like these." She pointed at *The Kama Sutra* and *The Joy of Sex* laying partly open on the coffee table.

"What was it like?"

"The first night was a bit nervous for my husband and I, but we loved and learned. With practice and good communication, we found ways to bring each other to fulfillment. Sex is like every other good thing. You need to learn and experiment to be first-rate."

"I am confused about this word orgasm. I do not believe I ever had one. Did you have orgasms?"

Margy felt a great sadness — to know the woman had never had that experience — a shameful reflection on Désirée's husband, lovers, and the era in which she had reached adulthood. Taking her hand, Margy said, "Yes, most of the time with my spouse. Have you ever tried with only yourself?"

"Oh no, that would be sinful, although the therapist does not think so."

"Dear, good sex is part of a healthy, rewarding life. Do not be afraid to discover where you are sensitive. How else will you be able to instruct your partner?"

"Should I look for my G-Spot?"

Margy wrinkled her forehead. "There is a lot of argument whether such a 'spot' is real. Wherever nerves exist, they can be stimulated, not just one place." She laughed, "Honey, if they ever prove the G-Spot is real, I will certainly be among the first to check it out."

The Hugh and Aubert worked side-by-side, naked from the waist up, backs and chests shining with sweat, as they cut firewood. Ten even rows of young trees shimmered green in the early afternoon sun. Resembling black locust, the plantings stretched out fifty yards. The two men worked with axes and saws to drop the twelve-foot tall trees, remove their limbs, and saw the four-inch trunks into stove-size billets. Stored under open-sided roofed sheds and stacked to allow airflow, the cords of wood would be stockpiled to dry until ready for the cast-iron cookstoves and ceramic fireplaces of the mansion.

Hugh stopped and leaned on his axe. He had temporarily removed the restricting patch over his right eye. The Mother-tree's attention had regrown the eyelids and lashes, but the new skin lay sunken over an empty socket. He rubbed the spot. Sometimes it itched or tingled as though the eye was still there. He turned to his companion.

"Father, surely we could avoid this labor by heating and cooking with a more modern fuel."

"We have considered alternatives. A power line or natural gas pipeline would sacrifice our independence. We would be reliant upon a source easily cut – by storm, landslide, or enemy. Alternatively, no propane truck could navigate our switchbacks. Besides, food cooked over wood is tastier. This way is also renewable, from each stump a new sapling will grow up fed by the Mother-tree's roots, providing an endless supply of free wood energy."

Hugh raised the axe and completed felling a four-inch diameter tree. Straddling the trunk, he began lopping off the limbs, muscles in back and arms flexing in an axe-man's age-old rhythm.

Another fifteen minutes and Aubert called a break. The two men sat in the shade with their backs against two of the saplings and drank Rickard's Shandy, a mixture of premium lager and lemonade. The lemon-beer smell cleared their nostrils. A short-breathed breeze tickled the hair on their chests and evaporated sweat.

"Your Uncle and I have gone over your recommendations on weapons and defensive updates. They seem reasonable and well-thought-out."

Hugh had done the research as requested. He still hadn't decided whether he would remain in the bizarre and extraordinary world of his family. Yet he had brought Fahad, an implacable enemy, home with him. An obligation to at least see the coming battle through before making a final decision on staying or leaving sat heavy on his shoulders.

He nodded. "I took an inventory of the equipment in the armory. Looks like the ancestors never met a weapon they didn't like. Polearms and bladed weapons from the Thirteenth Century to the present, pistols and long-guns starting with matchlocks up to Korean War semiautomatics, along with some nicely preserved fully-automatic WW II MG 42s, Sturmgewehr 44's and Thompson's."

"Anything useable here?"

"I've always liked the MG-42's: simple, reliable, 1200 rounds per minute, quick-change barrel, and can be fired from a mount, bipod, or from the hip. Old Alphonse, the armorer, has kept everything oiled and operational and even stocked spare parts. In my opinion, some of the combat knives, the MG 42's, and the army issue .45's are the only useable weapons."

"I suspected as much, and I have already ordered the purchase of …" Aubert pulled out a much-folded list from his jeans' pocket, "…night-vision devices, helmets equipped with tactical radio, sniper rifles with day/night-vision scopes, armored vests, grenade launchers, automatic shotguns, and assault rifles. All have been purchased in single or small lots at various places in various states to avoid attracting the attention of various government agencies."

He tapped his thumb on the paper and his brow lowered. "Procuring the claymore mines may be impossible. One of our straw companies is a pawnshop. They will connect with their friends operating near military bases and see what can be done. Deliveries should commence Monday. You recommend nothing heavier?"

Hugh shook his head. "We start acquiring air-to-air missiles and antitank weapons, and Homeland Security or the ATF will be all over us. I believe the fighting will take place within the confines of our surrounding thornwall. The only way to hit us with surprise and shock is from the air."

"They will land airplanes on our front lawn?" asked Aubert, raising a brow.

"Unlikely. Only small airplanes could land in that space, not large enough to carry many fighters. Large troop-carrying gliders haven't been manufactured since the 1940's, so I believe those are out. Soldiers trained in the use of modern parachutes could mount an assault, but it takes much experience to drift into an area this small. The updrafts and arbitrary winds pushing around our mountains would probably scatter them into ineffective packets."

"That only leaves…"

Hugh rubbed his nose and completed his father's sentence, "Helicopters. They'll be training their own pilots and buying their own machines."

"*Fait chier*," Aubert sighed. "Should we be purchasing radar and antiaircraft guns?"

"Probably ineffective. They will fly very low to avoid local airport and government radars. On their final approach, the pilots will terrain-hug down the valleys using our mountains for cover, gaining height only at the last to leap over the thornwall and land inside. There will be no time to interpret a radar image or fire at their approach."

"So, what is our response? You are the man most intimately acquainted with the demands and requirements of modern close combat."

"We'll need radio-equipped lookouts with clear lines of sight on the probable air routes — probably three or four different spots — to give us five-or-ten-minutes warning. My suggestion is that we prepare a very innocent-looking, but very hot landing zone inside the chateau proper covering all the open ground. The situation can be turned to our advantage. After all, we want to confine the action and its aftermath to the unobserved interior of the thornwall. We can't have flaming wreckage, and the remains of heavily armed men scattered down the mountainside and into Port Henry for the locals to find. All the gold in our coffers wouldn't be enough to quiet the subsequent investigation. Everything the de Gracie's have worked for over the last five hundred years would be lost."

Aubert nodded, satisfied with Hugh's analysis. "In the meantime, life must go on. We host some annual events here to make sure the locals know the family well enough not to mistake us — in our isolation — for a coven of witches or a nest of vampires. Next month, a six-week summer music camp for high school students will start, followed by our traditional buffet, dance, and fireworks display for selected townsfolk and other invited guests. The students will form an orchestra for the event. We have already sent out the invitations.

"In addition, the word is out that you are back and still a bachelor – the most eligible bachelor for miles around. I am sure the local matrons will be parading daughters, accoutered to display their charms in ways to attract your favor."

Hugh shook his head. "*Mon cul!* My ass! You're kidding."

"No, and given your age, you should be thinking about taking a wife and starting a family. Perhaps, there will be one among the throng of townies and relatives who will command your attention. Do you need refresher ballroom dance lessons?"

Hugh rolled his eyes. He flicked a sugar-curious bee from the lip of his bottle and took a deep draft of the shandy.

❦

Again, Hugh was caught up in a dream-memory, courtesy of the Mother-tree.

Far off to their left, the pilot could see flashes as bombs detonated on the French city of Caen. He envisioned massed formations of high-altitude B-17 bombers making their runs, rising slightly as loosed bombs lightened their load, the air around them speckled with puffs of smoke from exploding antiaircraft shells. His squadron of MK VI de Haviland Mosquito fighter-bombers was on its way to targets in support of the just-commenced D-Day landings.

He shivered as he remembered his squadron flying escort duty for nightly British bomb runs over Berlin. Thousands of antiaircraft guns located in massive centrally located flack towers and in the suburbs and surrounding countryside created a twenty-thousand-foot inferno of flame and steel. Viewed from altitude, it was simultaneously the best fireworks show he had ever seen and the most horrifying. He would never forget its terrifying asymmetry. The heavy lumbering bombers became priority targets for the antiaircraft gunners. Almost every ten minutes, one of the big four-engine Lancasters lost wings or engines, and in gravity-eating drops to earth spewed smoke and flame.

Putting aside the memory, Paul-Henri de Gracie placed a hand on the floor of his plane, and stroked it like one would a favorite dog. He and his navigator Bran Conan Wallace flew the fastest, most versatile plane in the Allies' inventory.

The Mosquito's two seventeen-hundred-horsepower Rolls Royce engines could accelerate the plane to over four hundred miles per hour, a greater speed than the best enemy fighters could manage. Loaded with two thousand pounds of bombs or equivalent weight of rockets, its nine fuel tanks allowed it to punish targets the length and breadth of Germany. The four 20-millimeter guns in its belly and four .303 browning machine guns in the nose made mincemeat of any aerial or ground targets in its sights.

The two men had taken flight training in Canada. Paul had followed his father's World War I example and ran off to join the fight against the Nazi's while the United States once again fussed with neutrality. Bran had volunteered to serve his home country, traveling to Canada's industrial east from his birthplace in Alberta. Their "Mossie," as the planes were affectionately known, was named the *Graceful Raven* in honor of its crew, Graceful coming from Paul's last name and Raven from the Scottish meaning of Bran.

The men were proud of the Mossie's reputation for unimpeded and daring action, even spitting in the face of Hermann Goering. In January of 1943, Mosquitos from the 105th and 139th squadrons knocked out the main Berlin broadcasting studio tower during the Chief Reichsmarschall's speech celebrating the tenth anniversary of the Nazi seizure of power. Pilots, navigators, and ground crew all laughed over the great man's frustrated response:

"In 1940, I could at least fly as far as Glasgow in most of my aircraft, but not now! It makes me furious when I see the Mosquito. I turn green and yellow with envy. The British, who can afford aluminum better than we can, knock together a beautiful wooden aircraft that every piano factory over there is building, and they give it a speed, which they have now increased yet again. What do you make of that? There is nothing the British do not have. They have the geniuses and we have the nincompoops."

Old Hermann was correct, Paul thought. The forty-foot long aircraft was over ninety percent wood, its shell composed of layered plywood of Peruvian balsa and European birch. In his opinion, the plane was also a "looker." The shoulder-mounted wings and protruding engine cowlings gave it a hunched prizefighter appearance.

Their squadron's mission for today – drop cratering bombs on a Luftwaffe airfield's runways, then to cruise east along French rail lines to destroy any supply or troop trains headed towards the Normandy beachheads.

In Paul's earphones came the flight leader's shout of "Tallyho!"

"Here we go," Bran yelled, and cut loose with a Scot war cry, a scream that rose from deep bass to high falsetto. One by one, the planes banked out of formation for bombing runs. Their low-level treetop approach caught the enemy unprepared, and only the last two planes received any serious flak. Unfortunately, that included the *Graceful Raven*. The left engine sputtered, its electrical and hydraulic systems shot out by the bursting shrapnel of a lucky forty- millimeter shell.

"This is flight leader to *Graceful Raven*, now the *Ruptured Duck*. Return to base, you cannot keep up. Over."

"*Graceful Raven* to flight leader, Roger, leaving formation, out."

The two friends nursed their one remaining engine as they sped over blurred farm fields and wooded patches, keeping at treetop level in an attempt to avoid the attentions of enemy fighters. It quickly became a false hope. A series of splintered raps announced the penetration of the rear fuselage by enemy bullets and a bang from an exploding twenty-millimeter shell made them aware of a German Focke-wulf 190 on their tail. Paul threw the plane into twisting, jinking maneuvers. The rattle of bullet strikes continued.

"With one engine, we are too slow!" shouted Bran.

"I have a plan. Hold on." Paul threw the throttle full forward. The plane gained speed.

The oil pressure gage of the remaining engine pinned itself at its max position. "We cannot take this beating for long." Bran sang out.

Paul let the *Raven* gain altitude. More bangs. The tip of the right wing broke off. Streams of tracers flashed by.

A high-pitched quivering voice said, "Hurry man, do the plan."

The pilot pulled back the stick and put the plane into a nose up stall, slowing its forward motion as though it had panic-braked.

From the navigator's seat, a low respectful voice recited the Lord's Prayer in Scot-Gaelic, running all the words together. The Fw-190 flashed by. Paul lowered the nose of their plane and pulled the gun triggers. Knife blades of .303 and twenty-millimeter rounds stabbed the enemy fighter beginning with the German cross on its tail then slicing forward to where its right wing joined the fuselage. The gas tank blew. High-octane fuel cremated the pilot and flamed chunks and pieces of the Focke-Wulf.

The *Graceful Raven* flew through the spinning wreckage. The three-bladed propeller on its last engine hit something solid, deformed, and shook the plane.

"Could we not have had a better plan?"

"Hang on, you thick-headed Scot, I'm looking for a soft landing."

The aircraft bounced off the top of a belt of elastic close-planted pines, and then nosed down into a vineyard. Paul pulled up the stick. The belly of the Mossie slapped the earth, making the men's teeth click. It skimmed along the ground, ripped up grapevines with its muzzle, plowed up pillows of dirt, and shed speed. It tore across the field, the interior echoing with screams and curses from the occupants, and rammed a copse of fir trees. The fuselage groaned and rattled as it slid between close-packed trees. Trunks snapped off both wings. Branches and limbs rained down, rasping across the canopy. The remains of the Graceful Raven came to a jerking halt completely encased in the fallen green of the grove.

"Whoa." Paul looked at his companion and began to laugh. "Bacchus, the god of wine, was with us today. Those vines acted like big nets to slow our rush."

Smelling gasoline vapor, Bran unlatched his side door. "Let us get the hell out of here before we become charbroiled."

The pair crawled over and around broken trees. Upon reaching the open field, they were surrounded by a dozen women from the nearby village armed with hoes and rakes. The oldest and leader, a toothless, smelly, prune-faced crone later introduced as Madame Jacquard, kept them covered with a shotgun that was modern when Napoleon was a toddler. The firearm in her stick-thin, age-spotted arms did not drop until their nationality was confirmed. Two of the women took them to the village while the others remained to cover up the skid mark left by the airplane.

Paul was able to use the de Gracie French on the way, learning this small rural community was at least thirty miles from the nearest town and German garrison. Its population consisted entirely of women of various ages. Most of their husbands and sons, in the army at the beginning of the war, remained in POW camps in Germany. The last of the village's able-bodied men and boys had been swept up for labor battalions to man military construction projects and factory assembly lines. The two decrepit grandfathers left behind had passed on, due to the poor state of food supplies and medical service in occupied France.

"Bran, these women have not had male company for the last three years. This could either be heaven or hell."

"I wondered why all the giggling and playing the *coquette*. How many are we talking about?"

Paul turned, "*S'il vous plaît, Madame, combien de femmes habitent dans le village?*"

"*S'il vous plaît,*" she responded, gently mocking his politeness. " *il ya en a trente, monsieur.*"

"The answer is thirty, my friend."

Arriving at a cluster of buildings, the men were sequestered in the main winery barn. Pastel wool blankets and quilts embroidered with flowers and vines arranged in the haymow would serve as beds. The women insisted on filling two cutoff oak wine casks with hot water for the men's baths. During their wash, Paul and Bran heard a lot of tittering and whispering outside, spotting eyes and arched eyebrows sneaking peeks through cracks in the weather-shrunk wood siding.

With the coming of dusk, two women dressed in their prewar best and the last drops of hoarded perfume brought a thin vegetable stew, brown bread, and a dusty bottle of wine. The foursome ate, drank, and laughed. After dinner, the females climbed the ladder to the beds in the loft and began shedding clothes.

"*C'est quoi ça?* What is this?" Paul asked, while Bran blushed.

"*Nous avons organisè une lotterie. Nous allons tous prendre notre tour.*"

"Jesus, Bran, they have issued raffle tickets, and we are the prizes. Not only that, but the whole gaggle of them is going to take turns."

Looking at slender, but prime female flesh, Bran grinned and responded, "Well, I think we should accommodate our allies, if for no other reason than to promote the war effort."

"Yes, but who gets Madame Jacquard?"

❦

Hugh awoke from the dream with a painful erection. It had been over a year now for him. He sympathized with the French women. Paul-Henri de Gracie should have stayed in the village instead of rejoining the allied cause. After returning to North America for a brief home-leave and assignment to a new squadron, he and Bran had departed for Europe. This time the comrades were not lucky. Their lives ended while providing close air support during the Battle of the Bulge in the fog surrounding Bastogne.

But the Mother-tree had gifted Hugh with this record of his great uncle's life for some reason. He added it to the memories of other dreams awaiting revelation.

❦

Margy had been giving flirting lessons to Désirée, not that she was an expert, but *La Grand-mère* had never learned the art. Confusing the issue, any Victorian era female-to-male enticement she might try to resurrect would not raise an eyebrow in this modern, looser era. Lifting your skirts to expose your ankles, a sign of a wanton woman in her time, would pass completely unnoticed in this age of short-shorts and bikinis. Also, knowing when to break off or cool down the siren song before things got out of control took experienced insight. They discussed words, phrases, and body language with double meanings used to send signals of come-hither or stay-away. Margy knew few of these and Ojas gave no help, his memories of such innuendo dated back centuries and did not translate well from Mohawk.

Several occasions allowed practice. The de Gracie attorneys and investment managers arranged invitations to parties, music recitals, and receptions. The few attempts at flirting at these allowed events had not gone well. Désirée did not have her heart in the process. The visits to the sex therapist had brought her back from borderline frigidity, but she remained cool and confused about the contemporary courtship process. However, Margy sensed in her charge a great growing potential to give and receive love, only waiting for the right combination of man and moment to run free.

Well, they were about out of time, she thought, one last party yet to attend this evening. Three more days and they would be back to the family holdings. Then everything depended on how well Désirée and Hugh would meld.

*

Désirée took a sip of a strawberry Daiquiri and wished she had earplugs.

The spacious high-rise apartment sprawled over two floors with stairs to the second level bedrooms hidden behind a stone fireplace. Persian rugs with thousands of wool and linen knots had been rolled back, exposing light Birchwood flooring. Couples shook and wiggled to the latest rock, heavy metal, and rap. Others clung together in twos and threes around the bars, one at each end of the room, or nested together on couches and overstuffed leather chairs scattered at random.

Désirée wore one of her favorite new outfits, consisting of a black silk blouse tucked into an above-the-knee khaki skirt complemented by a brown Berber weave jacket with black-banded cuffs. Gold Grecian sandals with straps up to her calves exposed matching gold-painted toenails. Her hair, parted down the middle, rolled over her shoulders front and back, long blonde curls bringing out the tans and browns in jacket and skirt.

She glanced around the room expecting to see Margy and Ojas staring from one corner or another, but they were keeping their promise. Their hovering presence, especially that of her fire-eyed tattooed Native American bodyguard, put a damper on any conversations with the opposite sex. After several contentious arguments over the space of a week, the trio had compromised.

The guardians would allow her the illusion of being unescorted. Arriving at the party, Margy and Ojas took positions in the apartment's kitchen, out of sight, with occasional furtive glances from the doorway every ten minutes or so.

Bored, Désirée examined the prints and gewgaws that decorated the apartment walls and nooks, none of them original, but this was the pad of a young man still on his way up. And, from the selection of art, one who promoted his sexuality.

The host, John Walters, a licensed investment advisor, moved close and looked over her shoulder. "Anything here you like?"

Désirée did not bother to turn. The man's breath tickled her neck and the heat of his body could be felt on her back and hips. She took a moment to translate her answer from the Victorian words that formed in her mind to more smooth modern English.

"There is an interesting sprinkle of movie poster reproductions: *King Kong, Indiana Jones*, and *Conan The Barbarian*, scattered among what is otherwise an eclectic collection of mildly erotic art."

"There are classics." He pointed to scaled-down print reproductions, "Hieronymus Bosch's painting of *The Garden of Light*, Maurice Dennis's nude *Woman in A Walled Garden* and Goya's *Naked Maja*."

"But not Goya's companion piece *The Clothed Maja*," Désirée replied, finally getting to use the information garnered in recent lectures and tours of New York museums.

"Are you a fan of the Old Masters or does your taste run to more modern themes?" Walters raised an arm towards three framed naked Vargas calendar girls with their extra ribs and non-human proportions.

He placed a hand on her right shoulder, pulled their bodies closer, and whispered, "I have a private collection of hand-painted Japanese scrolls upstairs that might prove interesting to an art devotee such as yourself."

Both eyebrows up, Désirée spun on her heels. At the three-quarter turn, she angled her glass downward and stopped abruptly. The centrifugal force of the movement threw the red slush of her drink in a mass to slop against his belt-line. The semi-liquid crystallized ice penetrated his clothes and dripped down into his groin.

"Jesus!" he exclaimed, bending over and brushing at his clothes. "I am so sorry." She said with hidden satisfaction.

"Don't go anywhere. I'll change and be right back."

She tried a dance with one of the wallflower computer nerds. The modern dance movements made her feel like a marionette, the strings of a puppet master jerking arms and legs. These epileptic spasms were not nearly so elegant as the two-steps, waltzes, and cotillions of her time.

A tap on her shoulder announced Walters' return, dressed in khakis, a Hibiscus flowered Hawaiian shirt, and sandals. He offered a new Daiquiri, this one apple with cinnamon.

Sweaty from the dance, she accepted and drank about half the contents. Fifteen minutes later, dizzy, woozy, and physically impaired, Désirée allowed Walters to support her as they climbed the stairs to his bedroom.

She obeyed his order to sit on the bed while Walters removed her jacket. Unable to resist, she watched him undo the buttons on her blouse, exposing a black lace bra. On his way to the dresser, he peeled off his shirt. Pulling out a hand mirror and a razor blade, Désirée watched him pour out white powder from a plastic bag and cut it into four parallel lines on the reflective glass surface. Rolling a crisp dollar bill into a funnel, he sniffed two of the lines, one in each nostril. He held up the apparatus. "Here you go, Baby. It'll help you feel better."

In an act of defiance, Désirée raised lead-heavy hands, caught the mirror on one side, and knocked it to the floor – the short-cut shag rug absorbing the powder.

"Damn, woman, that's a lot of cash lost." Walters slapped her on one cheek, pushed her back on the bed, and rolled up her skirt. He grasped the elastic edge of her panties and pulled.

The black lace bikinis came down past her hips. Désirée felt him pause, the back of his fingers lingered, feeling the soft, warm flesh beneath. She felt repulsed, the man actually had to swallow to keep from drooling.

The expression on his face reflected his anticipation of what was to come, physically engorged, and emotionally thrilled.

The door to the room crashed open, flung with such force the interior doorknob penetrated the plasterboard of the wall behind it and remained stuck there. A piece of shattered lock spun across the room to ricochet off a lampshade.

Walters had time for one yelp.

Ojas grabbed the man by the neck and tossed him into a walnut recliner.

Chair and man fell over backward.

The bodyguard kicked the seducer in the right kidney.

Walters curled up into a fetal position.

Lifting him up by the hair, Ojas' black eyes caught his. "This woman not for you, asshole druggie." He grabbed the little finger on Walters' left hand, applying pressure where it joined the palm. "I help you remember."

A snap and Walters rose on his tiptoes, mouth distorted in an anguished 'O'. Released, he gasped for air, and turned in circles cradling his finger, which now pointed upward.

❦

A mixed bag of de Gracies, including The Father, Uncle Frank, Jeannine, old Alphonse and others sat around a long oil cloth-covered table that stretched half the length of the armory. On fuzzy absorbent shop-towels lay fieldstripped assault rifles and pistols. The shipment had arrived. Cosmoline and heavy grease must be cleaned from the disassembled weapons, their parts re-assembled, and the actions checked. Later in the afternoon, they would be test-fired in one of the family back meadows on the mountainside away from the village. The smells of gun oil and solvent mixed with the friendlier odors of coffee and citron.

Hugh had selected Barrett Rec 7 assault rifles chambered in the legal-for-hunting Remington 6.8 SPC cartridge. With an eight-inch barrel, the six-pound weapon came in a matte black with an adjustable stock. An upgrade of the army's M-4, the weapon's larger slug flashed out of the muzzle at 2,650 feet per second. A flat trajectory made for accuracy, high velocity for better penetration, and at a weight of 115 grams, the projectile had plenty of knockdown power. In fact, it was the round of choice among the followers of the fastest growing sport in Texas, wild boar hunting. The bullet immediately dropped running wild hogs in man-heavy weights of one hundred fifty to four hundred pounds. A selector switch allowed the weapon to fire in semi-automatic or fully automatic modes.

Jeannine set aside an assembled Saiga 12-gauge Taktika semi-automatic shotgun and started work on a second. The gun fired a wide variety of shells, including frangible rounds, hardened double O buckshot, and slugs for door busting.

Uncle Frank attached a bipod to a green-mottled Marine Corps issue M-110 sniper rifle with a ten-round magazine. Properly sighted and adjusted for wind direction and bullet drop, it could hit a target the size of an eyeball at eight hundred meters.

Hugh stopped work on a Barrett and refocused his one blurry eye on a distant spot, allowing it rest from close-up work.

"Father." He pointed upward at the ceiling globes, illuminating the workspace with warm-white radiance. "We don't have a generator and no connection to the area electric net. Where is the power coming from for these light fixtures?"

Aubert set down a cleaning brush and the receiver group of a 1911 A1 forty-five caliber pistol. "Your great, great Uncle Arnaud became a disciple of Nikola Tesla during the early twentieth century. I don't know how he did it, but upon his return here, he convinced the Mother-tree to grow low-current, high-voltage Tesla coils and the vapor-filled globes you see throughout the mansion. The whole project took ten years of detailed man-plant hours."

Hugh tilted his head. "So, if my memory of my science tutors' lessons is correct, Tesla used the coils to broadcast electricity through the air, in one case, to excite gas in isolated glass tubes to fluoresce, creating useable illumination. Same principle we use today in millions of hard-wired fluorescent lights. Back to my original question, where does the power come from?"

"Your great, great uncle and the Mother-tree built a series of dedicated underground condensers to collect and store power from natural sources, primarily cloud and water-generated static electricity."

"This sounds dangerous. Tesla coils are still used to generate synthetic lightning. Couldn't someone get zapped?"

"Exactly why inventors decided to move electricity in wires instead of broadcasting it. However, our wood walls and floors are good insulators. I cannot believe there is any danger, unless someone breaches the system and becomes well grounded."

Jeannine de Gracie re-entered carrying a pitcher of coffee. She refilled cups. Placing a caressing hand on Hugh's neck, she asked, "Do you need a refill?"

Aubert shook his head and waved her off. She had been warned once already. They would have a serious *tête-à-tête* later. They did not need Hugh sexually sated at this time. He changed the subject.

"I have a team digging the foxholes in the 'L' shape you requested. The long leg of the 'L' paralleling the front wall of the mansion and the short leg at a right angle along the inside north section of the thornwall."

"That will allow interlocking lines of fire without friendly fire incidents," Hugh concluded. "Have you sandbagged the command bunker in the central tower and machine gun positions atop the two end towers?"

"A block and tackle arrangement is positioned. After we finish here, we need strong backs and weak minds to fill and hoist the bags." Aubert laughed. "You and your uncle should be first in line."

"All these... improvements need to be hidden, the pits covered with plywood and sod lids or in the case of the towers, camouflage netting." Hugh tempered his command tone in deference to his father's familial position. "We don't want the enemy to know our dispositions, nor any of next week's music camp participants accidentally falling in a hole."

Hugh took a sip of Kona coffee and made up his mind to take a verbal end run into territory both he and family members had been avoiding. "Father, what is our medical capability, if we have casualties?"

"Our folks would need to stabilize the wounded and then get them connected to the Mother-tree."

Hugh swallowed and continued. "Real combat can produce fragmented limbless bodies, not like the clean wounds in movies and TV. What's her capability?"

"The Mother-tree has a detailed, micro-cellular-level picture of each of us in her memory. She will try to return a wounded or sick body to match that record. It is possible she can stimulate the regrowth of entire limbs, although I have only seen it done with missing fingers or toes lost through occasional wood chopping accidents. However, those with significant organ damage and, of course, the already dead cannot be brought back."

Hugh pressed his lips together. "Is that what she did with my virus, damaged feet, and shrapnel-laced legs and back?"

"Yes, in fact, most of the cells in your body now resemble their eighteen-year-old condition, the last time she recorded your characteristics."

Hugh homed in on his hidden goal. "Is this why you are eighty-seven, look like fifty, and move like a twenty-year-old? Does the Mother-tree confer immortality, like it says in the legends?"

Hugh noticed Aubert purse his lips. Obviously, they were headed into an area his father did not wish to enter.

Aubert weighed an answer in his mind. Too much background information might come home to haunt them when Désirée entered the picture. To know her age might disclose her relationship. He decided to equivocate.

"Like most plants, the Mother-tree produces hormones and chemicals to regulate her growth and health. While our human hormones cannot affect her, her exudations can affect us. Her growth, stress, and immune hormones, properly applied, promote our longevity and health."

"Can you be more specific?"

"It is a simple thing for her to produce estrogen to regulate women's cycles, and other chemicals to maintain female reproductive fitness and extend their fertility. Osteoporosis is unknown among us. Almost as simple, she can detoxify our bodies, even producing chemicals that eliminate cancer cells." Aubert hesitated, broke eye contact. "Some of her hormones also directly inhibit senescence."

The old son-of-a-bitch is putting together a lie, just like he did in my early days, Hugh thought. "Father, don't try to hide behind science. I know that word. You're dancing around the immortality thing again."

"Cells divide and reproduce, over the years new cells eventually deviate from the original, become flawed, and replicate badly – our bodies deteriorate. Mother-tree produced cytokinins and other chemicals injected into our bodies ensure each new cell is a faithful reproduction of the original – aging is slowed. We do not live forever, but short of death in accidents and combat, we live extended lives."

"What does 'extended' mean?"

"Think one hundred and eighty to two hundred years."

Hugh tried to prevent his skin from flushing, Father would notice his anger. The old shit was still holding back information. This father-son mendacity had been building since he was thirteen. Partial truths took the place of complete knowledge. If only he knew the right questions to ask.

"So, during the last half of that time, we get to experience a longer period of age-related mind and body failures than our peers in the outer world. Extended dementia and Alzheimer's?"

Aubert looked sheepish. "It does not work that way. In addition to the quickening of wound healing that you experienced, the Mother-tree's treatment prevents muscle wasting, improves organ function and memory retention, lowers serum cholesterol, and, an added bonus, gives you tighter, more supple skin."

Hugh rubbed his empty eye socket, stared at the far wall, and tried to douse the anger that kept rising. He would deal with the implications. "Who is the oldest among us?"

His question caused the others in the room to put down their cleaning tools and listen.

Sensing a possible breakage in the plan, Aubert made a quick decision. This must be handled carefully. There were two measurements here. Actual age versus passage age, the first measured the number of years spent walking around active, and the second the total of actual age plus time spent in suspended animation. Uncle Frank was the oldest by both measurements with a passage age in excess of five hundred years. He decided on the usual presentation of a half-truth. "In actual age, your Uncle Frank burned past one hundred and ten last February."

📎

Désirée, Margy, and Ojas exited from a yellow cab at the corner of Fifth Avenue and 57th Street into bright sunshine. While their male escort handed cash to the cabby, the two women admired the building's iconic granite and limestone facing. Mounted over the door, painted to mimic a weathered bronze patina, a nine-foot-long wood statue of Atlas shouldering a four-foot diameter clock stood guard. On this final day, they had a mid-morning appointment at Tiffany & Co., the place where dreams were created. Désirée, the time traveler, knew of the store and its products, which even during her era, had been popular with the rich and elite.

"How do you feel, dear?" Margy asked.

They had lost yesterday, allowing Désirée to recover from the drugging. She had bounced back in spite of the worst hangover imaginable, consisting of headache, dizziness, and shooting pains throughout the body. Alcohol and Rohypnol taken together magnified the effects of both.

On the plus side, she had no memory of the events after drinking the poisoned Daiquiri, and no resulting trauma.

Margy pointed at the Atlas clock. "Past time for our call," she said, and placing a hand in the small of her charge's back ushered her through the stainless-steel door with its wheat-leaf motifs. Inside, they moved past glass display cases, their crystal and polished metal contents illuminated by tiny full-spectrum spotlights.

In spite of being ten minutes late, the trio paused before the case displaying the 128-caret yellow Tiffany diamond, currently set as a pendant attached to a necklace whose strands were encrusted with hundreds of white diamonds of various sizes and cuts. Lighting in the case was subdued with tiny lights set at angles to prevent the jewels' reflections from causing temporary blindness in the observers.

A tall balding man in a navy pin-stripe suit, red tie embroidered with a spray of miniature cherry blossoms, and spit-shined cap-toe Oxfords broke the spell of their diamond hypnosis. "Madame de Gracie, please, you and your companions follow me. We have the items you requested displayed on the fifth floor."

After the elevator doors shut, their escort turned a key in the control panel and pushed the button marked five. "Since the remodeling some years ago, we use the fifth floor as our entertainment center. A side room is scheduled for your use for the next two hours."

A fresh wax smell flowed into the elevator as the doors slid open. The group followed their guide across an open area encompassing two-thirds of the available floor space. Their steps on the underlying light wood parquet echoed off the high ceiling with its recessed incandescent lighting. Their host stopped before a gray-suited security guard, whose jacket had been cut large across the chest to allow for a shoulder holster beneath. He stood aside while the guide punched a code into an electronic door lock.

Holding the door open, the Tiffany representative bowed them in. "When you are finished let us know by using the room phone. Please help yourself to refreshments."

The trio advanced into a room with cream-pastel walls and generous windows. Light from the mid-morning sun was augmented once again by full spectrum bulbs in the overhead fixtures. In one corner, a honey-oak table of Frank Lloyd Wright's Prairie design held a four-legged sterling silver coffee pot with ornate handle and spout, accompanied by matching sugar and creamer. A linen-covered tray displayed a variety of cookies and house chocolates. Three Louis Quatorze chairs upholstered in red leaf-patterned silk clustered in the opposite corner. In the center, two tables had been set with black velvet covers. Blue boxes of various sizes and shapes formed asymmetrical patterns on their surface.

Margy and Désirée looked at each other, grinned, and moved up to the tables. Ojas glanced at the contents. In each box nestled a piece of jewelry with an accompanying card explaining its composition and history. He grimaced, and headed for the chairs and coffee. Their escort would settle in while the haggling took place.

"Oh, Margy, all this. *C'est merveilleux.* Can we buy something? A little ring, perhaps?"

"No need to buy. This is part of the de Gracie family hoard. Tiffany's stores and maintains these items for us. Let us select some baubles to augment your ball dress."

Désirée began by picking up a delicate gold chain with three small solid-gold bees affixed – wings, multifaceted eyes, and exoskeleton to proper scale. The card described them as awards for valor given to soldiers of ancient Egyptian Pharaohs, circa 1536 B.C.E. A yellow-gold ring caught her attention next. According to the card, the inch square plaque on its top was inscribed with the cartouche of Thutmose III (1475 – 1425 B.C.E.). Her hands wandered to a third piece of Egyptian origin. With a gasp, she held up a coiled snake bracelet. A representation of an asp, its coils fit around the forearm and wrist. The head straightened and stretched out against the back of the hand to stop an inch short of the knuckles. The age guessed on the card was 90 C.E.

With a sigh, she said, "Surely, these cannot be from the past. They are too perfect, too clean. Are they reproductions?"

"All of this," Margy's arms opened to encompass the stacked items on the tables, "has been handed down from mother-tree humans generation to generation. They have never been in tombs or dug up from the dirt. You remember mother-trees produce seeds every century and a half or so, requiring some of the existing humans to establish a new colony. Jewelry is one of the portable assets taken with each new group. It remains a link reminding us of our past and can be easily bartered or converted into cash if there is an emergency."

Désirée quickly did the math. *"C'est fou!* This must mean Mother-trees have been around for at least three thousand five hundred years."

Margy spoke a little louder, making sure she was heard over the deep rumbling snores now coming from Ojas. "The little gold bees are our oldest tangible link, but Aubert speculates the human-tree relationship must go back much further to have evolved into the oneness of today, say over three hundred thousand years. A time the fossil and stone tool record indicates the beginning of Homo Sapiens."

After an hour and a half, and much adding and subtracting of items, the women signed for their final selections on release forms provided by the Tiffany man. Out of all the rings, chokers, tiaras, and bracelets, only three items were selected. The 18-karat snake bracelet cast of an amber-colored alloy of gold and silver known as electrum went into its cotton-padded blue box. A pair of three-inch-long earrings from the Byzantine period followed, featuring dangling gold wire baskets holding thumbnail-sized pearls. The chains and loops connecting the baskets to the earpieces were set with square-cut emeralds.

Much to Désirée's amazement, she had found her own broach from the Civil War among the treasures. A two-inch-long oval gold frame held a cameo of her in three-quarter profile carved in ivory, the hair, engraved in detail, had been impressed with gold leaf to match her blonde tresses.

6

A time to seek, and a time to lose;
a time to keep, and a time to discard;
Ecclesiastes: 3:6

RECENTLY RETURNED FROM NYC, Margy added billets of fuel. Heat poured from the thick iron walls of the ovens. Today she, Hugh, and Jeannine were baking. In three days, two-dozen-plus hungry teenagers would be invading to attend the annual music camp.

Margy, Jeannine, and Hugh had been at work since six am. The character and décor of the great kitchen of the House de Gracie had not changed much since his childhood. Consistent with the décor throughout the mansion, its artifacts and fixtures were a mishmash of styles and ages. Attired in a white T-shirt and blue jeans, protected by a neck-and-waist-tied linen apron, Hugh stood belly up to the twelve-foot-long worktable in the room's center. A brazed metal chandelier, the same dimensions as the table, hung overhead from heavy chains fixed in the ceiling. Its design, originally possessing cups and linen wicks to burn lard oil and later modified to hold candles, testified to an advanced age.

The family's inventory of skillets, Dutch ovens, and copper pots hung from hooks festooned on its outer edges. An ancient six-burner cast-iron stove squatted up against the opposite wall, its double oven and multiple nooks and shelves designed to cook or keep food warm. Three separate fireboxes allowed a portion of the stove to be used without wasting fuel heating the entire construct. A water jacket with faucet welded to the range's backside provided a limited supply of hot water when it was in operation. The stove's exhaust pipe curved back, penetrating the brick of an ancient open-hearth fireplace to vent up the original chimney. Nearby a metal frame held forearm-length billets of firewood, mostly the mother-tree-grown version of hawthorn, but hickory and fruitwood were handy nearby to flavor the air and food while cooking.

Two refrigerators and a top lid freezer stood across the room, all powered with a twelve-volt battery system kept charged by photovoltaic panels mounted on the roof, or a backup propane powered generator. Hugh's ancestors and current living relatives, while on the surface appearing old-fashioned, weren't averse to adding modern conveniences when the harmony of the House and its tastes weren't threatened. The worktable was another example, its three-hundred-year-old maple top recently encased in modern stainless steel.

Supplies poured in from Port Henry stores, butter and cheese making accelerated, and dust-covered jars of jelly and pickles came up from storerooms. Family members picked, washed, and bagged early fruit and vegetables from orchard and garden. Necklaces of garlic, onions, and peppers hung among the pots on the rectangular chandelier, adding a spicy, homey scent.

No matter how demeaning on the surface, there was no job in which all the de Gracie's didn't take a turn. At least, the family had no need to clean latrines or sinks, Hugh thought.

These were all integral parts of the Mother-tree who efficiently absorbed and reused the refuse and gray-water. This was a great relief to Hugh, whose many personal indiscretions during his first months in the Army had earned him a close relationship with the cleanliness of the barrack's toilets.

Putting the memory away, he turned to the work at hand. The trio had organized the kitchen into *une boulangerie*, with bread, pies, and rolls the products. The women pushed him into the scut-work of hauling materials from here to there, retrieving bowls and implements from top shelves of cupboards, and mixing ingredients. Although the powers-that-be thought refrigerators were good, their beneficence didn't extend to electric mixers. All ingredients must be mixed or beaten with heavy wooden spoons, or kneaded with hands.

Margy removed a pie from the oven, set it on a cooling rack, and waved a hot pad. "Hugh, *mon cher*, run down to the storeroom and bring up another twenty-five-pound bag of flour."

"*D'accord*, and wipe the flour off your nose," he tossed over his shoulder as he started down the steps into the first level basement.

The kitchen heat grew oppressive. The women tied headbands around their foreheads. Perspiration tickled as it trickled down their ribs and soaked their clothes. Jeannine opened the hinged canopy windows set into the outer wall near floor-level. Margy undid a chain from a wall-hook that allowed a spring-loaded skylight cover to open in the roof. Hot air exited through the skylight, drawing in ground-level cooler air from the outside – the temperature dropped five degrees, still hot but bearable.

Hugh returned, the flour bag over his shoulder, exaggerating every step while chanting the Volga Boatman song. The women laughed and booed.

"Hurry up you slug, no sympathy here."

He smacked the bag down on the tabletop and pulled the string, which allowed the purse-type mouth to open. Two pounds of flour went into a yellow earthenware bowl, which he mixed with salt and yeast. Jeannine brought a pan from the stove, poured a hot solution of milk, water, and honey into the mix. Hugh cradled the bowl and put the spoon into action beating the wet and dry ingredients together while periodically scraping the sides.

At her position across the table, Jeannine worked with once-raised dough, punched it down, divided it into loaves, and placed it into pans to rise a second time. She took one loaf-sized lump and rolled it out into an inch-thick four-by-ten rectangle. Using wooden spice shakers, she dusted the surface with cinnamon and sugar, sprinkled a handful of raisins, and jelly-rolled up the dough, pinching the ends shut. The soon-to-be cinnamon-swirl bread was a favorite on the family breakfast menu.

Over her shoulder, she saw Margy leave the kitchen on an errand. Adjusting her apron to hang further down her front, Jeannine's fingers undid the three top buttons on her blouse.

Quickly rolling out a second loaf, she used her index finger to smudge her lips with sweet powdery cinnamon and sugar. Moving in front of Hugh, she bent over, exposed the curves of her breasts, and pushed her hands into the sticky dough he was kneading. As her fingers caressed his hands, Hugh glanced up. Skin-to-skin contact inside the warm gelatinous flour felt very sensual. Her eyes caught his. The green in them turned a mysterious aqua. The irises cycled open, drawing him in.

He felt a shiver flush out from his spine to his torso, spreading to arms, legs, and head.

Without volition, he bent from the waist to meet her at mid-table. Their heads turned. Lips pressed together. A little flicker of female tongue pushed a sweet rush of cinnamon-sugar into his mouth. The heat, the spice, smell of bread baking, soft flesh to flesh, all conspired to arouse him in rare fashion 150 all the senses engaged. His muscles clenched.

A shout came from across the room. Margy rushed the pair. "That is enough, you two." A wooden spoon smacked Jeannine on the neck and ricocheted to sting Hugh's shoulder. "Get back to work, we have no time for your... your... dithering." Margy waved the two-foot-long implement, a threatening wand. Jeannine fluttered back to her workstation.

Hugh tried to withdraw from the sexual fug the episode had generated. He felt as though someone had smacked him in the forehead with a boot sock half full of wet sand. Feeling a little shaky, he hefted the heavy sack of flour and prepared to pour some out.

The interior kitchen door banged, and a rush of footsteps made him turn, bag in hand. A human whirlwind of gold and black smacked into him. A corner of the paper bag tore off. Left-handed he suspended the sack, his right hand tried to find a new grip and failed.

The bag tore out of his fingers and fell. It abruptly slapped the faux-stone floor. The energy accumulated during the drop fountained finely ground flour up into an eight-foot-high pillar. Hugh caught the majority of the blast. Bleached powder coated his apron and clothes and the exposed skin on his arms and head. Stepping out of the ground-zero cloud, he sneezed and coughed. He blinked and caught the silhouette of the culprit who caused the accident exit through the patio door.

Anger replaced sexual frustration. Hugh ran after, leaving a filmy trail of gauzy-white. With each stride, his apron-ends flapped puffs of flour. Outside, he shouted and closed on his prey. From the hip movement and the yard-long blonde braid that swung across her back, the perp was definitely female.

She stopped on the gravel walk near two of Ojas's restored 1950's shovelhead Harleys. Turning upon hearing his shout, she rested one hand on the handlebars of a bike with fenders and teardrop gas tank painted canary yellow.

Hugh stopped six feet away and sneezed again. "What in the hell are you doing? Who are you?"

The woman looked at him, first with an expression of suspicion, then with anger-pressed lips and knitted eyebrows. She paused for a moment, obviously seeking words, winding herself up.

"I do not have to explain myself to any jack-a-dandy ragamuffin."

Hugh bent his neck and looked closer. He thought she was cursing him, but he had never heard those words in spoken English, only in old novels.

Her outfit conflicted madly with her speech pattern. She wore a waist-length black leather biker jacket over a matching boat-neck silk blouse. Skin-fitting pants showed every interesting curve of her body all the way down to where feet tucked into black-strapped Wellingtons. She picked up a black-visored helmet and removed a pair of driving gloves from inside.

"Well," he replied, dredging up a few old period words, "at least, I'm no hysterical strumpet." He took two steps forward.

The woman made a fist and shook her gloves at him. "Do not come closer, you plug-ugly scoundrel. You had best skedaddle before my guardian arrives."

A tickle of humor began in Hugh's mind – the exchange seemed so out of time. He looked at the hair on his forearms, coated in flour to twice the normal diameter, and he bet the same was true of his eyebrows and hair. The scene before him became ridiculously surreal.

Viewed from a distance, it would look like a Saturday Night Live skit featuring the 'biker bitch from hell' versus 'the Pillsbury doughboy.' Laughter started as a grunt through his nostrils. He took a deep breath and let it out in raucous snorts.

The woman stared.

The hilarity caused a cramp. Tears made a little doughy rivulet from his good eye down his cheek. He bent over. If this was a movie satire, so be it.

He rushed forward and grasped the biker in his arms, dipped her to the left, and stared amorously into her eyes. He recited Bogart's famous airport lines to Bergman from the movie Casablanca. The words spilled out about love gained in Paris, its loss, and recovery.

She writhed in his grip. "Let me go, you… you contemptible blackguard. *Tu me fais chier.*"

The woman freed one hand and slapped his cheek with her gloves, raising a puff of white powder. "*Fils de salope.* Release me, you bone-headed buffoon. Has the French-pox affected your intellect?"

Hugh delivered the parting Bogart Casablanca movie line with what he thought was deep savoir-faire. "Now, now. Here's looking at you, kid."

Released from his clutch, she clapped on her helmet and mounted the bike. Kicking the starter produced no action. She lifted her body and stomped down again. Hugh stood patiently behind and to one side as she made a third attempt.

She threw up her hands, raised her head to the sky, and shouted, "*Fuck!*"

Now that old fashioned word he understood. Moving forward, he reached over her lap to the far side of the gas tank and turned the key. With a smug smile, he motioned her to try again.

One kick and the engine roared to life. The biker twisted the right handlebar grip, as though it was his neck she was wringing.

The cycle spun out, the back wheel snake-twisted, loosed a seven-foot-tall rooster tail of pea gravel and powdered stone directly into Hugh, who managed to turn sideways to the buckshot rush of particles. Now he looked like an escaped European domino circus clown: all white on the right and dark gray on the left.

Ojas, dressed neck-to-foot in well-used distressed leathers, walked up to the second bike, looked him up and down, smiled, and winked. One kick and the motor of the black bike roared. Hugh jumped back, avoiding a second gravel-shot. Ojas cruised down the path, followed the dust trail left by the first bike, and exited through the front gate. Hugh walked back to the kitchen. He wiped his forehead. Flour had mixed with his salty sweat and formed a primitive dough.

Margy met him at the door, a worried look on her face.

"Who was that masked woman?" he asked. *"C'est une femme formidable."*

Margy frowned and pressed her lips together. She would have to tell him something.

Aubert would not be happy with the results of this premature meeting. "I believe the woman is an offshoot of a distant branch of the family, here visiting and becoming acquainted with us. You will see more of her later."

Hugh replayed his impressions of the biker babe. A Shakespeare quote from *Much Ado About Nothing* came to mind: 'The tongues of mocking wenches are as keen as is the razor's edge, invisible, cutting a smaller hair than may be seen.' Damn, though, if she wasn't pretty when pissed, he thought. She had felt good in his arms, the tight leather allowed body heat and the uninhibited play of muscle to be felt. Those great legs. A man with imagination could do a lot with those legs. Blonde hair, hazel eyes, black leather – a fascinating combination. Then he remembered in that particular Shakespeare play the male and female antagonists' relatives trick them into getting married.

*

Désirée knew she was in bed, asleep in her room on the third floor of the Mother-tree. A small inner voice told her she could not be in this place, but the vision – so full of color and sensation demanded her full attention. A hot July sun illuminated the Virginia countryside. The other senses engaged: the smell of the grass, the feel of the Swiss-muslin day dress between her fingers.

"More chicken, my dear?"

Eyes focused, Désirée's mind passed completely into the dream.

Senator Washburne's wife Adele held out a serving platter. "Uh, no, thank you." She looked down at her plate at the remains of fried chicken, deviled oysters, coleslaw, and succotash.

"Abel," Mrs. Washburne waved at a servant, "you can serve the apple pan dowdy and peppermint cake now."

The Right Honorable Senator from Illinois, Elihu Benjamin Washburne held up a bottle of wine, "More of the red, Madame de Gracie? Oh, and save room for champagne when our men have driven the rebels off."

The Washburne party was one of many hundreds spread over some poor farmer's pasture that July 21, 1861 morning. Men, women, and children settled themselves on oilcloths, spread to keep the moisture pulled out of the ground by the harsh sun from damaging fashionable clothes. Women and girls spinning pink-beribboned parasols and men and boys with thumbs inserted in vest pockets strolled in twos and threes between little picnic islands. Condemnation of the repressive heat was their opening remark to both friends and strangers. As the day wore on, the voices blended into a high-pitched buzz, the consensus predicting military and political disaster for the upstart Confederate States.

Earlier in the week, the crowd had watched the troops march out of the capital, centipede legs of the long blue-clad columns lifting and falling. Everyone in the cheering throng, except for the thick sprinkling of Southern spies, believed the Union troops would route the secessionist rebels and end the war in this one glorious battle. Invitations to parties and balls had already been delivered. Huge quantities of wine, beer, liquor, and food had been stockpiled awaiting the return of the victorious army. The troops had camped in the field for six days before contact between the two armies. Mixed parties of civilians had flocked out after hearing telegraphed reports that the battle would soon commence.

The thirty-mile drive by carriage over backcountry roads left passengers disheveled and bruised. The thirty-five-thousand-man Federal army with all its marching boots, caissoned field artillery, hoofed cavalry, and wheeled supply wagons had cratered and potholed the road. The general feeling among the ragtag crowd of civilian observers was the discomfort was bearable in order to witness firsthand the historic whipping the rebels were about to receive. Désirée pulled a lace hanky from her sleeve and dabbed her forehead, then adjusted her parasol. The last five days had been unseasonably warm.

The crash of massed musket fire and thunder of cannon drew all eyes. Men raised telescopes. The crowd broke into cheers and hat waving.

'I see black powder smoke. It is on! It is on!" the Senator shouted. "Those damn secessionist bastards will pay the price now."

"Eli, stop your cussing, there are ladies present."

Ignoring his wife's imprecation, he babbled on, "General McDowell will advance in three columns, two to hold the rebels by the nose while the third advances around their right flank."

More rolling thunder raced up from Bull Run and vibrated the air among the watchers.

"Whoopee!" shouted the Senator, "Give them hell, boys. Madame de Gracie, your man will be herding prisoners back before the days over."

The Désirée outside the dream knew her husband Lieutenant Charles Louis de Gracie had been in the thick of it. He had rushed off after hearing of the attack on Ft. Sumter and used his business connections to gain entry into the 14th New York State Militia. He posed for pictures in the unit's distinctive uniform, modeled after a French 'chasseur' outfit, consisting of ashy red baggy trousers, white leggings, a blue jacket, scarlet chevrons, and shoulder knots. A French style kepi with blue band, red above with blue top, covered his light brown curls. Rebel General Stonewall Jackson himself would name them those red-legged devils for this day's work.

The general lot of troops were green but eager. Unfortunately, their three months of training proved inadequate to establish military discipline. On the march, men had struggled to pick blackberries, smoke pipes, and talk with civilians. In spite of these deficiencies, when the fighting began, they initially performed well.

In her dream, Désirée gasped as the hillside scene faded and she was thrust into hellfire and brimstone. A small frightened hitchhiker in the back of her husband's mind, she watched him rallying his men for a charge up Henry Hill. Only hours earlier, the 14th New York, along with the 11th New York, and the 1st Minnesota had advanced with orders to protect two batteries of cannon, and to assault if an opening provided itself.

The Lieutenant had learned what the expression the fog of war meant. Advancing rebels in blue uniforms were mistaken for friendly troops and in the ensuing confusion, had captured the Union guns. His men had charged and pushed them back, volleys of buck and ball from the unit's smoothbores nearly buckled the enemy flank. But their opponent's forces had rallied and been reinforced.

This would be his unit's fourth charge, the men were tired and needed to pick their way through the dead and wounded carpeting the hill, slowing their movement. Charles' knees shook, he hoped not from fear. He tried to shout, but words came out only as a croak, his capability of speech lost.

No water remained to wet dry throats. A sergeant handed him a grit-covered, sulfur-tasting pebble to suck on. With no voice, example would have to do. He raised his sword, managed an incoherent scream, and charged up the hill.

The Virginia rebel unit at the top fired a ragged volley, he heard the silken whisper of lead balls fly past, the thunk as some hit flesh and generated surprised yelps and groans. The rebels ran before his men could engage them. On top among the recaptured cannon, he noticed Confederate reinforcements poised to counterattack. They raised muskets.

"Down, boys. On your faces."

A white-bearded corporal near him whispered, "For what we are about to receive may we be truly grateful."

A rattling flurry of explosions announced the beginning of another Rebel attack. Soft lead bullets deformed from hitting cannon barrels hummed and buzzed – a cloud of angry hornets. Those hitting the wooden wheels and carriages of the Napoleon guns released fans of splinters. One three-inch needle of oak pierced the wool of Charles' uniform and stuck in his right bicep.

The rebels dropped their muskets, pulled eight-inch long Bowie knives, and charged. They would regret that, Charles thought. The 14th, while in their first real battle, were veteran street fighters, having put down numerous New York City riots.

His soldiers leaped up. Those with charged weapons fired. The two mobs crashed together. Charles' saber chopped down, taking off a hand holding a knife. The bayonets on the muskets of his men gave them extended reach. Attackers groaned and screamed as rifle-mounted seventeen-inch bayonets pierced chests and stomachs. One man broke off the buttstock of his musket, smashing the head of his rebel opponent. Blood and brains sprayed over the Lieutenant – fragments entered his open mouth. He spit, repressed the urge to vomit, and vowed to keep his mouth closed in the future.

The rebel crowd thinned and disappeared. A pile of twitching bodies, entwined in tattered heaps, lay in front of the Regiment. The survivors drew in huge shuddering breaths. The men on either side of him dropped to their knees. The iron-and-shit stink of torn bodies assaulted his nostrils.

A dagger of pain, repressed until now, went through his right arm. He tried to move his sword to his left hand. The fingers molded into a death grip on the hilt would not obey his command to let loose. The muscles were too cramped and the coating of dried blood acted like glue. His corporal used spit to loosen the blood-bond, and helped pry his fingers loose from the grip. The splinter removed from his arm; the wound was bound by a Havelock removed from a dead soldier's cap. The men found the long piece of cloth attached to the back of the kepis did little to cool the neck as its design intended. It was more useful as a bandage.

Charles blew his nose into a handkerchief. The linen cloth caught a wad of thick red-black mucilage formed from inhaling a reek of black powder discharge, dust, and blood splatter, its composition a chemical microcosm of the battlefield. Staring at the substance, he wondered what the inside of his lungs looked like.

The order came to retreat. The men formed up and marched out. On the road back to Washington, Charles wept over the extent of their defeat. Dazed and confounded, he watched Federal soldiers abandon rifles and equipment, steal horses, and fight over seats on wagons. The loss of cohesion grew worse when the Confederates managed to put artillery fire on the bridge over Cub Run.

A Union wagon overturned, blocking the roiling, panicked mob coming from behind. Ambulances, horses, cannons, and men piled up in one confused mess. Shells landed and exploded, flinging disconnected torsos, arms, and legs among the panicked mob.

The 14th regiment moved off the road and waded the stream. Once across they resumed their long walk in the pasture to one side, the road being almost impassable. The litter of rifles, cartridge boxes, broken-axle wagons, packs and bags were so thick on its mucked-up surface that the men could have walked the thirty miles back to Washington without their feet once touching dirt.

🍃

Désirée awoke from the Mother-tree's husband-wife dream of her early life. Covers kicked off, her nightgown was soaked with sweat generated by the all-too-real vision. Plugged into brain and spine, the mother-tree's hair-fine projections brought all bodily systems into play, force-feeding organs and senses to create a past-reality as current-reality and, in this case, as horrifying as the original experience. The terror of the combat produced chills, both physical and mental, that shook her body and soul. Pulling up the blanket disturbed the Spanish cat at Désirée's feet. She hugged the hot little furry bundle.

The Battle at Manassas had convinced her and other witnesses that the war would be long and costly. Her husband's regiment would fight at Antietam, Fredericksburg, Chancellorsville, and Gettysburg, where Charles was killed. Before this vision, she had never physically or mentally experienced battle. The hybrid he/she nightmare had stripped any sense of glory from her concept of combat. However, living Charles' experience, every sense engaged, gave her a veteran's perspective. The modern de Gracies would soon be fighting an implacable enemy. If it was the Mother-tree's intent to harden her symbiotes to combat, she was succeeding.

Hugh and Uncle Frank cursed as the rope they were pulling slipped out of the pulley wheel and fouled itself. The two men were part of a work party preparing the great hall for the grand finale of the music school – an evening buffet and dance. The three chandeliers with all their brass work and crystal needed to be lowered from their two-stories high perch for cleaning.

Frank shook a fist. "*Casse-toi!* You obstreperous duplicitous old bitch!"

The frustration left Hugh's mind replaced with an inner smile. His uncle's nose had been in the dictionary again. Several de Gracies ran over and put their shoulders under the eight-foot diameter lower ring of the stuck chandelier relieving the strain on the rope. Hugh let out four foot of slack and then snapped it like a whip. A ripple rode up the rope, the line lifted, and looped crosswise over the pulley. He moved to one side and gently gave a simultaneous twist and pull.

Rope back in the pulley groove, he and Uncle Frank resumed the lowering of the chandelier to the canvas-covered floor.

The eight-foot-tall artifact's cut-crystal fobs, pendants, and beads tinkled as the workers cleaned out the cobwebs and polished each individual piece. The chandeliers looked like a layered wedding cake. From the wide circular base ascended four smaller concentric bands each two feet in height. Large diameter cut-glass pendants hung from the bottoms and ends of the rings, while ropes of smaller crystals ran from the central column to the ends of harp-shaped arms. The facets of these thousands of diaphanous teardrops in conjunction with those strung on matching wall-mounted sconces would both reflect and refract light, filling the great hall with an ocean of radiance and rainbow star points.

Frank stood back, admiring the chandeliers. "Magnificent, are they not? I remember when they first arrived, early 1700s. The Czechs had just entered international markets with their glass blowing and crystal cutting."

Hugh's eyebrows came together and lifted. There was something wrong with that comment. A worker broke open a box of fat forearm-length candles.

Uncle Frank misinterpreted his nephew's puzzlement. "Not to worry, *mon bon homme*, these are beeswax candles. They will not drip on you as you dance."

Thoughts of the ball drove the analysis of his uncle's remark out of his mind. His father and Margy planned to use the occasion to introduce him to the locals. "I'm not looking forward to this event. I don't want to be meat on display."

His uncle responded. "An old comrade of mine said, 'When I hear music, I fear no danger, I am invulnerable. I see no foe. I am related to the earliest times, and to the latest.' I believe I heard it for the first time in 1847 from Henry David Thoreau during a visit to Walden

Pond. However, Henry loved to repeat his sayings in lectures and newspaper essays, and especially when we attended dinners with the Emersons."

Hugh reacted. This couldn't be right. A shiver ran up his spine. Could Frank really be that aged? The old man must be having delusions or was playing with him as usual. He would check dates. "You knew Thoreau and Ralph Waldo Emerson?"

His thoughts and Frank's response were interrupted by a medley of piano music coming from low risers set up for the orchestra along the outer wall. The musicians and their instruments would enter and leave through the numerous French doors from the garden rather than having to wend their way through the guests. There would be a last rehearsal later this afternoon. Engaging his attention, he heard *My Old Kentucky Home*, followed by *Lorena*, and as he moved around the chandelier, *The Battle Hymn of the Republic*. He slipped past other de Gracies polishing the human-height mirrors mounted shoulder-to-shoulder along the walls and strode across the forty-foot width of the ballroom.

Seated at the pianoforte was the woman he had confronted yesterday while in his full body flour makeup. The Biker Babe was now transformed. Dressed in faded blue jeans rolled up at the cuffs, a red 'I (heart) the Big Apple' T-shirt, and yellow Reebok sneakers, the woman tickled the keys, producing old favorites. She spotted him walking her way, and switched into *When Johnny Comes Marching Home Again*.

His back straightened, feet and arms clicked automatically into a military stride, complementing the rhythm. Ten years in the Army had embedded the left-right-left of the march deep into muscle and bone.

Stepping up on the stage, Hugh admired the fan of hair gathered and knotted with a simple blue silk scarf at the back of her neck. As he neared her side, the music changed into a low-key version of *Jeanie with the Light Brown Hair.*

"You look like the girl next door. Very different from your biker persona."

Brown-gold eyes flashed. "So, it was you yesterday. I did not recognize you cleaned up. Margy told me the accident was my fault. I apologize."

Hugh admired her blush. Unknown to him, the incident had generated a nasty scolding from The Father as well. At any rate, she was back on target now.

Désirée grinned, "You look better without all the dandy sprat powder and paint."

Hugh paused, raised one eyebrow at the comment with its out-of-time adjective, and spoke. "I like your playing. And your smile."

Her fingers stumbled on the keyboard, a dissonant chord sounded, obvious as a pimple on a smooth cheek. "Mother insisted each of her children master an instrument. But I have been away from music for many years." She began to play *The Minstrel Boy.*

"Such old songs. Do you know anything more modern?"

A tap on his shoulder interrupted. "Hugh," Jeannine said. "You have a visitor waiting at the entrance foyer. The Father wants you to meet him immediately." Hugh gave a little bow, turned, and left. Hands on hips, Jeannine furrowed her brow, squeezed her eyes shut, and stuck out her tongue at a startled Désirée.

Hugh dodged past the caterer's staff wheeling in flatbed carts loaded with cases of wine, coolers, and boxes of buffet ingredients. As outsiders, they, their equipment, and supplies had been searched and examined by both de Gracie people and the family dogs. It was always possible Fahad would try something sooner than they anticipated.

A thought hit him. He had talked with this mystery woman twice and still didn't have her name. His game wasn't up to standard. Yet, there was a big helping of *deja vu* here, she seemed remarkably familiar to him. Had he met her before? No, certainly he would remember.

Hugh passed through the hallway and entered the main tower's rotunda. Sun pouring through the great outer double doors backlighted two human-curved silhouettes. Temporarily blinding him, the flood of light into the entryway brought alive the cream and brown swirls of the mother-tree simulated faux-marble floor. His eyes adjusted. Chin dropped. Standing before him, army issue duffle bag in one hand stood…

The heavy canvas bag sailed forward. He barely got his arms up in time to deflect it to one side. A commanding voice vibrated the rafters, "Coup, you son-of-a-bitch."

The Father skipped to one side as Hugh and the second man began to circle. They leapt together, hands chopped and parried.

Hugh dropped, spun low on one foot, his other leg stuck out to sweep his opponent off his feet.

His assailant rolled and popped up, snapped a high-kick aimed at the chin.

Hugh dodged, but it was a feint, allowing the man to close. An elbow to the ribs, followed by a hip throw, left the de Gracie heir gasping on his back.

His opponent leapt again.

Hugh flipped the man over his head, foiling a pin. The two regained their feet and rushed into each other's arms, hugging and dancing.

"Jonsey, you bastard. Did the Army finally wise up and boot you out?"

The new man nodded towards Aubert. "Your father sent me an invitation and filled me in on your situation. Took a thirty-day leave. Couldn't have you in terrible danger from all the local maidens without me to watch your back." Leaning forward, he gave him a wolf-grin. "I also want to help you all kick Fahad's ass."

Father stepped forward, holding Jonsey's plastic-wrapped Sergeant

Major's dress uniform by the hanger hooks. "I have given him the room next to yours, Hugh. Get him settled, give him a tour of the place, and after lunch you two meet Uncle Frank and me in the library."

✐

Hugh came early to the meeting, heard an animated conversation in the library between Uncle Frank and Jonsey, and paused in the hallway to eavesdrop.

"Then there was the time we'd been assigned temporary duty at NATO headquarters.

"Early in the morning, after a night shift analyzing the latest Russian military exercise, we went to this fancy cathouse on the outskirts of Brussels. They served us breakfast first, which consisted of a variety of toasted and untoasted breads, sliced meats and cheeses, and boiled eggs. Besides the marmalade and jams you'd expect, they served chocolate, your choice of sprinkles, flakes, or syrup. Oh, and they had a loaf of coconut stuff, served in thin slices. Called it *kokosbrood* or something like that."

"And afterwards?" Frank asked, moving the story along.

"Well, most of the girls were sleeping off the strenuous activity of the previous evening, so old Coup got one just returned from vacation by the name of Justine. Stacked brunette in her twenties and a Sorbonne grad 150 long-legged like a chorus girl. I got Bess, the madam – not their real names, I'm sure. Mine was in her late thirties and starting to thicken a bit in the hips but still one hell of a woman – big-boned, nicely fleshed Nordic type. You can't beat experience. We were entertained in two side-by-side garret rooms on the top floor."

Hugh risked a quick glance into the library. Jonsey looked down at his empty mug. Frank grabbed a pitcher of small beer and poured a refill. The storyteller took a drink, set the mug down, and licked a foamy mustache off his upper lip.

"Go on, go on," his attentive companion urged.

149

"Bess and I had just slipped between the sheets when we heard this giggle from the other room. The walls in that place weren't too thick."

In the hallway, Hugh blushed and continued to listen. He hadn't realized the occupants of the other room had eavesdropped on the proceedings.

"After several more giggles came through the plaster, I said to the madam, 'he's conducting a scout of enemy territory.' Justine's sniggers broke into a deeper stuttering laugh. 'Now he's doing long-range reconnaissance mapping the terrain in detail.' "

"Then came a series of 'oh, oh, oh's.' Bess looked at me. I told her, 'He's called in artillery and air strikes – prepping the objective."

Hugh's shoulder muscles twitched, he took another look and almost decided to enter the room.

"Groans and moans followed. 'The ground attack has begun,' I said. Bess caught the sequence of events and looked a little worried. There was a long rasping gasp from the other room. The *Schwerpunkt*, or focal point of the attack was driven home."

Uncle Frank smacked a fist on the table. "*Formidable*. That is *mon petit coq*."

"The bedsprings started squeaking, the legs slammed the floor like a battalion of marching men. 'Aha.' I said, 'hand to hand combat.' Then what started as a high-pitched female whimper fell into a contralto ululation. The battle was over, both sides won."

Jonsey grinned, "Bess turned to me and said, 'Damn, now she won't be good for anything the rest of the day. I should charge you double.'"

"So, did you get charged double?"

"No, I managed by quick and victorious action of my own to convince the madam the experience itself possessed significant value."

"Your story reminds me of a similar time in Paris, when Ojas and

I squared off with Jeanne Bècu and her maid. The four of us were on a lubricious mission as members of *Le Secret Du Roi*. Of course, that was before she became the Comtesse Du Barry and Louis XV's official mistress."

Hugh felt Aubert clasp his elbow. Father and son entered the library together. Aubert spoke, "It sounds like you two are getting along entirely too well. Do not take Frank's fantastic stories to heart."

"Sounds to me like someone was relating classified information." Hugh added. "I was just instructing Uncle Frank on the latest military terminology."

Aubert pointed to the diagrams and sketches laid out on the table, "So, sergeant, what do you think of our plans?"

"I believe you are correct. The attack must come from the air. The problem is not knowing how they will be equipped. Light machine guns, assault rifles, grenades, and explosives they surely will have, easy enough to get, but what else? Fahad is familiar with our tactics. He has been on the sharp end of them himself. My guess is he will have at least one bird set up as a gunship, to make runs over the attack site to bring suppressing fire down on specific points of resistance."

"You know how we are armed. Will it be enough?"

"Once the slicks, the choppers transporting the troops, start their drop to the ground they will be vulnerable to attack. However, when we open up, our positions will be exposed to the gunship. Three things to remember. We can't afford to be surprised, there must be more of an air defense, and we need reliable intelligence on enemy numbers, equipment, and plans."

7

A time to tear, and a time to mend
a time for silence and a time for speech.
                                    Ecclesiastes: 3:7

AUBERT, MARGY, AND SAM, the music camp's maestro, sat at a small table in the de Gracie kitchen dining room, their heads close together. The satisfying smell of pancakes, bacon, and maple syrup invaded their nostrils. The buzz and teenage slap-and-tickle in the room hit new highs when the last of the thirty music camp students dashed in, filled breakfast plates, and took seats in their favorite spots. This was the big day. All the previous two-weeks rehearsals and coming together as an orchestra would be on display at the ball tonight.

Not too bad this year, Aubert thought. Listening to the sour, disharmonious music coming from the group's first three days' work, he had despaired of them achieving a professional performance. Their conductor, Samuel Markowitz Rothschild, shock of white hair snapping back and forth, baton-swishing incantations in the air, had performed real magic.

During their dress rehearsal last night, Aubert had only to close his eyes to feel as though he sat in the front row at the New York Philharmonic. This was their tenth annual session with Sam in charge, and it had become his labor of love. Each year the maestro selected thirty high school seniors — equal numbers of both genders — from an eager national field of applicants. Graduates of the program boosted their chances of early entry into the professional music world.

"Our young guests have been better behaved than customary, or we have been less vigilant," Sam remarked.

As usual, females and males had been separated and isolated in dormitory-style sleeping rooms located as distant as possible from each other. Aubert responded, "I agree, the night watch, old Alphonse and his dog, have caught only three couples canoodling in the garden. The fountain in the middle of the maze is a popular romantic spot."

"Canoodling, forgive me, but I am not familiar with that term."

"It does not mean eating noodles while canoeing. Old English term for cuddling, petting, fondling, etc. – dates back to 1859. Do we need to discuss this evening's program further?"

Margy broke in. "We have the dance cards preprinted. Each of the eligible invitees will get their chance with one for-sure dance with Hugh. After the poor boy has worked his way through fifteen dances, it will be open season for the remainder of the night."

Sam excused himself, stood, and shouted to his charges. He announced there would be a quick run through for the tango and rock groups. A clatter of plates, cups, and chair feet scraping the floor marked the exit of the students.

Aubert huddled closer to Margy, "The attachment between Hugh and Désirée must be fixed tonight. I have handled one possible distraction. Jeannine will be one of three pairs of de Gracies guarding the gate or walking the perimeter of the thornwall. You have Désirée and Hugh set for dances five and ten?"

Margy smiled and patted his shoulder. "Relax my friend, already there is mystery and curiosity between them – the beginnings of romance. I have closely examined the field of candidates and set things up. Désirée will look like an angel after Hugh's first four partners."

"And the Mother-tree and I have added chemistry to the moment. Their pheromones will be triple the normal strength and quantity."

"*Jèsus, Marie et Joseph!*" Margy placed hands together in mock prayer. "You are not going to turn Hugh loose in a hall packed with women already half-crazed with Prince Charming fantasies and him wafting irresistible fragrance in every direction?"

"Calm down, the chemicals are coded to interact strongly only between the two of them. There may be a little poof-over effect on the innocent, but not enough to cause a riot."

"Aubert, have you never heard of Murphy's Law?"

Pinning on emblems of rank and unit designations, Hugh fussed over the uniform jacket hung from a valet stand near his armoire. In his ten years with the military, he had never owned official mess dress. Father had surprised him, insisting he and Jonsey wear the most formal of Army uniforms. He looked at the open book on the side table, its stiff pages held open by his lamp, and a pet rock from his preteen years. Army Regulation 670-1, 24-3 was clear in its intent: The blue mess uniform is worn for black tie functions and corresponds to a civilian tuxedo.

Well, he thought, it was either a tux or this. Given his decade in the service, he would feel more comfortable in a uniform than a monkey suit. At least, the old man had spared no expense. The cerulean-blue plain-front wool trousers had been fitted with two-and-a-half-inch side-stripes of real cloth of gold. Tucked into the pants would be a white, long-sleeved formal dress shirt with a stiff bosom, French cuffs, and a wing collar. The shirt was held together with buttonhole studs in the shape of fleur-de-lys and cuff links bearing the de Gracie crest. Margy would have to help him tie the old-fashioned black silk bowtie and wrap the cummerbund around his waist into the required five-pleat pattern.

Dark blue, almost black, the jacket fit him in a way that emphasized his shoulders and slim waist. It was cut on the lines of an evening dress coat slightly curved to a peak front and back, and riding just above the hips. Infantry blue silk panels overlaid the wide lapels. Two buttons, joined by an eighteen-caret gold metal chain, held the jacket together while allowing the cummerbund to be exposed. All the buttons, trefoil sleeve braids, shoulder knots, major's leaves, and miniature medals were solid gold. Hugh was grateful for the black compression socks, which would help keep the blood circulating during all the standing and dancing.

The custom made soft-leather shoes had interesting details. Chamois leather inserts in the soles where the balls of the foot pressed would allow him to glide across the polished dance floor with minimal friction. The uppers had been finished in small grain leather, allowing a high polish. Except for the distortion caused by the curve of the toe, Hugh felt he could have shaved in the reflection.

Jonsey would be envious. At least his old friend would also be in mess dress, so they could share the stares. They had managed, by impassioned argument, to convince Father that wearing sabers would be more of a hindrance than help even though he had tempted them by offering three-hundred-year-old Egyptian *Mamaluke* curved scimitar blades in jewel-encrusted sheaths.

The doors of the armoire stood open. Mixed with ties on a rack were a half dozen eye patches. Three black ones for day-to-day use, a camo patterned one that matched his battle dress, and for tonight, an Infantry blue silk patch matching the lapels on his jacket. A good touch, he thought. He adjusted the tailor's hand-stitched creation over his empty eye socket and buckled it in back, leaving no loose ends to dangle.

A knock on the door. Jonsey's sergeant voice rang out, "Let's go, Major. Time to conquer or be conquered."

"Be right there." Hugh slipped on the jacket, fastened the chain between the buttonholes, and took one last look in the mirror. He experienced a moment of discouragement. The total impression looked somewhat like the uniform of a posh hotel bellhop minus the pillbox hat, as portrayed in old movies. He sighed and joined his friend.

The pair slipped down the back service-stairs. This route allowed them to avoid the guests spilling out of the de Gracie family carriages to gather on the rotunda and porch. They passed through the kitchen and an adjoining prep-room occupied by hustling catering company employees opening boxes and preparing dishes.

The action stopped for a minute. People stared.

Hugh thought he noticed a look of panic on one face and of anger on another. Why those reactions? He slowed.

Jonsey grabbed his elbow, "We're late, man. The reception line needs us."

They moved through the garden. All eight pairs of French doors into the ballroom stood open, allowing the maximum flow of air and people. A shadow spread over the house de Gracie as the mountain blocked the setting sun, creating, as it always did, a false dusk. Blended perfume rose from beds of roses, peonies, and the angel's trumpet vines crawling up the porch columns. Light from hundreds of candles lit up the ballroom door entrances and open skylights.

Hugh and Jonsey took the steps up to the loggia two at a time. Old Alphonse gave them a passing wave from deeper in the garden where he and his guard dog would be stationed for the evening.

The two uniformed soldiers marched in with synchronized steps and took their places, assuming the position of parade rest, hands clasped behind their backs. They would be third and fourth in the reception line with Aubert and Margy, acting as lady of the mansion, the first to greet the guests and pass them on.

Hugh's old man in tuxedo and tie looked like the high-fashion male models featured on the covers of 1950s Esquire magazines.

Hugh thought his old nanny *trés chic* in an empire-waistline ankle-length dress of soft blue satin, square cut décolletage, and short puffed sleeves. A light silk shawl over her shoulders allowed a greater element of modesty. Her hair had been piled and pinned with a cut-short spray of peacock feathers. Elbow-length white gloves and rhinestone-dusted pumps completed the outfit. Hugh bent over her hand with a small bow.

"Will I get a dance with *la comtesse du manoir?*"

Margy shushed him, blushed, and responded, "Probably not, you need to give our guests precedence."

"Je suis désolé."

Hugh glanced around the ballroom. For the first time in his memory, it was decked out in all its finery.

Overhead the forty-foot vaulted ceiling sloped upward to a peak. Fortunately, the distance was too great for the assembled guests to discern that the great roof timbers were Mother-tree branches.

The murmur of guests waiting in the entry hall brought his eyes back to human level. It didn't seem possible that the combination of candles, crystals, and mirrors could illuminate the ancient place so brightly.

The orchestra gathered on risers, students at rest, talking in low voices and shuffling music. A large violin section sat next to violas, cellos, and double basses. Light reflected off polished tubing and the flared mouths of French horns, trumpets, trombones, and a tuba. Hugh also spotted flutes, oboes, bassoons, and a substantial drum and percussion section. Given the size of the orchestra and the acoustics of the ballroom, amplification wouldn't be needed.

The perimeter of the room was set with clusters of chairs and small tables. A bar at each end of the hall offered wine or non-alcoholic punch. The scents of spices, fruit, and cooked food caught his attention. Long tables set up at the far end nearest the kitchen held the buffet offerings: egg or shrimp tartlets, smoked salmon on triangular-cut dill bread, petite slices of goat-cheese pizza, *frittata*, *paella*, and sturgeon caviar. The dessert table allowed a choice of orange-frosted scones, cherry tarts dabbed with whipped cream, or German chocolate cake.

Being a host, Hugh would have time for maybe one pass at the buffet. He consoled himself with the thought that he could stuff himself on the leftovers tomorrow.

The main ballroom door opened, and the first guests entered. He heard Margy welcome John Duryea, Port Henry Mayor and owner of the Ford dealership, his wife Susan, and eligible daughter Tonda. The man passed a few words with Aubert, who quickly turned.

"Permit me to introduce my son Hugh, recently retired from the military."

Establishing eye contact and firmly gripping Hugh's hand, in the manner of an experienced politician and used car salesman, the Mayor said, "Thank you for your service. Glad to see you back among your friends and neighbors. Will you be staying? If so, I have some really great cars in my showroom I'd be delighted to let you test drive."

"Good to meet you, sir. Haven't made that decision yet. Let me introduce my best friend Sergeant Major Emile Jonsey."

Hugh remembered from his military experience that the theory behind reception lines was to make each person feel favored but to keep them moving. Those desiring a lengthy schmooze would have to wait until later in the evening.

Mrs. Duryea stepped forward, wearing a low-cut cream-yellow

gown with full skirt. The curves of surgically endowed breasts peeked out. She looked sideways at her husband, who was laughing at some remark of Jonsey's. Taking a deep breath, her nose twitched. She paused and her eyes widened. She gave a loose semi-drunkard's grin, and then leaned forward and squeezed his hand. "It's great to have handsome young men back in our community. I'm frequently at home during the afternoons. Call me if I can help you in any way."

Hugh raised one eyebrow, nodded, and passed her on.

The daughter moved to face him, glowering at her mother.

"Pleased to meet you, Tonda. I'm looking forward to our dance."

The eighteen-year-old took a sniff, and then blinked rapidly. The frown melted into a lascivious cat-fang smile. She said, "I'm sure I can show you a good time."

✿

The last three invitees waited patiently. Hugh's back and hips ached. He needed to walk around and get the kinks out of his muscles. His observations and interactions with the guests caused some conclusions to form. Number one, he wondered if there was something wrong with his scent. The women passing through, whether married or available, would sniff, sometimes several times, their irises would expand, and they would get all squirmy. Secondly, he had never seen so many bustiers. Stores for miles around must have empty lingerie selves.

Not that he was complaining, the experience resembled touring an art gallery with each sculpture getting its share of admiration. In addition, he mused, the bell curve was in action here. The numerous women could be arranged along a curve by weight, vivacity, boob size and lift, and body-configuration. There would always be a few at each end of the selected curve, with the majority stacked in the middle. None, however, quite seemed to have put it all together.

A wisp of familiar perfume snapped him to attention, the aromatic, aged whiskey scent of Clinique Aromatics Elixir. He turned.

His father presented the next guest. "Hugh, *permettez-moi de vous présenter* the widow, Catherine Désirée Terrenèe. She is a distant relative of House de Gracie." Aubert thought he could say that with a clear conscience, since she was truly a distant relative – distant in time.

Aubert continued to speak.

Hugh tuned the words out, focused entirely on the five-foot-four woman looking up into his eyes. She was no longer the biker or girl-next-door, but presented another more sophisticated aspect. Finally, he knew her name. The Terrenée last name, different, unique – translated strangely as 'born of the earth.' He took a breath. Something mixed in the scent went directly to his brain. His lungs demanded more oxygen. Blood veins expanded. Heartbeat increased. The surface temperature of his skin warmed. Colors grew more intense. Their hands touched. Clammy palms exchanged molecules.

Hugh shook his head to clear it and looked her over. A classic face eyed him back.

Her features, mostly devoid of cosmetics, were composed of high almost Asian cheekbones, the long aristocratic de Gracie nose, and hazel-gold eyes. Blonde hair put up in a Swedish braid left a slim but muscular neck exposed and allowed the free play of gold and pearl earring bangles.

His eyes moved down. She wore a hi-low jet-black halter dress, the 'V' décolletage almost to the navel.

The cutaway of the skirt-front rose up from ankles to mid-thigh. When she walked or danced, her long legs would be exposed. There was no bra, either separate or built-in – those breasts didn't need support. Capezio T-strap shoes with two-inch heels announced her readiness to dance.

He realized they had been standing without speaking for what seemed a long time. "Catherine…" he started.

She leaned forward.

He caught more of the perfume and her heat on his skin.

"Désirée," she whispered. "Call me Désirée."

An elbow jarred him in the ribs. "Don't hog the best one yet," came Jonsey's voice.

Upon her move to his right, Hugh noted the dress was backless, and a fine backside it was. His hands trembled. From the small of her back, the dress draped over tight curves and flowed down, stopping at the ankles. Her hair, figure, and dress reminded him of the statues on the Parthenon's porch of maidens. He felt shaky and took a deep breath. The calves of his legs quivered.

Father grabbed his arm, offering support. "Hugh, are you all right?" Aubert led him off towards the buffet. "Let us get some food into you. The dancing begins in twenty minutes."

Sam tapped his baton on the music stand before him. The orchestra settled. Making a few magical passes, the maestro led the brass section through a fanfare. The trumpets drew the attention of the guests and hushed their chatter. He turned to a crowd now tense with expectant silence.

"*Mesdames et Messieurs*, the first dance will be a foxtrot entitled *Maria Elena*. Written by Lorenzo Barcelata in 1932, the song was dedicated to the wife of Mexican President Emilio Portes Gil."

Hugh didn't have to search for his first partner.

Amanda Greenstreet, daughter of the local grocer, bare-shouldered in an ivory gown, pounced. Her three-inch high heels and piled-up hair attempted to compensate for a four-foot ten-inch height. She sighed and nuzzled her breasts into his stomach. The beehive hairdo tickled his chin.

Hugh noticed the mother possessed a few extra pounds with the daughter not far behind. *Pas de probléme*, he admired the infinite range of women's bodies.

He rehearsed the dance step in his mind, two slow steps forward starting on his left foot and then bringing the feet together quickly.

They moved a bit mechanically at first, and then both caught up the music and began a smooth glide. Two minutes into the music he felt the fabric of his partner's strapless gown loosen. The dress appeared to be a rental, and a half-size too large. Temporary stitches parted. With no shoulder ties to hold it in place, the heavy fabric started to peel down.

Amanda looked up with panic on her face. The gown with its built-in bra would be around her ankles in seconds.

Hugh lifted his hand from her waist and pushed his thumb down between the zipper and the flesh of her back.

She let out an "Oh."

Closing his fingers, he gripped the cloth and pulled up. They continued the dance with no accident.

With a flushed but grateful face, Amanda rushed off to her mother, both hands holding the dress at the armpits.

"And now that you are warmed up, something a bit faster. Let's try *Runaround Sue*, a hit song by Dion in 1961. You can find it among Rolling Stone magazine's five hundred greatest songs."

A hand took his. He faced Dr. Sammy Delong, a woman his age, oldest daughter of the village pharmacist. Like Hugh, recently returned to Port Henry, she worked as a GP at the local clinic. As they danced, the hem of her high-necked ruffled frock flared out exposing a nice pair of knees.

"How'd you get the name Sammy?" Hugh asked with a slight grin. "A nickname? A parental endearment?"

"I think they wanted a boy, cause the name really is S-a-m-m-y."

"It's a bold name," Hugh said as he spun her out in a twirl.

She returned to his arms. "The principal's office could never get it right. Every year, the first day of school, I was assigned to the boys' gym class."

"I'm sure the boys didn't mind."

"I'm glad to be here tonight. I have so many questions about the

162

de Gracies. You all look so young and healthy. I can't detect even a pimple, a blemish, or male pattern baldness." She pointed her head towards his uncle, dancing with one of the guests. "The family musculature and joint movements are unbelievable, almost ballet quality. My grandmother says your Uncle Frank was one of her beaus seven decades ago. She's almost ninety now and could no way dance like that."

Hugh's skin began to goosebump. Doctor Sammy was trained to be observant.

"I came back on Amtrak the same day you did – in the same car. I'm glad my diagnosis was incorrect. I would have said that you were in seriously bad shape, yet here you are a few months later as sprightly as a spring chicken."

"Well, Dr. Delong, we inherit good genes."

"Of course, I have read your father's occasional papers in the medical journals, a famed surgeon and geneticist." She laughed, "Are you folks genetically modified organisms? If so, I'd like to know the secret."

Hugh joined in her laughter. His guffaw sounded artificial. He mumbled something about the weather and turned her in a series of pirouettes, leaving her too dizzy to ask more questions.

Dance number three was a slow two-step, done to the music of *Unchained Melody*. A tenor vocalist sang the lyrics in a sugary voice. For this one, he drew Tonda, the Mayor's daughter, who, besides getting powder all over his cheek and lapels, did a bump and grind across their joined abdomens. During the process, she managed to lick his right ear lobe – quick reflexes prevented a nibble or an inserted tongue.

Hugh was starting to feel worked over by dance number four, introduced by the Maestro as a *bossa nova*, *The Girl From Ipanema*, a Grammy winner written in 1962 by Antonio Carlos Jobim. This partner quickly became a challenge.

Sue Wilfred owned and operated Sue's Dance Studio. During the dance, a variation of the *samba*, he tried to keep up with her heel-toe, heel-toe hip popping maneuvers. Fortunately for him, she became so caught up in improvisation that they separated and while she sambaed off solo into the crowd, he snuck over to one of the wine bars.

The white-jacketed attendant stiffened at his approach.

The reaction puzzled Hugh. He filed the man's face in memory.

He filled a cup with sangria. He tasted oranges, mangos, honey, and brandy. Guarding the drink, he shuffled through the crowd to where his father, Margy, several of the townsfolk, and the mysterious Madame Terrenée stood. He spotted Jonsey across the hall. With a here-I-come grin, the Sergeant Major sidled up, and offered a glass of wine to Dr. Delong.

Lifting his glass to Désirée, Hugh asked. "Aren't you dancing?"

"We have managed to protect her from most of the wolf pack so far." Margy said.

Speaking defensively, Désirée responded, "I have taken a turn around the floor with your father and your best friend." She reached up and brushed powder off his lapels.

Aubert smiled, the skin at the corners of his eyes crinkled. "How are you holding up? All your body parts still seem to be attached, although one ear seems a bit worse for the wear."

Hugh shrugged and took a long drink of the *sangria*.

Over his shoulder, the Maestro ended the *samba* with a flourish and placed fresh music in the stand before him. The orchestra shifted positions into a new configuration.

"It is our pleasure this evening to present an Argentine *tango*. The *orquesta típica* will be composed of violins, piano, double bass, and *bandoneon*. For those of you not familiar with the last instrument, it is a member of the *concertina* family."

A student stood, walked forward, holding up the *bandoneon* for examination. A wave of the Maestro's hand and the student played a demonstration of chugging chords, the action of the bellows pushing air over tuned reeds in the interior of the accordion-like instrument.

"And now, select your partners for *El Choclo*, written by Angel Villoldo and first performed in 1903."

Hand-in-hand, Hugh and Désirée moved onto the dance floor, the violins played a three-second pizzicato before the music swelled up to engulf them. The tango was an intuitive dance, combining basic steps with lots of room for improvisation. Hugh remembered the man led with the chest, not the arms, and much depended upon the couple allowing each other time and space to add flourishes and gestures. He stood straight — torso centered over the abdomen — an easy stance for a soldier.

Désirée looked confused and awkward. The dance fell outside her experience, except for a few hours' instruction at the dance studio during her trip to New York. The *Tango's* introduction to the United States came fifty years after the start of her long sleep in the Mother-tree's vaults. The music began its pulse-pulse-pulse. Hugh took her in his arms and started a *sube y baja*, forward-together and back-together movement with a pendulum action of the hips. She moved uncomfortably, resisting his direction and the beat.

Leaning forward, he whispered, "Let the music go in your ears, skip the mind, and into your body without resistance or critique. Allow sound to become motion."

Her body stiffened, and then relaxed as they danced forward and backward executing a not-so-bad *ocho*, a figure-eight walking step with flexed knees and feet together while pivoting. Their bodies begin reacting spontaneously with the bass beat. They broke apart.

Désirée executed a *cuatro*, her right leg flicked up against the opposite leg, with the knee bent, briefly creating the profile of the numeral 4.

She spun on the balancing foot to make full-body contact with Hugh, which allowed a series of steps with arms held at the sides, bodies pressed together. With the music, the synchronized movement, the heavy syncopated beat, Hugh felt his ego drift into a composite creature with his partner, *yin* and *yang*, equal parts male and female.

He breathed her perfume. Something peppery rode along with it, smoldered in his lungs.

Fiery tendrils striated his blood. He resisted, pushed them apart. Désirée took control, pulling him back with a *gancho*, her right leg hooked sharply around his left leg, making calf-to-calf contact then flexing the knee and releasing. The invitation almost more than he could bear, Hugh attempted to escape with a *barrida*, his right foot sweeping the inside of her left foot into a new position.

It was a mistake.

She blew past his last weak resistance with a *mordida alto*, clasping her partner's still extended knee between her thighs. The area above his knee felt her soft fleshy pressure as though it were skin to skin. The orchestra stopped, a *bandoneon* solo blew out waterfalls and butterfly wings in husky Technicolor notes.

The heat of her upper legs caught him, raced upward to flush his face and engorge his lips and another part of his body.

Désirée rose on her toes, sliding pliant, resilient breasts up his rib cage. Her arms extended around Hugh's neck. One hand massaged the short bristle hairs above his shirt collar. The other cupped his head, pulled it down and forward. Lips met. Bodies and minds completed their fusion. Primitive emotional walls cycled shut, excluded awareness of everyone and everything except this new self-indulged hybrid creature. The last notes of *El Choclo* reverberated off the curved ceilings.

Five seconds into the silence, Hugh disengaged Désirée's lips and arms. She spun out—a throbbing echo of the music still inside her—spun back, and pulled him to her for a second kiss.

From the sideline, Aubert said, "I believe Prince Charming has made his choice, I hope she will not run off at midnight leaving a glass slipper."

"Prince Charming, humbug," Margy squeezed his arm. "Cinderella did the choosing. In the meantime, *mon cher*," scanning the crowd, she pointed out angry female faces, and finger-hooked claws, "you had best protect her from the ugly stepsisters."

Hugh drudged through the next four dances, the kisses still feather-soft on his lips, trying to be the polite host and dance partner, while fuming over each minute's delay keeping him from Désirée. His reaction to her had solidified into a runaway blend of basic emotions, both instinctive and primitive, on a level not attained by the others. The dances played out – The *Cha Cha Cha*, another Two-step, the *Rumba*, and a Foxtrot.

The courtship competition of the evening picked up momentum. The kissing episode added an overlay of desperation to the remaining women's strategies.

His first two partners, after feeble attempts to attract his interest, gave up and relaxed into the dance music. The next one, the Unitarian preacher's daughter, tucked a card into his cummerbund.

Hugh read the scrawled script after they parted. It listed her phone number and an interesting package deal involving both her and her divorced minister mother. Eyebrows up, he glanced across the hall at the two women, to be rewarded with smiles and waves.

Partner number four, the city librarian, spent the four minutes of their dance whispering things that she had read in various 'bodice ripper' novels, things she'd like them to try.

His refusal earned him a quick 'woman scorned' kick in the left shin disguised as a dance step.

Désirée squinted in the lady's room mirror and tucked in errant wisps of hair that had come undone from the heavy braid on the back of her head.

The door squeaked open. The sound of high heels clip-clopped on the Mother-tree's faux-marble floor, stopped, and then moved faster. She turned in time to deflect a hand slashing a lipstick like a dagger. Désirée recognized a tube of Clinique Angel, a bright red-coral.

The woman tried again to smear her face.

Grabbing her opponent's hand with fingers on the palm and the thumb just below the back knuckles, she twisted. The girl involuntarily dropped the lipstick to clatter and roll off under a stall door.

Maximizing the twisting, locked the arm straight and put her challenger on her knees.

"Are you going to give up?"

"Yes. Yes. Stop the pain."

"What is your name?"

"Tonda," she gasped.

Désirée allowed the girl to rise.

Tonda immediately launched a roundhouse swing with eyes closed. Dodging inside the inept blow, Désirée counterpunched as Ojas had taught—a fist smacked below the sternum into the girl's solar plexus. She helped her wheezing, bent-over opponent into a stall and left her to throw up.

In her day, women, regardless of class, did not wear lip colors. Only actresses and prostitutes displayed such paint in public. Of course, a woman of her time would not have known those defensive moves. Not a repressed Victorian female any longer, Désirée liked how she was changing. She would seize this new life and new man. Secondly, Ojas must be thanked for his instruction.

She patted the wall, her gratitude to the Mother-tree, whose repeated visions with accompanying body stimulation of hand-to-hand combat and weapons firing gave her the grace, reaction time, and muscle-memory of a veteran. She had the highest scores with the sniper rifle, the moves, and techniques absorbed from recorded visions of Hugh's army training becoming second nature.

As she exited the restroom, the Maestro announced the next dance. Désirée rushed to find Hugh.

"Our last ballroom dance will be a Viennese Waltz. After this tenth dance, the orchestra will retire. However, we will Rock and Roll until midnight to tunes provided by WXZO radio DJ, Wild Karl."

Cheers erupted from the crowd.

Karl stood from his seat at a perimeter table and shook clenched hands over his head.

Sam waited until the noise died. "Our host wishes me to remind you that a pyrotechnics display will be held on the front lawn immediately after the ball concludes, accompanied by the orchestra playing Handel's *Music for the Royal Fireworks*."

Sam gave a knowing wink to Aubert, this dance another link in the romantic conspiracy. "Now it is our pleasure to present *Tales from the Vienna Woods* composed in 1868 by Johan Straus II, one of only six of his pieces that feature a virtuoso part for a concert zither."

A young woman stepped forward and sat in a chair at the front of the riser, a flat box-like instrument across her lap. With a wave from the Maestro, she fretted the strings with her left hand and plucked using a plectrum on the right thumb, demonstration notes rose and fell metallic and clear, reminiscent of a harp.

A nod of the head, a wave of the baton, and the lengthy introduction of the waltz began with horns and oboe creating pastoral and woodland notes.

Hugh faced Désirée, stepped forward, and placed his right hand around her waist. As her arm moved to his shoulder the gold and ivory cameo broach pinned to her halter-top flashed in the candlelight. Something metallic touched his fingertips. Hugh raised their clasped hands to examine the curious yellow-gold snake bracelet he had first noticed in the reception line. Small emeralds simulating its eyes flashed green as it lifted. The creature's three-quarter inch thick body curved three times around her forearm and wrist with the snake neck and head straightening to extend along the back of her hand.

The orchestra ended the introduction with a rolling march, replaced with the soft gentle music of the theme.

Hugh and Désirée, bodies close, moved in the one, two, three — forward side-together — and then four, five six — backwards side-together, the pattern forming a box. They turned and turned, another of many couples enclosed within the large arc of dancers circling the ballroom perimeter clockwise. The rising on the toes for each step created an overall effect similar to the up-and-down glide of a carousel.

Désirée had waltzed many times before, starting in her teens and extending through her married life and widowhood. However, the dancers never held each other so closely. The gowns were vastly different. In those old days, bodies could not touch, separated by voluminous petticoats and bustles. Any man trying to make body contact would be bounced back by whalebone or metal springs.

She felt Hugh signal a *ronde*, and on the fourth step, he guided her out with his left hand.

Désirée moved away, completed an underarm *pirouette*, before returning to him. The contra body movement and effortless sway made her feel like the two of them were pair skating on ice, gravity and friction releasing their hold.

The couple moved in total sync with the music, dawdling when the tempo slowed, and increasing speed when it escalated. At the times when the music paused, they froze for the moment, hearing the blood rush in their veins. Then the instruments would begin again, releasing a tumbling silvery rush that caught them up in an avalanche cloud of sound and flurried snow, a music box couple twirling in a glass water globe.

The orchestra stopped to allow an animated *cadenza* from the zither, each plucked note a sugar cube dissolving into sweet crumbles upon their tongues. The solo ended, breathed itself back into the orchestra. At the maestro's command, the tempo increased from the normal fifty-eight bars per minute, slowly climbing to sixty-eight bars.

Couples started to fall out and leave the dance floor, most incapable of articulating the steps at a pace only expert ballroom dancers could maintain.

Hugh and Désirée became a creature joined at the arms and hips. Bodies and legs moved in patterns and at a speed only achieved by intuition and complete submission to each other. To think about, preplan, or signal each move became impossible at such velocity.

Brown eye and hazel eyes locked to each other. Brightness refracted by the crystals overhead altered their shades. Brown to cinnamon, darkening upon the turns to chocolate. Hazel to grass green, then to sandy gold in harmony with light and shadow changes in the twirls and spins.

The tempo slowed, the solo zither made another appearance, liberating again its earlier melody, creating pictures in the mind of velvet-antlered deer moving among green-leafed woods. Its notes submerged into the finale. A crescendo crushed the tranquility.

The couple shuddered, caught up like storm-blown leaves, swirling in the rhythm. The concluding passage ended with a brass flourish and snare drum roll leaving Désirée bowed in Hugh's arms, one ankle lifted and exposed.

"That was… was… beyond measure," Hugh stammered in a choked voice.

Désirée watched a tear form and run down his left cheek. Slender fingers went up to catch it. Her response came up from low in her throat, "*Te me rends heureuse.* You make me happy."

The couple heard one person begin clapping, then another, and then the entire room reacted, the sound rising like a flock of startled pigeons to echo back from the ribbed organic curves of the Mother-tree's vault.

They looked up. They were alone on the ballroom floor.

Hugh grabbed Désirée's hand. They rushed up to Jonsey.

"Hey man," he slapped his uncompleted dance card into his friend's open palm, "cover for me."

The couple stopped by the closest wine bar. He grabbed an open bottle of champagne, and she gathered two fluted glasses. They flew out the French doors into the garden. The pair shared a silent moment near the trumpet flower tree, the purple irises planted around its roots black in the moonlight.

Désirée held up the glasses, whose long stems kept warm hands from affecting the temperature of the champagne, while tall, narrow bowls resisted the loss of effervescence.

Hugh poured, emptying the bottle and placed it on the edge of the path.

They held hands, walked, and sipped, each wondering how to begin. The strains of the Beatles' *A Hard Day's Night* came from the direction of the ballroom.

Two shadows approached and materialized into Old Alphonse and Alys, his companion guard dog of the evening.

Hugh spoke, "Is all well, my friend?"

"Right well, Master Hugh, only a few lovers to chase out of the garden." Alys placed her cold nose in Désirée's palm, to be rewarded with a scratch behind the ears.

"Well, we're taking a stroll, having some conversation."

"Strange, my ears must be getting old. I heard only the whisper of your feet moving on the path and the swish of a dress against young legs."

"We were just getting started."

Alphonse hid a grin, and moved off with flashlight, dog, and camo-painted, 12-gauge semi-automatic shotgun.

As he strode away, the old man recited,

"For all our words Are short and lame of breath and stumble, And you surpass them though I know not why. Shy love I think of you as the day wanes And as the sun sinks deep into the ocean And as the stars turn round above in silent motion."

Hugh and Désirée faced each other and said simultaneously: "Shakespeare."

"Part of a sonnet," she continued. "I do not know which one."

They laughed. The silent awkward wall broken.

Hugh spoke first. "Tell me about your parents, about yourself. You seem so familiar yet still a mystery. I don't remember anyone ever mentioning the Terrenée branch of the de Gracies."

"My family, all gone years ago – father, mother, husband, and two children." Désirée felt sadness revive. Even though she had experienced their lives through the Mother-tree's stored memories, she had not been there for her children.

Hugh spoke in the interval, "I am sorry for your loss."

"The loss feels both immediate and distant, though somehow I still feel their presence." Désirée studied Hugh, seeing something of her children in his features, now five generations removed. A simultaneous synthesis of motherly affection and a lover's craving conflicted with her ego. She closed her eyes and shivered.

The first notes of *Moon River* whispered in the air.

Hugh led Désirée between spiraling wooden columns into the garden maze, its eight-foot tall Green Holly hedges masking them from any other wanderer's glance. He told her about the death of his mother, his years of loneliness, the fear and discipline of combat – blood-soaked ground and the bewildering sudden vacuum of friends lost.

Setting the story in modern times, she responded with the inadequacies of her first marriage, her breakdown upon the battlefield death of her husband, and the resulting drug dependency.

"I have been away a lengthy time recovering. So long, that I now experience everything as new and different, both exciting and frustrating."

Avoiding the maze's last dead-end passage, they turned left and entered the open heart of the warren with its central fountain. Water spouted from an eight-foot-high center pillar cascading down to overflow through the mouths of gray-patinaed faux-bronze facemasks grown by the Mother-tree to resemble foxes, badgers, and rabbits. Excess liquid chuckled down a series of ever-larger basins until it spilled over into the three-foot deep reservoir. The circular twelve-foot diameter base of the fountain rose knee-high before curving outward to form a circular bench.

"I played here as a child," Désirée recalled, "a favorite place. It seemed bigger then. Did you know half of the holly bushes are female and half male? Over the centuries, they have twined together until they are inseparable lovers. Only when the females flower and produce bright red berries can you tell the difference."

Hugh added, "During the spring, blackbirds, thrushes, and robins make predator-proof nests among the prickly leaves. Their singing makes quite a symphony."

"Do you not feel safe here? No animal or force of nature could crash through these walls."

"I would guess you and I are close to the same age. When were you here? Did we meet?"

Désirée hesitated. At some point, Hugh would have to be told more, but not tonight. "You were living your Spartan life, and my family was overly protective of its women. It was not our time to meet."

She shivered. The skimpy dress, the cold champagne, the clammy night mountain air, and the physical awareness of her partner brought chills from toes to chin.

Hugh removed his jacket and placed it around her shoulders.

Désirée felt the moist residual warmth. The sultry musk of male scent mixed with his Polo Black aftershave. Its blend of tangerine, sage, and sandalwood pleased and relaxed her.

The conversation continued, punctuated by periods of meditative silence, both content to just share the same air, moon, and water.

Finally, Hugh asked, "Why did you kiss me?"

"The music, the dance, your presence, evoked a deep response. There was no forethought, no plan. I felt the spirits of all my lusty ancestor women rise to grasp the moment. Does that make any sense?"

Hugh responded by cupping her chin in his hand, bringing their lips together.

She closed her eyes and snuggled in closer.

Multiple popping noises drew their faces upward.

Chrome-colored chrysanthemum blossoms burst over the garden. The fireworks had started. Time had passed so quickly. Booms and cracks produced fans of light and showers of blazing powdered metals in blues, green's, and golds. The sky over the mansion split open and overflowed with exploding shapes of palm leaves, sparkling diadems, and weeping willows. The entirety of their vision, direct and peripheral, filled with radiance.

It reminded Hugh of the dense flak-filled atmosphere he had witnessed through the long-dead eyes of his WW II pilot relative. Then he understood the reason for the Mother-tree sharing that vision. Damn! This was the air defense they needed.

A shout from outside the maze disrupted the thought.

"*Que diable!* What the hell are you doing?"

Old Alphonse's shotgun boomed.

A wave of overpressure pushed against Hugh's spine and neck. Mother-tree enhanced reflexes took over. He pulled Désirée in close with his back between her and the disturbance.

An explosive roar savaged their ears.

Fragments of metal, glass shards, and green leaf bits blew past him. A three-inch slash opened on his right cheek. He jerked as something stabbed into the triceps of his left arm. Dozens of tiny holly-leaf darts pierced his shirt and stuck into the flesh of his back.

Ears ringing in the following silence, Hugh fought dizziness while his brain screamed IED! IED!

Désirée squirmed out of his embrace. *"Mon Dieu, mon Dieu!"*

He stood, staggered, and caught her shoulder for support, exposing his side and back.

"Hugh, you bleed." She tore at her dress, ripped off a strip of the hem, and bound his arm. She gasped, "Your back…"

Désirée picked at the fragments of holly leaves, their needle-tips stuck in random patterns in his back flesh, each one marked by a growing point of blood on the white shirt.

The holly hedges had absorbed the big fragments, leaving him pin-cushioned but with no large disabling wounds. The cumulative effect still hurt like hell.

Hugh wiped the sweat off his forehead, refused to go into shock, and filled his lungs with air.

"Find Father or Jonsey and get them back here. The explosion will have passed unnoticed among the fireworks."

They parted. He raced behind her out of the maze. Hugh stumbled over debris at the detonation site. Ground zero was the caterer's prep room. The explosion had been channeled out the open French doors into the garden. Two bodies lay half-in, half-out of a flowerbed. A wash of familiar battlefield scent rose to assault him — hot copper blood and the sewer smell of shredded bowels. His knees shook. Hugh knelt by what had to be Alphonse, the entire front of his body ripped and torn. Shirt, skin, and meat had been flayed away from his chest and face exposing white ribs and cheekbones. The body moved. He can't be alive, Hugh thought.

The lips gone, skeletal teeth opened, "Waiters, the waiters…" A convulsion and the body went still.

Hugh heard a whimper.

To his right, a fur bundle writhed then stopped. Alys lay on her side, a leg missing, intestines torn into purple-red rags spilled from her stomach. Hugh knew she would not recover. The pain must be intense. He reached into the back folds of his cummerbund and pulled out a switchblade. Thumbing the safety off, he pushed the release button. A six-inch blacked-out stiletto blade snapped out and locked in place. Caressing a ragged ear, he held Alys's head steady. Hugh made a soothing murmur – she recognized his voice and relaxed.

"Peace, warrior, peace," he said, as the blade snaked through her eye into her brain.

Hugh shook off a wrenching, almost incapacitating wave of sadness. This was why father and uncle had whipped him during his childhood for displaying emotion. You must not sob, laugh, or panic. The military had built upon that conditioning, making it stronger. During a crisis, during fighting, only the cool, unemotional brain of a warrior could make the life and death decisions needed to accomplish the mission. He would cry later.

Emotion must be suppressed. Loss of comrades, terror, regrets, and guilt must be encapsulated and dealt with during later haunted hours. Hugh found the conditioning weakened from repeated exposure to battlefield conditions. When the suppressed rush of memories returned, your trainers' half-job left you shaking and alone to contain the aftermath as best you could. He hated it.

A year ago, he decided not to "suck it up" any longer. Hugh began allowing himself the emotional release of tears or rage in private. Catharsis was an instinctive human release from trauma. He concluded that only psychopaths could deal with the repression demanded by his family and the military.

He stepped cautiously through the spray of wreckage. Inside the caterer's prep room laid the disassembled parts of another human

177

body. Hugh shuffled around a disconnected shoulder complete with arm. A pair of shoes stood together next to a heavy Maplewood table – feet and ankles still laced in them.

Clothed in the rags of a white waiter's jacket, a bloody headless torso slumped against the back partition. From the room's misty smoke came a mosaic odor of burnt cloth, blood, and something else that he could not identify. Water dripped and trickled from gashes in the Mother-tree's walls and ceiling.

A peppery, cinnamon smell came from thick sap oozing from the cuts that had already begun to seal the wounds. The scent made his blood race, chemicals, and hormones flooded his body. He was at once both hyper-alert and without pain. The Mother-tree was releasing stimulating vapors, alerting and strengthening its symbiotes for battle.

A hand touched his shoulder. He leaped, hands blurred, and cut with the switchblade.

Jonsey's open palm caught the blade on its flat side and pushed it into empty space. Aubert and the sergeant major stood by his side. "It's the caterer," Hugh spit out. "Some of his help are terrorists. Jonsey, are you packing?"

"Yes, of course." The sergeant bent over and rolled up one pant leg exposing an ankle-holstered Browning .380 automatic.

"You and I will round up the caterer and all his people." Hugh remembered the faces of the waiters that had expressed fear or anger at his presence earlier in the evening. Why hadn't he done something? He pushed the guilt, and residual pain from his wounds to the back of his mind. They would return unbidden later. "Be careful, there is more than one infiltrator among them.

"Father, send the guests home. Make sure none of the enemy get away with them."

*

Jonsey and Hugh moved together down the dark first-floor

hallway, clearing rooms as they went. They had found the puzzled caterer and all of his help except four new ones especially hired for this event. Ojas guarded the innocent employees sequestered in one of the tower rooms. Given one killed in the bomb blast, and another shot minutes ago by Jonsey while trying to escape up the back stairs, two of Fahad's assassins remained.

They flushed the final pair out of the kitchen.

Pursued and pursuers raced out of the mansion into the garden. The two enemies split left and right.

Jonsey followed one into the darkened ballroom, its hundreds of candles now burnt out.

Hugh chased after the other heading for the bombsite. He sidestepped around a peony-filled flowerbed and stopped. In the moonlight stood a composite creature – the white-jacketed terrorist, a long-bladed knife scavenged from the mansion kitchen, pressed against the throat of Désirée.

"Jesus!" A raging, almost crippling anger, raced through Hugh's mind, then, shock at finding the woman with whom he had fallen in love in such danger. She must have come back looking for him. It was unfair. He had waited many years to find her.

The situation was also ridiculous. Here they stood immersed in a scene reprised hundreds of times in movies and on TV. That they could find themselves in such a clichéd state – impossible.

Hugh stared at the stolen knife held by the assassin. He knew the weapon. It was old, even older than the Mother-tree herself. Uncle Frank had once told him a fairytale about a damascened scimitar, brought back from the Holy Land by a crusader ancestor, booty of war. The hilted blade sharpened repeatedly over the last nine hundred years grew shorter and more slender with each passing year, until it was finally relegated to kitchen duty. Now, the Muslim-forged blade had completed the circle returning to the hand of another believer in *jihad.*

Hugh inched forward, bringing up the switchblade, and putting him within seven feet of the hostage-taker.

The man hissed and pressed the knife more tightly against soft skin.

Désirée caught Hugh's eye. Her left index finger pointed to her right hand, the one with the entwined snake bracelet.

Hugh's legs began to quiver. The effects of his own adrenaline spikes and whatever Mother-tree drug he had inhaled was wearing off. Forcing his body to relax, he moved slowly, held the switchblade out to one side and let it drop.

The man loosened up. The blade pressure on Désirée's neck eased.

The trio saw two flashes and heard the sound of gunshots from the ballroom. Jonsey had finished a game of cat-and-mouse with the third man.

The terrorist grimaced as he realized the last of his comrades was gone. His knife-hand began to shake.

Hugh grunted.

The man's eyes focused on his one.

Désirée's snake-clasped hand moved up.

Hugh raised his eyebrows and shook his head. He must keep the man's attention.

In his peripheral vision he saw Jonsey push through the peonies, raise his pistol, and then lower it – the distance too great, no way to make a for-sure headshot.

Désirée's flattened hand, fingers extended and closed, moved into the open space between the blade and her shoulder.

Hugh tensed. His right hand formed into a small fist, knuckles making a blunt wedge. Hugh saw that his love had positioned the metal neck of the snakehead bracelet against the blade.

She screamed and pushed the knife away – yellow snake-scaled gold against the steel's razor edge.

The man drew the blade crosswise as she spun out of his grasp.

Hugh lunged forward, the wedge of his tapered fist punching the *jihadi* in the larynx.

The hostage-taker crumpled to the ground.

Hugh leaped to Désirée. No blood. The blade's cutting edge had slid across the snake metal, gouging the gold but missing the flesh of hand and neck.

Another flash of anger flashed through him. His body used it as fuel. Picking up the switchblade, Hugh moved to finish the coughing, gasping man. He knelt on the stone flags to insert the blade up under the ribs.

Aubert grabbed his hand. "No killing. This is the last one left alive. We need to interrogate him."

The heat of the moment, the Mother-tree assisted blood chemistry, and all the old unresolved anger and resentment against his father flared in his mind. Here was another attempt at manipulation. Hugh threw off his hand. "Fuck you!"

"Son. *Arrête!* Stop!"

Jonsey grabbed his shoulders and pulled him back. "Major de Gracie, get control. If you must, you can take him out later."

Military conditioning took precedence – Hugh quit struggling.

Aubert examined the gasping captive. "I believe he has a partially collapsed lung. I need to prevent it from fully collapsing or we'll lose our only chance at interrogating him."

8

HUGH WALKED INTO THE LIBRARY, now a war-room. His body felt better after four hours of Mother-tree-assisted profound sleep. She had swept all the toxins and accumulated fight or flight hormones from his blood, leaving him calm and analytical. A flattened 00 shotgun pellet had been removed from his left arm, all the holly darts picked out, and the healing process for his wounds accelerated.

His father, Ojas, and Désirée sat around the circular table in the room's center, eating a late breakfast. The smell of *huevos revueltos* with green *jalapenos*, cilantro, and salsa drew him to a side table. He filled a plate with eggs, sausage, and hot muffins. Désirée motioned him to a chair beside her. An innocent-looking unopened bottle of champagne stood at the center of the table.

Father said, "A close examination of the blast site and the

interrogation of the surviving terrorist has presented us with a reconstruction of last night's events and a smidgen of real-time intelligence."

Hugh stopped eating, laid the fork down, the memories of last night flooded through his mind. As though still sticky with blood, his palms rubbed against his pant legs. He shivered as he looked at Désirée. He had almost lost her.

"From what we can tell, the four infiltrators were not here to kill, only to complete a detailed interior reconnaissance and plant these," Aubert spoke as he picked up the champagne bottle. "It looks like a standard 750ml glass wine bottle – label, cork, and the foil around the top, what you would expect, even with a close examination." He hefted it in his hands. "However, it is heavier than usual. The original liquid has been removed and replaced with two cups of 00 buckshot, the remaining space packed with Semtex, a Czech-manufactured plastic explosive notoriously popular with your Afghan friends."

Hugh commented, based on his military knowledge, "The dark olive green of the bottles hid their contents. With the containers sealed, scrupulously cleaned, and re-foiled there was no vestigial scent to alert the dogs." He paused. "But they would still need detonators."

"We discovered the detonators packed into one of the German chocolate cakes. The plan was to de-cork the explosive bottles, insert an electronic blasting cap, and connect it to harmless-seeming cell phones. Hidden in key places, the bottles would be remotely detonated to cause casualties and confusion during their forthcoming main attack."

A wave of understanding flashed through Hugh's brain, "One of them had just begun to wire one of the bottles when Alphonse and Alys spotted him. Alphonse fired. Fahad's man fumbled the job and set off the explosive by accident."

Aubert's head bowed. He let out an audible breath. "At least all the students and guests departed ignorant and unscathed. They heard the blast as part of the fireworks display. Losing two of our own was bad enough, but it could have been worse. Only one bottle went off, the other five were still in the case under the rock maple table which shielded them from sympathetic detonation."

"What about Jeannine, Alphonse's daughter?" Hugh asked.

"She is being tended by Margy and Jonsey. The bodies of Alphonse and Alys are being prepared for the funeral. She is desolated, a complete sobbing breakdown."

In one night, Jeannine has lost her father to a terrorist act and the man she loved to another woman. She might have to be put in stasis – suspended in one of the leaded glass caskets to safely dream away her hurt over the years.

Aubert spoke again, "I have placed her on suicide watch. She will be examined again in a few days. *Elle me fait pitié.*"

Hugh sat silent. Hate, repulsion, sadness percolated in his mind, twisted his face. Their home had been violated. A beloved man and dog murdered. His woman almost killed. He had brought Fahad to them.

Beneath the table, Désirée grasped his hand.

Aubert pointed at his son's still full plate, "Eat up. You need the calories. We have an offensive to plan. Our prisoner did not possess the recessive genes needed to clearly communicate with the Mother-tree. However, with the help of drugs, she and I extracted enough fuzzy memories from our captive's mind. We now have their staging location and a sense of Fahad's timing. The attack will come within the next five to seven days."

"Are we through interrogating the son-of-a-bitch?"

Aubert nodded, a pleased smile on his face, "We do not suffer enemies to live and tell tales or possibly strike again. He and his three friends are feeding the Mother-tree. *Nous somnes satisfaits.*"

"Open your briefing files and examine the photo we pulled off the realtor's website." Hugh stood before the group dressed in SWAT style black fatigues and boots. "Our objective will be the forced entry and elimination of all terrorist personnel and equipment within the warehouse you see before you. We will also remove any papers, personal effects, and other useful intelligence."

"Will we take prisoners?" Ojas asked.

"We will not endanger ourselves by hesitating to shoot. No prisoners. These *jihadis* will not surrender. Even the wounded will try to kill you. This operation is intended to disrupt their plans and weaken their organization through the destruction of assets, both human and materiel."

Hugh continued after a moment of silence produced no further questions. "The enemy has leased a portion of a rejuvenated Brooklyn, New York Civil War-era warehouse. Like many of its kind, it was constructed in 1864 on an earthen pier built out into New York Harbor and has sixteen-inch diameter redbrick walls. Man-thick old growth yellow pine posts hold up its roof timbers. During its first days, the facility stored grain, coffee, mahogany, nuts, and tea."

He took a breath, continuing to keep his thoughts articulated, pushing out all extra so he could focus on the task at hand. "With the advent of container shipping, the city's old warehouse and manufacturing district became obsolete. The area around our objective is now surrounded by a mix of empty lots where rotting buildings have been torn down and its remaining structurally-sound sister buildings. Ten years ago, it became fashionable to buy and renovate these old abandoned buildings."

Hugh eyed the group, making sure to keep full attention. "This one was fully leased when Hurricane Sandy hit. While the walls and roof survived with little damage, the original arch-shaped metal doors allowing access to the partitioned interior were blown off their hinges and water flooded inside. Guess who the first and currently only lessee is in the newly refurbished building?"

Looking at the harbor water surrounding the building on three sides Jonsey commented, "Now I can see the reason for yesterday's kayak orientation at Port Henry Beach."

"Right you are. Notice the riprap, the stepped piles of stone framing the building's waterside foundations protecting it from wave surges. You will be scaling those. Watch your step. We don't want any twisted ankles or broken legs. Please go to page two."

Hugh waited until everyone had their pages turned to continue. "Our six fighters will form into three teams. Ojas and Uncle Frank will form assault team one, assault team two, myself and Jonsey, and the sniper team, Margy and Désirée. The sniper team will find a position with a clear field of fire covering the landside door. They will take out any outside guards and later, any enemy trying to escape landward. The assault teams will blow doors, one each on the north and south walls, enter, and moving from west to east terminate any enemy personnel. Turn to page three."

This was well laid out, maybe even overdone, but nothing could be left to chance. Every little thing, every contingency, had to be thought of to ensure they could be victorious.

Hugh pointed at Margy. "Equipment will be Barrett Rec 7 assault rifles with six thirty-round magazines for all except you, who will carry a medic's pack. Désirée will take a sniper rifle. Everyone will carry a pistol and fighting knife of your choice. Teams one and two will carry door buster C-4 explosives and remote detonators. All will be equipped with night-vision devices, local maps, and a hand-held GPS unit. Flashlights with red and white LEDs will be issued for signaling and illumination and we will all be connected with two-way tactical radio. Team leaders — myself, Uncle Frank, and Margy, as the sniper's observer — will have day/night binoculars. In case of incapacitating wounds or death, overall command will descend from me to Jonsey and then to Uncle Frank. No one will carry any identification, papers, or mementos that could be used to identify them if killed or captured."

Hugh nodded to Jonsey, who stood and announced, "Check page four in your file for our schedule. Breakfast at 0600 hours tomorrow and immediately following at 0700 a final inspection of gear and radios. We will depart at 0900 hours from the Port Henry beach utilizing a rented amphibious plane, which will drop us at New York Skyport's Seaplane base. Vans will move us to New York Kayak Company's headquarters on the Hudson River's pier 40. At approximately 1200 hours, we will take our kayak flotilla downriver past Governor's Island to Brooklyn's Red Hook neighborhood, landing at Louis Valentino Water Front Park."

Jonsey switched to his guidebook voice. "After having kayaked the gorgeous — but filthy — Hudson and East rivers and taking great pleasure in observing the skyline of New York, we will enjoy a picnic at one of the most beautiful yet least visited Brooklyn parks. Its green- grass slopes a blush with flowers and its magnificent view of the Statue of Liberty will entertain us until dusk when we will cease being addlepated tourists and turn into the highly-skilled and efficient raiders your Mother-tree training has made you."

Jonsey flashed a grin a Hugh. "After a short paddle further down river and under the cover of darkness we will climb the riprap and attend to business. I estimate our arrival at 2000 hours and our departure at 2025. We will return to Valentino Park, leave our kayaks, and depart in waiting vans for the return flight. Any questions?"

"What if we get separated?" Margy said.

Hugh nodded. "A good point, the fog of battle and Murphy's Law could prevail. In that case, toss your weapons in the river, come ashore anywhere you can, find the nearest phone, and call our emergency number, which you should already have memorized. You will be given instructions. If for some reason the vans have to move before we return, we will meet them at our secondary rendezvous, The Red Hook Winery. Its location has already been programmed into your GPS devices."

Uncle Frank stared out a window. His thoughts went back to his time as a supervisor in the Brooklyn shipyards during the 1870's. He remembered the scent of fresh worked pine and oak, tar, and hemp rope. The harbor water, even then, smelled bad. "I worked in that area years ago and there can be stiff tidal- and river-generated currents. Have we planned for them?"

"Tidal charts have been consulted. Our daytime journey downriver to the park will be with the current. The few kilometers paddle to the objective will be against a two to three knot inflow. Nothing we can't handle. The return will be with the tidal inflow. Any other questions?"

The members of the group looked at each other.

Hugh nodded. "All right, you are on your own until the funeral at 1800 hours."

Hugh, Jonsey, and Aubert sat drinking coffee across the table from Rick Brown, president and owner of Brown & Sons Fireworks Display.

Hugh started the conversation, "We were greatly impressed with the program you folks put on two nights ago."

"Thank you. We aim to please."

"We'd like to plan another. What would it take to put a continuous interlocking dome of fire over the entire expanse of lawn in front of our property? For, let's say, ten to fifteen minutes?"

Brown looked surprised. His facial expression turned calculating considering the timing, type of ordnance, positioning of the firing tubes, and personnel needed. He tapped his fingers on the tabletop, silently summed up the costs, and added a profit margin.

"Continuous with multiple simultaneous bursts? That will be costly in terms of employees and material."

"Price is not an obstacle," Hugh replied.

Eyebrows rose. This was not the miserly haggling normally experienced with the senior de Gracie. He glanced over at the head of the household.

Aubert nodded.

Brown's imagination opened. He resisted rubbing his hands together. "Well then, we'll need to place mortar tubes in a ninety-degree arc all along the inside edge of your great wall.

"Three times the normal amount. The angles on each launcher will be separately calculated. Fuses won't work – too slow. We'll need to detonate the propelling charge electrically."

"What type of shells will completely fill the sky?" Jonsey asked.

"The best for this occasion will be those with multiple breaks."

"Breaks?"

"The initial airborne explosion lofts out sub-munitions that explode separately after a very short delay. These combined with other bursting shells, such as salutes, peonies, chrysanthemums, and willows should completely fill the sky with loud bangs and powdered burning metals. When do you want the performance?"

"You've got three days," Hugh replied.

"Whoa. That'll take everything I've currently got in my bunkers. I'll have no stock left to fill my other orders, unless I buy high-priced stuff off the retail market. I also have too few employees."

Hugh repeated, "Price is no obstacle. We'll provide extra people-power."

"I won't have the time to train your folks and do all the setup."

"Can you find a way?"

Brown had been thinking, "Well, we could do a cake. We'll wire the entire cluster of individual tubes to chain-fire with a single fuse. You press one button to get it started, and then each tube pops off by itself in a preset order. My people would wire it and you set it off when ready."

"And this cake can be configured to completely fill our sky for ten or more minutes?" Hugh queried.

"Yes, some cakes we've engineered have had a thousand connected tubes. In addition, while we're at it, how about ground effects? We can engineer a ground-level firework called a mine that expels small reports, shells, stars, and other garnitures into the air, to fill the interior of the dome created by the overhead display."

The two de Gracie men and the sergeant major blinked and looked at each other. Jonsey and Hugh, in mirror image, picked up their coffee cups, sipped, and smiled. Brown shivered, reacting to the two sets of feral canine teeth exposed.

Hugh said, "By all means, we want our guests to be amazed."

Hugh, and five other de Gracie men, synchronized their steps as they passed out of the great front door of the mansion, down the steps and entered a five-foot-wide path marked by strewn cut-flowers.

Squinting in the bright sunshine, Aubert led them down the newly created *Chemin de l'Égalité* (the Path of Equality) since all life is equal in death. The symbolism was not lost on the mourners, who in spite of the Mother-tree's gift of longevity became aware again of their mortality. The men acting as pallbearers hefted the cross-handles of a flat assembly of planks long and wide enough to hold the linen-wrapped bodies of Alphonse and Alys. A banner embroidered with the blue and green de Gracie crest draped the bodies.

Hugh wished his best friend could be with them. Strictly a family affair, Jonsey had been sent off to Port Henry on a make-work errand. It wouldn't do for him to gain insight into the true nature of the de Gracie symbiotic relationship. Aubert had been rigid on this point.

Rung for this purpose only, the soul-bell in the central tower clanged out a slow measured peal.

Black-dressed mourners placed a foot down with each bong. Feet crushed the path's carpet of peonies, irises, roses, and hydrangeas, releasing a mix of perfume normally pleasant to the nose, but now a reminder of sorrow.

Behind Aubert and the pallbearers marched the remaining dozen active de Gracies, the dog pack trotting at their sides.

Jeannine, a bent, sobbing, wrung-out figure supported by Margy, stumbled along following the bodies. Hugh witnessed for the first time the family's *les obsèques*, an accumulated mix of death rituals and customs — eons-old pagan practices grafted onto more recent Christian belief. Men and women had their hair cut short, all mirrors in the mansion had been turned to the wall, and pitchers and jugs holding liquids had been emptied. A single window left open allowed an escape route for the victims' souls. Death masks, crafted by a de Gracie artist, would be added to the shelves in the catacombs beneath the mansion.

In a concentric circle paralleling the inside of the thornwall were what appeared to be evenly spaced, boxy stone benches. Removing their lids allowed access to the Mother-tree's root recycling system. In this day of satellite and drone photography, a shielding canopy tent had been set up over the selected entry site.

The pallbearers stopped and rested the end of the plank on the lip of the open stone rectangle. Its lid flat on the ground to one side. Family members and dogs gathered in a circle.

Aubert stepped forward. He chanted, "*Nous servons, que nous soyons servis.*"

The group responded with, "We serve, that we may be served."

"Here is Alphonse de Gracie and Alys, two who passed before their time. At one hundred and one years, Alphonse possessed yet the potential to be with his daughter for another eight decades and Alys another twenty years. Their time cut short defending us. They fulfilled a sacred duty bred into flesh and bone."

A breeze passed over the thornwall, tousled the women's shortcut locks, molded the fabric of shirts and pants against warm fleshy curves beneath, and rippled the tent top.

Out on the grassy sward, creating long shadows in the late afternoon sun, a knot of sheep and one donkey, heads down, moved in mincing-steps.

A dragonfly, mottled black and jade, rode the air current, landed on the tree of life insignia, and twitched its bifurcated wings.

Aubert went on. "We have our own little Darwinian island here. We birds have fostered our own mutations. There are few of us. Over the centuries, we have developed as a group apart, dependent for understanding, kindness, and continuation upon each other. When one is lost, no matter the reason, we are diminished more greatly than any other human branch." Aubert paused, raised his palms.

The dragonfly tensed.

"The Tree of Life possesses no double nature, no good and evil, no light and dark, no duality. It is just a oneness. We come from and return to that oneness."

His hands dropped.

The dragonfly flew off.

The pallbearers raised the end of the plank bed. Shrouded bodies slid from beneath the flags and entered the Mother-tree's care.

"Alphonse de Gracie, Alys, you have returned to the oneness as we all shall in our turn.

Nous servons, que nous soyons servis."

Hugh harmonized with other male and female voices, "We serve, that we may be served."

He felt Désirée entwine her fingers into his.

The emotion-packed events and funeral had finally broken his resistance. This was family and whether he was willing or not he had finally come home. The desire for oneness with all this became overwhelming.

*

Rain pattered down, making rattling snare drum sounds on the polyethylene hulls of the kayaks. In the reflections, created by shore lights on the water, Désirée could see dimples rise as drops smacked into the river surface. Her muscles, adapted to the necessary rhythm, dipped the kayak paddle on one side then the other. Thin leather shooting gloves kept blisters away. Making progress against the current was easier than she had anticipated, thanks to the double cockpit kayaks, which allowed two paddlers. She blinked a splashed drop of rain out of her right eye and focused on the red guide light to the front – the convoy of three kayaks should be close to the objective. They approached a dark mound thrust out into the harbor. Red lights moved left and right.

Over their earbuds came a crisp voice: "Objective to the left. Team Two, take position. Over."

"Roger that, Team One," Désirée responded. "Moving to the north wall, out."

The remaining two boats continued around the earthen pier to the opposite side. "Team Three, take position and report when ready. Over."

Désirée heard Margy acknowledge and respond. The drizzle stopped. Rain-rattle ceased, allowing the collective hornet-hum of the massive urban area to surround them. A small iridescent bow wave hissed against the hull. The dark hulk of the warehouse slipped by as their craft ghosted through the water.

The two women back-paddled to lose momentum. The kayak's bow thudded against the riprap covering the bank. A swirl of current pushed the boat sideways, laying it alongside the piled rock. Margy held their position with a paddle jammed between boulders while Désirée tied off bow and stern. They exchanged hard-plastic kayak helmets for soft ranger caps, crept up rain-wet head-and-chest sized boulders. Hands and feet sought safe grips.

Clambering over the top, they left the riprap behind, low-crawled through thick uncut grass soft on their knees and elbows. Désirée cradled the sniper rifle across her forearms. Rain pearled on blades of grass and soaked through the knees, elbows, and chests of cotton-polyester battle dress, leaving skin cold and clammy.

Stopping in a miniature thicket of weeds, they spotted the warehouse main entrance forty yards off. A single industrial light fixture mounted at the building's peak broadcast a cone of light over the front door. Armed with pistol belt and shotgun, a single guard stepped into the circle of illumination, emerging from the roof overhang where he had sheltered from the rain.

Margy located the power cables where they entered the building and traced them out to an electrical transformer mounted on a pole twenty yards distant. She tapped her companion's shoulder and pointed, receiving a nod.

Désirée pulled the waterproofing condom off the barrel of the M-110 sniper rifle and snapped out the bipod. She lifted the front and rear caps on the night scope, snuggled the butt into her shoulder, sighted on the guard, and then on the transformer. The distance was short and there was little wind. No adjustments needed, she thought. Reaching forward, she checked the suppressor tube nested over the barrel. Not like the movies, her cheeks dimpled in a half smile, these devices did reduce the noise and hide the muzzle flare, but they were not silent.

She glanced at Margy's striped leaf-green and urban-gray camouflage face-paint and wondered if they both looked that silly. Désirée tapped her companion on the shoulder and nodded.

Margy whispered into the mike, "Team three reporting one hostile. Ready to proceed, over."

"Acknowledge, team three. Break. Team one ready. Out." came back in Hugh's voice. Ojas's rasp reported, "Team two ready, over."

"Acknowledge, team two, Break. Team three initiate. Over."

"Team three will initiate in one mike. Out."

Désirée brought the night-vision scope crosshairs down onto the head of the guard. The sight picture flickered. She looked up.

The man was moving.

Did he suspect something? She looked again.

The sentinel swatted the air in front of his face. The light had attracted a cloud of moths and other night-flyers. Dozens swirled and danced in the illuminated cone, more arriving by the minute.

The guard took a step outside the brightness, whisking insects from his cheeks and neck.

She waited until he settled and reacquired her sight picture. The safety clicked off. Désirée fought an adrenalin surge. Sniper training calmed muscles, regulated breathing, and placed a forefinger on the cold metal of the trigger. Waiting until her heart was between beats, she pressed.

A click. Nothing happened.

Damn! A green soldier's mistake. No round in the chamber. She felt her cheeks and neck turn red. She slowly pulled the bolt back and guided it forward, stripping a cartridge off the ten-round magazine and chambering it. Resuming position, she reacquired her target.

Margy rubbed her back and neck, helping the muscles relax.

The shot — a bass chug noise — came as a surprise, just like in training.

The weapon punched into her shoulder and click-clacked as the bolt moved back then forward. Désirée watched the guard's brains and fragments of skull blow out, cutting a fan shape through the cloud of insects. Knees collapsed. The body slumped forward. The man's chest and what was left of the face smacked into wet mud.

Sniper and spotter heard a thwack as a rubble pile one hundred yards off finally stopped the 51mm bullet.

Margy reported, "Team three, one shot, one kill. Over."

"Acknowledge, team three, out."

Désirée sighted the rifle on the electrical transformer. Another bass chug and sparks burst out of its cylindrical housing. The light over the door went black. The sniper team adjusted their night vision equipment and watched the front door.

"Team two, this is team one, on my mark blow side doors – three, two, mark."

The two women heard the explosions, so close together they sounded like one. A few seconds of quiet passed, the inside of the warehouse lit up with flashes. The high-pitched burr-r-r of the Barretts was answered by the brief stutter of an AK-47.

A man raced out the front door.

Désirée fired, and missed, the terrorist's panic-run too fast for her to track.

Margy stood, squared her body to the target and raised a pistol to her dominant eye. The 9mm Glock banged.

She emptied the seventeen-round magazine with spaced controlled shots. Long range for a handgun, she got lucky, one of the slugs ricocheted off a rock and smacked into flesh. The fugitive tumbled, rose, gripped his right buttock, and limped forward.

Désirée pulled the sniper rifle tight into her shoulder, and fired twice.

The *jihadi* threw up his arms and fell.

A hand stuck out the front door at knee level and blinked a red lens three times – the all-clear signal.

8

What profit has the worker from his labor?
Ecclesiastes: 3:9

"WELL, THERE'S GOOD NEWS AND BAD NEWS."

Hugh stood in the library turned war room, olive drab cup decaled with a U.S. Army crest in hand. Mid-afternoon of the day following the warehouse assault the room smelled of coffee, tea, and apple-filled bear claw pastries.

War paint scrubbed from faces, the raiders sat around the tables dressed in an eclectic mix of civilian and military clothing.

Uncle Frank, as usual, surpassed everyone else in strange fashion choices. He wore moccasins decorated with a firebird in yellow, red, and blue beadwork, light green doctor's scrub pants, and a wrinkled black T-shirt with a skull and crossbones front and back.

Hugh's opening comment had interrupted his uncle's once-upon-a-time conversation with Désirée concerning an old sea captain he had sailed with named Teach.

Hugh cleared his throat. "The bad news first. We did not do enough damage to Fahad's people and materiel to stop or even delay his attack. Our raid came too late. Although we racked up a score of six terrorists killed at no cost to ourselves, we only caught the last group staged out of that location. The fire set upon our departure destroyed five thousand rounds of small arms ammunition, a case of AK-47s, and a dozen RPG warheads – small potatoes for an operation this size.

"However, the photos we took of the warehouse's contents, captured invoices, letters, and a personal journal have given us a cogent picture of the enemy's build-up of men and materiel." Hugh nodded to Jonsey, "Give them the benefit of our analysis, O mighty sergeant major."

"Yes sir, your high holiness," Jonsey rose holding a wad of papers and spoke to Aubert and the members of the raiding party. "From the looks of the rumpled cots, abundant fast food wrappers, and abandoned dirty clothing, the warehouse was only a way station. In order to avoid being challenged at regular ports of entry, small groups of men and some matériel were secretly dropped off boats entering the harbor. Personnel and supplies were consolidated and transported by vehicle to somewhere else.

"Much of what they needed had been purchased on civilian markets in New York or surrounding states." Jonsey slapped documents down on the table one at a time. "We have paper receipts for armored vests, AK-47s complete with conversion kits allowing fully automatic fire, shotguns, pistols, military fatigues, socks and boots, knives, and food – enough to equip and feed a force of fifty fighters. Rifle and pistol ammunition had been purchased in small lots, so as not to attract attention, from stores and gun shows in the surrounding states."

Those gathered listened to his report.

He waved additional papers. "Receipts for the payment of rental trucks indicate they had been driven an average of eight hundred miles. Assuming round trips, the half-mileage would limit them to a circle bounded on the south by Durham, North Carolina, to the west as far as Akron, Ohio, and north to Montreal, Canada. No sense worrying about them holing up to the East, since traveling any such distance in that direction would put them in the Atlantic Ocean."

Uncle Frank, fresh from a morning read of his dictionary, broke in. "So where are the ignominious, obsequious bastards?"

Hugh fielded the question. "Our previous conclusion still stands. They will come in by chopper, probably from the north. Supporting that view is a six-month-old letter sent by the Canadian Ministry of Natural Resources to a Saudi Arabian straw company confirming the sale of their retired firefighting Bell 204 and 205 aircraft – the civilian versions of the Huey helicopter. We know these machines cruise at one hundred and twenty-five miles per hour giving them a range of two hundred and sixty miles. If they want to get here, do their business and return to their original location, they must be based within one hundred and thirty miles. Given the amount of men and equipment they have assembled, they will be flying four or five war birds from someplace south of Montreal."

"It makes sense," Ojas responded pointing a bear claw pastry, with a big bite missing, at a map of North America on the wall. "The border is mostly wilderness. Bears, moose, and raccoons will not be reporting the movement of strange flying objects without filed flight plans to the authorities."

Hugh nodded. "If there are no other questions, let's get to work. We have three to four days before the attack. The fireworks defense should be dug in and connected by late afternoon tomorrow. We have time to put overhead cover on the foxholes and excavate the connecting trenches a bit deeper. Aubert assures me the Mother-tree's minefield of pit-traps and stingers is ready to be activated."

🌿

Désirée lay in bed, hands clasped over her stomach. Conflicting emotions generated by the attack on the warehouse had foiled her initial attempt at sleep. She had killed. *Mon Dieu*, fellow human beings. The rifle's recoil punch to the shoulder, brain and bone fragments flying through the cloud of insects – replayed again and again.

A body bereft of animation became an awkward bag of bone and meat tumbling forward into the mud. Her skin flushed hot. Sweat prickled. The training and the Mother-tree conditioning let her make the kill, but only partially, inadequately, prepared her soul for the real thing.

Désirée rose, slipped on a gauzy linen robe, and opened the window. Moving air bathed her, evaporating moisture on her skin. Cooler and at last tired, she returned to a bed of fitful sleep and a Mother-tree vision.

*

"I think I see a koala bear down there."

Lieutenant Lewis Clark de Gracie almost lost his grip on the gunship's stick. He turned to face Dale Grabowski, his warrant officer co-pilot. Assuming an exaggerated Aussie accent, he said, "I think you are about four thousand miles off, mate. Now, if we were farther north, say close to the Chinese border, we might find some pandas."

Dale twisted the ends of a red handlebar mustache, "But I'd really like to see those cute little koalas."

Lewis shook his head. It was difficult to determine when his second was serious or just screwing over his mind. He chose serious. "This is the Central fuckin' Highlands, my man. You need to improve your grasp of the local geography. I've got a copy of the U.S. Army Area Handbook for Vietnam, NO. 550-40 in my footlocker. It's yours when we get back to Kontum."

The helicopter gunship platoon normally flew support for Republic of Vietnam and U.S. troop operations, but today targets of opportunity took precedence. Intelligence sources had picked up a significant increase in NVA supply and troop movements into their sector. The Central Highlands, 18,600 square miles of up and down terrain 600 to 7,280 feet were considered essential by both sides to the domination of South Vietnam.

"Lew-assss," Dale said, drawing out the end syllable. "I have been curious for the longest time. Why did your mammy and pappy name you Lewis Clark? Doesn't seem to fit, attached to that aristocratic French moniker."

"My father, Frank, claims to have made the westward trek with the famous explorers of the same names. His high regard for them expressed in naming this mother's son."

"As I recollect, and my memory is fuzzy on this point, that expedition took place over one hundred and sixty years ago. Your dad involved in some kind of reincarnation thing?"

"Highly likely, the old man is a strange one."

"Given your permanent tan, are you related to Sacaga… Sacagawea?"

"No, my mother is Mohawk, Sacagawea belonged to the Shoshone."

Lewis scanned the rainforest below and checked the chopper's place in the platoon's staggered trail formation. He slowed the aircraft to maintain position with the other five gunships. A glance to his right checked the status of the unit's mascot, George, a dusty-brown rhesus macaque monkey. Still a young one, the primate measured eighteen inches long and weighed fifteen pounds. In his six months with the men, pointy-eared George had bonded with the group, eating corn flakes with raw egg, rice pudding, and locally grown fruit in the mess hall and getting drunk on the Vietnamese brewed *Ba Mu'o'i Ba* served in the enlisted men's club.

After a few beers, the monkey's normally fur-less pink face would turn red.

George squirmed and let out a *chit-chit-chit*. The macaque looked like a little soldier, clothed in a set of tailor-made fatigues complete with buck sergeant's stripes. The maintenance folks had created and bolted a facsimile helicopter pilot's seat just his size to the chopper floor. Tugging at the straps securing him to the chair, George curled lips to expose teeth and cut loose a long multisyllabic monkey sentence.

"Dale, the monk wants food."

A handful of lychee nuts dropped into the mascot's lap kept him busy. Lewis smiled when he looked at the parachute wings recently sewn on the mini-uniform. After a four-hour bout of drinking, the unit had decided to let George earn his wings. Someone had secured a miniature hand-made silk parachute to the macaque's back. The men marched along the runway to the three-story control tower chanting "George, George, George of the jungle. Watch out for that tree." The screaming monkey sailed off the tower's balcony. The chute inflated. He touched down and ran up a tree just off the airstrip.

Lewis vocalized his thought. "Boy, George was really pissed after his first jump."

"You said it, El Tee. Took us an hour to coax him down from his perch. Hey! Did you see that? I caught the flash of a face in the tallgrass clearing to our right."

"Rattler flight leader, this is Rattler Five, possible enemy activity in the clearing below. Over."

"This is Rattler One, Rattler Five and six recon clearing. All other units follow me. Out."

The two tail-end gunships descended to treetop level, increased speed, and blew over the open space. Lewis's eyebrows lifted. "Whoa, Dale, the place is crawling with NVA. We've caught at least two companies out in the open."

Over the next twenty minutes, the six gunships exploded 2.75-inch rockets into the tree line to kill stragglers and to pin the majority of the enemy in the open. Making passes at different angles to confuse the target, they raked the hapless troops with fire from side-mounted dual M6 machine guns, while door gunners shot up enemy officers, NCO's and crew served weapons.

Leaders dead or disabled, isolated soldiers lost unit cohesion, dropped weapons, and ran back and forth in terror stumbling over windrows of their comrades' bodies.

On Lewis's fifth pass, a smart-ass on the ground got off a burst from his AK, one of which turned out to be a golden bullet punching through the chopper's Duralum alloy skin to damage the hydraulic system.

"Rattler One, this is Rattler Five going down. Over."

The chopper crunched into the middle of the clearing, rattling the teeth of the crew.

Overhead blades geared down, reducing vibration through the airframe. Their steady whop-whop dropped to a hum and then to a swish. The pilots and crew felt exposed and vulnerable without the protective force field tremor.

"Rattler Five, this is Rattler One, a heavy lift helicopter and two slicks with infantry will arrive in fifteen mikes to bring you back. We will fly cover until bingo fuel. Set up a perimeter and stay alert. Over."

"Roger, Rattler One, can we order a beer and pizza delivery? Out."

Dale clipped a leash to George's collar, drew a Smith & Wesson .357 revolver, from his shoulder holster, and exited. Lewis followed, struggling against the aircraft's forty-degree sideways slant. The door gunners fired bursts of six rounds at any sound or movement among the scattered mass of intertwined bodies. They weren't about to allow a wounded enemy to take a last-minute shot. Lewis jumped out of the cargo bay .45 automatic ready, discovered the helicopter's strange lean was due to one landing strut resting on a three-foot pile of bodies.

Streamers of smoke from burning trees and brush fluttered across the clearing. They carried the nitrate smell of expended ordnance, wood smoke, and cooked flesh mixed with human excrement and the puke of partially digested food released from sliced entrails. A mist of fire-vaporized liquid droplets of human fat puffed across Lewis's body, condensed, leaving an oily coating on his fatigues and the exposed skin of arms and cheeks. Their boots and clothes would stink of this place no matter how often laundered.

The body he stood on jerked and writhed. Completely by nervous reflex, the lieutenant's .45 came up and fired into a preteen boy's bloody face. Lewis sickened, bent over, and added his stomach's contribution to the massacre. In the background, came the involuntary cries of NVA wounded between bursts of machine gunfire.

He heard George shriek. Death in the macaque's world came quickly and didn't hang around to sicken the survivors. Members of the troop vanished in the jaws of leopards or the claws of black eagles. The monkey jerked the leash free, ran and leapt over the heaped dead, finally disappearing into the surrounding woods. Their good luck mascot had deserted.

*

Désirée bolted upright, disconnecting the thousands of micro-thin connections to the Mother-tree. The linen night-wrap fluttered around her thighs as she ran out the bedroom door and down the dark hallway. Would such hellish machines destroy them all? Her heart continued to pound during the dash up the manse's stairway to the third floor and Hugh's room.

She fell and slid the last few feet. Leaping up, her arms slammed open his door. "Afraid! I am scared." She stood at his bedside. "*Je suis effrayée.*"

Hugh closed the switchblade and placed it back under his pillow. One arm raised, sheet and quilt in invitation, Désirée slipped under and pressed against his nakedness. Drawing the covers around them, Hugh shivered as cold, demanding female hands and feet stole his heat. The peppermint perfume of her breath tickled his cheek. Unfettered breasts tight against him transmitted the close-spaced, panic-thump of her heart.

Désirée's gave a last shiver. The goosebumps deflated. In the warm nest of sheet, blanket, and masculine flesh, muscles relaxed. The fear eased. Gathered in strong arms, she felt an instinctive protective aura engulf her. Realizing any threat must pass his defense before reaching her, she snuggled in closer, wiggled arms under and around his chest in a tight hug.

Surprised at how well they fit together, a second realization surfaced. The entity they formed was powerful, more resilient, and intellectually and physically more capable than when separated.

She wondered if it could potentially become more satisfying and emotionally fulfilling. Her experience with men denied it.

First, there was the husband, an inexperienced youth, and product of his time, who took his pleasure from a wooden unresisting, dutiful wife. Their bedroom episodes, lacking in tenderness and compassion, ceased entirely after the birth of two children. Greatly relieved to be released from the burden, Désirée offered no objections to his frequent trips to the brothels and whorehouses, behavior common to the Victorian age of male dominance. Alone and depressed, his death at Gettysburg shattered the thin crust of her composure. Guilt descended. Perhaps, if she had loved him, cared more about him, he would have survived. Emotionally strung out, and hooked on the laudanum that helped her through each day, she collapsed into full-blown addiction, which allowed other men to take advantage of her desolation and misery.

She felt Hugh's body stirring, becoming aroused. A decision needed to be made and quickly. His hands pulled down the linen robe, lips pressed behind her left ear, moved down her neck, and feathered her shoulders. The shivers returned. Her mind wanted to continue, but her body revolted, generated a wave of nausea.

She pushed, separating them. "No. No. Oh, God."

Hugh's body tensed, signaled surprise, then relaxed. His hands and lips withdrew from what he sensed as rejection – not what she wanted. The sessions with the sex therapist had convinced her rational mind that men and women could form desirable, durable relationships. However, her body, the animal shade, remained unconvinced. Increasing the space between them, she rolled over on her back. In the silence and dark, she pleaded, help me, *Aidez-moi*. someone help me. *Soutenez-moi*, I want this. I cannot deal with the loneliness any longer. This is my last opportunity.

Désirée felt her back and side prickle as the Mother-tree's hair-thin cilia entered her pores. In a great upwelling of light and rainbow color, the spirits of her female ancestors and descendants flowered in her mind. Their confidence and determination dissolved the demon of badly conditioned youth, banished hesitation and fear. Mother-tree chemicals and hormones flooded her veins.

The mental block replaced with anticipation, Désirée drew Hugh to her.

He remained silent and unmoving, body language projecting bewilderment. Hands remained inert at his side, arms, chest, hips, and legs stiff and unresponsive.

She grasped his wrists and placed his hands on her waist. He remained reluctant, unmoving. A moment of panic, she thought, what else can I do?

A chuckle emerged from the relatives sharing her mind. An idea formed in the collective consciousness. Becoming the aggressor, Désirée pulled Hugh's head down. A kiss, the tip of her tongue emerged to lick where lips met lips, and then pushed between teeth to probe deep in his mouth until tongue met tongue. The taste like sugar and pepper combined. She sighed as his tongue followed hers back.

Its thrust a sweet prediction of what was yet to come.

Two pairs of hungry nostrils inhaled Mother-tree augmented male and female pheromones. Hugh's palms traced slow swirls up her arms then progressed to sides and hips. Her fingers spread and kneaded his back. Hugh's lips moved to her nipples, evoking a spasm of pleasure new to her experience.

Désirée's female mind-companions moaned and whispered advice. Her hands moved down, massaged slim male hips, and cupped his flesh. Mother-tree released endorphins flushed into the lovers' circulatory systems. Kisses loosed vines of fire between her breasts and down her stomach. Heart contractions doubled. Her body reacted in strange ways, knees came up, cradling her lover. The personalities inside her writhed, their anticipation filled her – became her anticipation. Hands stroked her calves and inner thighs, tested her readiness. The visitors inside exuded an electric tingle.

This was normal. A river of rightness and assurance touched every atom. Désirée knew this was what should happen. She needed to feel this way. A last cogent thought danced among the delighted laughter of her forbearers and descendants – *Je suis libre*. I am free!

The way of bodies took over, the joining a joyful ravenous movement. Contractions generated budding ripples of elation. The female spirits moaned. Their voices raced into syncopation with the world's oldest rhythm. Time defeated, Désirée let crashing waves go on and on, building and building.

Gasping at the peak of tension, a hesitation, then she leaped. Deep inside Désirée's core, a blossom spun open and blazed. It produced tremors of shuddering bliss. The sensation grew, hurdled to a glorious height, and then diminished. Her rasping contralto groan echoed from the throats of the others. A small scrap of Désirée's rationality said, No, do not let it stop now.

But it was only the beginning. Out of the expended rapture of the first joyous husk rose a second explosive seizure. Nerve synapses snapped shut. A clutch of fire filled her, billowed out into her arms and legs. Hands grasping her partner's back squeezed into fists whose nails drew blood. Legs kicked. Toes curled. Over five hundred years of de Gracie women chorused in an eclectic warbling howl of ecstasy.

Désirée lay panting, the first afterglow she had ever experienced, leaving her relaxed and at peace.

The lovers remained joined.

He made a movement.

No way she was going to give up this sensation. Legs locked around his hips held him in place. She arched her back and stretched under him like her kitty, Spanish Cat, and decided to savor the feeling for as long as it would last. A part of her mind wondered how much time it took for a man of Hugh's age and physique to recover. She had a lot of catching up to do.

9

I have seen the task that God has given to mortals to keep them occupied.

Ecclesiastes 3:10

A PROCESSION OF THREE DE GRACIE MEN descended stone stairs and passed through the second level storerooms beneath the chateau. Aubert led, holding a bright LED lantern. Uncle Frank brought up the rear swinging another battery-powered lamp. Shadows of the men and their legs projected on the wall by the moving light blended together.

A stunted one-dimensional centipede creature with rippling feet kept pace with the party. Between the two men marched a stiff-legged and impatient Hugh.

"I know you feel the pressure of the coming attack, but there are things you need to know in case something happens to your Uncle and I. Besides, preparations are complete. Any last-minute fussing will only confuse things," Aubert said as he opened the door to the third level stairway.

"You've never been honest with me," Hugh retorted. "Why start now?"

"When you were young, even at an early age, your goal was to leave us. You had the right to choose that path, but we have not survived the centuries by entrusting full knowledge of the Mother-tree and our relationship to the uncommitted. We will do anything necessary to protect our secrets – our way of life."

Dressed in a green cotton T-shirt and black jeans, Hugh shivered.

Outside, a sunny Indian summer day with a temperature in the low seventies blessed the tan and cinnamon walls and towers of the mansion. In contrast, the lower depths of House de Gracie were below the frost line, where contact with the rock heart of the mountain kept the walls and humid air a constant fifty- five degrees year-round.

"You think I am going to stay here?"

"I believe you're starting to feel– I think you are concluding– that this is your place, your responsibility. Your education, training, and experience in the wider world have all prepared you for this." Aubert gave a thankful quiet prayer to *le bon Dieu* for the love evidenced between Hugh and Désirée, another bond to the family.

Hugh's silence confirmed his hopes. Aubert sensed his son had reconciled with the family, a good first step, but not with him personally. Well, that would not be a problem in a decade or so.

The trio's footsteps echoed down the narrow hallway. The men stopped at the door to the fourth and final level. The lanterns lit up the surface of a door made up of four-inch rough-sawn planks.

The youngest of the three de Gracies ran his fingers over the surface of the wood, its tight grain characteristic of ancient old-growth oak. The black iron-strap hinges and lock-work still showed pockmarks where a smith had hammered out the fittings from bar stock. He tapped a knuckle against its surface. No noise. He guessed the door must be hundreds of years old, the atmosphere of the tunnels slowly petrifying its wood until it would become as solid and impenetrable as the surrounding rock. He turned and noticed no effort on the part of his companions to proceed.

His father spoke. "My son, the first of the major things you must know – fifteen years from now, when the Mother-tree has produced a seed, I will be the one to lead the break-off group to a new location. After the coming battle, all surviving de Gracie women will become fertile. Children born and raised will be divided among those who stay and those who go."

"My God, you mean…"

"Yes, the conflict between us will be ended. You will be left in charge. Adhering to our tradition of secrecy, no one left behind will know where the new colony will be established."

"But those who leave will know where we are."

Aubert unsnapped the ring of keys from his belt and inserted a snaggle-toothed skeleton key into the door lock. "The new Mother-tree will fuzzy-up our memories. While our love for you will remain, we will not be able to return no matter the circumstances."

Hugh set aside further questions and a swirl of emotions, as the door opened and the men descended a dozen steps into a large barrel-vaulted cavern.

Evenly spaced across its center stood thirty waist-high tables, each crowned with a beetle-like carapace formed of metal-framed glass panes in the width and length needed to cover a human body. His first impression: a burial ground, some kind of catacomb, but this wasn't the way the de Gracies handled their dead. Mother-tree roots, the size of his thighs festooned the walls running down to corduroy the floors, then rising to form the support columns and flat tops of the tables. His companions moved him along, the atmosphere in the cavern colder than the higher levels — he guessed low forties — a few degrees above freezing. The men's breath huffed out in white puffs. Hugh raised eyebrows and looked at his father.

Discerning his question, Aubert responded, "The Mother-tree possesses great nets of roots immersed in icy underground streams – heat exchangers, if you will. The chill radiating in the sap circulating in these connected roots absorbs heat, maintaining the preserving cold." He held up both hands, palms upward. "The process lowers the temperature in this chamber another fifteen degrees."

Looking through the glass panels as they passed, Hugh determined ten of the coffin-like containers were empty. Moisture condensed on the others hinted at occupancy. Aubert and Uncle Frank unlatched and removed one cover to disclose a naked, longhaired man whose elongated curved fingernails would not have been out of place in an old Fu Manchu movie. The body was fully fleshed, not a shrunken mummified corpse as Hugh expected. The man's legs twitched, initiating a ripple of contracting muscles that flowed up the pasty white of the body. Hugh stepped back.

"This container," Aubert waved an arm behind him, "and the other occupied platforms, contain relatives. Let me introduce Lewis Clark de Gracie, one of Frank's sons, and to you a cousin."

Hugh broke in, "What the hell is this?"

"In words you will understand, this is a place of suspended animation. One of the most wondrous talents of the Mother-tree is the capability of placing and maintaining humans in stasis. The years roll by, and they age but little."

"What are he and the others doing here?"

"A Vietnam veteran, Lewis was placed here in 1975 because he needed rest and treatment for PTSD. His cure is almost complete. The others are in suspension for a variety of reasons. Diseased ones await cures that do not exist yet, others because they are surplus to the dozen humans the Mother-tree can support. And a few because they wish to time-travel – to awaken in ten years or ten centuries to experience whatever delights and sorrows the future brings."

"So, we have the capacity to produce Rip Van Winkles?"

Uncle Frank spoke in a wistful voice. "I told our leader at the time it was a mistake to let old Rip loose. Fortunately, we were able to confuse the story and it became a fable rather than a believable biography."

"What!" Hugh felt more than a strong sense of shock.

"Well, you know, *mon petit coq*," Uncle Frank responded with a sheepish grin and a Gallic shrug of shoulders, "there is always a little nugget of truth in all the old tales."

Aubert pointed at Frank. "Here is your example of a dedicated time traveler. Tell him."

Frank rubbed his right eyebrow. "I was born in 1431 on my parents' farm near the French village of *Montcorbier*. My uncle *Guillaume de Villion*, a priest, raised me after my father's death, my mother being poor and illiterate."

Completing the math, Hugh said, "You are over five hundred and eighty years old?"

"Let me finish," he pointed to Aubert, "and we will explain. Sent to the University of Paris, I studied hard and played hard, earning a Bachelor of Arts degree and a Masters of Arts. I developed a taste for drink, money, and women as strong as any addict's need for opium. At twenty-four, I killed a man in a tavern fight – good with a blade, as you know. Imprisoned and tortured once for murder and twice for robbery, the authorities always found an excuse to free me."

"Wait, this sounds familiar." Hugh remembered the fevered vision from his train ride home. Whose poetry had he recited in the dream dojo? His subconscious mind had been sending a message. "Villon – François Villon. You? My Uncle Frank is the infamous medieval poet?" Information from school days flooded his mind. "You took the last name of your uncle. I remember the story. A street brawl on top of a robbery got you banished from Paris in 1463, and no one ever saw you again."

"Twenty years after being taken into a French Mother-tree's

family, I left with the colonists, your ancestors, carrying her seed to the New World. I am the last of those."

"But you can't be almost six hundred years old."

"No, he is not," said Aubert. "Your uncle has been awake and active one hundred ten years — a decade here, a decade there — the in-between times have been spent in suspension on one of these tables. And the same is true to a lesser degree with Désirée."

The two men replaced the cover over Lewis and opened the empty capsule next door.

Hugh caught a sparkle of gold thread reflected in the lantern's light. He held up the remnant. Not thread, but hairs, gold-blonde hair the color of Désirée's locks. Shaken, the cold of the room did not keep sweat from appearing on his face and armpits.

"How old is she?" He asked, almost afraid to hear the answer.

"A mere child," Uncle Frank responded, "only twenty-two years active, but one hundred and fifty years asleep with the Mother-tree."

The clues came back to Hugh, his Mother-tree dream of the golden-haired woman in the Civil War era drawing-room, the antique terms that crept into their conversations, and her initial lack of knowledge of modern events and technology. His jaw tightened, tongue grew thick, and he had to ask a question. More afraid than at any time in his life, a stutter broke his first word: "A-a-are we related?"

This is the tricky part, Aubert thought. He must be given the nugget of truth in this tale and no more. *La grand-mère* will know when to tell him the whole truth, if ever. "Yes, of course," Aubert replied. "However, it is of no concern. She is a distant relative, five generations remote."

Muscles Hugh didn't know he'd tensed relaxed. His happiness returned.

🖝

Fitting together spoon fashion, her front to his back, Désirée extended a questing hand under a sleeping Hugh's arm, feeling the sensuous tickle of chest hairs on her forearm. She found his right nipple and rubbed it with a fingertip. It grew hard. Hugh gave out a low hum and wiggled his butt. She rubbed it more. His shoulders begin to twitch. Her fingernails traced a line across his thick pectorals, down his sternum, and into his pubic area. Things had already started to come alive there. He turned and pulled her close. She realized then that nipples on a man do have some value after all.

Two days had passed since her sexual awakening. Given the wartime atmosphere, Hugh's father performed *le cérémonie de marriage*, being among other things, a local justice of the peace. The family jewel vaults provided *une bague de fiançailles*, a diamond and ruby-encrusted engagement ring, and a matched set of *des alliances*, simple gold wedding bands. Uncle Frank, Jonsey, and Margy had played the various roles of father of the bride, best man, and bridesmaid. The certificate had been signed, witnessed, and registered at the Essex county courthouse in Elizabethtown.

Time did allow for the traditional removal by the groom of *la jarretière*, a sexy black, lace-flowered garter. Hugh made sure Jonsey caught the prize. A beaming Désirée tossed *son bouquet* as well, stimulating a swirl of hands and elbows among the de Gracie women. The couples' *voyage de noces* would have to wait upon completion of the nasty business to come. Aubert promised a large formal wedding at a more peaceful later date.

Aubert moved them into a suite of rooms no one had occupied since the year of Hugh's mother's death. Although the knotted silk Persian rugs, dressing table, chairs, armoires, and other furniture had been cleaned and scrubbed, Hugh had dismissed the ensemble as outdated. Désirée, however, thought two rooms of well-preserved Louis Quatorze antiques suited her time and taste, the pieces would have been perceived as the height of luxury during her early life.

Hugh came around a bit after viewing Désirée's leggy *dishabille* poses on the red velvet upholstered chaise lounge. Its high back, a four-foot diameter spread of carved gilded peacock feathers with blue lapis lazuli inserts, framed her short, tousled gold hair and white skin as though in a Goya oil painting. The other pieces were highly decorated with geometric designs picked out in ebony and metal inlay, many also veneered with dark green tortoiseshell. She thought the dressing table a marvel with eight drawers, two with secret latches to safeguard jewelry. Its only flaw, the silver backing on the three hundred and seventy-year-old mirror had begun to peel. On its top rested matching combs, hairbrushes, and cosmetic containers all crafted from tortoiseshell.

A marvelous six by seven-foot bed dated from Elizabethan times. Bare-breasted Greek goddesses were carved into each of the oak end posts and the full headboard supported a wood-paneled top. Rails ran inside the tester, which allowed damask end and side curtains to be pulled to shut off any drafts. Désirée particularly liked the mattress, which was a Mother-tree pedestal growing up from the floor to fill the interior dimensions of the bed, its firm spongy material when activated by body warmth conformed to human curves. She ran a hand over a silk quilt filled with eiderdown.

While she and Hugh had been discovering each other, tension had reached critical mass in the rest of the de Gracie household. Special sound pickups had been installed on the mountaintop. Parabolic antennas focused any sounds coming up the valleys between mountains into pin-drop sensitive microphones. Listeners with earphones operated the positions in four- hour shifts around the clock. The mansion death-bell would be rung when the mics detected the sound of helicopter blades. After countless random drills and exercises, the de Gracies could reach their defensive positions in under three minutes. A scheduled "foxhole jump" was held every morning thirty minutes before sunrise since dawn was the traditional time for an attack.

The guesstimated date of the attack had come and gone, leaving everyone frustrated and resentful of both the enemy and the de Gracie leadership. As professional soldiers, Hugh and Jonsey remained calm, remembering only disciplined and experienced troops managed to make things happen at preset deadlines and even then, strict adherence to a timetable was a rare accomplishment. Fahad was likely having trouble coordinating his never-worked-together-before assemblage of men and machines.

10

He has made everything to suit its time; moreover,
he has given mankind a sense of past and future.
Ecclesiastes 3:11

0615

The attack came early. Audio pickups reported the staccato noise of helicopter blades forty minutes before sunrise. Two separate microphones in two of the arrays caught sound, a faint hum rising from the east and a larger blended collective noise from the north. Hugh's interpretation — a single aircraft, probably a gunship would attack first from the east, hoping the de Gracies would be blinded by the rising sun. It would strafe the landing zone to suppress the defenses for the larger troop-carrying group coming from the north. Given the estimate of speed based on the increasing magnitude of sound, the first gun would be fired in five minutes.

0616

The death-bell clanged. Booted feet made the wooden floors of the mansion rumble. The metal of gun barrels clacked against door jams as people collided at these choke points. Outside, black-clad leaders waved and shouted, directing their helmeted charges into place, moving from position to position to take roll.

Jonsey, in command of the left flank, laughed and sang beneath his breath the repetitive mantra he used to relax before combat. Sweet violets, sweeter than all the roses/covered all over from head to foot/ with shit.

0617

In the center, behind the mansion's great main portico now sealed with a barred cold-iron portcullis, Uncle Frank assembled the reserve, a three-person squad consisting of himself, Margy and Ojas. They would reinforce where needed as the action developed.

"Lock and load," Uncle Frank commanded.

The trio snapped magazines in place and jacked rounds into their weapons, Barretts for the men and a tactical Saiga twelve-gauge shotgun for Margy, its magazine alternately loaded with slugs and buckshot. She sighed, looked at her companions. Besides the assault rifles, they had strapped on pointy-bladed short swords called Arkansas toothpicks and long-handled tomahawks. Ancient warrior personalities revealed, half their faces from hairline to chin were slathered with non-regulation paint of solid white, the other half teal blue. The pair began a ritual warm-up – tugging on shoulder straps and belts, grunting, and punching each other in the chest and stomach. Frank winked at her. He and Ojas filled their lungs with air. Mouths jerked open. Heads went back. A bass-pitched howl emerged racing up the scale to an ear-busting falsetto scream.

Margy shuddered. They had loosed the ancient Mohawk battle cry, reputed to freeze strong men in their tracks. It did not seem to have much effect on strong women, she thought. The two blood brothers hooted, ready now for whatever might happen.

Not needing reassurance, Margy brought her weapon up to port arms and clicked off the safety. She had killed early in her married life.

A memory came to mind of the surprise grimace on the man's face as the shotgun slug blew through the screen door of the isolated farmhouse and tossed him onto the hardscrabble dirt yard. Kicking the shattered remains of the door open, she pumped the Remington twelve-gage and put another round into his chest. A man intent on rape should know his victim better.

She and her supervisor husband Charles were living near Kilgore, deep inside the East Texas Oil Fields. A roughneck fired off the rig decided to get revenge by attacking her. Margy would have left the husk for coyotes, buzzards, and ants, but Charles fetched the Sheriff. Self- defense was the decision. Local men and women treated her with considerably more politeness when the word got around.

0618

Aubert shuffled the last of his fighters into their defensive positions on the right flank, before activating the Mother-tree's buried minefield. He heard Jonsey and Frank report in over the headset mounted in his Fritz-style Kevlar helmet.

The only person he was unsure about was Jeannine. Still too depressed and suicidal to fight, they had moved her to the underground armory for safety, and he had not had time to check on her this morning. He reported his sector ready.

0619

From a bunker atop the central tower, Hugh received ready reports over the radio from the flank units and the central reserve. The MG-42 machine guns sandbagged in the corner towers to his left and right called in green-light readiness. He went over the de Gracie dispositions in his mind once more. The fourteen defenders were spread thin with two each on the tower guns, three in reserve, and the remainder situated in foxholes spread in an outward pointing 'L' shape across the front and left flank of the mansion thornwall. They had anticipated having one more person each on the machine gun teams, but the death of Old Alphonse and his daughter's emotional incapacity scotched the plan.

They had reverted to bluff to appear more numerous. Placed in the windows along the Mother-tree's front, scarecrows and dummies fashioned out of old clothes stuffed with pillows and blankets stood or kneeled armed with black-painted broomstick weapons. Backlighted with battery-powered lanterns they produced threatening silhouettes.

0620

Hugh could now hear the approach of the gunship with the naked ear. Fahad's timing was off. The attack would commence before sunrise, when the light of the sun would have partially blinded the defenders. The fight would be decided one way or the other in the twenty minutes of darkness remaining before full light. He snapped the protective covers off the switches that would activate the firework globe and mine. Green lights showed the electrical circuits to be active. Hugh blinked, what looked like a hunched human shadow moved across the lower part of the thornwall near the front gate. He squinted, but caught no further movement.

A single gunship leaped over the thornwall, door-mounted thirty caliber machine guns sprayed suppressive fire at mansion windows and doors – the first mistake. Titanium netting in the walls and Lexan paned windows absorbed or deflected bullets that, if penetrated, would have hit only scarecrows and mannequins. The real defenders in foxholes and bunkers waited for Hugh's command to fire.

Enemy tracers twisted through the darkness in spiraling hose-like lines as they tattooed the walls of the Mother-tree. Ejected from the helicopter cargo bay, small shapes spun out to thunk on the earth or bounce off the mansion's ramparts before exploding and flinging shrapnel to rattle against the walls and thump into sandbags. The chopper roared over Hugh's head. It would have time for one more pass before the jihadi-carrying slicks landed on the front grass.

Hugh shouted into the radio, "Lock and load! They don't have rockets. Keep your heads down. We'll fire when the *jihadis* come in for a landing."

He looked through the firing port to his left, night vision binoculars searching for the next wave. For maximum effect, the fireworks defense must be triggered at a moment when the troop-carrying choppers would not be able to veer off and yet not so late that it wouldn't catch them still in the air.

The howl of turbines from the mic pickups became so loud it hurt his ears. Chopper blades appeared over the top of the north thornwall. Hugh slapped the switches activating the fireworks. Plastic mortar tubes chugged and barked. A fusillade of eight, ten, and twelve-inch shells arced up over the open area in front of the mansion, propellant charges set to loft them five hundred to one thousand feet. At ground level, the massive pyrotechnic cake began its program with twenty-foot high fountains of blazing silver and gold earthbound fireballs.

The descending troop-carrying slicks moved across the vision port in Hugh's bunker: momma duck, papa duck, and three fat baby ducks flapping along in single file. The first of the sky shells burst. Four hundred to six-hundred-foot diameter globes of red, blue, and green blossoms merged to dome the sky.

"Guns free, I say again, guns free. Pour it on!"

Fire from the de Gracie machine guns in the towers hosed down the lead and rear aircraft. Barretts stuttered from foxholes and bunkers, muzzle flash and tracers lost in cascades of flaming powdered metal. The fire from both legs of the reverse 'L' bunkers crisscrossed, creating a merciless kill sack.

Horsetails and pillars of powdered copper, iron, and cobalt mushroomed and volcanoed in plumes five to sixty feet high across the grass expanse. In combination with the aerial bursts, they created a great crucible of flame. Combatants on both sides tore off useless night vision devices.

Pilots of the incoming helicopters became disoriented and lost sight of the ground. The first chopper smacked into the grass. Its right-side landing strut broke off. Belly sheet metal screeched against the earth, blades leaned to one side and chopped turf. The large surface area of the aircraft slid across the ground and triggered a Mother-tree stinger. Underground roots tensioned like catapult springs launched an eight-foot long shaft of iron-hard wood. It pierced the cargo floor, then the roof, poking into the still revolving rotors. Two blades broke off. The third chopped against the now fractured lance. The turbine engine belched a ten-foot flare of flame then stopped with a grinding noise.

In the aircraft, Fahad's men hesitated to leap out into clouds of metal embers that burned exposed flesh. They slapped and rubbed sparks off bare forearms and necks. Explosions of black powder and Pyrex added to the buzz-saw din of automatic weapons, damaged eardrums, and made verbal communication impossible. Nostrils wrinkled with the rotten egg smell of sulfur.

Crystals of potassium nitrate soured tongues, gritted against teeth. Men tumbled out of the helicopter cargo doors. Disoriented ones stumbled into bullet streams.

Hugh felt elated, the *jihadis'* attack became disrupted. Five choppers had landed, one more than he anticipated. The last one, crosswise in the right angle of the 'L' shaped ambush caught bullets from both legs. Out of its ten-man lift, two or three survived, now returning fire with their AK's. Good but bad, the remains of the chopper blocked the sightlines and targeting of his folks in the small leg of the 'L'.

The next Huey's troops had dismounted but lay pinned to the ground.

His eyes moved on.

Hugh gasped as yard-long gun barrels flared out of the cargo bay of the third aircraft. "Jesus!" He shouted into his helmet-mounted mic. "They've got fifties!"

Fahad had surprised them with what could be a knockout punch. The middle chopper contained no ground troops. Instead, a pair of pintle-mounted fifty caliber machine guns raked the front of the Mother-tree. Thumb-sized armor-piercing bullets punched through walls and windows, penetrated interior petitions, and blew out the back, not stopping until they ricocheted off the heart-rock of the mountain. Uncertain of the location of the defenders' fire, their crews sprayed the front of the building trying to gain fire superiority.

Hugh knew they would soon spot the de Gracie's tower-positioned heavier weapons.

Next to him in the bunker, Désirée leaned on one elbow, loading a fresh magazine into her sniper rifle. She had been taking out pilots. The helicopters would not be lifting again.

He grabbed her wrist. Shouted in her ear, "Middle chopper, crew-served heavy machine guns."

She nodded and brought the weapon down, snuggling the stock into her cheek and shoulder. The flaring light required the use of open iron sights. Gaining a sight picture, she squeezed off a round.

Hugh saw the left gunner's head snap back. The fifty's muzzle went dark and dipped.

Hands pulled the wounded man back and the gun began firing again. This time in tandem with its twin, they raked the machine gun bunker on the right tower. The combined thousand rounds a minute chewed through the crenelated parapet and into the bunker. In a wind-milling spray, Hugh identified splintered baulks of timber, sandbags, human bodies, and the barrel of the MG42 blow off into the air. Relieved from the tower's rain of bullets, the surviving jihadis from the first two choppers rushed the mansion's south face.

Hugh keyed his radio. "Uncle Frank, they are about to turn our right flank. Hold with your reserve or they will roll us up." He thought he heard, "Roger, wilco."

The intensity of the fire from the enemy's center slowed, Désirée had nailed another gunner. Again, the triggerman was quickly replaced.

"Shit," he cursed aloud. The gunship overhead was starting another pass. They'd be machine gunned from the ground and the air. He lifted his Barrett.

This time the armed chopper roared in from the north. Fireworks continued to crack and burst, shaking the aircraft as it made its pass. Hot powdered metals sucked into the turbine engine's air intakes melted on its fuel injectors. A nervous pilot yawed his sputtering, slowing machine. A ten-inch firework shell fresh out of the mortar tube flipped through the cargo door, smacked the ceiling, bounced off the back wall, and lodged behind the copilot's seat. Ignited seconds ago by the lift charge, the delay fuse in the passfire tube set off the twelve-pound main explosive.

The helicopter lit up like the inside of a Chinese lantern.

Hugh's mouth dropped. For a second, he could see the face of each crewmember.

Men started screaming as burning metal powder entered nostrils and lungs, melted eyes, and set clothes on fire. An unguided missile, the aircraft veered off to crash and embed itself in the top of the outer thorn wall. Blades swept down to break and shatter against the dense interlocked wood. Crew members flew out of the interior to be impaled like shrike's prey on the dagger-length thorns, arms and feet thrashed, jaws stretched open – their incoherent bawling inaudible against continuing weapons' fire and exploding black powder fireworks shells.

Hugh froze, goggle-eyed.

The pyrotechnic displays reached their peak. Cascades of silver and gold mushroomed from ground and sky. Amber tracers and fist-sized fireballs from roman candles raced at crazy angles bouncing and spinning. Bengal flares emitted plumes of red, orange, and yellow.

Everywhere within the giant globe of raging embers and rippling veils of powder smoke, men ran, crawled, and leaped – writhing devils from hell seeking the damned.

Wet, fresh blood pools from the dead and wounded reflected the riot of color.

It was the most beautiful and hideous scene he had ever witnessed. Someone wanted his attention. He couldn't respond. Hands shook him. "Go away," he shouted. He looked out. The middle chopper gunners walked the fire of their terrible fifties up the central tower towards him and Désirée. Leafy fragments and fist-sized chunks of the mother-tree spewed out directly under their position.

Husband and wife would be dead in seconds.

A flicker of motion at the base of the thornwall caught his eye. He remembered seeing a human-sized shadow near there before the attack. Unnoticed by gunners focused on the target to their front, a camo blanket wrapped person jumped up and ran towards them. Hugh thought the face familiar, but the body was too stocky and thick around the middle.

The face! It was Jeannine. Nearing the back of the enemy aircraft, she threw off her cover.

Hugh screamed, "Oh, Jesus!"

Duct-taped around her mid-section were the five captured champagne bottle-bombs. She held a detonator switch in one hand.

"No! No!" A memory of baking day in the kitchen. Their fingers interlocked in sticky dough – a soft stolen kiss tasting of cinnamon and honey. Hugh stuck his Barrett out of the firing port and emptied it full auto into the enemy bird.

Jeannine hurdled into the cargo bay. Her arm came down.

The windshield blew off. Flame billowed out of every opening of the Huey. Metal bits, plastic parts, disconnected arms and legs spewed out. The tail section bent like a pipe cleaner. One of the eighty-pound fifties clanged off the front portcullis, spun, and stabbed its barrel into the ground. The chopper burned. Ammunition cooked off. A series of secondary explosions sent out a spiked witch's wig of fiery tracers.

Hugh crumpled to the floor sobbing.

One foot below his position, the last-fired fifty-caliber bullet hole oozed Mother-tree sap.

🍃

Uncle Frank, Ojas, and Margy took positions in the dark kitchen. Fortunately, the enemy attack on the right flank had been delayed. The gunship's earlier aerial bombs had liberated the de Gracie livestock. Miniature sheep, donkey, and carriage horses had panic-thundered out of the broke-doored barn and torn across the lawn scattering the advancing eight attackers. The ram, more angry than frightened, attempted to round up his ewes. Strange men kept getting in the way. He lowered his head, ran, and every muscle straining butted one of the intruders directly in the gonads, lifting the man's body a foot off the ground. Feeling much relieved, he turned and pranced off into the smoke.

A second *jihadi* triggered a Mother-tree stinger. The rod sprang upward faster than human eyes could follow. The sharp end entered the man's anus, raced upward, impaled his intestines, stomach, and liver, scraped along the upper spine and exited out the back of his neck. Pinned like a beetle on a specimen board, his nervous system caught up with what had happened. He shrieked and waved arms and legs.

His companions mewed in horror. An experienced *jihadi* shot him and forced the others to move.

Six terrorists entered the kitchen, single file. In dark corners, blue sides turned to the intruders, Uncle Frank and companions waited for their opportunity. They started with the rear of the formation. The tail-end man caught a flash of a white ghost face a second before a cold steel blade punched through his temple. The body was lowered to the floor without a sound.

A *thwock* noise, something sharp hitting something semi-solid, startled the four front-most men. They turned. "Ali, are you there?" A stumbling form stepped forward, a flash from an outside strobe of fireworks passed light through windows, exposing a collapsing man with a strange shaped hatchet embedded in his skull.

The inexperienced fighter behind the leader panicked, flipped the auto switch on his assault rifle, and went full rock and roll, emptying the thirty-round magazine. His spray of bullets chopped down his two rearmost comrades. In the ensuing quiet, broken only by the empty AK's clicking trigger, the two remaining men heard banshee screeches of what could only be daemons of Shaytan. The panicked shooter felt his sphincter muscle relax. Pants filled with excrement. A pint of the liquid portion trickled down the inside of his pant legs. The pair raced back towards the door.

A female silhouette stepped out from behind the kitchen's massive worktable and said, "Welcome to House de Gracie." The shotgun at her hip recoiled four times.

⌒

At the front of the mansion, a kneeling Fahad surveyed the wreckage of the attack. All he wanted was to kill Hugh. He could still do that. The last of the fireworks burned themselves out, but the flames eating three of the helicopters lit up the area. The sun had begun to rise. They needed to get out of there while darkness and shadow would still cover their move. He rallied six survivors. A seventh refused to move and was promptly shot. At his command, an RPG team fired a round into the first floor of the mansion. The explosion opened a man-sized hole.

A sniper from somewhere high up shot the rocket team's loader through the temple.

Fahad signaled the remaining men – they rushed forward.

One stepped into a pit-trap. The ground gave way, and he fell down a twenty-foot deep vertical shaft. Hitting bottom broke both ankles. Dirt in clumps and fine grains rained down the sides of the hole and filled the area around his legs, then waist, then chest. Clawing at the sides increased the fill rate. Too far down to be heard by his preoccupied comrades, he coughed and spat mud as the dirt packed the space around shoulders, neck, and mouth. More dirt dropped. Six inches over his scalp, the surface covering of loose soil gave a last shudder then went quiet.

Stunned and concussed by the proximity of the rocket grenade explosion, men and women occupying foxholes near the mansion failed to stop the jihadi squad. Fahad, the RPG gunner, and a third man entered through the opening into the mansion. Outside came a flurry of shots and yells – a delayed counterattack. Fahad caught a fragment of a crazy song, something about 'sweet vio-lets'.

His men on the exterior would not be following.

The explosive warhead's cone of fire had wrecked the contents of the room and blown a second hole in the inner wall. Fahad thought, all this wood, paper, and cloth, why wasn't it burning? In answer, water continued to spray from the walls, soaking the ruins, puddling on the floor, and trickling down the outside walls to the earth beneath. A broken light flickered overhead. He and a companion slipped through the hole in the back wall, crossed the portico, and disappeared into the garden.

Still, within the room, the RPG gunner felt water leak through his boots, soaking his socks. Pulling a new rocket from his backpack, he inserted it into the steel launcher tube. He lifted it upright.

Deep in the bowls of the Mother-tree the electricity stored in the barrel-sized condenser that fed the broken overhead Tesla coil lamp sensed a path to ground. It discharged. A man-made lightning bolt snapped out of the lamp filament, found the piezoelectric fuse in the tip of the RPG rocket.

A split second before the round detonated the man's brain boiled, bloody steam lifted off the back of the skull. At the speed of light, the electrical charge continued down the terrorist's body and blew off the meaty soles of the man's feet on its way to the ground. The explosion that followed blew out the Lexan windows in the rooms on each side.

❧

"Hugh, Goddamn it! Coup, answer me, come in. Over."

Hugh's ears received Jonsey's radio voice, but his mind did not. On a closed loop, a vision of Jeannine with bottles taped to her body ran and jumped into the Huey. A fireball. It played over and over.

"We have a penetration. An unknown number of jihadi's made it inside. As soon as its daylight, we'll make a sweep of the outside grounds and clean up any left-over enemy. Can you organize your reserve to take out the intruders? Hugh? Over."

Désirée held Hugh's head to her breast, rocking him back and forth.

11

I know that there is nothing good for anyone except to be happy and live the best life he can while he is alive.

Ecclesiastes 3:12

HUGH COULD ONLY STARE into the smoke and fire, his body numb, mind miles away. All physical sensation shut off. If nerves were still firing, he couldn't feel them. Shuffling deformed ghost shapes emerged out of the battlefield's smoldering gray curtains. The first, Specialist fourth class Gruenwald, his blond hair and uniform mud-caked from the fast-current Bosnian river where the pontoon bridge under Hugh's command had collapsed and threw him to his death. Others' shades followed, friends and enemies. Some with faces he remembered, others' ghouls with egg-smooth features, the human detritus of combat. Known and remembered by mothers and family, not by Hugh, his brief contact with them ended with bullet or knife.

A hundred Iraqi villagers, a mixed bag of armed men, women in *hijabs*, and children in shorts, wandered by. Victims of the artillery and airstrikes he had called in during Desert Storm. Hugh's heart stopped then beat again as Sergeant Murphy, the Riddler, sniper-killed in Afghanistan, stepped through the curling mist. She stood to one side and spoke, "What has nine circles? Sorrow without torment. Mute without light.

"Eternal rain, maledict, cold, and heavy. Weights roll back and forth.

"Teeth-torn flesh, mouths gurgle in black mud. Limbs of women, hair of serpents.

"Blood boils poison fruit. Wallow in human excrement,

"Winds freeze ice far from all light and warmth."

A squad of men in loose Afghan clothing stepped forward, interrupting the chant.

Thin Nazim, who would never recite another poem.

Abdul, the farmer, lost to grain fields and domestic animals.

Uncle Maahir scowling and clenching his hands, never to experience again the exhilaration of battle.

Aziz, mouth full of bat excrement, centipede tails wiggling in its mass. The dead Saudi held out his hands, eyes begged. He wanted his *jambiya* dagger returned.

The present caught up, clots of newly dead men filtered forward, rising from twisted positions among the smoldering wreckage to the mansion's front. Three quivered and strained, trying to pull themselves off blood-slick impaling stakes of the stingers. Black-crusted ones, human fat still aflame flopped out of helicopter seats, crawled to join up. On the thornwall, activated corpses ripped muscle and skin from barbs and spikes, fell to the ground, rose, and advanced.

Hugh's soul writhed. So alone, so alone. He had killed so many.

Last of all came the de Gracies, a handful of men and women in black uniform and helmets.

Old Aphonse and Alys limped forward.

The immediate dead – a pair of machine gunners — male and female — and a rifleman.

Then, finally, Jeannine shuffled forward. She raised her arms. Hugh's spirit persona moved – floated towards her. Her face grew larger, filling his vision, torn lips parted. She could not have him in life; she would have him in death.

Hugh felt a shock. His movement stopped. Another shock. Jeannine's face shattered into mirror shards and tears. A third slap to the face wrenched his skull, nerves on the left side of his head and shoulder shrieked. Soul and body reunited. Another whack sent a needle of pain down his neck. He blocked a hand from a repeat slap.

It came from Désirée. Her voice strong, demanded, "You are mine. You cannot leave me. I love you."

Hugh lay on his back. Désirée straddled his hips. Her arm lifted. His hand grabbed her wrist on the down stroke. "All right." He croaked. "I'm back. Thirsty."

A canteen held to his lips produced the Mother-tree's citron cut with dark rum, tasting like all the world's best sweet fruit distilled into nectar. Its formulation of carbs, sugars, and protein energized muscles.

His wife dismounted and stood. Hugh raised an arm. Désirée grasped his hand and pulled.

Hugh let out a half-gasp, half-laugh as scattered pains surfaced throughout his body. Standing on trembling legs, he fussed with his shirt, sweat-glued to back and underarms. A solid bar of light from a risen sun, compressed through the bunker's front-firing port, blinded him. Fingers automatically rose, shielding his eyes.

"How long was I out? What's happening?"

"It's pretty much over out front. Aubert deactivated the Mother-tree's minefield and is in the clinic working on the wounded. Jonsey, the dog pack, and Uncle Frank's forces are cleaning out the last resistance and putting out fires. Two or more of the attackers remain inside, probably in the garden."

Hugh released the GI .45 from a black leather shoulder holster, an extra magazine sheathed in a small pocket on its front. "Stay here. I'll take care of the infiltrators."

"I'm coming. You need backup."

For her benefit, Hugh put on a grin more grimace than smile. It failed to reassure. "Stay here, wife."

She slapped him again.

He shook his head and commanded. "Listen to the radio. Get Jonsey or Frank to send help."

Désirée reached for her rifle.

"Stay here." He pulled her in with his left arm, his right holding the pistol down and away, and emphasized his order with a warm selfish kiss. Her tenderness and enthusiastic response swept the last of the bad memories out of his mind, locked out the spirit world. *I needed that*, he thought. *I wish every order I give a woman could end with a lip-lock.* Releasing her, he eased out of the bunker and started down the stairwell, knees still shaky from the power of the adrenaline-enhanced vision.

Hugh moved in a crouch, stopping every thirty seconds to listen. Light filtered into the garden, but the three-story walls of the mansion still blocked much of the sun's illumination casting long east-to-west shadows. He circled the garden inside the portico, moving from pillar to pillar. The *jihadis* must be holed up in the center, probably behind the thick walls of the maze. No indication yet of their number.

Avoiding open paths, he snaked around trees and low-crawled through beds of sky-blue phlox, fox-tailed decorative grasses, and purple lavender. The plants crushed by his body perfumed his clothes, covering his sweat-stink. As always, the anticipation of immediate combat affected his bladder. He stopped to urinate.

Fingers dug into the freshly moistened dirt and smeared black muddy humus-heavy soil over cheeks and forehead. Approaching the maze walls, he noticed the normal musical trill of the Mother-tree's fountain had changed. Now lower in tone, its falling water made glugging and slapping noises. He figured it loud enough to cover the sound of his movement on the pea-gravel of the labyrinth's corridors.

Keeping his silhouette low, Hugh did a forward roll coming to a stop next to the maze entrance. Still, nothing to see or hear.

If they weren't familiar with mazes, the enemy had a small chance of taking the correct turns to find the middle.

Standing back to the holly wall, he held the forty-five in two hands barrel up, a perfect mime of the combat stance in which he and Jonsey had been trained. The pistol came down, pointed left and then right as he entered the maze. No bad guys in sight. Moving to the right seemed the best strategy. If they had gone left, he might beat them to the center and be waiting. If they had chosen the right, he would at least know they would be positioned at the fountain.

He stopped, listened, and led with the Colt at each right-angle turn. Dropping to the ground before the last opening to the center, he tried to look under the holly wall. Perhaps a glimpse of booted feet would tell him the enemy's location. No openings — no information. He stood and prepared himself for a rolling leap through the last opening.

A grunt of surprise caused him to spin in place.

A strange face behind an AK-47 triggered conditioned reflexes. Hugh's pistol roared, the barrel lifted, then dropped back for a second shot. The first round entered the man's neck, below the larynx. The second round would have entered a quarter-inch higher, making a nice tight grouping of which his advanced training instructor would have been proud.

However, the target's head snapped back allowing the follow-up bullet to shatter spade-shaped front teeth on the way in and neck vertebrae on the way out.

The dead man dropped to his knees.

Hugh heard a shout and felt air pressure on his bare neck. He turned.

Rushing full tilt around the corner, Fahad crashed into him. The impact sent Hugh's pistol and Fahad's AK flying. Locked together, the combined bodies pushed deep into the opposite holly wall. Hugh felt the plant's stickers pinprick his back and arms. It gave him an extra boost. He flung Fahad back, freed an arm, and punched the Afghani in the left kidney.

With a twisted face, his opponent staggered back through the entryway and into the open space around the fountain.

Hugh followed.

The two crouched and stared, eyes broadcasting hate. In his peripheral vision, Hugh noticed the fountain had lost its upper two feet. One of the fifty caliber bullets must have given it a crew cut. The basin at its base now overflowed onto the surrounding slate tiles, making a slippery surface.

Fahad jerked a *Pesh-kabz* Khyber knife from a side sheath. The full tanged eleven-inch blade was razor sharp from its hilt to the point.

Hugh responded. Reaching behind his back, he pulled the sickle-shaped double-edged *jambiya* dagger he had taken from Aziz in the bat-infested cavern.

Fahad's face and green eyes paled as he recognized his departed brother-in-law's property.

Almost as one, the two men leapt forward, knives flashing and rasping together in thrust, parry, and repost. Even drunk with adrenaline, the human body's endurance in hand-to-hand combat lasts only minutes.

Evenly matched, the pair pulled back beyond knife range, lungs pumping.

An unemotional judge in Hugh's head assessed the exchange. Fahad had a six-inch diagonal cut across the forehead. Blood trickled down into his eyebrows and around his temples. He would have to be careful not to be blinded by his own fluid. A sting on Hugh's right forearm disclosed a similar length gash. In an extended fight, the wound might weaken his primary hand. Another reason to be careful. Fahad was a lefty, which automatically allowed his knife inside a right-handed opponent's guard. The critic in Hugh's mind declared the first round to be a draw.

"I have damaged your house and killed your people. Now you die."

"Your attack has been crushed."

"There is a blood debt between our families. If I fail, they will send others. Let me kill you, and perhaps I can convince them to leave the rest of your misbegotten *firangi* kin alive."

Hugh flicked his blade. "Only one response to that. *Bouse tizi!* Kiss my ass!"

The action began again.

This time they managed to get a hand on each other's weapon-wrists. Fahad's straight-bladed weapon was bent upward and out at an angle, Hugh's down and inward. Curved tip, bowed up like a filleting knife, Hugh's blade gave him a positional advantage. Against his opponent's resistance, he pushed the curved tip in and up.

The point and upper edge caught in Fahad's shirt. The tough cloth absorbed the disemboweling stroke, leaving only a long cursive scratch across his belly. The pain seemed to generate a burst of adrenaline. The Afghani threw his opponent off.

The back of Hugh's knees hit the fountain edge. Feet slipped. While he wavered seeking to regain his balance, Fahad locked an arm around Hugh's chest and heaved them both into the water-filled basin. The two thrashed in the three-foot deep pool. Hugh smacked Fahad's wrist against the Mother-tree-formed stone seat circling the basin. The Khyber knife flew off. Fahad bit Hugh on the wrist. His blade fell, lost in water mixed with debris.

The pair revolved in the fountain, two sharks circling and rolling. Waves crashed over the edge. Fingernails and teeth opened wounds. The water took on a pink tinge.

Hugh's legs twisted together.

Fahad's hands found his head and neck, pushed him underwater, and pinched off his air. Hugh shoved. He arched his back, but couldn't throw off his opponent or get his head above water.

Fahad sat on his opponent's locked-together legs.

Hugh could exert no leverage. Hands free, he punched his enemy's kidneys and stomach. Resisted by the water, lacking the additional power and weight of his body, the blows had limited effect. His body was in diving reflex, which like dolphins and seals, allowed the body to conserve oxygen. But air was running out. Normally able to hold his breath five minutes or more, the high burn rate of oxygen exhausted in hand-to-hand combat had already left him short.

He let some air bubble out of his lungs – tricking his body into thinking a breath was forthcoming, delaying the breathing muscles' desire to spasm. Using his father's relaxation techniques, he reduced his body's need for air and forestalled its automatic reaction to gasp.

Everything he did only slowed the inevitable by seconds. His hands rose and grabbed handfuls of Fahad's shirt. Hugh's still-twisted legs moved into the Afghani's crotch and pushed him forward. The combined effect of hands and legs rocked the upper man's head into the fountain shaft.

He had waited too late, the move not powerful enough to stun or knock the *jihadi* out. Air gone, muscles all over Hugh's body shook and seized. Lungs burned. His open eyes caught one last look at Fahad's distorted face above the water. A smile of green-eyed triumph began to replace a contorted scowl of hate. Contracting irises spiraled Hugh into darkness.

12

Indeed, that everyone should eat and drink and enjoy himself, in return for all his labors, is a gift from God.

Ecclesiastes 3:13

HUGH STOPPED RESISTING. He lay supine, flat against the fountain bottom. Any second gasping mouth and nostrils would fill his lungs with water. He willed peace into each atom of his corpse. Death rushed in, offering freedom from dreams and respite for the spirit.

As much as he desired the release, it wasn't going to happen. The faux-stone fountain being part of the mother-tree, he felt hundreds of thousands of her cilia pierce cloth and enter pores everywhere his body touched — scalp, back, buttocks, thighs, and calves. Oxygen infused into tissues, turning hemoglobin in capillaries red. Carbon dioxide was extracted; the whole process something plants do as well or better than humans. Her waste product became his salvation and his, her treat.

Oxygenated blood back-flowed into veins and arteries, bypassed lungs, which, for the moment, became useless, empty sacks. Endorphins injected into his bloodstream erased his depression, elevated his mood. He wondered how long it would take before his enemy figured out this drowning thing wasn't working.

The water about him quivered, Fahad's body shook, and then shook again. Hands released. The weight of his body fell off.

Hugh's head and chest breached the surface of the bloodstained water. Next to him, a dazed Fahad tried to sit up. Désirée stood knee-deep in the fountain, her rifle butt jacked back and snapped down on the Afghani's head for the third time.

Realizing he was okay, she said, "I told you– you needed backup." The *yous* were emphasized with another up and down butt stroke.

Hugh took a huge breath, reactivating his lung. "Well, I probably didn't need it quite as much as you might think. Nevertheless, I am grateful, my love. You can quit pummeling the man. He needs some brain left to question."

❧

The smell of cinnamon rolls glazed with melted sugar covered the ammonia and vinegar odors leftover from the intensive scrubbing the kitchen had received. The removal of six bodies and the fluid and pieces of them scattered by knife, tomahawk, and shotgun had received first priority in the cleanup following the battle.

House de Gracie survivors needed hot food. Five de Gracies and Jonsey sat on one side of the central worktable. Men and women poured sugar and milk on bowls of steaming homemade oatmeal spiked with raisins made from the mountain's wild Labrusca grapes.

Hugh took three quick spoonfuls. "We can eat while we talk. There's a hell of a lot of work before us. Jonsey, what's our security situation?"

"Over the last twenty-four hours, we've swept the battlefield four times and conducted room-to-room inspections of the mansion. I'm satisfied that there are no enemy combatants unaccounted for. We have a guard duty rooster set up requiring observers in the undamaged two towers around the clock."

Hugh's spoon lifted the last bit of cereal to his mouth. The spoon clicked against the blue flowers painted on the interior of the empty porcelain bowl. He grabbed one of the fast disappearing rolls from a tray. "Do we have a final body count?"

"Kind of hard to tell. Some of the jihadi's were in bits and pieces." Jonsey paused a moment, then continued. "Our best estimate – the four troop-carrying slicks contained ten men and two pilots each for a total of forty-eight. The gunship — two crew-served 7.62 caliber machine guns and two pilots — six personnel. And the close support chopper, the one with the twin fifty-caliber guns, contained eight counting pilots. Total attacking force numbered sixty-two."

"Father, what's the count on casualties?"

Aubert took another sip of honeyed tea. "All wounded are secure in the *valetudinaria*. We are keeping three surviving enemy immobilized and under sedation. One is in a coma, tomahawk cut to the head, and will be euthanized today. The second is a puzzle. No wounds, but his testicles are swollen to the size of grapefruits. I cannot deduce how that happened. Fahad is fine. Remarkably, I have determined he possesses one of the two recessive genes needed to talk to the Mother-tree."

"Damn, does this mean we might be related?"

"Possible, but thousands of years distant. The family mythology has mother-trees originating in the Middle East eons ago. If so, the gene would be more widespread there."

Hugh's thoughts returned to more practical matters. "We need to discover and neutralize his Saudi bankrollers. Fahad's expedition, counting all men, materiel, and logistics must have cost over two million dollars. Will his genetics make it easier to interrogate him?"

Aubert gave a thumb's up sign. "Certainly. The Mother-tree is already sampling and recording his memories. With only one of the genes, they'll be blurry and in black-and-white, but readable."

"So, out of sixty-two attackers, only three survived? How can that be? What about our casualties?"

"When we swept through the battleground, we gave mercy to any *jihadis* with wounds, about a third of their original number, through morphine overdoses. Injections large enough to fell an ox. They drifted into sleep, never to reawaken. A few of the lesser-wounded attempted to resist and were shot."

Hugh's expression turned sour. This was not how he had been taught to treat enemy wounded in the army.

His father noticed the emotion. "As our French ancestors said, '*qui sème le vent récolte la tempête*', who sows the wind, reaps the whirlwind. We do not let attackers live to use up our resources or escape to communicate what they have learned about us." Aubert moved on. "Our dead so far consist of Alphonse, Jeannine, René and Élise who were the left flank tower machine gun crew, and Gustave, one of our foxhole soldiers. We also lost a horse, two sheep, and Bonaparte, a second dog."

"*Nos blessés*, our wounded?"

"Light. Shrapnel gashes, a busted eardrum, and one leg wound — your Uncle Frank took an AK round in the calf — nothing the Mother-tree's ministrations cannot cure within the week. We began this war with sixteen actives and now are reduced to eleven."

Hugh tilted his head and looked at Uncle Frank with a wrinkled forehead.

His uncle gave a Gallic shrug of his shoulders, and mumbled through a mouthful of cinnamon roll, "It is a through and through. *Pas de probléme*. I am exuberantly copasetic."

Hugh made a mental note to take away Frank's dictionary.

Margy put a hand on his shoulder, refilled his coffee cup, and whispered in his ear. "*Au contraire*, he and Ojas are both feeling down because I outscored them on kills."

"Okay. Lessons learned? Jonsey, your analysis."

"Things we did correctly were surprises and force magnifiers consisting of the fireworks artillery, home turf advantage, and the minefield. Errors were not enough heavy weapons, no defense against their close-support fifties, and too few fighters."

Désirée finished buttering a roll and waved her knife. "But we won," she volunteered. "The fog of battle generated through the fireworks dome, our ambush, and the mines kept Fahad from organizing his men and attacking us in strength. In the first minutes of confusion, our MG 42's and Barrett's took out over forty percent of the attacking ground force. The remainder we handled in bits and pieces." Her enthusiasm waned. "Even so, without the lucky shell burst inside the gunship and Jeannine's sacrifice, it's likely we would have been overrun. We can't count on such fortune next time."

Jonsey glanced out the kitchen windows and checked his watch. "Now, if you'll excuse me, I need to check on the status of the smudge pots we've got burning outside to hide the battlefield from aerial and satellite observation."

Hugh waited until he left, pushed back his chair, crossed an ankle over his knee, and took a sip of coffee. "What's the status of Mother-tree damage?"

Margy straightened in her chair, brushed back a gray-shot lock of hair, and as the official housekeeper reported. "Wounds that broke her bark damaged food and water conducting tissues. As with most plants, the small penetrations will seal and then heal. The extensive damage to the south tower and the two large holes blasted in her sides may make her susceptible to bacterial and fungal infections."

"What's your prescription?"

"We need to build scaffoldings of living tissue taken from elsewhere in her body to build bridge-grafts across the openings. We will use the same technique to construct a framework to recreate the tower top complete with crenellations. Otherwise, she will seal off the edges of the wounds and the injured areas will never reform in their original configuration. Once the cellulose transplants are in place, they need to be covered with nylon window screening to keep off the bugs and plaster to keep out the elements. This needs to be done immediately. The many dead deposited into the Mother-tree's root system with the addition of balancing chemicals should stimulate rapid growth in the spring. But it will be three to five years before she will regain her former beauty."

"All right," Hugh said, pulling a spiral-bound notebook and pencil stub from his shirt pocket, "I want a command group consisting of myself, father, Uncle Frank, Margy, and Jonsey to meet at this table every morning at 0600. We will plan and review progress."

Hugh entered items in his notebook as he spoke. "First things first. Uncle Frank will supervise a work detail to give all enemy bodies and parts to the Mother-tree. These cool late October nights help, but it won't be long before the stench, insects, and the possibility of disease will make it unhealthy for the living. While you are at it, recover all weapons and live ammunition. Store them temporarily in the armory. Keep our dead in the underground third level cold suspension area until we have time for a proper ceremony."

Nods of agreement followed.

"Margy, select assistants," Hugh went on. "Do what needs to be done to repair the Mother-tree."

He turned to his father. "Aubert, select two helpers and awaken enough sleepers to refill our ranks. Make sure Lewis Clark de Gracie is one of them. We'll need our own helicopter pilot to lift out the remains of Fahad's choppers."

Aubert nodded, looking impressed by Hugh's strategizing.

"Jonsey will be in charge of logistics. Father, set up a checking account for his use." Looking around the table, Hugh addressed the group in general again. "Everyone, submit verbal requests to Jonsey for supplies. We have no time for paperwork." Hugh imagined his friend's greedy grin when he heard he would have *carte blanche.* "The sergeant-major will also set up schedules for guard and kitchen duty – to include all of us."

More nods from those present.

"Another thing, we are through with defensive tactics. One way or the other, we will be taking the initiative – striking back. In the meantime, an old army expression applies. For the next two days, all I want to see are elbows and assholes."

Next morning, the leading family members met for status reports and their next planning session.

Hugh slid a ham and cheese omelet out of a frying pan onto a plate. He handed it over the kitchen table to Aubert. "Okay, who's next?"

Désirée spoke, *"Poivrons verts, oignons, fromage suisse pour moi, s'il vous plaît."*

Hugh repeated the order: "omelet with green peppers, onions and Swiss cheese–"

She smiled. "Oh, yes and drizzle some caviar on top – not the red stuff, the black."

He glanced over his shoulder with an exasperated look.

His wife's wide grin greeted him. "Okay," she said, graciously waving a hand, "drop the caviar."

His face relaxed into a smirk. It was his day for kitchen duty. He added oil to the frying pan, ladled in beaten eggs, then opened the oven to check on trays of biscuits. The smell of sausage gravy bubbling on the stovetop mixed with the fragrance of baking bread.

Two helpers clattered out plates and silverware, pitchers of *citron,* milk, and coffee.

Hugh folded the browning omelet and turned to face the command group. "We're into day three. What's our progress?"

"We have completed phase one of cleaning the battlefield," Uncle Frank said. "Only the husks of helicopters are left." He looked out the window at the curtains of soft rain, drenching the grass. "The weather is helping wash away traces of battle."

"The resurrected ones are doing well and should be available for duty in three to four days," Aubert reported, shuffling a handful of three-by-five cards then referred to them as he continued. "Besides Lewis, we have awoken Ahladita, Frank's original Mohawk wife, an excellent cook and organizer." Aubert waved a hand. "An additional benefit, she will bring your wild uncle under control. *Les autres* include Gaston, a language expert, actual age forty-five, asleep with the Mother-tree on and off since 1830. A midshipman aboard the USS Philadelphia, he was captured by the Barbary pirates during the American naval blockade of Tripoli in 1803, ransomed back fifteen years later. He speaks Turkish and Arabic fluently. We woke him after 9/11 for two years to assess the terrorist threat, so he is reasonably up-to-date."

Hugh glanced several times at his father as he continued to list off the several family members.

"Aimée, a farmer and gardener, thirty-five, received her baccalaureate degree in agriculture from the University of Pennsylvania in 1870. Declared surplus to our needs nine years later, awakened in 1960 to receive her master's degree in animal husbandry and returned to Mother-tree sleep immediately after."

Hugh poked at the sizzling skillet, trying to take note of each one and write them to memory.

Aubert continued, "Valentina, weaver, chemist, and jewelry maker, twenty-four, apprenticed at Tiffany's. Declared surplus to our needs in 1945, then resurrected in 2006 to receive her doctorate in chemistry – returned to suspended animation two years ago."

Frank leaned forward and pointed at Aubert. "Don't forget about Bertrand."

"Ah, yes. Bertrand, twenty-five, hunter extraordinaire, weapons expert, and veteran of the Spanish-American War in Cuba and the Philippine Insurrection. A time traveler, his request to sleep with the Mother-tree granted in 1909."

Hugh flipped Désirée's eggs onto a plate and slid it down the table. Using the tails of his double-linen apron, he pulled trays of gold-brown confections out of the double ovens and placed them on cooling racks. "Anyone for biscuits and gravy?"

Jonsey raised his hand. "Not as desirable as SOS, but it'll have to do."

"What is this SOS?" Désirée asked.

"An excellent military food served in mess halls and field kitchens for the last one hundred years," Jonsey expounded, "known in full as Shit on a Shingle. The dish consists of a piece of toast — the shingle — covered with a bland white gravy, crumpled hamburger mix. Also known in some circles as 'Same Old Stuff' or 'Save Our Stomachs.' The addition of the cooked meat turns the gravy corpse-skin gray." The sergeant-major wiggled his eyebrows. "If you don't look at it too close on the way in, it's quite tasty, especially with lots of hot sauce and pepper."

Hugh spatula-loaded biscuits into a basket, filled a large gravy bowl, and set them on the table.

Jonsey retrieved and broke apart two biscuits, slathered them with butter, and ladled out sausage-specked white gravy to be topped with a quarter bottle of red Louisiana hot sauce.

Kitchen helpers and the group at the table stopped to stare.

"You can always tell a man who's found a home in the army. You're a damned lifer all right." Hugh laughed. "Who's next?"

Jonsey took a bite and swallowed. "It burns so good," he hissed out in a single breath. "Back to our situational progress, Lewis and Ojas will be leaving for Canada tomorrow. They have located a Huey model 214 medium-lift chopper for lease. The aircraft has a sling load capacity of almost 15,000 pounds, more than enough to lift out the gutted shells of Fahad's helicopters, some of which have burned down to turbines and blades surrounded by piles of powdery ash." Jonsey glanced at Uncle Frank as he continued. "Uncle Frank recommends we deposit the wreckage into an existing fifty-foot deep crevasse on the backside of the mountain. A few sticks of commercial-grade dynamite set off at the top will loose rock and dirt cover. In the spring trees and bushes can be planted to hide the scar."

Margy raised her hand.

Hugh nodded.

She handed him a hand-written report, careful not to look at Jonsey.

His friend frowned and gave him a strained look.

Putting on a poker face, Hugh read it silently.

The bridge-grafts on the holes had been completed. Rolls of soft nylon netting and plaster would be wagoned up from Port Henry this morning. Light brown latex exterior paint will waterproof the plaster casts and blend the patches to match the mansion's color. Work on recreating the tower top would take another three days. Lexan window panels had been ordered to replace those damaged in the battle. Margy had also begun to tease the Mother-tree maze fountain to regrow its top.

He folded the sheet and placed it in his breast pocket. "How is morale? Everyone holding up okay?"

Heads nodded.

Aubert spoke, "We have yet to achieve emotional closure on our losses. But the victory, hard work, and the Mother-tree enhancing our sleep and chemistry has all but one of our people feeling good."

"And what's wrong with the one?"

"Your Uncle Frank is heavy with disappointment that neither one of the fifty caliber machine guns survived for him to play with."

Frank's fingers twitched as he held the imaginary spade grips of a heavy machine gun, his thumbs pushed against an invisible butterfly trigger. "Can we not buy those devil's tools for our use?"

"No promises, *mon oncle*. We'll see when we plan the refortification of the mansion and grounds. Now, Father, any reaction from Port Henry?"

"Only a question from the sheriff, asking if we had a permit to set off fireworks. We didn't, so we will have to pay a fine." Both Hugh and Aubert grinned at this, recalling the extent of the de Gracie fortune. "Besides confusing the enemy, the pyrotechnics covered the explosions and the battle noise. Most local folks will believe that this was just another weird party thrown by the eccentric de Gracies."

Hugh nodded, some of the worry lines in his face relaxed. "And the status on squeezing information out of Fahad?"

"I should have the last of it by lunchtime."

Hugh nodded. "Let's you and I meet at the clinic at 1500."

13

I know that whatever God does lasts forever; there is no adding to it, no taking away. And he has done it all in such a way that everyone must feel awe in his presence.

Ecclesiastes 3:14

HUGH STOOD IN THE HALLWAY of the first level basement. Holding up a lantern, he noticed for the first time the word *valetudinaria* carved into the gray rock over the door of the combination clinic and med lab. He wondered why the family used the name of roman military hospitals dating from 100 BCE. Almost every day he discovered de Gracie cultural anomalies, traces of which petered out in historical dust.

Perhaps they were part of the curse or blessing of inhabiting a creature whose life span could stretch out for thousands of years. Hugh had read of non-symbiotic trees, such as bristle cone pines, yews, and chestnuts whose age exceeded four thousand years. On that scale, the family tree, so young at five hundred years, still left his extended human life, twice the normal, a mere flash. Hardly time enough to wave hello and goodbye to such a long-lived entity.

Unlatching the iron-studded oak door, he entered and found Aubert standing next to a pedestal upon which a supine Fahad lay in a Mother-tree induced coma, eyes closed, straps buckled across neck, chest, waist, and legs.

"Father, before we start on the terrorists, I need to talk about Jonsey. Can he become a permanent part of the family?"

"He is a hero, a man of merit, but I have already checked. Jonsey does not have the recessive genes."

"We owe him. I owe him. We have shed blood together. He could be a productive part of our group."

"Yes, but he would remain an outsider. His memories and experiences cannot be recorded by the Mother-tree to enrich our library – add to our survival. Nor could he be allowed to breed with de Gracie women. Any offspring would become second-class citizens. We cannot afford a permanent underclass. His life with us would surely turn bitter."

"Is there nothing we can do?"

"A similar dilemma faced me after my service in the Korean war. My best friend, Doctor Alfred Jeskie, who you met at the Army hospital in Germany, could not be permitted to join us for the same reasons. However, we can give the gift of an extended healthy life."

Hugh started at this. "I wondered at the time how the Colonel, a contemporary of yours, in his eighties, could still be on active duty."

Aubert smiled. "Well, I am sure the old fox has found ways to fiddle with his 201 file. However, the Mother-tree and I have already done some preliminary work on Jonsey. He has another two weeks leave coming, yes?"

Hugh nodded.

"In that time, we will take care of several things we have discovered. Your friend is HIV positive. He also has the beginnings of prostate cancer. You boys must pay the consequences with your passion for loose women and exposure to the chemicals and radiation of modern weaponry. We will eradicate those before he departs." Aubert smiled then continued. "In addition, we can ameliorate an old knee injury, which has not healed well. If you can get him to visit periodically, we can give him over a hundred fully-functioning years. Besides giving him a cash bonus, it is all we can offer. May this be reward enough?"

At a rap on the door, the two men turned their heads. "Come in," Aubert said.

Gaston de Gracie entered, nodded to Hugh. "I have assembled the information you requested. It is a compilation of Fahad's memories, general internet information, and stolen classified U.S. State Department assessments I purchased from Wikileaks."

Hugh took a minute to give Gaston a close look over. The man's fiery red hair stuck out in clumps and cowlicks, resistant to comb and brush. Frequently the case with this coloration, a cloud of freckles dotted cheeks and neck. Pale green eyes peered through a pair of oval-cut wire-rim Franklin reading glasses. This configuration was unusual for de Gracie's, who normally ran blond to light brunette hair and blue or brown eyes. Of average height for the 1800's, about five-six, Hugh thought the cousin looked comfortable in a blue and gray flannel checked shirt and jeans.

Noticing Hugh's study, Aubert said, "His mother was Irish."

"And never received into the protection of this family," Gaston injected.

"Gaston's father married an outsider without permission. After his birth, she ran off, leaving him to be raised by his father and, I'm sorry to admit, by de Gracies of the period that refused to fully accept him."

"To relieve me from this house of gloom, father got me a berth as a cabin boy aboard a merchant ship at age twelve. I had been around the horn three times before the piracy of American vessels caused Congress to establish the first serious United States Navy and build the heavy frigates that became famous in our history."

"Tell me of your capture," Hugh said.

"Given my experience, the family's influence, and a bit of gold passing hands, at sixteen years of age, I received the senior midshipman post aboard the *USS Philadelphia*, 1300 tons and thirty-six guns, when she was recommissioned in 1803. We left in April, passed Gibraltar in August, and fought our first action, capturing the twenty-four-gun Moroccan ship-of-war *Mirboka* and retaking from the pirates the American brig *Celia*."

"If I remember my history, the Philadelphia ran out of luck in Tripoli Harbor."

"Right you are, Master Hugh. We ran aground while on blockade duty. Our Captain Bainbridge had us throw all the guns and excess equipment overboard. We even cut down the foremast. In spite of all our efforts, we remained stuck fast. Surrounded by Tripolitan gunboats, the ship surrendered. Three hundred Americans became slaves."

"How did you survive?"

"They worked us during the day dragging blocks of stone to reinforce the harbor defenses or cleaning out city sewers. Poorly fed, and beaten for any infraction, or perceived infraction, we still rejoiced when a month later our people recaptured the Philly and burned her to the water line. The enemy would not have the use of her. Yet another horror faced us when a fireship loaded with six tons of gunpowder sent by our American forces to destroy the enemy fleet exploded prematurely. We captives were forced to watch while the Tripolitans fed the dead bodies of the crew to packs of dogs."

Shoulders slumped, hands rubbed pant legs, tears filled Gaston's eyes. Hugh and Aubert waited in silence for his recovery.

"A peace treaty signed in June of 1805 and the payment of $60,000 freed all of the surviving crew except myself. Fluent in speaking, reading, and writing in English, French, Latin, and Greek the *Pasha* kept me for his personal secretary. The family hunt for me started soon thereafter, but was interrupted by conflict. Only allowed back into the Mediterranean after the end of the War of 1812, my father began his search again. The de Gracie family gold loosened tongues and paid a sufficient ransom to free me in 1818."

Hugh placed a hand on Gaston's shoulder, "We remain glad to have you back. I hope you now feel at home and comfortable with our family."

"I do indeed, Master Hugh, the passage of time, and the passing of certain individuals has allowed me to purge any false feelings of inferiority."

"Only one thing may put you back into disgrace, if it isn't corrected." Hugh grinned. "Stop calling me Master Hugh. Major de Gracie will do, but just Hugh will be best." He placed a hand on Fahad's brow. "Now, have you determined our *jihadi's* source of support?"

"That I have Master, uh— Major de Gracie, his source is Prince Abdulluh al-Nabir, head of a populous branch of the Saudi Royal family."

"This doesn't sound good." Hugh tried to imagine the handful of de Gracies going up against a powerful regime capable of asserting immense political and monetary pressure on most of the world's governments. Their riches allowed the hiring of an unending stream of well- equipped mercenaries.

"Bad enough, but not as bad as one might think. Abdulluh is head of a lesser cadet branch of the Saudi family and one currently in disgrace. Evidently, he and his faction tried to get too involved in determining the last succession to the throne."

"So," Aubert interjected, "we do not have the entire Saudi nation after us."

"In fact," Gaston replied, "if the Royals ever caught wind of one of their own financing a military operation on American soil, they would be very upset. Heads might literally roll. One of our options is to expose them."

Aubert looked thoughtful, and then pursed his lips. "Not good for us. A U.S./Saudi government investigation would lay bare all our secrets. In addition, both countries would be under extreme pressure to sweep the facts under the rug in order to maintain an unblemished alliance. Give us more background."

Gaston continued. "The Saudi royal family, the ones that figure in the succession to the throne, are descendants of Muhammad bin Saud or his three brothers Farhan, Thunayyan, and Mishari, the original group that established the kingdom. All other relations are the cadet branches, and while they may hold powerful and influential positions in the family and government, their members cannot be considered for elevation to the throne."

Gaston paused, glancing at the ceiling for a brief moment, then continued. "Fahad's connection to the house of Nabir is two-fold. First, the Saudis have vigorously promoted their strict *Wahhabi* version of Islam, especially in the funding of *madrasah* or religious schools in Pakistan." Gaston paused and pointed at their prisoner. "This inconsequential but ambitious leader of a few Taliban fighters converted to their brand of Islam and was rewarded with funds, marriage, and promotion to the big-time."

"Will they continue to persecute us?" Aubert wondered aloud. " We have defeated their first attack and hold Fahad captive."

"Abdullah is a very religious and fundamentalist patriarch. His name means 'slave of God.' The blood feud is dominant in his culture and his family. The Old Testament and Qur'an both have passages advocating "an eye for an eye" justice. And it's a family affair. Both you and Fahad could be dead, but previously uninvolved family members would step up to continue the fight."

"In Iraq and Afghanistan," Hugh wrinkled his brow in memory, "the Army paid out hundreds of thousands of dollars to families for innocent casualties and property damage resulting from military operations. I administered payment for losses numerous times. I remember the legal phrasing. '*Solatium*'—from the Latin for "solace"—is defined by the military as 'monetary compensation given in areas where it is culturally appropriate to alleviate grief, suffering, and anxiety resulting from injuries, death, and property loss with a monetary payment.' Can't we offer something similar here?"

"Well, there is the concept of *diya* mentioned in the Qur'an, which is an obligatory payment of blood money used in cases of accidental killing, which is not applicable here," Gaston pondered. "Perhaps, *fasil*—a term for negotiated settlement—could be invoked. In this instance, a payment is accepted even after intentional killings. It might consist of both money and other non-financial items."

Aubert looked thoughtful. "So, the mechanism for a peaceful settlement is there, but the question is how to open negotiations."

"This will be the most difficult part. Other peoples have no idea of the concept of shame or loss of face that permeates the Arab culture." Gaston glanced at Hugh. "Major de Gracie, and now our entire family, has shamed the al-Nabir, first by the killing of Aziz and now the absolute defeat of their air attack. They will not be open to listening."

"No offer of negotiation, either direct or through influential third parties, would be accepted?" Hugh thought of the vast network of connections around the world that the de Gracie family must have.

"Such an offer might make things worse. The more public the knowledge of their shame or loss of honor, the worse it becomes." Gaston's voice took on a lecture's tone. "Let me tell you the classic Arab story of a rich man traveling across the desert, who spent a night in an oasis. He pulled his cloak around him and fell asleep under some palm trees. During the night, a thief crept up and stole his cloak. The next day the man had his servants chase down the thief and bring him before the nearest local judge. The townspeople all turned out to observe.

As the story goes, the thief said, 'I am the thief. While a man was sleeping, I had sexual intercourse with him and then ran off with his cloak.' All faces in the courtroom looked at his accuser.

With a red face, the man replied. 'That is not my cloak.' The guilty man went free."

Hugh's face betrayed his consternation as he asked Gaston, "Is there no option, or cultural loophole we can use to stop this conflict?"

"If you can get Abdullah to negotiate, which does not look probable, then there is one possibility. The lie. Al Ghazali, the medieval Muslim theologian, stated: 'It is sometimes a duty to lie... if lying and truth both lead to a good result, you must tell the truth, for a lie is forbidden in this case. If a lie is the only way to reach a good result, it is allowable. A lie is lawful when it is the only path to duty... We must lie when truth leads to unpleasant results, but tell the truth when it leads to good results.' "

"I don't get the concept."

"Right now, the al-Nabir feel a loss of honor, shame over their defeat. If they can be induced to accept a lie — that they have actually had revenge or the equivalent — their honor is restored, and peace may result."

Both Hugh and Aubert looked confused. Hugh exclaimed, "How in hell do we do that?"

"Your first step, Major de Gracie, is to find a way to get them to talk to us. In the meantime, I will put together possible scenarios for successful negotiations. The WikiLeaks information stolen from State Department emails gives us detailed information on his family and a personality sketch of Abdullah. There was also the mention of him and a large entourage traveling every ninety days to the Mayo Clinic in the last year. Aubert, can you get us access to his medical records there?"

"I have lectured there, cooperated on research projects, and have management contacts at the highest level," Aubert mused. "Friendship and money should prevail."

14

Whatever is has been already, and whatever is to come has been already, with God summoning each event back in its return.

Ecclesiastes: 3:15

ABDULLAH IBN MOHAMMAD AL-NABIR sat in his study. His desk, supported by cut-to-size marble columns of an ancient Roman temple, was topped by six eight-foot slabs of yellow-brown native limestone one and a half feet thick. Convoluted fossils of middle Jurassic period brain coral rose in bas-relief from its top, observed through a pane of glass supported by rubber disks around its periphery. Three layers of wool and silk Persian rugs rested over the central area of a floor of polished oak inlaid with walnut and zebrawood. Oil paintings of landscapes from the world's major ecosystems covered the walls from floor to ten-foot ceilings.

He hated the palace, always had. His great grandfather had started the construction, and succeeding sons enlarged the grounds and made them increasingly luxuriant. In the miss-spent days of his youth,

Abdullah had followed their example, believing these material things buttressed the family honor. The walled quarters now covered almost seventy hectares.

The palace in the center contained two hundred and three rooms. Besides living quarters, there were libraries, conference rooms, theaters, separate swimming pools for men and women, billiard and game rooms, kitchens, and maintenance facilities. Outside, within mustard-hued razor wire-topped walls, stood stables, kennels, falconry mews, orchards, barracks for security guards, and gardens replete with plants and flowers from around the world. Polo and soccer fields and large expanses of irrigated short-cut green grass stood ready to play and picnic on.

Yes, he mused, Abdullah had raised the family to their highest achieved position of wealth and political influence. He and his minions had fingers in every pie in the kingdom – construction, hotels, shopping malls, and even desalinization plants. Using straw companies and not-for-profit foundations, the family invested in businesses in other countries. Lately, he had even purchased a significant interest in Fox News, if they only knew. The intricacies of the family business still kept him occupied, but there was no longer any thrill or pleasure in the running of it. In his seventies, there remained nothing left to prove, although he had failed on several counts.

He raised his cup and sipped his afternoon coffee, a perfect brew from his cook of many years. Abdullah remembered an old saying: coffee should be black as hell, strong as death and as sweet as love. His latest failure, attempting to influence the choice of a successor to the throne, had missed by the narrowest of margins – the last-minute betrayal of an ally ruined his ploy. His family would face years of isolation as punishment. Nothing would be made public. No cracks must appear in the royal family façade to provide an opening for the internal terrorism and extremism that attempted to manifest itself every year. The Arab spring might rear its ugly head here also.

In addition, he had no son until recently. In spite of his devotion and prayers to Allah, the forgiving, the merciful, his wives produced only viable daughters. Boy babies terminated in miscarriages or died soon after birth. Giving to charity, building mosques, financing madrasah, making the *Hajj*, receiving blessings from Imams and holy men – nothing worked. Eight years ago, desperate at the age of seventy, he had fertility doctors in Switzerland try in vitro fertilization. An egg quickened by a centrifuged accumulation of his seed implanted in his youngest, strongest wife produced an initially healthy-appearing boy. He remembered with a smile the three days of feasts and parties celebrating the birth.

A soft-toned gong rang from a speaker on his phone. Abdullah glanced at the clock, 10:00AM, time for his first appointment of the day and news he probably did not want to hear.

He pushed a green button on the phone. A knock on the door followed, a pause, and then Claus Reimer, his tow-headed chief of security entered, portfolio tucked under one arm. The man stood six foot three and one hundred eighty slim pounds, dressed in the household uniform of dark blue shirt covered by a waist-level long-sleeved jacket, sand-colored cummerbund, and slate-gray pants bloused paratrooper style into black leather boots. A seven-inch long knife scar ran at an angle down his right cheek; a parting gift received in his eighteenth year while defending the palace from an intruder. After he had put the burglar down, he rubbed pepper and wood ash into the cut, making a permanent visible sign of his first combat success.

Claus was the ultimate product of a program that started when Abdullah first came into control of the family. An admirer of the Turkish use of *Janissaries*, disgusted with the poor security material provided by the males of his family, and not trusting outside mercenaries, he set up his own orphanage. Starting forty years ago, his agents had stolen lost male children from three to six years of age from war zones throughout the world, careful to select non-Arab physical types. Converted to Islam, and trained in physical security, the orphans formed a fifty- man guard unit.

Besides mental conditioning designed to generate feelings of loyalty, their reliance upon his house for their needs, and being obvious physical strangers in a land of Middle-Easterners reinforced their dependence. He allowed none of them to marry or form attachments — no relationships allowed — to detract them from their focus on his family's safety. Even their names had been changed to prevent them from seeking possible family connections. Claus's German name was such an invention. Abdullah remembered he originally came from Australia.

The head of security's opening remark broke the silence. "Your Highness displayed wisdom in deploying a secret observation team at Port Henry to observe Fahad's attack." He waved an inch-thick multi-page paper printout and a DVD disk. "Their report and video of the attack arrived at 08:00."

"You have conducted an analysis?"

"Highness, I am the bearer of bad news. Our initial tentative conclusion, based almost exclusively on the team's report is that the attack failed. Further attempts to collect intelligence have been unsuccessful. There have been no reports from members of the expedition. Once over the battle area, intercepted communications traffic between our radio-equipped elements degenerated into panicky shouts, curses, screams, and silence. The landing site has since been covered with clouds, or de Gracie generated smoke, so no satellite or aerial photos can be taken."

"Any further intelligence from the ground team?"

"None. Our unfamiliarity with a landscape full of interlocked downed trees, brambles, jagged jutting rocks, and the enemy's aggressive patrolling preclude getting close to the infidel's home. Our four-man ground team took two casualties in trying – falls from being chased down the mountain resulted in a broken leg and a concussion."

Abdullah felt anger, astonishment, and shame fight for dominance. "And what of survivors? Any chance the coming days will see stragglers appear?"

"Highness, I fear the odds are vastly against that. Once you have viewed the DVD, I believe you will agree."

"Let us see it."

Claus moved to the office's electronic console and inserted the disk. After a brief warm-up, an image full of odd-shaped grays and blacks appeared on the forty-eight-inch screen.

Abdullah leaned forward. In the recorded predawn darkness, the light gathering ability of the camera lens allowed a better picture than unaided human eyes. The terrain consisted of mountains and valleys, all heavily forested, but with bare rock bones protruding here and there. An elongated shadow flitted across the screen. Abdullah recognized the silhouette of a helicopter. The camera followed its movement. Cresting the mountain peak opposite, yellow tracers from machine guns spurted from its sides. Explosions flashed, backlighting the high wall surrounding the enemy mansion. No return fire came.

"The gunship attacks to soften up the landing zone for the aircraft carrying the assault troops," Claus offered.

"The de Gracies do not shoot, did we catch them asleep?"

"No, Highness, they wait for the main attack."

The camera panned right, catching five pewter-gray shapes climbing out of the north valley. The old man's heart fluttered. He could see the exhaust flares coming from the helicopters' turbine engines. From the DVD player's speakers came the blended stutter of five sets of chopper rotor blades. The line of aircraft swished across the screen up and over the enemy's wall. The camera zoomed in. An eruption of fire and flame filled the entire screen, blotting out any recognizable feature. Abdullah blinked and gasped.

The firestorm of blazing metal went on and on, punctuated by explosions and cascades of flame. In that roiling conflagration of light, no details could be seen. At one point the gunship came swooping in for another run. It shuddered like it had run into a wall. A terrible burst of radiance flooded its interior before it spun to the earth. Fragments of its airframe and the bodies of its crew made tiny whirling black spots against the continuing inferno.

Finally, the sky darkened. The camera zoomed in and focused on the wall. Burning equipment on the other side cast flickering light and shadow through small natural openings in the hedge barricade. The rising sun colored clouds of smoke yellow and pink.

A knot in his throat, Abdullah pursed his lips and shook his head. "Can any of this be traced back to us?"

"The expenditure of funds took place through several sets of intermediary straw companies established for that purpose only. The men involved never knew their true employer. We hired only outsiders — Iranian pilots and Yemeni, Palestinian, and Afghani infantry — no Saudis. The only person dealing directly with us was Fahad. If he survived, which I doubt, his hatred would prevent him from giving any useful information to the de Gracies."

Abdullah clasped his hands together to stop their quiver. He stared at the blank screen. "I did not wish it so, but this will be a long war now. Maybe several generations will pass before completion. Given our greater wealth and larger family, we should still win, *inshallah*."

"Highness, I will prepare options for your consideration."

⌖

Hugh sat in the library. Legs spread one to each side of a reversed chair, his arms folded across the back. He felt vibration and heard the sound of Lewis' helicopter headed for the crevice with wreckage from the attack suspended from its underside. Two days into the planning of offensive action, he had spent the morning connected to a selection of Fahad's memories plucked out by the Mother-tree, especially those disclosing details of the al-Narib palace and grounds.

There was not as much information as he needed, Fahad's time there limited to specific areas only – conference rooms, a theater, dining rooms, a bedroom, and hallways.

Jonsey sat across the table drinking heavily creamed coffee and eating *Aqras Mukarrara*, Hugh's favorite boyhood pastry and ironically a recipe Uncle Frank claimed to be of Arabic origin passed from Spain into Europe in the 1400s. The honey-coated disks consisted of leavened white flour, mixed with eggs, butter, almonds, dates, and rosewater fried in raw sesame oil.

His friend took another bite, licked his fingers, "I don't believe your ancestors were too concerned with cholesterol buildup. The only thing lacking is the doughnut hole. By the way, don't think I haven't noticed the fact you and your family are holding back information."

"I don't believe the doughnut hole was invented until the late 1840s," Hugh responded.

"Come now. Don't try to put off an old friend."

"The family has secrets – many I didn't know until recently. Not sure the old man has shared all of them with me yet. Compounding the situation, they have had five hundred years to learn how to keep their mouths shut and bury any embarrassing skeletons. We're alone for the moment, so if you have questions, ask me. I'll answer where I can."

Jonsey grimaced. "Where shall I start? Everyone is way above norm healthy. Old or young, they move like college athletes. Wounds heal quickly, too quickly. No one has any allergies, and they don't appear to ever catch cold. In addition, the house – a dozen fifty-caliber slugs came through this library, turned books on the shelves to confetti, yet the holes have sealed and the wallpaper appears to be growing back. Growing!" Jonsey raised a hand to his chest. "I've never felt better. Muscles are in top tone, and my joints are almost as flexible as a baby's. Any further improvement and I'll be able to bend over, stick my head between my legs, and give myself a blow-job."

Hugh stared at the table, refusing to look his best friend in the face. He'd never lied to him before, but there came a time for everything. A great weariness wept through his flesh and bones. "My father and some of the others come from a long line of engineers and geneticists. Over the centuries, they have developed additives to the food, water, and the very air within the enclosed circle of our mountain. Selective breeding contributes. I can't explain it any further, since, as you know, I was raised to be a soldier, not a scientist. However, I can testify no matter how long you live here, you will not ever be able to achieve an autoerotic blow-job."

"So, Major," Jonsey's voice rose into drill sergeant range, "I've been sent on chickenshit errands to exclude me from planning sessions. During the meetings I have attended, notes are passed, and sneaky side conversations keep me ignorant. You and your kind have isolated and rejected me. I'm not going to be trusted with any real answers, am I?"

"I will write you a check for combat pay. And, as a gift for your acceptance of the status quo, come back and visit us for a week every year. This isn't the fountain of youth, but it's close. You'll gain a long healthy life, a reward well-deserved for your help, and being the brother I never had." Hugh sighed. "You must see, we would be overwhelmed by outsiders if the benefits of our lifestyle became common knowledge."

Jonsey rose, started for the door, paused, and said, "I have a top-secret clearance from Uncle Sam, and if that's not good enough to be read in, then damn you and your entire family. My leave is almost finished. Can you drop me at the train station this afternoon?"

Hugh felt a frigid hole open in his heart. His last contact with the contemporary world severed. Family appeared to be all that remained. Events were pushing him in a direction he didn't desire. The price for symbiosis with the Mother-tree and family loyalty came high – almost more than he could bear. If it wasn't for Désirée, he'd pack a duffle bag and walk out shoulder-to-shoulder with his best friend. Family and a woman had been the death of another buddy relationship. Unable to speak, he nodded. The sergeant major clenched his fists, stiffened his back, and left the library.

A rattle at the door, an eager Gaston entered, accidentally smacked his shoulder against the jamb, and dropped a portion of his burden. Papers cascaded onto the floor while he struggled to retain his grip on Désirée's battery-powered combination DVD player and TV set. Glad of the interruption, Hugh slid off the chair and rescued the machine, which he placed on the table.

His recently-revived relative went on hands and knees to reassemble the pages of his research.

Given the twisted past-present relationships the Mother-tree's suspended animation produced, Hugh voiced a curiosity question, "Are you one of my ancestors?"

"No, Major de Gracie, I have not had children yet. Without consulting the family blood-line chart, I would guess we are some kind of cousin many times removed."

"A blood-line chart?"

Gaston nodded, looked guilty, and changed the subject. He clicked on the TV and inserted a disk. "Our luck holds. I have discovered a video on YouTube that explores the interior and grounds of the al-Narib palace. Three years ago, a French TV program called *Fabuleux Motifs* did an hour-long program touring Abdullah's palace, both the interior and the grounds. We have pictorial footage of the kitchen, hallways, Abdullah's bedroom, and the nursery, almost everywhere but the women's quarters."

"I'm surprised he would allow the filming, given his secretive nature."

"I believe it became a matter of honor. At that time, most of the other Saudi families similarly showed off their wealth. And I heard his envious wives nagged him into it."

Hugh pressed the stop button, freezing the current frame. "What are these alcoves spotted in the hallways? Looks like lighted display areas for art."

Gaston nodded. "The art, such as the four-foot-tall pedestal with bronze camel sculpture in that picture, actually hides access to utility shafts. Arabesque-carved doors on the back wall of the recess open up to allow repair and maintenance work on plumbing, HVAC ducts, and electrical conduit." Gaston consulted his notes. "It is a signature element of the French architects, Acy & Picot, who designed the palace. They build hollow weight-bearing concrete shafts up from the basement that run the full height of the building. Open ports on the sides at each floor allow takeoffs of piping to service the rooms."

"Hmm, how interesting. Is Aubert capable of getting us fake passports and travel arrangements to Riyadh in two weeks?"

Gaston nodded. "The Father says, yes."

"Have you found a line of attack to get us inside?"

"On my scouting trip there last week, I found a way."

"Good. After lunch you, Aubert, and I will put the final polish on the plan. We will now take the offensive."

15

Moreover, I saw here under the sun that, justice where ought to be, there was wickedness; and where righteousness ought to be, there was wickedness.

Ecclesiastes: 3:16

THE HIGH-DESERT SUN BURNED through the tinted glass windshield, turning the black vinyl-covered dash into a heat sink. Hugh adjusted the air conditioning vent on the van's passenger side to blow around his right side rather than directly in his face. The chilly air made both his eyes uncomfortable in different ways. The muscles in his empty eye socket now embraced a prosthetic glass eye, rather than covered with his usual black eye patch. The blowing air made his left eye too dry and the solid material of the artificial right eye transferred cold into the sinuses centered above his brows.

Glancing out the window, he watched the white lines on the six-lane highway flash by, then turned to Gaston crouched in the back behind the split front seats and pointed at the familiar red-themed paint and golden arches on a two-story sand-colored building. "Add McDonalds to Riyadh's list of fast food joints. It joins Burger King, KFC, and Papa John's."

"The Saudis also have home-grown quickie places. *Al-Baik* is the most popular, serving take-away chicken, shrimp, and fish dishes."

Hugh raised his arms, changing the subject. "Tell me again how this subterfuge is going to get us by the guards?"

From behind the seats, Gaston clapped a hand on the driver's shoulder. "Our friend here, John Paul Mercado Reyes, is the reliable foreman for the Ma'mum Company that provides luxury and *halal* food and drink to the al-Narib family, been doing so for the last ten years. John Paul is originally from the Philippines and one of many thousands of migrant workers that do the scut work of the Kingdom. He has been trying to go back to the home islands for the last three years."

"And why is he still here?" Hugh asked.

"Migrants coming to work in Saudi Arabia need a sponsor to get an entrance visa. They also need an exit visa approved by their employer. His boss values his work too highly to let him go. His terms for helping us, besides monetary payment, are to get him out of the country and back home. He'll leave with us on the private plane waiting at the airport."

John spoke for the first time. "The guards will let us through the gate, *Señor* de Gracie. They know me well from our weekly deliveries. Islam requires prayers five times a day. Our arrival will be thirty minutes before *dhuhr*, the second prayer held at noon. They will pass us quickly, so we can unload and exit before the call to prayer. All those of the Moslem faith, men and women will enter the on-grounds family mosque. Numerous non-Moslem servants will remain in the palace. Distracting them is your problem."

Gaston and Hugh both grinned.

"And you're sure your boss won't be around the next three days?"

Hugh asked.

"The man is spending a week in Dubai, away from the eyes of his wife and the faithful, spending the money I earn him on high-class whores and the horses at the Jebel Ali Race Course. I am completely in charge of the company during regular absences."

The highway necked down to four lanes. In the side mirror, Hugh could see the capital city's receding Kingdom Tower, at nine hundred and ninety feet, the tallest building in the country. Its notched-out top was bridged by a skywalk, which allowed a panoramic view of Riyadh. The van passed through the eastern edge of the city, where buildings shrank to one-and two-story structures separated by empty lots filled with the sand and the bleached rock litter of the surrounding desert. Irrigated patches of green grass shaded by a variety of palm trees became less frequent.

Hugh turned his attention to the slab-sided commercial van, a rented bone-white Mercedes Sprinter whose all-wheel-drive allowed a degree of off-road capability. The Ma'mum Company name, which translated as 'trustworthy' in Arabic, address, and product line had been painted on the sides in water-based yellow and blue Arabic snake-like script."

"Okay, John." Hugh breathed out. "You get us in the palace, we do our thing for three days and then depart. Tell us again what your role will be."

"After dropping you off today, I return to the garage you rented and hide the van and myself. I wash the truck removing the lettering, put the original rental license plates back on, and three days from now," John pointed at the dash-mounted GPS, "engage the all-wheel-drive for a trip into the desert to await your arrival three miles east of the al-Nabir palace. I pick you up and we proceed at normal highway speed to the airport and departure on your rented jet."

Gaston leaned forward and checked the GPS coordinates. Their cell phones' similar software would direct them to the same location.

"Remember," he said, wagging a finger at John, "no baggage, only what you can carry on your person. No one must suspect you will be leaving."

The road devolved into two-lane traffic. The van passed through a procession of gray-brown gullies and wadis, emerging into a mustard-colored plain spotted at random with scrub brush. In an effort to keep his mind distracted, Hugh read the invoice listing their cargo. He recognized most of the foods, which included long grain basmati rice, fava beans, boxes of various lamb and chicken cuts, onions, pine nuts, and olives. Spice replacements included cloves, cardamom, saffron, black lime, and bay leaves. Some items were a puzzle.

"What are *labneh*, *sultanas*, and *puck*?"

John replied. "Puck is a popular local brand of cream cheese. Sultannas are golden-colored dried grapes. Labneh is a common Middle East staple, made by removing whey from salted yogurt. You spread it on bread and choose your topping – olives, mint, cucumber, and such. That reminds me of an old Arab women's joke. Men wonder why women buy so many cucumbers in the market, but none appear in the salad."

"Your company advertises *halal* products. Explain to me again what this means."

"Halal means lawful or permitted. Its opposite is *Haram*. While religion and custom apply these words to all facets of life, this company is only concerned with their dictates in relation to groceries," John explained. "Generally, all food is considered *halal* except pig products, animals improperly slaughtered or dead before slaughter, alcoholic drinks, carnivorous birds and animals, or food contaminated by any of those."

"That seems fairly straight forward."

"Given the great use of additives in modern processed food, it becomes more difficult. Because the origin of these ingredients is not known, foods containing additives such as gelatin, enzymes emulsifiers, and flavors may be classified as *mashbooh*, which means doubtful or questionable."

Hugh had a lot to learn about Saudi speech, culture, and customs. Connected to the Mother-tree, he had studied the replay of Gaston's early memories as a captive, especially those of him learning Arabic. Chemical stimulants flowing from her roots allowed him to speed-learn and retain much of what he observed, but the time had been short. His grasp of Arabic remained at the eight-year-old level. Gaston had said this would not to be a problem since many migrant workers rarely progressed beyond that level.

John turned his head towards his passengers. He checked their appearance once more.

Hair blackened, skin dyed medium tan, eyes color corrected with brown contact lenses, white high-collar jackets with company name embroidered above the right pocket, and gray slacks with black boots — no suspicious equipment bulges — all correct.

"You had best get in the back now," John suggested. "We are nearing the turnoff. The guards expect the strong back and weak mind servants to ride in the rear, as befits their status."

The van's left turn signal blinked, alerting the BMW 528i and Toyota Land Cruiser behind them. The truck passed under a pillared arch and followed a narrow macadam road. A mile later, the pavement gave way to a sand and gravel surface. Dust billowed out behind the vehicle for a half-mile until hard surface pavement began again.

"It's a security measure," John mentioned to his companions. "The cloud of dust alerts the guards to the approach of vehicles. They won't be overly concerned, however. They know our schedule."

Several quiet minutes passed as the men mentally prepared themselves for the deception. The van rumbled over a series of metal grates and popped up over a rise.

The two de Gracies gasped.

Before them, filling their vision, were the mustard-brown twenty-foot tall crenelated walls surrounding the al-Nabir palace and grounds. A minaret topped by an onion-shaped dome rose an additional ten feet from one end of the complex. As intended, the walls' height blocked a view of anything else within the compound.

"That last rise of ground blocking the complex from sight is artificial." The Filipino driver, John, waved a hand. "The builders want you to be impressed by the sudden appearance of power."

Gaston pointed towards the tower, "The name minaret comes from the Arabic *manāra*, meaning lighthouse. In the old days before air-conditioning, hot air rose in the towers, which pulled cooler ground-level air into the mosque providing ventilation."

"I'd hate to have the job of climbing that high five times a day to call the faithful to prayer," Hugh added.

"Now, they use a speaker, with the microphone safely installed below on the ground floor," Gaston said. "However, in the old days, they did have some compassion for the *muezzin*, especially as the towers grew higher. Some had stair steps cut wide and shallow enough to allow a donkey to carry the prayer-caller to the top. A small stall housed the poor lop-eared creature until the return trip."

The van crunched to a stop, its bumper a foot from the massive front gate.

Wall-mounted cameras and human eyes scanned the vehicle. After a lengthy pause, the three men watched the doors, engraved cedar-wood panels over steel grating, cycle open. They ran smoothly on metal tracks embedded in concrete.

John goosed the van past the gates and stopped before a second set of doors. The front gates closed, trapping the visitors inside high walls.

A man with a mirror on a long pole circled the vehicle, examining its underside. A dog handler allowed his charge to sniff around the tires and fenders. The Mercedes' back clamshell doors were opened.

Uniformed man and Alsatian peered in, stared at the pair of lackeys.

Gaston and Hugh raised their eyebrows and relaxed their facial muscles.

The dog lifted its body by the front paws intruding into the cargo area, snuffled its distaste at their foreign scent, lost interest, and turned away.

John, Hugh, and Gaston were motioned out.

They stood with arms out as hand-held metal detectors ran over their bodies. Pocket contents and cell phones were examined. No contraband discovered, the guards allowed them back in the van. Front and back doors clicked shut. Through the windshield, they noticed the inner gates retract, and the guard with the pole-mounted mirror waved them through.

The van's tires rumbled over pale yellow pea gravel following a service road that wound through stands of date palms heavy with chains of browning fruit. Building and tree-mounted cameras moved to follow their progress. The smell of freshly clipped grass came through the vehicle's air ducts. Someone had been busy preparing the polo field.

As they passed, Hugh could see the flash of blue and yellow jerseys as helmeted riders swirled around the ball, long-handled mallets S-curving as they swung between horses.

He had played a bit in the Army, and done well, mostly because of a string of specially trained horses, usually thoroughbreds, who provided seventy percent of the skill needed to excel in the game. He wished he could be out there feeling the signals going back and forth between his body and pony through double reins, knees, and thighs, evoking the exhilaration of a game dating back to the fifth century BCE. He watched two teams of mounted pairs race down the three-hundred-yard field, horses and riders riding off against each other. The ponies looked neat and streamlined with roached manes and braided tails, their legs wrapped in team colors.

The sight was cut off too soon as the truck approached a second fortified gate, set in a ten-foot wall at the rear of the main palace. It slid open, allowing the van to enter without stopping.

John pulled to the right, stopped, and backed up against a loading dock. An assistant cook and a guard with clipboard waited. John shut off the engine, exited, and moved to the rear.

He opened the cargo doors and shouted, "Crisanto, Ruperto, get your asses out here and unload." He pointed to the cook, "Put the parcels where Achmed wants them."

Hugh and Gaston carried boxes and bags upstairs and into the kitchen, stopping at the top so the guard could check off each item.

John checked his watch. "Hurry it up, ten minutes until the call to prayer."

The guard stopped Hugh as he carried up the last box. He frowned and motioned John over, waved the clipboard, and said in Arabic. "What is this? Not on the list."

John yelled up, "Come now, man, you know every trip the owner includes a little present. Something he hopes the customer will like and buy in the future. Crisanto, set it down and open it for the man's inspection."

The top unfolded, John drew out one of six dark-green wine-shaped bottles with wired cork and silver foil wrapper. The guard muttered something complex in Arabic. Hugh caught the word *haram.*

"No," John replied, "It's *hallal,* only carbonated apple juice, no alcohol. Can you read the label?"

The cook and the guard examined the bottle and argued.

John pointed to his watch, reminding them of the few minutes remaining before worship.

Throwing up his hands, the cook replaced the bottle and waved Hugh inside.

He threaded his way through the kitchen; currently a demanding place with various sous-chefs, sauciers, and their white-aproned assistants chopping, whisking, and blending food on long stainless-steel tables. A meal would be served immediately after *dhuhr*. Stoves and grills steamed with meats and vegetable combinations. Exhaust fans rattled and voices in Spanish, Arabic, and Slavic combined to fill the air and make the pots and pans hanging from overhead racks hum. The smell of cardamom, garlic, and lime masked the heat-sweat odors of the workers until Hugh and Gaston passed close.

Outside, John glanced at his watch. Right on time came the call to prayer, the *muezzin's* amplified song of devotion penetrating the walls and rooms of the complex.

The man possessed a professional's voice, reminiscent of the older throaty Sinatra. The range of notes the man produced ran from a tenor falsetto to a deep bass. Abdullah could afford the best of everything, John thought.

The faithful started streaming outdoors and down steps, finding familiar paths to the mosque. The women dressed in variations of reds and blues, satins, and silks from head to foot, chattered and swayed – clusters of gaudy butterflies. John closed the doors, jumped in the driver's seat, and drove away. Sweat dimpled his forehead and armpits. The timing was crucial.

Hugh and Gaston moved among the kitchen staff mostly unnoticed, or cursed and pushed aside if they got in the traffic flow between cookstoves and prep-tables. They positioned the case of fake apple juice in an out-of-the-way corner centrally located in the elongated kitchen.

Opening the box's false bottom, they pulled out two fanny packs. Reaching inside, they activated a time fuse and moved to the far inside end of the room to crouch behind two of four tri-legged forty-gallon electrically heated kettles.

Gaston pulled up the sleeve of his jacket, exposed his watch, and began an internal countdown.

Hugh heard a pop and spotted a spurt of gray mist in the direction of the bottles.

Then a series of bangs and thick puffs of gray-black smoke billowed out into the room.

The two infiltrators pulled cut-down gas masks, only goggles and mouthpiece, from the fanny packs, strapping them over their faces.

Shouts and a smoke alarm started simultaneously. Pans, spoons, and knives clanged, spanged, and rattled on metal tables and brown-tiled floor as twenty kitchen staffers dropped their tools and raced for the doors.

Gaston produced a tube of Krazy Glue and squirted its contents into the controls of the two hind-most kettles.

He and Hugh stood and reversed their jackets, turning them from white to al-Nabir gray. Removing their high-collared shirts exposed navy-colored turtlenecks. They pulled blue berets and lion-colored cummerbunds with Velcro fasteners from inside pockets. Blousing their pant legs in their boots, they completed costumes mimicking the guards' uniforms. They moved quickly through the smoke-filled abandoned kitchen, passing the adjacent dining room, and into a large hallway. Smoke clouds, warmer than the air, drifted up into the main living areas.

Pleased with the effect created, Hugh made a mental note to reward Valentina, the sloe-eyed recently revived de Gracie chemist.

Racing up the stairs to the second level, they passed empty hallways and rooms, the occupants already outside on the way to the mosque. Acting as though they were real authority figures, they helped a pair of disoriented non-Moslem housecleaning maids to evacuate. On the second floor, within the heart of Abdullah's personal family living quarters, they prepared their previously selected hiding place.

In the van, John heard the alarms and in the rearview mirror spotted wisps of gray-black mist rising from the palace's open kitchen doors. He passed four of the gate guards running towards the source of the smoke. The remaining two guards hurriedly motioned him into the sally port, their attention distracted by the unknown happenings at the palace. A quick look-over and their familiarity with him and ten years of routine Ma'mum Company deliveries allowed him to exit without a detailed inspection. On the road out, he fought with the adrenaline in his blood to keep the van's speed at a normal pace.

Six hours later, Abdullah ibn Mohammad al-Nabir sat, hands clasped together, forearms resting on the top of his desk, a sour look on his face. The joints in his left hand felt tender, hot, and stiff. The progress of rheumatoid arthritis made it more painful and less flexible every month.

The smoke had not penetrated his sanctum, which also served as a safe room, sealed and isolated from the rest of the complex. Huge fans brought from the stables and arranged in the palace had blown out the gray-black particulates. An additional complication came as a result of the panicky evacuation. Abandoned food on stoves and grills in the kitchen had caught fire, activating overhead extinguishers.

His steward reported minimal injury. A sprained ankle and bruises resulting from the clumsy fire drill seemed to be all the human damage. Extinguisher water had shorted out some electrical appliances, including two of the large kettles. The kitchen and the informal dining room would need cleaning and repainting. The remainder of the palace was untouched.

Sandwiches and fruit had been substituted for the lost lunch, but the head cook believed he would be able to produce a normal hot menu for dinner with only a small delay.

The telephone pinged. From its internal speaker, a voice asked if he wished to receive his head of security. He pushed the button, releasing the lock on the door.

Claus Reimer strode in, his face relaxed, but his legs moved more stiffly than usual.

Abdullah interpreted this to mean his man expected a dressing-down. The news Claus brought was probably not good.

"Highness," the security chief launched into the facts without preliminaries, "This was no simple kitchen accident." He laid a picture on the desk.

Abdullah noticed a charred cardboard box appearing to hold six de-corked wine bottles. Wrinkles appeared on his forehead. There was something familiar about it.

Claus continued. "Achmed, the head cook, claims the case supposedly contained carbonated apple juice and was delivered as a gift from the Ma'mum Company, our normal food supplier."

"Instead of juice, it contained smoke bombs?"

"Yes, Highness, and a letter attached to its side."

Claus stood at attention and handed over a Xerox copy of the note.

Abdullah's eyes opened in surprise as he read the nine lines centered on a business-sized sheet of paper.

> *He will judge between many peoples and will settle*
> *disputes for strong nations far and wide. They will*
> *beat their swords into plowshares and their spears*
> *into pruning hooks. Nation will not take up sword*
> *against nation nor will they train for war anymore.*
> *Micah 4:3*

00-41-22-722-1617
Code: Aj33n27

"My English is good enough to understand and recognize this verse. It is from the holy book of the Jews, but what is the series of numbers?"

"Highness," Claus remained boot heels together, spine straight, and arms held rigid at his side. "The first line of numbers is an international phone number."

Abdullah tried to control the flash of anger that burst in his mind and failed, "*Ibn metnakah!* Son of a bitch! And whose number is it?"

"The number will connect to a phone in Geneva, Switzerland, Highness." Claus hurriedly continued to prevent his boss from commenting further. "A detective contacted by us in the Swiss capital finds the number rings a phone in an empty office in a building on the *Rue du Grand Pré*. The code number punched in once a connection is established will transfer the caller to another location."

"It must be the de Gracies sending us a message."

"Highness, that is also our supposition, which is supported by the fake bottles. Fahad tried to detonate wine bottle bombs in the de Gracie's mansion, snuck past their security through a caterer. They are replying in kind."

"This look like a peace offer to you?"

Claus's face paled. His voice took on a higher pitch. "Highness, those could have been explosives in the case."

"Have your men checked to make sure no other presents were left?"

"Every box and container in the entire complex has been thoroughly examined, Highness. We have twice swept the buildings and grounds for infiltrators and found nothing."

Abdullah nodded his head. Claus, if anything, was a master of detail. "For tonight, double the guard on the palace and relieve them every hour on the hour. I do not want any of them falling asleep. Establish random roving patrols on the grounds and send scouts into the desert adjacent to the walls."

"Highness, it will be as you command."

"And, now into the matter of the Ma'mum Company. What have you discovered?"

"The foreman of the company, his assistants, and the delivery truck did not return to the company warehouse, Highness. The owner is out of the country. We questioned the few employees and discovered nothing. When we used harsher means of interrogation, we got made- up stories that did not correlate. From his absence, we infer that the supervisor is involved in the plot. Without involving the police our chances of finding him are slim."

"No. No police. The Royals would love to possess something more to hang us with. *Moor-jāk!* Fuck it! The de Gracies have found us. They must have broken Fahad."

Abdullah ibn Mohammed al-Narib lay in bed, his sleep pattern disrupted by yesterday's events. The air in the room smelled fusty with his own perspiration. From cracks around the curtains, ribbons of light ran across the floor and ceiling telling him morning had arrived. Four hours of sleep and four hours of tossing and turning had left him grumpy and achy. The protector of his family and its retainers, he felt he had failed in his duty. They had lost the initiative with the de Gracies. He must find a way to strike back and keep them running.

A muffled scream came through the doorway. He recognized the voice of Karimah, his son Haytham's nanny, shouting for the guards. Her high-pitched cries soon joined by those of Fikriyah, the boy's teacher.

Ice ran in his veins as he threw aside the sheets and raced for the door dressed only in his nightgown. His bare feet slapped across the black and white checkerboard tiles in the hallway, past a decorative alcove, its bronze camel statuette perched calm and undisturbed on its plinth. Gouty toes and arthritic knees sent a needle of pain upward each time a foot hit the floor. The cedar wood nursery doors, their carved Arabic script invoking supplications to Allah, stood open.

Near the entrance stood a tender tableau, Karimah kneeling holding his pale-cheeked son in her arms. In front, Fikriyah, legs spread like a wrestler, brandished a brass vase as though it were a weapon. He relaxed. Haytham was safe and unharmed. A half-dozen guards rushed around them. Two of the men hustled the women and boy out of the room. The remainder checked furniture, rummaged in closets, looked behind curtains, and opened chests.

A guard near the bed stiffened. He whistled and pointed.

Abdullah pushed him away.

Something glinted in the morning light coming through the window. He moved closer and squinted. A fine gold chain hung from the bed's canopy, directly over where his son's face would rest. Attached partway down, a scroll of paper twisted in air disturbed by the search. On the end dangled a glittering two-inch wide bangle. Abdullah reached for the object.

A just-arrived Claus intercepted his hand, "Highness, it may be a booby trap."

The pendant swung around exposing its flat front. Both men gasped. The gold pendant, sparkling with diamond chips, bore the shape of a fleur-de-lis, the symbol of the House de Gracie.

❦

Claus stood trembling before Abdullah in his office. A flood of curses still vibrated in his bones. He had reported no luck in finding how the necklace had been placed. Arabic is the best of all languages, he thought, for cursing and for poetry. The old man had cut loose with all the foul words and word combinations seventy years of life had allowed him to accumulate, and a hefty inventory it was.

Claus shared anger and frustration with Abdullah. The penetration of the palace in spite of all its guards, cameras, and alarms left them feeling as though a rape had been committed. His enemies had demonstrated how easily they could get to his master's greatest treasure.

The flood of invective slowed, and then halted. "Show me the message."

Claus handed over a copy of the single sheet of paper recovered from the necklace. "Highness, we have determined that the chain and pendant are pure electrum gold, the alloy an exact copy of ancient Egyptian formula. The chips are from Herkimer diamonds, a de Gracie specialty."

Abdullah held the paper out at half an arm's length, he wiped grimy eyes, and read the note twice.

> **Blessed are the peacemakers, for they will be called children of God.**
> **Matthew 5:9**

> **"Put your sword back in its place," Jesus said to him, "for all who draw the sword will die by the sword."**
> **Matthew 26:52**

00-41-22-722-1617
Code: Aj33n27

"Quotes from the holy book of the Christians," Abdullah said aloud. "They invoke the prophet Jesus. How in the name of *Shaytān* did they get into my son's room? Where were your guards?"

"Highness, the guards were vigilant, no one got over the wall. My people have again searched the palace, the outbuildings, and the grounds with extreme vigor. We have reviewed all the camera tapes—"

"And found nothing." Abdullah completed his sentence.

"We believe it must be an inside job, Highness. Someone we trust within these walls."

"Question the staff. Use whatever interrogation techniques you deem necessary to loosen tongues, but get me answers. In the meantime, how fast can we strike back?"

"As we have discussed, Highness, there are few ways to attack the de Gracie stronghold without attracting unwanted attention by their government and ours. Even small asymmetrical warfare actions such as kidnappings, car bombs, and snipers are extremely difficult, given their defenses and the support of the townspeople surrounding them. We just can't get close to them. However, another option remains to continue to use the airways. We have a man preparing at a secret location not far from Port Henry."

"Yes, yes, project DuPont. How soon can we release him?"

Claus glanced at his watch. "It is 1000 hours here and 0200 at his site. With a phone call we can launch him at 0700, his attack to occur two hours later, or 1500 our time."

"Let it be so."

16

I said to myself, 'God will judge the just and the wicked equally; for every activity and every purpose has its proper time.

Ecclesiastes: 3:17

WILLIAM CARTWRIGHT FINISHED *FAJR*, the Morning Prayer required by his adopted religion, pushed himself to his feet, and began rolling up the colorful prayer rug. Raised Presbyterian in his native Canada, he had converted to Islam during a decade-long stint as a pilot for Saudia, Saudi Arabia's government-owned airlines. The last five years, he had served the al-Narib household as their senior pilot. The family had found his blond hair, blue eyes, and Canadian passport useful on a number of occasions.

He tied the rug ends with leather straps and stowed it in a nylon-sided duffle bag. Time remained for a quick meal before takeoff. His rented Toyota, a cot with rumpled blue polyester blankets, a small refrigerator, microwave oven, and a chair shared space in a dusty hanger, which also housed the queen of his attention. An AirTractor-

503 crop duster aircraft stood clean and shiny. Its bright yellow paint was bisected on both sides of the thirty-three-foot-long fuselage by a blue stripe. A mono-wing, like most modern dusters, its Pratt & Whitney PT6A turboprop engine could generate over 1000 horsepower, capable of lifting its human operator and five hundred gallons of fertilizer, herbicide, or pesticide.

In this case, the plane's tank was loaded with a commercial pesticide of the organophosphate class. The chemical affected both insects and people in the same ways. Derived from nerve gases developed in WWII, human exposure to the disbursed mist would initially cause difficulty breathing, irregular heartbeat, vomiting, and diarrhea. The end result would be seizures, convulsions, and respiratory failure. If a victim survived the first day, psychotic episodes, loss of memory, and inability to focus would occur.

In government-required classes, William had learned all about the attributes and effects of various farm chemicals before being granted a license to dispense the products. The more he learned, the more he questioned his commitment to the project.

Perhaps, the five-million-dollar bonus for a successful mission would allow him to forget what he was about to do. The conservative tenets of *Wahabi* Islam also bound him to protect his religion with *jihad* – a struggle requiring spiritual discipline. He opened the hanger door, allowing in the cold night air. Kissed by rays of a rising sun, the isolated winter-dormant brown grass runway, with its limp pole-mounted windsock, stood silent and expectant. A glance at his watch indicated a half-hour until takeoff. He picked up a clipboard with a pre-flight checklist.

*

At least four of the de Gracies were ecstatically happy to see the sunrise. A month ago, Hugh had finally argued The Father into springing for some almost cutting-edge technology. He shared a warning dream from the Mother-tree concerning the experiences of

Ojas and Alain Michel de Gracie with poison gas in WWI. Besides outfitting everyone with gas masks, Aubert allowed Lewis Clark de Gracie to purchase a bit of airpower.

Lewis found an old Vietnam War buddy, now in upper management with the Sikorsky Corporation. The company's military drone program had fallen on hard times, and their extended range unmanned aerial reconnaissance vehicle, known as Cypher, was available for purchase at bargain prices. Over a few cocktails, Lewis convinced his old comrade that since the military had passed, sales on the civilian market might help recover the R&D costs.

To the de Gracie team, the miniature aircraft looked like a six-foot diameter two-hundred-pound flying donut, the middle hole filled with a ducted fan consisting of two four-blade coaxial rotors. The drones could hover, or with the aid of a rear-mounted ducted propeller move forward at speeds up to seventy MPH. Controlled from a ground station, the latest mark of the machine could carry up to fifty pounds of cargo and could stay aloft for five hours at altitudes up to eight thousand feet. Detachable wings could be added to increase range, maneuverability, and time aloft.

Lewis, Valintina, Betrand, and, not to be left behind, Uncle Frank formed the team who learned to fly and maintain the six aircraft which now mounted thermal imaging and day-and-night-vision cameras. Onboard computers were programmed to provide flight patterns that allowed twenty-four-hour 360-degree coverage of a ten-mile perimeter around the mansion.

Images of surrounding valleys and mountains were tight-beamed back to TV screens in the ground control station. Three Cyphers flew patrol patterns at all times, while the remainder received maintenance and refueling.

But the team leader wasn't through yet. The UAV system could alert but not defend.

Besides machine guns mounted in the towers, they needed

something that could reach further out – provide a defense in depth. Lacking the ability to purchase military-grade antiaircraft missiles legally, Lewis innovated. He contacted a former aerospace engineer who specialized in designing custom remote-controlled miniature aircraft much in demand by hobbyists.

At $15,000 apiece, he bought a dozen model F/A-18 Hornet fighter jets, each an exact-to-scale replica of the full-size Navy fighter-bomber. The radio-controlled twin-tailed aircraft ran five feet in length with three and a half foot long wingspans. The twin-engine jets had controllable exhaust fans, which allowed them to be 360-degree thrust-vectored, just like their big brothers. At Lewis's request, the contractor had equipped the models with the latest internal kerosene-start P200-SZ turbine jet engines, capable of accelerating the small planes to speeds of one hundred and sixty MPH.

The de Gracie pilots could hardly believe the intricate maneuvers the planes could perform.

Arming the models proved to be more complicated, but Valentina's skill solved the problem. The plane's fiberglass-skinned foam-filled bodies were hollowed out in spots to compensate for weight additions, which included a micro-miniature TV camera mounted in the cockpit after removal of the little pilot and navigator figures. Images were broadcast back to virtual reality goggles worn by the ground controllers.

Copper cones surrounded by plastic explosives fitted into the pointy noses formed metal-penetrating warheads that could be detonated by contact or remotely by the controller. More plastic explosive situated in the toy drop tanks balanced the now heavier snout and were wired to explode simultaneously with the nose cone.

This still left the aircraft with one remaining disadvantage. The small fuel tanks meant a short flight time. The problem was resolved by attaching one of the twenty-pound aircraft to each of the Cypher's wings. If a target appeared, the Hornets would be carried close and launched from a mother ship.

Practicing maneuvering and flying unarmed models against each other was the most fun the four had experienced in an age – for Uncle Frank, several centuries. A rented Piper Cub, flown by Lewis allowed them to become experts at identifying and intercepting approaching aircraft.

✦

William clicked on the autopilot before pouring himself coffee from a stainless-steel vacuum bottle. He groaned to himself. Made from Arabica beans, the most popular grounds sold in North America, it tasted like weak dishwater. Only in the Middle East could one get the real stuff, coffee ground, brewed, and served with a little cardamom. The plane lurched. Hot liquid splashed over his fingers. A calm day in the flatlands, updrafts, and wind channeling in the valleys between the mountains made for unpredictable rough spots. He checked the GPS. They were closing on the objective – within twenty miles.

He clicked off the autopilot and took manual control. The current approach speed of 180 MPH would have to be halved to allow him the time needed over the target to dump his load within the de Gracie thornwall. Starting out liquid, the vapor and globules disbursed in the air by the drop would fill all the available space just like any gas.

Any de Gracies not in a sealed room would be killed or permanently disabled.

Pulling the throttle back, he nestled the plane into an approach vector, keeping the aircraft's belly only two hundred feet above the valley's trees. The GPS indicated ten miles to target. He pulled back the wheel, starting the upward climb to the three thousand eight hundred feet needed to top out over the de Gracie holdings.

He blinked. Something small, gray, and dish-shaped, a speck against white clouds and blue sky, moved across his vision. For a minute, the thought of a UFO flashed across his mind. The de Gracie

290

Mountain grew larger. Reaching the required altitude, he adjusted the flight path to cross over the center of the towers silhouetted against the sky and throttled back.

A projectile flashed through his peripheral vision – smashed into the engine cowling halfway between the propeller and the cockpit. A bang. Shredded miniature wings and a forked tail assembly blew by. A piece of the AT's cowling flew off and smacked against the windshield, leaving a large star-shaped crack in the glass.

An alarm beeped. The engine oil gauge registered zero. Smoke and liquid oil billowed back, coating the windshield and cutting off his vision. The engine sputtered. Unbalanced ragged vibrations shook the plane.

Williams was close.

Machine-guns in the towers opened up, sending finger-sized globes of light swishing past the cockpit. Noises, like hail hitting a metal barn roof, informed him of bullets puncturing the metal skin of the left wing. It retained its lift.

The mission could still be completed.

He turned the plane to circle the target. The prevailing southern wind would blow the smoke away from the plane and allow him to see. A second flash of a yard-long gray body followed a straight line to smash into his plane just forward of the tail. William felt an explosion rattle up through the aircraft's tubular frame. The pedal controlling the elevators went slack. He swore.

Muscling the plane to face east, he put the AT into a shallow dive. There was plenty of altitude and space. He'd make Lake Champlain and a water landing – live again to fight another day, he thought. Tree tops flashed by. A strange looking circular craft pulled up alongside his wingtip. Camera lenses glittered.

William spent no time speculating on what it was.

Ground cover opened disclosing roads and houses. Retail parking lots with scattered car-top rectangles of blue, white, red, and black rushed by. White faces looked up. A tail of fire blew out the back of the engine, shaking the plane, like a terrier shakes a rat. The propeller came to an abrupt halt as the overheated engine seized up. Vibration and noise ceased.

Silence, broken only by the whistling noise of wind over the cowling's jagged metal, settled in the cockpit. He swore and managed to bank the unpowered aircraft to miss a church tower by the width of a gnat's ass.

Over the water, he lowered the wing flaps and raised the aircraft's nose. The emergency maneuver slowed his momentum, but not enough. The fixed landing gear caught in the water, at that speed the consistency of liquid concrete, causing the plane to flip over. Contact at high velocity tore open the fuselage and smashed open the tank containing the pesticide.

William's head slammed against the instrument panel. Hanging upside down, he moaned and weakly fingered the safety belt release. A solution composed of fifty percent lake water and fifty percent pesticide bubbled up into the cockpit. William shouted, "No!" as fumes filled his lungs. The AT's yellow and blue cruciform body bobbed for a few minutes before disappearing beneath the lake's foam-flecked slate-colored water.

The white bellies of dead fish began to surface.

🍃

The de Gracie crew clustered around the TV screens mounted on the Cypher control station. There was no cheering as they watched the attacker's plane sink. A shiver passed through the group. The enemy's murder-attempt had been a close thing.

Uncle Frank wiggled eyebrows with a final comment. "That was a felicitous and efficacious encounter."

17

*I said to myself, 'In dealing with human beings it is
God's purpose to test them and to see what they
truly are.'*

Ecclesiastes: 3:18

ABDULLAH SAT AT HIS DESK AND GLARED at a seated Claus,
who had clasped his hands together to keep them from shaking. The
duo had been waiting for the last five hours for a report from
William. In desperation, they tuned in on the internet to stream Port
Henry's local radio station, WVTK 92.1 FM. The mix of uniquely
American music and a constant barrage of loud, obnoxious ads
touting the Ford Dealer's auto specials left them half-paralyzed with
alternating moments of boredom and rage.

Abdullah thought that if he died and went to hell, being assaulted
with such advertising would be his punishment for eternity.

At 1000 hours Saudi time, 1500 at Port Henry, a news reporter
cleared his throat and spoke:

"Residents of Port Henry were treated to an amazing sight

midmorning today. A bright yellow, light aircraft trailing a stream of smoke flew low over the heart of the city, narrowly missing the steeple of St. Patrick's Catholic Church before diving into Lake Champlain.

"The sheriff's water patrol arrived at the crash scene twenty minutes later. The site of the mishap was marked by thousands of dead fish floating on the surface. Water samples analyzed by the city utilities lab disclosed a dangerous pesticide had been loosed by the crash. The poisoned water has prevented any diving to examine the condition of the plane or to recover the pilot's body.

"A sheriff's office spokesperson has indicated that no aquatic sports or boating will be allowed until further analysis indicates the water is safe. Residents are assured that favorable winds and currents have prevented any contamination from reaching the shore. Authorities are checking all aerial chemical application companies within two hundred miles to determine if they have lost an aircraft."

Abdullah clicked off the computer. "It appears this mission has also ended in failure." He rubbed his eyes. "I can't think anymore tonight. Let's go to bed. We'll talk midmorning."

🌿

The rooms, halls, and grounds of the palace filled with dark shadows, thicker and blacker than usual, due to the absence of a moon. Exhausted sentries in hallways and towers had lost their edge after two and a half days of tension. The changing of the guards every hour and sending scouts into the desert had stretched manpower reserves, disrupted schedules, and resulted in a lack of restful sleep.

Two human silhouettes stopped at the top of the stairs leading down from the second floor, slipped over the side, and went hand-over-hand down the outside rail, their hanging bodies hidden from the guard leaning up against the wall at the bottom. They slipped through the dining room, shuffled through the kitchen and out the back door, narrowly avoiding the arriving breakfast shift of cooks and bakers.

The shadows paused in a grove of trees and bushes, shivered in the cool night air, and hoped the breeze would not carry the rancid scent of bodies that had been confined together for three days without a bath.

Halfway across the polo field, they paused to time the guards walking around the base of the walls. Low-crawling to the gravel perimeter path, they rose and strode along, mimicking a random patrol, arms swinging and boots crunching in military rhythm. Tower sentinels nodded as they passed, recognizing uniforms, but not seeing faces in the darkness.

Reaching the north wall, they crept up the stairs on all fours, and then crawled along the parapet to a point halfway between two towers. The pair squeezed between crenellations, hung full length from their arms, and dropped the remaining ten feet to the desert floor below. The shades crawled a dozen yards, paused to listen, and then crawled again, repeating the sequence until out of sight of the palace.

A long-eared buff-colored fennec fox, with a limp green gecko in her mouth, stopped to hide in a miniature thicket of *abal* bushes. The vixen had just detoured from her usual path to the den containing her three kits to avoid a prone human sleeping in a pocket of sand still warm from the day's sun. Creatures from the man-warren a mile away had invaded the area for the last two days, spooking prey, and nearly finding her hideout. Now here were two more, and she was caught in a small space between the sleeper and the active ones. Her heartbeat raced. She snuggled deeper into the plants' waxy leaves.

The two crawling ones stood, one limped and cut off a groan. The first knelt and checked the second's ankle.

Her large ears caught agonized breathing. The healthy one rose, bent over, and pulled the wounded one onto his shoulders, then jogged away. She could feel each heavy footstep through the desert floor. A night breeze ruffled her fur. The sleeper behind her mumbled, rolled on his side, and began to snore. Bushy tail up, a relieved fox trotted off.

❧

Abdullah woke and stared at the canopy over his bed. Last night's hot chocolate and a mild sedative had overcome the last three days of accumulated worry and fatigue, allowing a restful slumber. A servant knocked on the door.

"Come," he shouted.

"Highness, do you wish breakfast in bed?"

"No, open the curtains and prepare my bath."

He felt strong bladder pressure, threw back the blanket, and thought, if I didn't believe I was old, having to pee more often is a constant reminder.

The curtains on the east windows fluttered apart, the sun's rays reflected off something shiny on the right-side pillow. The reflection almost blinding, Abdullah shuffled out of the focused light. Eyes opened wide. A hand jerked to his beard. Nestled on the pillow lay a sheathed knife. Abdullah looked closer. He recognized it as a lost family possession — the curved *jambiya* dagger Aziz had lost in Afghanistan. It had been restored. The rhino horn sheath gleamed with polish — jewels sparkled in corals, cobalts, and ambers. A large Herkimer diamond had been fixed as a pommel to the hilt. Beneath it laid a sheet of paper.

He held the dagger in one hand the message in the other.

> **It may be that Allah will grant love and friendship between you and those whom you now hold as enemies. For Allah has power over all things; and Allah is Oft-Forgiving, Most Merciful.**
> **Quran 60:7**

00-41-22-722-1617

Code: Aj33n27

Aubert and Uncle Frank sat in the mansion kitchen, coffee cups in hand. A smile twitched across the Father's face.

Across from them, an aproned Margy bustled around the two returned men, a clucking mother hen, heaping their plates with fried eggs and hash browns from a still sizzling cast-iron skillet.

Désirée cuddled next to Hugh, an arm around the small of his back, her hand in the right pocket of his jeans.

Valentina sat next to Gaston, tearing and eating pieces from a cinnamon roll.

Slathering butter on a slice of whole-wheat baguette, Hugh began the story. "The entry, the smoke bomb distraction, and the modification of our hiding place – all went as planned."

"There was enough room in the utilities access?" Aubert inquired.

"Barely," Hugh replied with a grimace. "The alcove was two feet in depth. We undid the hinges and moved the access door another foot out into the nook. We folded ourselves into a space about three by three by ten."

"And none of the al-Narib guards or family noticed the modification?" Aubert asked.

"None. *Grâce à dieu*. They were so used to seeing the alcove in its original depth, their minds filled in the difference. The guards also knew that normally there would not be room there to hide one person, let alone two."

"And thanks to the flexibility of body, a gift from the Mother-tree and my isometric exercise program, you were able to withstand the confinement," said Uncle Frank.

"As you directed," Gaston said, "we spent the many boring hours pushing against the walls and against each other to keep muscle tone. Cross pipes allowed us to do pull-ups. We alternated sleeping – one sat and dozed while the other stood. Your gift of a miniature magnetized chess set was a God-send."

Hugh pushed a half-masticated mouthful of egg and potatoes into a side cheek and said, "The little hollow fang on the iron water spigot we had prepared penetrated the palace's copper water line as designed, allowing us to keep hydrated. Otherwise, the food bars, especially the chocolate chip ones, kept our energy levels up. Zipper lock plastic bags with hunter's scent neutralizer held our waste products."

Aubert took a sip of coffee and nodded. "You positioned all the artifacts and messages as planned?"

Gaston laughed and vigorously nodded his head. "The only downside was that we weren't able to see their faces when they discovered them."

"Obviously, the escape went expeditiously," Uncle Frank concluded.

"Timing the mission to end on a moonless night, after three days of running the guards ragged, worked very well. The only bad event – Gaston broke his ankle landing on loose stones after dropping from the wall."

"I could low-crawl, but not walk," Gaston added. "Hugh did the fireman's carry with periodic rest stops for the final six miles to the van."

"I better not find out that you were faking."

Gaston pointed at his ankle. "Tomorrow after the Mother-tree heals me. I'll shoulder you and run for a few miles. You can see how well you like the herky-jerky, slam-bam, up and down. My chest and stomach are still bruised."

The seven de Gracies laughed together.

Hugh's face grew thoughtful. "Have we heard from Abdullah?"

Aubert let the silence grow for dramatic effect. "Yes. His security chief called, and we have set up an encrypted Skype session for our first talk. Soak in hot water, love your sweethearts, and get a good night's sleep. We will need you listening to the conversation scheduled for ten hundred hours tomorrow."

🍂

Abdullah ibn Mohammad al-Nabir and Aubert Renée Phillipe de Gracie stared at each other's screen image. The picture they built in their minds still incomplete, but filling in as they took in faces, body posture, and dress.

Choosing his Korean War uniform, Aubert wore a green blouse, khaki shirt, and black tie. Numerous ribbons and badges tightly packed the space over his left pocket. Light reflected from gold oak leaves on epaulets and the winged caduceus on his lapels.

Abdullah recognized the message – the House de Gracie mobilized for war.

The American sat, shoulders back, relaxed, both hands purposely held open on the tabletop. A boxer's broken nose broadcast his willingness to take punishment. A military burr-cut head of salt-and-pepper hair and few wrinkles belied the reports of his almost ninety years.

Aubert observed a dark-skinned Middle Eastern man whose slumped shoulders, plentiful facial wrinkles, and hennaed beard told the story of a man well into an unforgiving old age. His hawk nose, black eyes, and thin lips in combination gave the impression of a still powerful mind and capable student of Machiavelli. The sheik of al-Narib wore the traditional Saudi dress of a *thobe*, a bone-white robe trimmed in gold. His head was covered by a matching scarf call a *gutra*, held in place by a doubled black cord called, according to Gaston's whisper in his earplug, an *igal*.

The returned brightly jeweled *jambiya* dagger lay crosswise on the tabletop, a symbol of their unresolved conflict.

Behind Abdullah sat advisors: his senior wife, closely veiled, and his new security chief.

The de Gracie elder broke the silence.

" 'Like sheep, we're doomed to travel o'er, The fated track to all assigned, These follow those that went before, And leave the world to those behind. As the flock seeks the pasturing shade, Man presses to the future day, While death, amidst the tufted glade, Like the dun wolf, waits his prey.' "

Abdullah raised eyebrows, recognized the verses of *On Life*, an ancient Arabic poem his early tutors had forced him to memorize. Some of Ebn Alramacram's fatalistic work, he thought.

Aubert continued, "The poem's sentiment of unalterable fate and doom should not apply to our families. We are locked in a struggle, two honorable adversaries, that can only result in deadlock for decades, or if one side prevails – what we call a Pyrrhic victory."

"A victory that leaves the winner so weak, they fall easy prey to lesser enemies. Yes, I know what that means," Abdullah responded in Arabic. Gaston's translation came through the earbud in Aubert's ear.

The Father continued, "In the old days, permanent peace was maintained between the community of Islam and non-Muslims who respected the ways of the faithful but maintained their own religion and identity."

The sheik replied, "Even if I wished to help create this peace, there is the matter of honor and the humiliation brought by your family upon the house of al-Narib." The voice from the other room tickled Aubert's ear.

He responded, "Throughout history tribes have fought honorable wars in which respected men on both sides have been killed and wounded. Yet, at the end, when wisdom dictated, they made peace. Ways exist to restore honor. Is there anyone else outside our families that knows about our conflict?"

"There is no one."

"Then, there is no public shame. What no one knows cannot be paraded in the marketplace. The longer our conflict lasts, the more chance of the details being exposed to the embarrassment of all parties."

A concealed shame is two-thirds forgiven. Abdullah whispered the old Arab proverb to himself, then spoke aloud. "Our losses have been great. Family members and retainers have been killed."

"By our count, you have lost a nephew and a son-in-law in honest combat with my son and most recently, a personal retainer attempting a poison gas drop. Your remaining casualties were mercenaries of no blood ties. We have lost five of our blood – an uneven score at this point."

"Still, if I felt in the mood to negotiate, what could you offer to compensate?" The sheik's tone was sarcastic. "Money, or other tokens of wealth? My tribe has billions and needs no more."

Gaston's buzz in Aubert's ear told him it was time to make the offer. "What about a gift no money can buy? I have spent the last fifty years of my life curing disease and developing longevity treatments. What about twenty more years of life, healthy life, that would allow you to teach and raise your son?"

Abdullah looked shocked. "You know about my illness?"

"Your prostate cancer has spread to many locations throughout your body. Your doctors give you another two to five years."

"Then you also know more life for me would not benefit my son or family."

Aubert responded, "Your child has a rare brain tumor, so little researched that treatment is mostly done by guess. Haytham has had radiation and chemotherapy, which have only slowed its growth – given him another half-year at most."

Aubert sat silent and waited, hoping the sweat dappling his forehead could not be seen through the camera. This was the moment of decision. Violence or peace hinged on Abdullah's next comment.

The sheik's thoughts bounced back and forth like a tennis ball from thoughts of revenging the family honor to the potential for his son.

His advisors remained mute.

He weighed the value of both options. The decision came to him. He had never liked Aziz and Fahad anyway, the *na-ghals* — bastards. They were to blame for all this.

"If… if… my son could be helped…"

"Twenty extra years for you and a lifetime for your son in exchange for peace eternal between us, Abdullah ibn Mohammad al-Nabir, on my oath as a physician and a de Gracie."

"So be it." The al-Nabir family patriarch removed the *jambiya* from the table and stuck it in his belt.

"You must make immediate plans to come to our house."

Abdullah's mind had already leapt ahead. Pleased to have the mental initiative, he smiled and said, "Hostages must be traded to guarantee safety. And… one last thing must be agreed upon."

Aubert raised his eyebrows. A cold, sinking feeling filled his belly. His face turned to stone. They had no more to offer.

Abdullah smiled internally. He recognized he had struck an emotional chord in the de Gracie. These brief seconds of the former enemy's discomfort were the only revenge he would receive. He enjoyed the moment as long as he dared. Black eyes stared into brown as he announced, "Adoptions must be exchanged."

In Aubert's earbud, Gaston's hushed voice said, "The old man is serious. It is a great tribute to be adopted into each other's tribe. It will seal the peace."

Aubert's shoulders relaxed. "I am greatly privileged. I will adopt your son and you mine. My son and his wife will travel to your palace and remain, while you and your child are within our walls. You may also bring a cook, Haytham's nurse, and one other retainer."

Abdullah's finger paused above the cutoff key, the wrinkles in his forehead eased. "*As-slāmu aleikum.* Peace be upon thee."

Aubert's lips formed a smile, he responded with the phrase

Gaston provided, *"Ma'a as-salāma*, go in peace."

18

Human beings and beasts share the same fate:
death comes to both alike. They all draw the same
breath. Man has no advantage over the beast, for
everything is futility.

Ecclesiastes: 3:19

HUGH ÉDOUARD AMAURY DE GRACIE Fatik ibn Abdullah ibn Mohammad al-Nabir stood atop the high middle tower of the family mansion, hands resting on the crenellations. A late February storm had deposited three inches of fresh snow on this portion of the Adirondacks. Escher-like shadows thrown by the thornwall's resistance to the rising sun-dappled and streaked the open field in front of the manse. As the sun changed position, the dark panels stretched and crawled across the virgin white blanket as they had done for the last five hundred years.

A breeze deposited a spindrift of flakes on his face and shoulders. Hugh wiped tears of melting snow from his cheeks and pulled the hood of the brown robe of handspun de Gracie wool over his head.

The ankle-length garment and the woolen long underwear beneath protected him from night cold yet to be dispelled by the day. His feet were kept warm by ankle-high winter moccasins, a wedding gift from Uncle Frank's Mohawk wife Ahladita, lovingly fashioned from rabbit skins, the fur turned inside. In this costume, a stranger spotting him on the tower might be excused for thinking the family home was a monastery and he an old-time monk or friar.

Rising early to greet the sun, he wanted time alone to meditate on the happenings of the last twelve months. A year and a day had passed since his return as a dying man seeking a father. He had found two.

Named Hugh by his de Gracie father, meaning heart or spirit, he had been awarded the second name of Fatik by his al-Narib father, meaning deadly or lethal. The combination: deadly spirit? Saudi family members also called him *Fatik 'abāni* or Fatik of the two fathers. The time he and Désirée had spent as hostages at the al-Narib palace had begun with apprehension.

◖

As the limo pulled through the front gates, each of them felt a nervous stomach tickle at entering what had been until recently an enemy stronghold. The welcome was polite, but initially reserved.

Désirée spent the days submerged in the culture of the ladies of the harem. Abdullah's wives and daughters used the visit as an excuse to introduce their guest to the female pleasures of Riyadh. Appropriately sheathed in *hijab*, *niqab*, and *abaya*, she was whisked off with wives and male escorts to the Al-Glaya district jewelry shops, women's cafes, and fashion houses of the capital.

Hugh discovered that Saudi women's outer coverings could hide a wide variety of Christian Dior, Donatella Versace, and Simonetta of Rome creations accessorized with locally designed gold trinkets encrusted with traditional coral, pearls, garnets, and amber. The world's great sophisticated clothiers and even the mundane Victoria's

Secrets found numerous willing customers in the Kingdom. Such concealed sights, of course, were only for the eyes of husbands and family members.

He particularly liked Désirée's purchase of a thick gold neck chain hung with dozens of little bells. A vision of her, face in an ecstatic smile and clad only in the necklace, came to him. She moved slowly above him, her hips, shoulders, and unencumbered breasts trembling in ancient rhythms. The music created when they made love this way better than any symphony. He wept at the beauty of it.

During the visit, Hugh filled his time with tutoring in Arabic, achieving twelve-year-old fluency, memorizing al-Narib family genealogy, studying the Qu'ran, and participating in a variety of men's activities. These included traditional desert sports of hawking, camel racing, and hunting with whippet-like hounds. Hugh also joined his new companions playing the Kingdom's adopted sports of polo, golf, volleyball, and soccer. The Saudis were keen aficionados of the last and he spent a companionable afternoon with new cousins in the al-Narib air-conditioned stadium box watching the national team, *Al-Saqour*, The Falcons, demolish the visiting United Arab Emirates team *Al-Abyad*, The Whites.

Meals were prepared with great care. The assistant chef, his boss Achmed off with Abdullah and son at the de Gracies, felt obliged to show off his skill. Hugh particularly liked the man's *kabsa*, goat or lamb rubbed with pepper, cloves, cardamom, saffron, cinnamon, lime, bay leaves, and nutmeg, then barbecued in a deep covered hole in the ground. Displayed on a bed of basmati rice with almonds and pine nuts, it was served hot with *daqqūs* – homemade tomato sauce.

Hugh's brows knitted as he remembered the one nasty experience that flawed an otherwise perfect visit. Min-jun Kim, the new captain of the guards, and he had squared off in the gym for a formal judo match. Known as the "gentle way," the rules allowed tosses, throws, pins, chokeholds, and joint locks. A slap on the back of your opponent when things got too rough would call a timeout. A crowd of onlookers, gathered in the balcony cantilevered out on one wall of the gymnasium, applauded and armchair quarterbacked each throw or pin.

The rules changed dramatically when Min got him on his back in a chokehold. A panic cacophony of warning shouts and yells came from the balcony. The men on the mat realized it was not the earlier admiring spectator garble. Min released his hold and looked up. The butt of a three-inch-thick wooden rod thocked against his temple. His eyes rolled up into their sockets. He collapsed, falling as dead weight over Hugh's hips.

Half-pinned, Hugh twisted as the end of the rod missed his head, cut his ear, and smashed against the gym floor. The crash of wood against wood made his ears ring and convinced him his skull would have been crushed if the blow had hit its intended target. Rolling Min's unconscious body downward, Hugh drew his legs back, pulled the body onto the bottoms of his feet, and tossed it towards his unknown opponent. The move allowed him a few seconds to roll and leap upright into open space.

Facing him across Min's body stood Claus, the disgraced former guard captain, armed with a six-foot-long wooden pole. Some version of a quarterstaff, Hugh thought. The choice of weapon meant Claus wished to inflict as many broken bones as possible before killing him.

"*Ibn metnakah*, you have ruined me. *Qawwad*, now I will ruin you.' Claus danced forward, holding the staff two-handed like a stabbing spear or bayoneted rifle.

Recognizing the Arabic words for son of a bitch and pimp, Hugh skipped back, seeking an opening. His Uncle Frank spoke in his mind, "An angry man will make mistakes. First, get control of your own emotions." His mind slipped into a cool mode, a collected Hugh would keep his adversary angry, "*Je m'en foutisme*. I don't give a fuck about your shame."

Claus shouted and lunged, staff threatening to impale.

Hugh took one calm step back and watched the pole-end stop three inches from his belly.

His opponent, slow on the recovery from the exaggerated extension, returned to an *en garde* position. The lunge with legs fully stretched out covered a lot of space, but the move was something only amateurs tried in real combat, Hugh noted. Such a pose left you dangling and vulnerable to a repost. Claus reversed the staff, slid his hands to one end, and advanced swinging it sideways.

"*Na-ghal…*" Hugh shouted the Arabic word for bastard and stepped forward into the swing, piercing the staff at the midpoint between his left arm and ribs. It stung and he heard a rib crack. He leaped up and brought his right arm palm down, hitting the staff just in front of Claus's grip.

Reinforced by the full weight of Hugh's body, the shock blew the rod out of Claus's hands. He stumbled back, rubbing numbed fingers.

Hugh spun the staff a few times propeller-like. He ran towards Claus, faked a strike, then used the rod like a pole-vault baton, and lofted himself off the ground. Hugh's feet came together on his antagonist's chest.

Claus sailed off to land hard on his back.

Talking like a teacher to a student, Hugh said, "You've never killed a man, have you? Your training treats combat like a sport with rules requiring you to pull your blows." Turning his back on Claus, Hugh walked over to the balcony and threw the staff up to a mob that had doubled in number. "I don't need this for you."

Hugh heard a gasp from the crowd and felt the vibration of feet moving across the wooden gym floor. Not bothering to turn, he watched the spectators' eyes as they tracked his opponent's forward motion. Earlier, Hugh had determined Claus was right-handed. He lowered his body and leaned to the left. A hand holding a boot knife passed over his shoulder. Grabbing the arm, Hugh pulled Claus onto him. Taking advantage of his enemy's forward motion, Hugh pistoned his hips and legs, and threw his opponent.

Claus grunted as the floor slammed his neck and upper back, but he managed to convert most of the force into a roll. He regained his feet and knife fighter's stance.

Hugh threw words at his enemy. "No rules in this game, asshole."

A voice from the balcony shouted, "Fatik – Fatik – Fatik…" The crowd took up the chant.

Claus raised his head. This final betrayal of former friends and subordinates brought tears to his eyes.

It was Hugh's chance to finish it.

Claus made a fumbled sideways cut with the knife. The thick cotton material of the *judogi*, which would have yielded to a stab, resisted the slash.

Hugh spit in Claus's eyes, an additional humiliation. The de Gracie's hand snapped up open-palmed to catch Claus under the chin. As his blinded opponent's head rocked back, Hugh stepped to the side, then spun around, his back to Claus. Tucking his shoulder up under Claus's knife arm, he reached up and grasped Claus's wrist.

Claus stood stunned and unresisting as Hugh jerked down.

The man screamed as his arm popped out of its socket. The knife clattered to the floor.

🖝

Hearing the tale upon his homecoming, Abdullah had been appalled. A guest in his house assaulted? It went against centuries of Arab hospitality. The sheik had returned a man of joy. He looked and moved like a forty-year-old. The gnarled knuckles of rheumatoid arthritis gone, joints all over his body moved freely – no swelling or fever. After a week of treatment at the de Gracies, Abdullah had diverted his entourage to The Mayo Clinic for a second opinion. His condition and that of his son had confounded the doctors. Besides the diminution of his gout and arthritis, the prostate cancer had disappeared. The son's brain tumor had shrunk to pea-size. For the moment, it had ceased to be a threat.

In a rage over the unprovoked attack, the sheik would have put Claus to death.

Hugh interceded with Abdullah calling him *Abu'l Gadl*, Father of Grace. He asked that their first few weeks as father and son not be marred by an execution. Abdullah relented and settled for tossing Claus out the back gate clad only in a pair of boxer shorts.

The smell of biscuits fresh from the oven brought him back from memories of the polo field to the cold snow of the present. Smoke rising from the kitchen chimneys carried the scent of baking bread and biscuits and the crispy odor of frying bacon over a hickory wood fire. The breeze changed direction and his nostrils burned. The vapor spouting from the laundry vent brought a whiff of homemade lye soap.

The breeze changed again and carried the fragrance of blooming netted purple iris. He scanned the ground near the mansion walls, spotting a variety of early blossoming flowers. His ancestor's spring plantings ran to randomly scattered purple and pink crocuses and masses of buttercup-yellow winter aconite, in enough curvaceous shapes to be mistaken for the fictional yellow brick road. Scattered here and there, he recognized isolated clusters of blue and white glory-of-the-snow alongside spring snowflake with its bell-shaped flowers dotted green on the petal ends.

Coupled to the Mother-tree, like all plants within her root range, they never failed to blossom. Continuing to spread their seed or bulbs, they remained healthy through extremes of weather that would kill off or stunt unconnected varieties. They were also measurably larger and showier than their contemporaries, leading Hugh to wonder whether the Mother-tree had affected their genetics. If so, could she be doing the same to the animals and symbiotes under her protection?

Hugh squinted and held up a hand to shield his eyes. High enough to finally dispel the shadows, the sun's slanted morning light reflected off the snow. Through the radiance, the thornwall seemed to move in places. Cardinals, chickadees, juncos, nuthatches, and blue jays played in the tops, fluffing and preening, absorbing the growing warmth of the sun. He heard the double caw, caw of a crow sentry. He pursed his lips and imitated the call well enough to cause the local murder of curious crows to land on the tower to his left. Recognizing an old friend, their black eyes left his to scan the countryside for food or danger.

Hugh knew the secrets of the mountain, the habits and peccadilloes of its plants, birds, and animals more than the things kept from him by his own relatives. Upon his return from Saudi Arabia, his father had filled him in on more of the Mother-tree and family secrets. They had gone to New York City to conduct an annual inventory of de Gracie assets.

Hugh had expected to view the contents of a few safety deposit boxes. The bank guard opened the door to a mini-vault the size of a handball court. The accounting took three days. He remembered strange treasures. The earliest Egyptian, Hittite, and Phoenician artifacts composed of weapons, rings, jewelry, and modern paper copies of earlier records that had once been inscribed on sewn-together papyrus mats, cuneiform tablets, or stone.

"Father, where in the hell did we get this stuff?"

"Some are purchases made by our ancestors, but about two-thirds came with us to this country from the previous Mother-tree. You and I will mark some of the artifacts to be sent with the group that will carry our Mother-tree's seed fifteen years from now."

"Why aren't these things in a museum, instead of squirreled away? Shouldn't they be shared?"

His father pointed to another set of shelves heavy with books further down. "How would you explain the sudden discovery of the lost poems of Sappho? The complete histories of Adsinius Pollio, Herodotus, Thucydides, and Tacitus, as well as the Satyricon and books of navigation and geography collected by Ptolemy I?"

Hugh looked shocked.

"And there is more, much more. Unknown Greek plays, the earliest treatises on mathematics, ancient clockwork analog computers, and plans for mechanical devices designed by Hero of Alexandria and DaVinci. Eyewitness diaries and journals describe the fall of Troy, the truth about the Minotaur, Alexander the Great's campaigns, and the medical knowledge of the Druids before their destruction by the Romans."

Hugh opened his arms in an inclusive gesture. "Shouldn't we feel guilty about keeping all this locked away?"

Aubert's expression grew gentle. "It is like having a tiger by the tail. If released, it could turn and destroy us. People, corporations, and governments would ask too many questions. In this modern world, we would be uncovered. We only got away with it once. Our word-of-mouth tradition indicates that the anonymous release of portions of Mother-tree archives at the end of Europe's dark ages was the stimulus for the Renaissance."

Father had imparted other secrets during their isolation in the vault. One that bothered him concerned his new Saudi brother Haytham. While the Mother-tree possessed the capability of completely eradicating the boy's tumor, Aubert refused to allow it. The Al-Narib heir must be kept dependent upon annual visits to keep his cancerous growth under control. The peaceful attachment between the families must be maintained. Human history recorded too many examples of allies turning against each other, no matter how strong the bond, when ties of blood or mutual benefit waned.

Hugh had brought back a selection of the ancient books to read – a guilty pleasure. He heard shouting and high-pitched squeals of female laughter below him.

A half-dozen couples ran out of the kitchen, men chasing women through the virgin snow. All the women were fertile now, the Mother-tree activating their monthly cycles. The de Gracie lovers had paired up quickly. A number of children must be produced to replace those that would leave with the Mother-tree's seed.

Stable and kennel doors opened. Horses raced out nipping and kicking, white vapor blowing from their nostrils. A bay mare dropped and rolled on her back in the snow, mimicking several human women making snow angels. Dogs barked and cavorted about joyfully. The men began throwing snowballs. Wolfhounds bounded into the air and snapped at the hard-packed missiles.

Motion at the front gate caught his eye.

Uncle Frank and Ahladita, Frank's original Mohawk wife, entered, both dressed in mink coats, fur turned inside, and felt-lined sheepskin boots. They'd been to the barn, smokehouse, and the chicken coop. Uncle Frank carried two hams looped together over his shoulders. His companion, a hickory-bark basket carried over one arm, held up a sample of brown eggs.

Behind them came Loup-garou, the senior wolfhound, harnessed between the shafts of a dogcart, two five-gallon stainless-steel milk containers riding in the back.

Ahladita laughed and shook out her long black tresses.

Hugh noticed straw woven in her hair. The couple must have enjoyed the privacy and warmth of the haymow before tending to business. He made a mental note to give that a try when he and Désirée next drew milk and egg detail.

Another flicker of motion at the gate and Aubert and Margy strode in, dressed in long capes of patchwork white, gray, and brown – the de Gracie's winter hunting camouflage. Slung over their shoulders, the couple carried composite recurved short bows made of yew, bellies reinforced with thin strips of sheep horn and backs with sinew.

Hugh remembered making his own bow as an eight-year-old. The shaping of the staff, steaming of the wood to induce the recurve on the ends, and the gluing of the horn and other materials to add power had taken over a year of work.

The de Gracie bows, with their draw weight of eighty to one hundred pounds and four-foot length, worked well in forest choked with brush and fallen trees or from horseback. From his study of military history, he knew the family bows could be described as a hybrid of Native American and Mongol technology.

Margy carried two braces of rabbits strung around her neck, legs tied together with leather thongs.

A trumpeted *ee haw, ee haw*, announced the third member of their party. Koshan trotted through the gate, two deer hides stuffed with rough-cuts of venison meat tied to a pack frame on his back. Hugh's father and substitute mother had spent the night in the family's yurt further down the mountain. Its thick felt blankets stretched over a collapsible wooden frame resisted extremes of weather, and sheltered family hunting and work parties. They must have awoken before daylight and climbed to tree stands constructed close to deer trails. After bagging two of the larger prey, they picked off the rabbits on the way back.

Hugh's mouth watered. There would be a feast tonight. He turned. The crunch of small feet in the snow behind him drew his attention. With one brown eye and one green eye, he watched Désirée approach, her woolen underwear and light housecoat insufficient protection from the cold air. Spanish cat followed, carefully stepping in her footprints, stopping periodically to shake distasteful snow from its paws.

It was paradise for Hugh to see her curves with two eyes and binocular vision. Fahad had provided the new eye before his removal to feed the Mother-tree. Father had worked out how to complete the transplant. A small living fragment of the Mother-tree knitted the nerves and blood vessels together. No flesh of the donor interacted with Hugh's flesh so no rejection occurred.

Modern medical procedures still found it difficult to impossible for nerve tissue to be repaired or reconnected once cut. In this case, the mother-tree tissue acted as a conductor of impulses between the alien eye and Hugh's optic nerve. He supposed — in a small way — he was now a human-plant cyborg. An increased sensitivity to the Mother-tree, even when separated, seemed the only strange phenomenon resulting from the transplant.

Désirée shivered. She stooped to pick up Spanish cat, holding it to her breast.

Hugh opened the flaps of his robe, tucked his wife inside, their bodies pressed together spoon style in the warm cloud created by their merger. Blonde sleep-tussled hair tickled his chin. She smelled of sandalwood, jasmine, cedar, and pine, the natural perfume humans generated after frequent connection with the mother-tree. Perhaps the biggest mystery of all, this woman — this Désirée, the desired one — who fit him so well, more each day and hour. She was a mother to the child in him, yet her femininity complemented in every way his maleness, making him whole. An image drifted up into his mind, a flash from an earlier Mother-tree dream. A picture formed of a curly blonde head in a Civil War era drawing room, face hidden, sobbing into the hugging arms of two children.

Spanish cat's sputtering lawn-mower purr distracted him. He lost the vision. Drawing his right arm out of the robe's oversized sleeve, he reached down inside and gently rubbed the baby bump on her abdomen. He kissed her ear.

Désirée chuckled. *"Mon cour."*

Hugh whispered to her an ancient Egyptian poem culled from the vault book inventory:

"To hear your voice is pomegranate wine to me. I draw life from hearing it. Could I see you with every glance, it would be better for me than to eat or drink." He paused and ended the moment reciting *"Toz jors mes vous amerai."*

Désirée translated the ancient de Gracie house French into: "I will love you forever." She smiled. Not forever she thought, but with the help of the Mother-tree, for a very long time indeed.

THE END

ABOUT THE AUTHOR

DENNIS MAULSBY is a retired bank president living in Ames, Iowa with his wife Ruth, a retired legal secretary, and his dog Charlie, a retired CIA operative. A son and grandson live in the Pacific Northwest. His poems and short stories have appeared in numerous literary journals and anthologies, including *The North American Review*, *Mainstreet Rag*, *The Hawai'i Pacific Review*, *The Briarcliff Review* (Pushcart nomination), and on National Public Radio's *Themes & Variations*. Some of his poems have been set to classical music and may be heard at his website: www.dennismaulsby.com.

His Vietnam War poetry book, *Remembering Willie*, won silver medal book awards from two national veterans' organizations. His book of poetry, *Near Death/Near Life*, and a book of short stories, *Free Fire Zone*, both published by Prolific Press, won a gold medal and a silver medal respectively from the Military Writers of America. Maulsby is a past president (2012 – 2014) of the Iowa Poetry Association.

The House de Gracie is his second book published with NeoLeaf Press. His first NeoLeaf Press publication, the American Fiction Award finalist *Winterset: Short Stories of Pixies, Demons and Fiends*, was released in 2019 and became their best seller for that year.